Praise for *To Love a Liar*

'I adored this. A [...] beautifully written [...]
about the secre[...]
the past com[...]
Cla[...]

'A clever, provo[...]
of loyalty and lie[...]
couldn't turn the pages fast enough'
Chris Whitaker

'A tensely written, thoughtful thriller that will
stay with you long after you've put it down'
Jennie Godfrey

'A riveting and poignant read. Matthews has masterfully
rendered a tale of love, death and betrayal'
Oyinkan Braithwaite

'A spellbinding tale of deception and betrayal that asks
the ultimate question: how well do we really know
the ones we love? Fantastically twisty storytelling'
T. M. Logan

'An exceptional read. Nail-biting and utterly
addictive, fans of Lisa Jewell will love this'
John Marrs

'A masterful feat of storytelling, with a kaleidoscopic
plot that shifts your perspective with every
turn of the page. No word of a lie – this is one
of the best crime novels I've ever read'
Amy McCulloch

ABOUT THE AUTHOR

L. V. Matthews worked for ten years in both domestic and international sales for major UK publishing houses, before leaving to pursue a career in writing. She has always been fascinated by the grit of the human psyche, and what drives people to act in the dark ways that they do.

TO LOVE A LIAR

L. V. MATTHEWS

PENGUIN BOOKS

PENGUIN BOOKS

UK | USA | Canada | Ireland | Australia
India | New Zealand | South Africa

Penguin Books is part of the Penguin Random House group of companies
whose addresses can be found at global.penguinrandomhouse.com

Penguin Random House UK,
One Embassy Gardens, 8 Viaduct Gardens, London SW11 7BW

penguin.co.uk

Penguin
Random House
UK

First published 2025
002

Set in 12.5/14.75pt Garamond MT
Typeset by Falcon Oast Graphic Art Ltd
Printed and bound in Great Britain by Clays Ltd, Elcograf S.p.A.

The authorized representative in the EEA is Penguin Random House Ireland,
Morrison Chambers, 32 Nassau Street, Dublin D02 YH68

A CIP catalogue record for this book is available from the British Library

ISBN: 978-1-405-97470-7

Penguin Random House is committed to a sustainable
future for our business, our readers and our planet. This book
is made from Forest Stewardship Council® certified paper.

MIX
Paper | Supporting
responsible forestry
FSC
www.fsc.org   FSC® C018179

To my wonderful agent, Camilla Bolton.

On 12 October 2005, police were called to an abandoned council house in Derby, where the body of twenty-four-year-old Sophia Roy was found on the living-room floor, a needle in her left arm. The needle had administered a fatal dose of heroin, causing a pulmonary oedema, and police and the coroner concluded that Sophia had tragically taken her own life. However, nineteen years on, new evidence has been brought to light, prompting a relaunch of the inquest.

    – *Observer*, article by Caroline Bonner, 3 March 2024

I knew he had something to do with it. I *knew* it.

    – @LeilaRoyPR, X [Sophia Roy's sister]

At this time, any speculation out there regarding Christopher Fletcher is exactly that – speculation.

    – Statement from Jawad Khan, Department of Legal Services, 5 March 2024

I

They have come to the loch, where it is quiet, where it is wild. They're here for the inquest, but during the crawling days while they wait, they will try to rebuild their marriage. They need the time together. And Chris needs to hide.

They're staying in The Old Smoke House, which belongs to Jill's aunt: a dated eighteenth-century building, stone-built and rendered white with an uneven grey slate roof. It's on its own, overlooking the loch, among the roots of nature, and a mile from the village. Its remote position should make Chris feel at peace, but the inquest has stripped away any sense of tranquillity. There is an invisible grenade beneath him, close to explosion.

He leans back in the kitchen chair that he's positioned on the scrub of grass at the back of the house, and stares at the water that leads out to the sea. This is most definitely not a holiday, but at least it is the best time of year to come. Spring in the Highlands is beautiful and fresh and biting. Hopeful. Is that what he's searching for out here? Hope? Perhaps it is. Or perhaps it's closure he wants.

Neither he nor Jill wanted to leave the safety of their house in Sardinia, but the coroner called for it and so they came, along with Jackson, their Great Dane, who now lies at Chris's feet in half-slumber. Chris is glad they brought him over. It was a long process to get him a passport, and a very long journey in the car cooped up with Jackson's flatulence, but family is family.

'What will fate decide for us, Jacko?' Chris asks.

He digs into his coat pocket and throws him a biscuit. Jackson hoovers it immediately, and then stares at the ground, willing for more, like they fall from the sky and not Chris's jacket.

'No more treats until dinner. Mum would be cross.'

Jackson puts his head back down. Chris takes the cup of tea that he's balanced on the thick arm of the chair, the wind snatching away the steam, and watches Jill out on the loch, sailing the dinghy borrowed from her childhood friend. She's gone far today: sometimes she sails all the way to the mouth of the sea and into the north wind; other times she'll explore all the little bays and coves along the cliff edges. She's an adventurer, whereas Chris has never sailed and has never wanted to, even though she's told him over the years that she'd teach him. He much prefers to watch her from the bank, in awe of how she handles the water. This is the village she grew up in, and its familiarity is why they've come – for her comfort, because he owes her that while they wait for the inquest. Wait for the grenade to blow.

Beneath ice-clouds and stormy skies, I sail into tomorrow's fury.

It feels ironic, this line she'd penned years ago, as if somehow she'd known how their life would end up – caught up in a shitstorm.

She'll be gone for another hour at least, and in that time he could distract himself by watching a film or making lunch, but these things feel too normal. Besides, he needs to answer the emails he's been avoiding and force himself to scan social media. The internet searches are narcissistic and self-destructive, but he does them anyway because he needs to be vigilant, and he prefers to do them when Jill isn't around because he wants to give her the impression that he's confident in the justice system, and confident, too, in his own version of events. He wonders if she checks online for his name, or even her own, but in the week they've been at The Old Smoke House he's never once seen her looking at any news websites. Maybe she's pretending not to care, just as he is. Maybe at night by the fire, she's got her book open but she's not reading the words. Maybe her phone is laid in the crease of it and she's reading all the horrible things about him instead.

He watches her constantly, searching for clues on how she's feeling, but she's retreated into her head, writing words in her notebook that she doesn't want to speak aloud. And who can blame her? Since Caroline Bonner wrote that article, they have moved quietly around each other, all their layers of intimacy gone. He understands it – he's turned both of their lives upside down – but he misses her; God, he misses the way she snakes her hand around his waist, the way she whispers into his ear, the way she laughs. She's done none of those things for weeks.

He digs his phone from his pocket, and goes first to X, typing in the hashtag: #sophiaroy

Reams of chat come up and he painfully starts to sift through, like a panner in a river looking for nuggets of truth within the heavy opinion and judgement.

A step closer to the truth . . . How will they get out of this one? Who takes responsibility?

Who indeed? A question that's been asked over and over for years, with no clear answers, because that's how it all operates – in murky light and indiscernible sound.

I can't believe all the stories coming out about this.

Believe it, he thinks. There is worse to come – always

worse to come. The news about Sophia Roy may well tip the carefully constructed system, but the sole reason for his being here is so he can save it.

He clicks on his own name, famous now but for the wrong reasons, dissected by the media and by people who weren't there.

#christopherfletcher #findchrisfletcher

His name is out there, thanks to Sophia Roy's sister, Leila, but there's no picture of Chris yet. For how long will he have that luxury, he wonders. He supposes it depends on what comes out at the proceedings. His breath hitches at the thought of it, only a week away now. People will be watching like vultures from all angles. They love wrong moves, and he's made plenty.

Aggression radiates from the screen and heats his face as he scrolls on and on, until soon it becomes unbearable, and he clicks off and presses the email icon instead. Stacks of emails ping up – from old colleagues, from the legal team – and he starts to battle through them, answers some, deletes plenty. On and on until his fingers start to shake. Perhaps they were already shaking to begin with.

The image of Sophia Roy seeps into his mind, weighing him down like lead. He closes his eyes, exhausted.

'Chris?'

His eyes snap open. The sun has moved, and Jill is standing in the boat, twenty yards away, with the rope in her hand. He hurriedly shoves his phone, which is loose in his hand, back into his pocket.

'Did you turn the boat back around?'

'What? It's midday,' she says, glancing at her watch. 'I'm always back for lunch.'

6

He chastises himself. It was a mistake to be outside; he cannot afford to lose himself in sleep or whatever distorted state he was just in, even if the chair is sheltered from view.

Jill steps on to the bank, takes off the life jacket, and then bends to haul the boat slightly out of the water and on to a smooth rock, where it will wait until the next time she uses it.

'Any news from Jawad?' she asks.

Jawad is his legal representative – young but energetic and efficient.

'Nothing of importance. A few things to read.'

She ties the rope to a jutted stone. 'Do you want tea?'

He touches the mug on the arm of his chair and finds it stone cold. 'I – yeah. Thanks. How was the water?'

'Great. Some beautiful birds.'

'Oh.'

'Yeah.'

'Great.'

'Yes.'

When did they become a couple that talked about *birds*? But then, when did they become this age, late forties? He's spent too much time reflecting on the past and missed the present.

She walks towards him, puts out her hand for the mug.

'I love you,' he says.

She doesn't answer, looks out to the loch again. Strands of hair sweep across her face with the wind.

'What? What are you thinking?' he asks.

'It's my birthday tomorrow.'

He swallows, had forgotten. With everything going on, the days have melted into one another and he's lost track of the date. He's never forgotten in all the years they've been together. He always tried to be at home with her too, even if it was for just a precious couple of hours.

'Yeah,' he says hurriedly. 'My plan was to cook you something nice.'

She nods, but her face is neutral. Possibly because she can tell he's lying, possibly because he is, in fact, a bad cook and she's not at all excited by this prospect. Possibly because she doesn't want to be here, even though this is her aunt Meredith's place, and the village of Jill's childhood.

'We'd usually be in Marco's,' she says.

'I know.'

Marco's is their local restaurant back in the town of Palau. They go there most weekends, and always for birthdays. Marco and his family have become their family too. When everyone else leaves the restaurant on a Friday night, Chris and Jill go walking to the beach with Marco and Angela, his wife. Together they paddle in the silver waves and share a bottle of wine.

'What about if we went out tonight?' Jill says suddenly.

Chris frowns, confused. 'Out where?'

'I don't know. The pub?'

He laughs. 'Good one.'

But she's not smiling. 'Is it so stupid?'

'You want to go to Harris's?'

Harris McGowan owns The Black Horse and is an old schoolfriend of Jill's.

'Maybe it's stupid, but . . . I don't know. I'm beginning to feel like a lab rat.'

He tries not to let his frustration spill over into his voice. How could she be suggesting this, given the severity of the situation?

8

'We can't go out, Jill.'

'We've gone to the shops.'

'*You've* gone to the shops. People know you're here. No one knows *I'm* here.'

'Meredith knows.'

'Apart from Meredith.'

'And Harris.'

He blinks. 'What?'

She puts her hands on her hips, a gesture of confrontation. 'Harris asked me about the inquest, and I told him you were here. I couldn't lie to him, Chris.'

'You could have *tried*,' he says, and attempts not to seethe.

'He's my best friend.'

Chris goes to speak – isn't *he* supposed to be her best friend? But a best friend would never have been as deceitful as he has. He swallows his hurt and reaches for her.

'OK, I understand. That's OK. But we agreed you'd keep a low profile, yes? Susie's for food, and Harris because you borrowed the boat.'

She doesn't say anything.

'Shall we watch a film tonight? *Armageddon*?' He pauses, smiles. 'Too ironic?'

She glowers at him.

'We need to wait until all this blows over,' he says. 'You know that. We're doing fine here in Smoke House.'

'I feel like a fugitive, hiding away like this.'

'It's not a fucking holiday,' he snaps, and then feels bad. She looks like she's going to say something, but doesn't, and he's grateful. He reaches for her again, his fingertips grazing her hip.

'Look, I'm sorry, but we can't – we're here for the inquest. I can't . . .'

'What if we went in the back way?' she says. 'And stayed in the back room? No one goes in there much anyway. What if I text Harris and ask him how busy it is?'

'Jill—'

She purses her lips and then nods reluctantly. 'No, OK. I know, I know.'

'We've been so careful. Let's not upset it all now. When the inquest is over and everything is done – we can go for a drink, then.'

She looks him straight in the eyes. Her skin has tanned with the sailing, and her eyes are a brighter blue as a result. 'What if it doesn't go the way you want it to?' she says.

'What are you talking about? It's just going to be a few questions. Clarifications.'

'Fine.'

She turns away from him, but he catches her expression and she looks so sad that it pulls at his heart. He feels terrible; he's done this to her, upended everything she thought was true. Jillian is his rock, his support, his everything, and he hasn't even bought her a sodding birthday card.

She goes to walk away and he catches her arm.

'You believe that, right? That it's all going to be OK?'

'Yes,' she says, and she smiles, but it's thin and tight.

'Text Harris.' He says it before he's even realized. 'And if it's not busy, we'll go for one and sit in the back room.'

Her eyes light up. 'Really?'

His heart rate is spiking, but he ignores it. He takes her hands in his, notes the warmth of them, notes the longing in his chest for the emotional warmth of her, which has long been absent.

'It's your birthday,' he says.

*

They walk the twenty minutes to The Black Horse but leave Jackson at home because he is huge and will draw attention. They haven't needed to pass through the village itself because The Black Horse is set further out, the only building looking out over the small fishing harbour, and for that mercy, Chris is thankful.

They walk through the big pub garden and open the back door. Chris is relieved to see the room is empty. He can hear laughter coming from the main bar, wonders how many people are in there and who it is. They shouldn't be here. It feels so wrong. He forces himself to smile reassuringly at Jill, but she doesn't smile back. She looks decidedly worried.

He squeezes her hand. 'Are you OK?'

'I'm being selfish.'

'No, look, I promised you one, and we're here now.'

She's nervous, shifting on her feet like a skittish horse and picking at the skin around her fingernails.

'Hey,' he says gently. 'Don't do that. They'll bleed.'

She nods and stops, but she'll start up again, he knows she will. It's a habit she's always had, a tic exacerbated by stress, and this is probably the most stressed she's ever been. In the last few days he's noticed that she's been binding her hands in bandages when she goes out to sail because the salt in the water hurts like hell against the rawness of her fingers. Again, he's done this to her – hurt her physically as well as emotionally. He knows that she sails to be away from him, to have her own time and headspace, and he gets it; the pressure of keeping everything lidded is exhausting for them both.

He spots a table that faces the doorway to the main bar. He can see who comes in from here and can adjust himself accordingly. He's wearing a cap – not for fashion; it's too young for him – but he doesn't dare remove it.

'I'll take the table there,' he says. 'You go to the bar.'

She nods, makes to walk out, but a voice stops her.

'You came.'

Chris glances up and sees Harris in the doorframe. He's a tall, wiry man, wind-burnt and with a mass of black hair like a bird's nest on his head. Chris hasn't seen him in a long while, but he looks the same, albeit with a few more lines on his face.

Harris walks towards them, holds out his hand. 'Good to see you both.'

Chris half stands to shake it. 'And you, Harris.'

'Everything OK?'

'We're doing all right,' Jill says tightly. 'We thought we'd come out for a drink.'

'Aye. Your message was a bit of a surprise.'

Yes, thinks Chris. They are inviting trouble. If Oliver knew what they were doing, he'd blow his top.

'It's Jill's birthday tomorrow,' Chris says.

Harris smiles at Jill. 'I remember. You'll have a drink on the house, both of you.'

'Thanks, Harris,' she says.

'Who's in the bar?' Chris asks.

'Two couples from the next-door village – old – and some of Lorna's friends at the bar. They'll give you no issue.'

Lorna, his daughter, sixteen now. She is Jill's god-daughter, though Chris has never even met her.

'Usual?' Harris asks.

'Please,' Jill says.

'I'll take a half of Tennent's,' Chris says at the same time.

'I'll bring them through myself.' Harris looks at Jill. 'You've got good weather for the boat, Jillian.'

'It's a salvation.'

The word stings in Chris's ears, whether deliberate or not.

'Do you want to come fishing with me sometime?' Harris asks her.

'Doubt we'd catch another tope, like last summer.'

They laugh together, and Chris is momentarily jealous of the connection between them, and the ease that comes from years of uncomplicated friendship. He's jealous, too, of the fact that she's been able to maintain this friendship. She returns every year, stays at Meredith's house, but this is the first time Chris has been back in the UK for nearly two decades. He has missed so much, so many people and events, because of what happened. Everything balanced on a knife edge. A lump of grief forms in his throat – he missed his parents' funerals, for fuck's sake.

He smiles, tries to join in. 'You caught a shark?'

'Aye. We let it back in, didn't we? It wasn't for the table.'

'It was a beauty,' Jill says.

'There's a storm due in the next few days, but we'll just keep an eye on the weather. Are you eating tonight? I can recommend the bream.'

Chris shakes his head. 'No, a quick drink—'

But Jill nods, enthusiastically. 'Can we take a look at some menus?'

Chris stares at her. He'd agreed to one drink, and now she's playing happy families.

'Aye, I'll get some. I'll tell anyone else coming in that the back room isn't available tonight.'

Chris shifts and Harris leaves the room.

'I'm glad we came,' Jill says. 'Are you?'

Chris leans so he can see into the main room, sees someone's arm on a chair by the fireplace.

'Chris? It feels normal, doesn't it? Like when we used to come here together. It was so long ago, wasn't it? Do you remember? Twenty years ago or something? When Kate ran that Easter hunt and Cal's dogs ate all the eggs? When Duncan fell into the water?'

She smiles again, but this time he doesn't. How can he explain to her that he doesn't feel normal? That every day since 2005 he's been looking over his shoulder? He doesn't remember the eggs, doesn't seem to remember anything from that long-ago life except for the frightening scenes that loop over and catch him unawares in the strangest of places.

'Chris?'

'What?'

'This is nice. Isn't it? Being out.'

He smiles, and she must see the effort it takes to do so because, for a brief moment, she looks hurt, but now she is distracted, looking at her bag and taking her phone out of it.

'Meredith is calling me.'

'Don't answer it,' he says. 'Let's try to have a nice time without your aged aunt putting a flea in your ear.'

'It's probably about my birthday.'

'Can you call her back?'

'Why? Because we're having such a great time?' she says sarcastically.

She is shifting sand, veering from extreme anger to upset to blame and back again. He can't say anything to make it better.

She puts the phone away again, sighs. 'You're right. Sorry. It just feels odd being here.'

'I thought you said it felt normal?'

'Well, I was lying. It doesn't.'

'Happy birthday,' he says, also sarcastic, but gentle, like a peace offering, a joke. He holds out his hands across the table for her to meet them. He doesn't want to fight.

She takes his hands in hers but doesn't say anything. They sit there, the lighting low and ambient, the paint dark grey and flaking on the walls. There is a large frame of fisherman's knots above them, and a sailing boat lantern on the sill, a thick candle alight within. Even from inside, he can hear the boats outside, sails chiming like bells. In any other circumstance, it would be good to be here. He looks across at Jill, at the rope of blonde hair tied unfussily in a simple French plait over one shoulder. Effortless beauty.

'I didn't get you a present,' he admits. 'Or a card.'

'You don't need to. I'm forty-seven.'

'But I'm sorry. Everything just . . .'

'It's fine. I appreciate this, coming to the pub. I appreciate feeling important.'

He baulks internally at her last sentence – a barb because of everything he's putting her through.

'Oh!' a voice exclaims above them.

Startled, Chris looks up and sees a girl who has come through, dressed in black jeans and a yellow hoodie, her dark hair in a choppy bob. She's followed immediately by Harris.

'Lorna! I said I was shutting the area.'

'I *know*,' the girl replies. 'You just said. I was coming to shut it up for you. I didn't know that Jill and . . .'

There's an awkward pause. Jill is wringing her hands.

Chris's heart is beating fast. 'It's no problem,' he says, even though it is.

Lorna looks at Harris and then at Jill. 'Is this . . .'

'I'm Chris,' Chris says at the same time. Resigned, because of course she'll work it out.

Harris puts the drinks down. 'But no one needs to know he's here, understand? Get the menus.'

She leaves.

'I'm sorry,' Harris says.

'She was trying to help you. It's OK.' But Chris's voice is wooden and everyone hears that it's not OK.

'She'll know all the things about you are nonsense.'

Chris blinks. 'You think she'll be following it?'

Jill makes a face at him. 'Everyone is following it. You think I've been skipping around the village and no one has asked me about *you*?'

Harris walks away swiftly.

'I didn't know you'd been skipping around the village,' Chris says in a low whisper.

'A figure of speech—'

'So Harris knows I'm here, which we didn't agree to, and now Lorna.'

Jill bites at her finger as Lorna returns.

'Hello, Lorna,' Jill says, her voice now a bright singsong. 'So how are you?'

'Umm. I'm OK.'

'How's school? Are you studying for Highers?'

'Umm. Yeah. I started college last September.'

Chris is only half listening to their exchange, has one eye on the door behind Lorna. Harris has disappeared from view. Some of the younger group from the bar – Lorna's

16

friends – have moved into his eyeline. He looks away quickly and to Jill. She catches his eye.

'Are you OK?' she says.

'I—'

She looks over his shoulder, realizes what he's seen.

Three teenagers are hovering at the doorframe.

Lorna looks up then, frowns at the doorway. 'Go away,' she says, crossly, and shuts the door. She looks then to Chris and Jill. 'Sorry.'

Jill turns to Chris. 'Maybe we should go?'

Chris smiles tightly at her, feels it come out as a grimace. Every inch of him screams to get up and go.

'It's fine,' he says.

Please, he thinks. Please let it all be fine.

'Let's eat something that's not cooked by you.'

'I'm a great cook,' Jill says, indignant.

'I know you are,' he says. 'But *I'm* shit.'

She gives a half-smile. 'You are shit.'

'Guilty.' He laughs, and then stops abruptly.

Jill stares at him.

Chris clears his throat. 'I'll have the pork, Lorna. Please.'

Lorna nods, her eyes down at the pad in her hand.

'And I'll have the bream,' Jill says.

'They both come with new potatoes and greens. Is that OK?'

'Perfect.' Jill hands the menus back over. 'Thanks, darling.'

Lorna looks like she can't get away fast enough.

'You might want to stop declaring yourself "guilty",' says Jill as Lorna closes the door behind her. 'It's not a good look.'

'It was a slip.'

'Wasn't it just?'

Jill finishes her pint quickly, starts to tap her foot against the table. They sit in silence.

'Meredith is calling again,' Jill says after a moment, her phone in her hand.

He drinks, the cold liquid soothing the ache beginning in his head. 'Ignore it.'

'I shouldn't—'

'She'll text you if it's important.'

'She's just texted.'

He sighs. 'What is it then?'

She doesn't answer him, is tapping on the screen, and then her hand flies to her mouth in horror.

'What?' he says. 'What is it?'

She turns the phone around and the screen shows a picture of him – here at the pub – on social media, posted four minutes ago by an anonymous user.

#murdererattheloch #ourownlochnessmonster #justiceforsophia #christopherfletcher

It's all coming out of the woodwork. The great unmasking continues. #sophiaroy #justiceforsophia #christopher fletcher #nowheretohide
    – @Outtahere, X

Is that him?? Have you got a better photo? Where is this?? #sophiaroy #justiceforsophia #chrisfletcher #christopher fletcher #nowheretohide
    – @MMOP, X

Someone's having a laugh. That's not him.
    – @MinnieMoose, X

Where are you guys looking? I can't find any photo?
    – @bemorelauren, X

There's going to be an inquest, remember. Innocent until proven guilty. #sophiaroy #chrisfletcher
    – @booyakka, X

Inquests are legal inquiries into the cause and circumstances of a death, and are limited, fact-finding inquiries; a Coroner will consider both oral and written evidence throughout the course of an inquest. The purpose of the inquest is to find out who the deceased person was and how, when and where they died, and to provide the details needed for their death to be registered. It is not a trial.

– www.cps.gov.uk

2

They leave the pub, leave the drinks on the table. Chris locks Jill's hand in his, pulls her forward. Outside in the dark she fumbles to turn on the torch and he snatches it from out of her hand.

'No,' he says. 'They can't have any more pictures of us. People will know where we're staying because you always stay at Meredith's. And they'll have seen you out in Harris's boat.'

In the blackness, they half jog down the lane and across the field, down the grassy hill to the lone house, but with every step, he feels more and more disconnected, fuzzy. He keeps telling himself over and over that it was only a profile shot, and that he's changed from all those years ago. He is wearing the cap. But he can't erase the essence of himself. What if someone recognizes him? What if the person who took the photograph is going to betray their location? He needs to call Oliver.

They get home within fifteen minutes and shut the door, stand in the stillness and the dark, their breath short and panicky. Jackson stands to greet them, but they don't touch him yet, keep their arms around each other, and for a moment, he absurdly thinks how nice this is – that they're embracing, that he can feel her heart thumping against her ribcage. But it's for all the wrong reasons.

'I'm sorry,' she says into his chest. 'I've fucked it all up.'

'You've not done anything.'

'I *did*, Chris. I made us go there. Was it one of those kids? One of Lorna's friends?'

'I think it must have been.'

She sobs into him until his shirt is soaked through. 'I'm sorry,' she says.

'*I'm* sorry.'

Because he is. For everything.

Time passes, and no one has come to hunt them – no lanterns and pitchforks. Jill stands back to look up at him.

'Why did you stay?' he asks quietly. 'After all I put you through over the years?'

'Because I love you, fool.'

Love. It is the reason for all great things but also the reason for the bad. The things Chris has done to hurt Jill are insurmountable.

'I need to make a phone call,' he says, heading for the spare bedroom and shutting the door.

Chris watches Jill in bed, asleep now beside him, the silver light of the moon picking out the curve of her cheek, her long eyelashes.

He shouldn't have listened to her when she suggested going to the pub; they had been doing so well to keep his presence here a secret. The photo has now gone – dealt with by Oliver – but it's still on someone's phone and there's nothing he can do about it coming back online again, over and over. And asking Lorna which of them took the photograph would only fan flames. Perhaps Lorna herself asked her friends to take it.

He clenches his jaw.

He is too angry to sleep. He swings himself out of bed, grabs his dressing gown from the back of the door and goes downstairs. The wooden staircase creaks with his footsteps, but he doubts Jill will wake. He suddenly slams his fist on the wooden bannister, and the thud of it is like a crack of lightning in his ears. He wants to roar, tear everything up, but he must seethe in the silence, as he always has done. He's a man used to violence, but against the power of the internet and this unbending campaign to crush him, he is powerless.

He goes into the snug, doesn't bother turning on the light. Sitting on the arm of the sofa, he stares out of the window at the loch. The public don't know, he thinks bitterly. No one knows the whole truth. No one but him, and the others who lived through the same thing he did, can possibly understand the nuances of it all. Nobody wants to hear about those, though, or the context out of which all this was born, because everyone loves to hate the 'villain'.

There's a creak on the stairs, followed by Jill's voice. 'Chris?'

He doesn't want to answer her, even though it's technically now her birthday and it feels mean not to. He wants to hide away from her, from the world, because he is so angry, so lonely, and upset. Yes, upset, because of Sophia, of what happened to her. But he can't share that particular pain, and especially not with Jill.

He moves swiftly so he's behind the door and out of sight as he hears Jill moving in the kitchen.

'Chris? Are you down here?'

She sounds timid, nervous. He can tell that she's seeking his assurance, security, and yet he doesn't give it to her. He stays quiet, listens as her footsteps approach, and then feels her presence in the snug, even though he can't see her. He catches the faint scent of her: a rich citrus from the oil

23

she put in her bath after they returned. And then he sees her silhouette, sees the turn of her head as she looks this way and that in the gloom. But even if she switches on the light, she'll not see him here, behind the door.

'Chris?'

Perhaps she'll think he's gone for a walk. Perhaps she'll think he's in the downstairs bathroom. He hears her go back up again and he exhales into the darkness.

He was always good at hiding. As a boy he was obsessed with spy-novel heroes and true-life spies – encouraged by his dad, of course – and Chris would skulk around the house pretending to be one, hiding behind doors and under beds. He heard a lot of things that way – conversations between his parents that he shouldn't have been privy to, conversations his parents had with their friends. Teachers in their staffroom when the door was ajar. He wrote down all he heard in his black book (like all good spies did). Sometimes he repeated things back to them months later in an attempt to impress, like he was a mind-reader, a fortune-teller. A superhero.

'Don't forget that it's Uncle Harry's birthday on Friday.'

'Is Mrs Reynolds from the school unwell?'

'The swimming gala is going to be moved to next Saturday. I can feel it in my bones.'

His parents would look at him, amazed at his perceptions, at his observations, laughing when his 'predictions' came true. He learnt how to cover himself when they asked how he knew things they thought they'd kept private. Over time the act of lying became addictive. When he met Sophia Roy in 2002, he was an expert in the art because, by then, he'd had professional training in duplicity.

3

2002

Sophia Roy was late and had missed the talk entirely. An August downpour had snarled up all the roads and people's tempers; the bus driver had several arguments with people for not making space, and for treading dirt and dog shit all over his bus. She'd decided to get off early when there was a gap in the rain, but it was ill-timed and, in the ten minutes' walk between the stop and the pub, she got completely soaked. Droplets ran down her hair and her bare arms and stuck her thin cotton dress to her skin. She had no umbrella but couldn't have held one anyway, thanks to the pot plant balanced carefully in the crook of one arm.

No matter. She had arrived at the pub eventually, stepped into the fug and the noise and the buzz. Soho pubs, indeed the district itself, had their own particular energy, she thought. People full of burning ambition, desire, ideas. Full of *idealism*. And she was no different.

Cigarette smoke curled down the staircase as she walked up it, her wet trainers squeaking on the tread. She could hear Jude's laugh, a distinctive bark, from above, and then she was there – with her people. Carlotta and Paul were on the sofa, engaged in conversation, Jude and Johann were carrying beers from the bar to a table, and Esme, Peter and Jodie moving chairs to accommodate everyone. There were a few others she didn't recognize, and that was good: it meant that they were starting to make headway with their messaging. People were interested in what they were saying, attracted to the same ideology that had drawn her to Green is Go. That together they could make a difference to the world.

'Look who it is!' Johann called when he saw her across the room.

She smiled, held the plant aloft.

'Get yourself a drink,' he said. 'I put fifty pounds behind the bar.'

She nodded. She liked having friends who were older than she was – in Johann's case, he was twenty years older, and cash rich. There was a level of maturity, naturally, with having older friends, but there was also such diversity within the group, which she loved. Johann was originally from Frankfurt, Carlotta from Milan. Esme was a retired hippy (though still very much a hippy), there were several people who ran their own businesses, a few in the corporate world. Like Sophia, there were students. They had become a family of funny, quirky, good people. She fancied Jude, fancied Evan too. Sometimes Johann, if she was drunk.

She turned to the bar and waited to catch the barman's eye, but he was busy serving. She put the pot plant up on the ledge, shook her hair of rain and tied it up in a bun.

'What's your friend having?'

She turned to see who'd spoken. A young man with dark hair and liquid brown eyes who she'd not met before. He was slender, athletic, wore low-slung jeans.

'My friend? You mean the plant?' she said.

'Yeah, Vera.'

She laughed. 'You think she looks like a Vera?'

'Sure,' he said. 'Vera the Parlour Palm. See her sprawled across her chaise longue, with her glass of bourbon.'

She was impressed he knew what the plant was – she hadn't known before looking at the label in the store. Slim stems, feathering leaves. Yes, perhaps she *did* look like a Vera.

'Actually,' she said, 'she can't hold her liquor.'

He smiled, then, and it was so nice, so beautifully straight and warm, that she wanted to see it again, immediately.

'Poor Vera,' he said. 'Always the talk of the town after events like this.'

'Stop. You're making me not want to give her away. I'm worried Jude will ply her and she'll fall into ruin.'

'Who's Jude?' he asked.

She pointed. 'That guy. It's his birthday tomorrow. Vera is his gift.'

He looked over to Jude, who was still laughing merrily along with others. 'Ah, hence the singing earlier.'

'Did I miss that? Oh God, I missed the whole thing,' she said with a grimace. 'It was crazy trying to get across town. Were you here for the talk? Was it good?'

'Actually, yeah.'

She grinned. '*Actually*, yeah?'

'I mean, don't test me on it or anything.' He nodded to the rows of bottles behind the bar. 'Can I get you something?'

'I'm in need of a towel, but a Guinness would do.'

He smiled again, this time wider. He had dimples, and she was partial to a dimple.

'Do you always come to these talks?' he asked.

'To every one of them for the last two years. They're really inspiring.' She held out a hand. 'I'm Sophia, by the way. I'm studying Environmental Science at Kingston.'

He took her hand, shook it. 'I'm Chris.'

'Are you studying too?'

He shook his head. 'Nope. I'm a gardener.'

'That explains how you know my friend here,' she said, nodding to the pot. 'You study plants.'

'I guess I do,' he said. 'The pulse of nature.'

A moment passed between them. Something electric and wonderful.

4

It's early morning and Jill has been in the snug since dawn, writing. Chris brings her tea at eight, as he usually does, come rain or shine, wherever they are.

'Happy birthday,' he says, handing it over.

'Is it?' she replies flatly.

His heart sinks. Any warmth and togetherness after everything that happened at the pub last night is clearly now obliterated. Her mood is stark.

'Do you want to go out?'

She doesn't look up. 'I think it's best we don't go anywhere.'

Fucking yes, he wants to say. *Which is what I tried telling you last night.*

But he says nothing, instead tries to read some of her words over her shoulder, but she hunches over the pages. He wonders if they're about him.

'A walk in the woods would be OK,' he says. 'No one comes this way, do they? You said as much when we got here.'

'No,' she says.

'OK, great—'

'I mean, no, I don't want to go out for a walk.'

He waits for a beat, but she still doesn't look at him. He leaves and goes through to the kitchen, sits at the table. On his phone he flicks to the article written by Caroline Bonner in the *Observer*, even though he knows it by heart now. This is what kicked it all off – the piece that threw his careful life into absolute bedlam.

On 12 October 2005, police were called to an abandoned council house in Derby, where the body of twenty-four-year-old Sophia Roy was found on the living-room floor, a needle in her left arm. The needle had administered a fatal dose of heroin, causing a pulmonary oedema, and police and the coroner concluded that Sophia had tragically taken her own life. However, nineteen years on, new evidence has been brought to light, prompting a relaunch of the inquest.

The evidence presented is Sophia Roy's online journals, recovered earlier this year by her sister, Leila Roy, who, when clearing their family home, found passwords written in an old diary. The online journals date from 2004–2005 and are rumoured to shed significant light on Sophia's movements prior to her death, and the state of her mental health at that point.

'What are you doing?'

Chris jumps. 'Nothing. Did you change your mind about the walk?'

Jill leans over his shoulder. 'Why do you keep reading it?' Her voice is clipped. 'It's not going to disappear, is it?'

'I know.'

'It's like you want to torture yourself, Chris. And me. It's like you want to torture *me*.'

'No,' he says, and reaches for her waist.

She moves away, flicks on the kettle and busies herself – loudly – with cupboards and crockery.

'I'm trying not to think about Sophia Roy. You hear me?'

'I know, Jill.'

She crashes a spoon on the counter. For someone so graceful, she knows how to make noise.

'Hey,' he says. 'Come here.'

'I want my life back.'

Chris thinks of their house in the hills – burnt orange walls, white shutters. Tiles on the kitchen floor, thin white curtains. Plants everywhere. Is Marco watering them enough, he wonders. Jill will worry about that. In Palau, Chris is a part-time handyman out there for the locals, cleaning swimming pools, working in the garage. Jill does shifts at the local surgery, writes poetry, teaches sailing and English. Sardinia has become theirs – Jill is with him and they're a unit, the two of them and Jackson.

'Please stop reading about her, OK?' she says. 'It's my birthday.'

She pours hot water from the kettle into the mug, clangs the spoon against it, and then pulls open the fridge for milk. How did she finish the first tea so fast?

'How's your writing going?' he asks, awkwardly.

He never knows what to ask about it, feels clumsy that he can never offer anything. What should he be asking? *How's your word count?* He has no idea.

'You've given me a lot of material,' she says.

And then she laughs. She laughs and laughs until she cries, bent double and supporting herself with a hand on the back of his chair, and he thinks that, finally, they're going to be OK, they can weather this together, as they have weathered other things in their lives. But no sooner does she start than she snaps up straight and stops laughing.

'Over the years, when you were away, I imagined what you were doing, but I never imagined her. I never ever imagined that you would do that to me. To us.'

'Jill—'

'Stop,' she says, and bends her body again, this time her expression one of pain.

'Are you OK?'

She reaches and grips his shoulder, talon-like and digging into his flesh.

'When your old friend Oliver called us about that article, and every day since, I've thought about drugging you. How you would fall asleep, and I would drag your heavy, naked body out to the loch and fill your mouth with stones until it was all you were made up of – dark, slick, smooth stones clicking together as I pulled you into the water. And then I'd watch as you sank down into the depths. Into the blackness. Into nothing.'

He stares up at her.

'There, you see? A *lot* of material.'

And when the dawn comes, will you follow it here?
Step into old shoes, and on to the dew-grass of a new day.
Will I be waiting, still?
– Jillian Moore, 'New' from *Anthology of Madness*, 2005

He [Chris Fletcher] was a lot of fun, you know? I remember once when he came to stay with us, we'd have been about, I don't know, eight or nine. He came up with this game – there were two motion light sensors outside my house, but they were slightly angled. He was convinced that there would be a line between them where the light wouldn't go off, and so we waited until after dinner, and I kid you not, we spent over two hours on our bellies trying to crawl, commando style, up the front lawn of my house without the motion sensors going off. It's one of my favourite memories of our childhood together.

– Guy Fletcher, Christopher Fletcher's cousin, interview with Sadie Clarke, *Under the Cover*, 2025

He was always playing games. With Sophia. With everyone.

– Leila Roy, interview with Caroline Bonner, *Observer*

The man is sound. There's no one you'd rather have on-side than Chris Fletcher. Trust me.

– Oliver Hamilton, colleague of Christopher Fletcher, BBC True Crime Drama: *Into the Dark*, 2025

5

Despite the heavy tension between them, Chris has suggested making fajitas and cocktails because Mexican is Jill's favourite cuisine. At three in the afternoon Jill leaves for Susie's shop, has to buy the ingredients herself because Chris is chained to the house by invisible shackles.

He watches her drive over the ridge with a heavy sense of foreboding. Jill is going to the village like Little Red Riding Hood with her basket, and any number of wolves could be waiting.

Alone, he tunes in to some Radio Four drama to drown out the drama of his own life, but he doesn't really listen. Instead, he scrolls social media for any new shockwaves. He's relieved that the picture from the pub isn't back, and wonders what tricks Oliver would have had to pull to make it so. After a while, he puts the phone down, stares out of the window at the water and contemplates how the inquest might change their lives. If all goes as it should, they can return to Sardinia as soon as it's over. But if it doesn't, he can kiss goodbye to life as he knows it. He might even lose Jill, and the thought of that makes his skin shrink against his bones.

They have been together for decades – less for murder, ha ha. He was twenty-three and she was twenty-two and they met in a Soho club on a sticky July night, the rope of her shocking white-blonde hair seducing him from across the bar even before she'd turned her head. He'd been with colleagues and they'd dared him to approach her. They'd dared each other a lot in those days. Bravado and ego and all manner of stupid things that young men were made of. Chris had bought Jill a drink, danced with her a little, and then they'd talked outside while she smoked and told him that she was a nurse, working in St Thomas's Hospital on Westminster Bridge Road and really shouldn't be smoking. Social only, she insisted. She said that she liked to garden and write poetry in her spare time and, as she talked, he found that he wanted to keep listening. He liked her honey-ed Scottish accent, and the way she casually jutted a hip. Before he knew it, at two in the morning, he'd asked her out on a proper date.

A week later, they went to Hyde Park and sat on the grass. She'd brought two bottles of white wine and some strawberries; he'd brought a big packet of crisps and a Frisbee. They watched people out on the lake on rowing boats and drank the wine straight from the neck of the bottle. They talked about everything and nothing, then got up to play Frisbee. He was impressed by her speed; she beat him absolutely and beautifully.

'You said you were a poet,' he said, laughing.

'And what? Poets can't be good sportspeople?' she said, and threw the Frisbee with such elegance and strength that he had to chase it down a hundred yards.

Afterwards they lay in the grass, drank the second bottle, and became dizzy with the heat and with each other. She told him dark and terrible ghost stories, right there in the thickness of the summer day. He told her true spy stories that he'd been obsessed with as a boy. He could feel the tickle of clover on the back of his neck. He watched as she picked a daisy that was near the crook of her elbow and twirled it between her fingers. The stem stained her skin green, and he wanted to grab her hand and put it to his lips. They were still together, there on the grass, and yet he wanted to see her again already. At seven o'clock they went for dinner at a pub where a man played the piano. At eleven, they were the last ones there. They went to see a late-night play, but they didn't watch it, made it only to the foyer bar and spent the duration of it kissing in a corner. He hadn't wanted to find someone permanent – he was young, just been looking for a good time – but, as with all these things, fate had other ideas. She was charming, and sharp in her observations. She was sporty and could easily beat him at pool, at table tennis and squash, and he liked that. She dazzled him. They went hiking together in the Lake District, went to gigs across London, spent time with her father, Robert.

After a year they decided to move in together and found a run-down place in Queen's Park where the outside brickwork was crumbled and sun-baked. The blue door had flaked over time and had become all the hues of a brilliant sky. In the summer they dragged chairs up to the roof and spent weekend mornings with a portable radio, Jill's bare legs in his lap. She wrote poems, and he would listen to the football, the cricket, whatever was on, and they laughed. God, they had laughed so much. They were just so *good* together.

Movement catches his eye through the window. A figure is standing by the corner of woodland over the ridge, half hidden by a block of shade. At first, he thinks it's Jill on her return from the shops, but then remembers that she drove. It's a man – or rather he thinks it's a man, given the body shape – and Chris feels immediately nervous. Not many locals come out this way. He thinks perhaps a tourist hasn't noticed the 'Private' signs and has wandered past, oblivious. Or it could be a journalist. Surely not though, because no one knows where they are. Or do they? Is there something new online in the last few minutes? He steps back from the window, can't risk being seen or photographed through the glass, and drums his fingers on the kitchen counter, trying to slow his heart rate. After a moment, he leans forward and looks at where the man was, but whoever it was has gone.

'Jacko?' he says.

Jackson lifts his head.

'I'll take you out, come on.'

They see nothing and nobody on the meandering woodland path. The six acres of woodland beyond The Old Smoke House also belong to Meredith so the brief walks they've had in the last couple of weeks have felt safe. After crossing into the woodland, there are no roads, no villages, no people, only the mouth of the loch at the end, with its hypnotic lap of water against the bank. Out here it feels like the world is pushing against the edge of another.

He wonders if he should ask Oliver if they need to move house – somewhere more remote. Perhaps they were stupid to think that Jill's childhood village was safe enough.

He diverts from the narrow track and walks between the trees towards the sound of the water. He likes being on the edge of two such different environments, though he finds each of them suffocating, in its own way. Jackson zips this way and that, occasionally dipping into the water and sloshing around where it's not so deep. There are pieces of driftwood from fallen trees among the rocks.

Chris bends to pick up a thick piece of wood by his feet. From an alder, perhaps, one of the water-loving trees that doesn't rot when it's waterlogged, instead turns harder. Robert, his father-in-law, taught him that. Chris turns it over in his hands and then has an idea. He didn't get Jill a present, but he can whittle this piece of wood into a heart and give it to her.

After an hour, he and Jackson come out of the shade and into the bright sunshine and expanse of grass that leads back towards the house. Jackson tears up to it, and to Jill, who is standing by the side wall, with two full shopping bags at her feet. As he squints, he sees that her face is full of anguish.

'Jill?'

She turns and points to the wall, but the angle is wrong and he can't see what she's looking at. He starts to run, is by her side in a matter of seconds.

Written in huge red letters on the white stone wall are the words:

FUCKING KILLER PIG

'Oh, Chris,' Jill says. Tears choke her voice. She grips his arm. 'Oh, Chris.'

Over and over and over.

6

'Pigs don't sweat, did you know that, lad?'

Chris was sitting at the kitchen table – nine years old – and his father was above him, dressed in uniform. He looked smart, always so smart. Sometimes Chris snuck into his parents' wardrobe and tried on his father's jacket, with the gold buttons that shone, or his boots that were heavy and polished to such a sheen that he could see his own reflection.

'Some people call me a pig, but I take it as a compliment.' His father laughed. 'Because pigs have an excellent sense of direction, excellent memories. And they don't sweat. I don't sweat when I'm under pressure. You still want to be a police officer like me?'

Chris had nodded vigorously. 'Yes, Dad.'

And he did, with all his heart. Everyone in their suburb knew his father, handsome Edd Fletcher, who was invited to charity dinners, to open libraries, to speak at events, was interviewed by the press on local cases. He was smart, authoritative, straight-backed, and Chris was in awe of him.

'Just remember – no one goes into the police wanting to be the bad guy, but you'll be called one anyway. And a pig. You've got to let it all roll off you. Keep sight of the people on your side.'

Chris's mother came in then, and his father grabbed her by the waist. She squealed in surprise but laughed in his embrace.

Edd Fletcher kissed his wife hard. 'And your loved ones. You're doing it for them. Protecting the streets for them.'

'Get on with you,' she said, giggling.

'It's true, Marion. It's a job of servitude. And it sucks you in. Being part of the police is like having a love affair. It's a commitment, for ever.'

In 1997, Chris followed in his father's footsteps, walking out of Hendon training academy, a fresh-faced twenty-one-year-old. He had dreams – big ones – but he knew he needed to put in the time before they could be realized.

There was a strict hierarchy within the force, dominated by huge egos and a cult of masculinity, but he was smart enough to show the right facet of his personality depending on whose company he was in. He needed to be recognizable by having some spark, but having too much of it could mark him as volatile. He needed to be reliable, physically strong, needed to play along with the banter that involved the extreme denigration and sexualization of women. He needed to be able to hold his drink, though that was always a downfall he tried to keep hidden.

He worked hard at being the person he needed to be. God, did he work hard. It was like growing a shell around himself. He was like a dog for four years, at the beck and call of his superiors, always saying yes, always doing overtime, always partnering with officers who were lazy and knew he would pick up the slack. He earned a reputation as an independent thinker, as well as being unafraid of the challenges on the streets. He used a calming voice when talking to a drunk or an addict, but he didn't think twice about jumping people who needed to be jumped. Even faced with violence, he didn't quake, because he knew there would be no room for sympathy or empathy – both were seen as weaknesses, and any vulnerabilities in his character would shut doors on his career progression. He was driven by the praise of his seniors, and of course from his father.

In late 2001, when he was twenty-five and had recently moved in with Jill, a man that wasn't his sergeant came into the briefing room one day, called him out to one of the offices. Chris had never seen him before. Tall, lean, black-and-grey hair clipped short, and with dark, watchful eyes.

They studied each other for a moment, before the man finally spoke.

'You want to take the NUC.'

'Yes.'

The man held out his hand. 'I'm Oliver Hamilton.'

The national undercover course (NUC) is considered the police equivalent of SAS training – in terms of both the physical and mental fortitude required.

– [Name redacted], former SDS officer, BBC True Crime Drama: *Into the Dark*, 2025

SDS was the unit Chris Fletcher first joined. That stands for Special Demonstration Squad, which was a unit created in 1968 within the London Metropolitan Police. The role of its officers was to provide intelligence to enable the police to maintain public order.

– Oliver Hamilton, SDS officer, BBC True Crime Drama: *Into the Dark*, 2025

We infiltrated activist groups that were of interest. We lived and breathed them, became part of them, you get me? Yeah, at times it was genuinely terrifying – some of those groups were violent. But most of the time, I swear to you, I never felt more alive.

– Mike Emerson, former SDS officer, BBC True Crime Drama: *Into the Dark*, 2025

When I was an undercover officer, I was a lot of people. Sometimes I was a person for a few minutes on a call. Most often I was undercover for days, or for a few weeks. Once I was a completely different person for two and a half years. With hindsight, all of it was a total mind-fuck. You get some people – like Mike Emerson – who downplay it, act like it was all a bit of a laugh, you know? Either he never got posted to a job that scared the shit out of him, or he did and he's got good at hiding it. Other people – me and Chris Fletcher included – it screwed us up.

— Anthony Stewart, former SDS officer, BBC True Crime Drama: *Into the Dark*, 2025

Do you know what they did in that unit? They stole the identities of dead children to create passports, bank accounts. They invented new lives, and then they went underground for months, years. And what happened to us – the wives and our families – when they went away? Did anyone ever think about us? Of course they didn't. To hell with those who they'd vowed to love, and never deceive. I'm glad I divorced Mike before all the shit about him came out, otherwise I'd be like Jillian is now. God help her.

— Amanda Connolly, ex-wife of former SDS officer Mike Emerson, BBC True Crime Drama: *Into the Dark*, 2025

We did what we were told to. Hell, there were some senior officers encouraging us. Get close, they said. Closer than close.

— Mike Emerson, former SDS officer, BBC True Crime Drama: *Into the Dark*, 2025

I thought the police were supposed to protect the public?! Not exploit them? #sophiaroy #justiceforsophia #destroytheestablishment

— @livingonthewing, X

I predict a riot. #sophiaroy

— @shadowman, X

7

Harris McGowan comes over to inspect the writing on the wall of the house. They stand, the three of them, in a crescent, arms folded against the blatant aggression of it. It hurts Chris's eyes. It hurts Jill's feelings. They haven't yet dared tell Meredith.

'Thank you for coming, Harris,' Chris says.

Harris nods, and bends to pick up the length of tarpaulin he's brought. 'This will do for a couple of hours, in case someone comes over the ridge. Lorna will paint it over as soon as she's back from buying the tin.'

'I'll do it,' Chris says.

'You won't,' Harris says, firmly. 'She'll do it, and you know why? Because it was one of her idiotic friends that took the picture of you and put it up online. It'll be one of them that did this wall, too, I should think.'

'It wasn't Lorna's fault,' Jill says. 'It was mine for making Chris go out.'

Chris shakes his head. 'No, Jill.'

Though, also, yes.

'I'll keep my ear to the ground at the Horse,' Harris says, and looks at Jill. 'I said you'd both be safe here, and I meant it. Lorna will come and paint it over.'

Chris watches as Harris puts a hand on his wife's shoulder. He feels distant, as though he's floating above the scene and looking in. He can see the deep crease of worry on his wife's face.

'Will you stay for a tea?' she asks Harris.

'Another time,' he says, and squeezes her shoulder before dropping his arm.

Jill nods, disappears into the house. Harris and Chris watch her go in silence and then look at each other.

'Help me with this, Chris,' Harris says, and he unrolls the tarpaulin.

They secure it with long nails that Harris hammers crudely into the stonework. Every drive echoes in the stillness.

Afterwards, Chris looks back at the house. 'You should take her out.'

'What?'

'Jill. Could you take her out on your boat, like you were saying last night? She needs someone to talk to that's not me. Or her aunt. Jill's angry; we argued yesterday.' He gives a small exclamation of laughter. 'She said she wanted to drown me.'

He doesn't know why he's telling Harris this. It's unfair to drag him even further into the complicated mess of their situation. It's dangerous to talk about anything at all.

'But she's here with you,' Harris says. 'Doesn't that say something?'

Chris nods. Yes, Jillian is here with him, just as she always has been. She had to come in case she was called for the inquest, but she also said that she wanted to.

'I'm in this with you,' she'd said, but maybe all that meant was that she wanted to keep an eye on him.

'How can she still love me after this?' Chris says aloud.

As the light fades into dusk, Chris stands outside with his head tilted and his arms by his sides, breathing in the ghostly words which are still visible beneath the white paint that Lorna washed over only hours ago.

FUCKING KILLER PIG

Though the blind is down, the kitchen window is open and he can smell onions and garlic on the air. Jill is at the stove on her birthday, even though he was supposed to be making her dinner. She told him that she needed to be busy, wanted to cook. He hates that he feels so useless, so powerless. All the masculine bravado that he fought so hard to build up and maintain over his life has gone. He wasn't ever any of those things anyway – was always playing pretend.

He goes into the house.

'It's nearly finished,' she says without turning. 'I decided on a casserole.'

'You didn't want to do Mexican? We've got limes.'

Now she turns, and she looks angry. 'For fuck's sake, I don't care about the *limes*. I don't feel like celebrating at all any more. Do you?'

She doesn't let him answer. She undoes the apron, speaks on.

'There's bread too. Will you watch the pot? I'll take Jackson out.'

'Now? It's getting dark?'

'I like the dark.'

'Shall we eat together first and then I can come with you?'

She sits to pull on her boots. 'No.'

'But it's your birthday.'

'Yeah.'

'Can't I come?'

He sounds churlish, childish and self-absorbed. All the things he already hates about himself.

'No,' she says again.

He knows it's fruitless to keep asking. 'OK.'

She stands, pauses. 'About what I said. My . . . poetry. I'm sorry. But I really have thought like that. About putting stones in your mouth.'

'I don't doubt it for a second. And I get it.'

'You were your own person on those jobs, Chris. *You* could have made different decisions.'

She bites her lip, and he wants to hold her tight.

'You betrayed me.'

'I know,' he whispers. 'And I'm sorry, Jill.'

'So, *so* easily.'

He doesn't reply. Because to his shame, it had been easy to betray her. On the operations where he was really deep-swimming, he'd felt an ugly smugness that he could trick her so easily. Perhaps it was because he'd seen first-hand how it was done. Yes, Chris's father was a great man, a man who was revered within the community, but he had his secrets. Chris recalls one Christmas when, at the Fletchers' annual party, ten-year-old Chris saw his father with the woman from number fifteen, their faces very close. In his childhood innocence, Chris thought that perhaps his father was undercover, on a secret mission, thought that perhaps this woman was a villain. Imagine the dawning horror when two years later he eventually realized that it was an entirely different kind of undercover operation. He didn't tell his mother – knew that he had to protect his father's indiscretion, even from that early age. Perhaps that was how he'd duped Jill for so long: he'd witnessed his father over the years, watched the effortless switch between two women.

His mother had deserved better. And Jill deserved better too.

'Meredith is calling me every day,' Jill says. 'And Amanda

Connolly, you know, Mike Emerson's ex-wife. She got in touch a while back, via my agent, of all people.'

Chris blanches. 'Speaking to either of them will only fan the flames.'

She takes her raincoat and Jackson's lead from the back of the door. 'This morning I got an email from the *Sunday Times*. They want an exclusive interview with me.' She laughs, but it's without humour. 'Add them to the list, with the *Sun* and the *Telegraph*.'

He swallows. 'Have you replied to them?'

'Of course not. Any story I'd tell would be twisted beyond all recognition anyway. They'd want me to make you out like a monster. And you're not. I don't think.'

He smiles, and then wonders if he's supposed to.

'You're just a man – a stupid man – who made mistakes, right? Who got confused . . . Who . . . God, I don't know. Sometimes I want to pin it all on you. Other times I want to pin it all on the police, on a nameless unit, because to admit that *you* did it all as an individual person . . . it's too painful.'

She opens the front door.

'I need you to keep an eye on the food.' She gives Jackson a little whistle and he barges over. 'And then you can clean the bathroom. There you go – you didn't get me a card or a present, so *that* can be your present.'

For years it had been flowers and hours of sex that she'd wanted. Now it's a clean bathroom because they're middle-aged and he's upset her, possibly irreparably.

The door bangs shut and he's left alone.

He doesn't clean.

Instead he pulls the piece of wood that he found on the walk out of his coat pocket and takes a potato peeler from the kitchen cupboard. He doesn't have all the right tools here, but he will still make it as smooth and as perfect as he can. A gift worthy of Jill.

It had been Robert who'd taught him about trees, about wood, and had taught him, also, how to whittle. Robert Moore had been a man who loved nature, long walks and solitude. In the early days of his and Jill's relationship, Sundays were spent with Robert outside in his beautiful garden; the three of them planting bulbs and seeds, raking leaves, making bonfires. They would go inside only when the sun had sunk below the treeline. Jill went to write, and Chris sat with Robert in the glass conservatory, where they whittled pieces of wood while listening to sport on the radio.

'You try this one,' Robert would say in his gentle voice, passing over different parts. 'This here is beech. This one is limewood. You could make this one into a beauty.'

Robert was only fifty-eight when dementia overwhelmed him. He went to a care home in west London and gradually became mute, but he never lost his dexterity. Over the years Chris spent many hours sitting with him, the two of them just whittling wood into little hearts, and, in his lucid moments, Robert would look at him, and he would smile, reach a hand to Chris's forearm and grip it. Those moments, so tender and accepting, were so very different from the moments with his own father, who was strong and commanding but also relentlessly blunt. Sometimes Chris wonders if he took more comfort from Robert's silence than he ever did from Edd Fletcher's pride. If they were both alive now, it would be Robert that Chris would go to because it would be Robert who would tell him that it would all be OK, that he was a good man still.

Chris pauses. Forgiveness. That's what he's looking for out here.

There's a bottle of whisky on the side. Did Jill buy this from the shop? He gets up, opens it and pours himself a generous three fingers. It burns like fire down his throat. He has another and then carries on whittling.

Snapchat

FionaWilson: Oh my God, Rory! Was that you who graffitied on Lorna's dad's house?

LornaMcGowan: Why did you do that, you dick?

RoryCampbell: I didn't! It was Sean. I took photos though.

LornaMcGowan: Leave it alone, Rory, FFS!

RoryCampbell: Your dad shouldn't be allowing that copper in the house! Aren't you reading all this stuff online???

LornaMcGowan: Jillian Moore is Dad's friend. They've been friends for ever.

RoryCampbell: He should hang them both out to dry.

8

The sleeping pill Chris took hasn't touched the sides. It's three in the morning now and he's been in and out of sleep – he thinks – but now he's purely awake, restless and feeling disconnected from himself. He's drunk, too. The room is on an axis that he can't correct.

Earlier, Chris and Jillian had eaten the casserole in silence, but he hadn't been able to taste it. Too full of whisky, too full of worry. They'd put on *Golden Eye*, though Chris had been occupied by listening for unfamiliar sounds outside. He could tell Jill was distracted too because the television sound was so low that she couldn't possibly have made out any words. Instead, she'd sat there gnawing at the skin on her fingers.

'Jill,' he'd said after a while. 'Stop. They're bleeding.'

She'd ignored him and carried on. Moments later a bright red droplet had run down her finger.

'You know what?' she'd said.

'What?'

'You didn't even clean the fucking downstairs bathroom like I asked.'

He'd stared at the blood. 'I was – I was making you something for your birthday.'

'Where is it then?'

'I haven't finished it yet.'

'Too busy drinking my whisky. That bottle was a gift from Harris to me, and you've drunk nearly half of it.'

'Sorry. I didn't know.'

'Well, now you do,' she'd said, and got up to get a plaster.

'Jill?' he says now, to her sleeping form.

She's silent beside him.

'Jill.'

She turns. 'What?' she says crossly, wide awake. 'What's wrong?'

'I never once lied when I told you I loved you. In the years when . . . you know. When I was with her.'

'I *know* you loved me. What I didn't know was that you loved someone else as well.'

'I didn't—'

'Shut up.'

They're silent a moment.

'It's exhausting, being this worried,' she whispers.

She looks to the window out of habit, but tonight they've shut the curtains. They don't usually, because they like to see the moon in the sky, but the writing on the wall has upset them.

'You believe me, don't you?' he asks. 'That I had nothing to do with what happened to Sophia?'

'You were in Southampton and your unit has evidence of it.'

'Yes.'

She looks to him now, like she's examining him for cracks. 'But we left for Sardinia not even a week after she died.'

'That was a coincidence. Nothing more.'

'I hate this,' she says.

He sees tears pooling in her eyes.

'I hate it all.'

'If I could take it back—'

'But you wouldn't,' she interrupts. 'You wouldn't ever take it back because you loved that job. It meant everything to you.'

He is silenced. Because she's right, it did.

'And you loved her, too,' she says. 'I don't believe that Sophia meant nothing. I don't believe that.'

Not a question but a statement, and what can he say in reply? He would only give himself away in some capacity. She rolls over. He should have denied it. He stares at her: a silhouette under the duvet, hair splayed on the pillow in ribbons of gold. He wants to lean over and kiss her, but at the same time he wants to put a pillow over her face. Her disappointment in him is almost too much to bear and he wants to extinguish it.

But of course he doesn't touch her. Jillian is the love of his life, his strength and stability. He rolls over so that their backs are to one another, reaches to take another sleeping pill and hopes that oblivion will follow.

If he knew in that moment that he would never see her again, what might he have done differently?

9

2002

He started to attend their meetings regularly. In the early weeks he didn't speak, just listened, but as time went on he began to ask questions and contribute ideas that were smart and well considered. Then he began to stay for drinks after the talks, and Sophia would note how he moved among their tight group, finding things in common with them all. She also noted how he'd always end the evenings sat next to her with a pint and a bowl of chips. He seemed to sit closer to her than he did to any of the others, looked at her in the eyes, and she almost wanted to recoil from the intensity of it. He seemed to smile more often with her too, not that she counted. Did she count? Perhaps she did.

After a couple of months, people remarked that they liked having him around and, with this wider acceptance, he was invited to attend meetings at Johann's house in Fulham, where the core group made flyers and banners for upcoming climate protests, and where they discussed long-term strategies. Chris was logistical and practical, and he had a van for his gardening business and would clear it out to take them all to protests and meetings.

There were nights where they would stay up till the early hours, some vibrant with conversation and others quietly and peacefully working on a task. Sophia would watch Chris with his headphones on, with a paintbrush making protest signs, or a pen and paper making notes, deep in concentration. Occasionally, he caught her looking at him and he would smile and she would blush and look away.

She started to wish the weekdays away, hungry for the weekends, when she would see him at meetings. It was pathetic, she thought, because she didn't know him, but in a short space of time he was all she could think about. He was like a ghost at her shoulder when she flirted with boys at clubs, and he was in her head when she took those boys to bed. His smile, his eyes, his casual effortlessness. Those boys at university had nothing on him, didn't know how to play the game as he did. Didn't even know how to open the box to the game. Where before she wouldn't care a jot how she looked coming to the meetings at the pub, she now took great care in what she wore, made sure that her make-up was delicate and her hair curled in a way that looked like she hadn't really curled it at all. Stupid, she knew, to care at all, but he gave her feelings no one else ever had – fancies, girlish excitement.

'Who's got you all pepped up?' her sister asked her when they were at their parents' in Kent one Sunday.

'His name's Chris,' Sophia replied.

'God,' Leila said, and mussed Sophia's hair. 'You said that all breathy. When do we get to meet him?'

Sophia smiled. 'Nothing's even happened.'

'Is this a boy from uni?' their mother asked.

'No,' Sophia said. 'He's from Green is Go. A proper man.'

Leila laughed. 'What does that *mean*? Is he made out of iron and steel?'

Sophia nudged her sister's arm, grinned. 'I just mean he's different.'

'*Different*. OK.'

'Maybe you'll meet him soon.'

Their father raised his eyebrows and passed the gravy.

It was in October 2002 that Sophia saw exactly what Chris was made of. There was a combined group march for climate change where over a thousand people walked the streets of London, clogging traffic, forcing people to cram the pavements. They blew whistles, chanted, banged drums.

Sophia walked with Johann, Carlotta, Jude and Chris, each of them holding picket signs which read *Green is Go* and *We Need Change Now*. Johann, Carlotta and Jude were in good spirits: high on weed, singing loudly and bouncing along the road. This was their bread and butter, the reason why they'd founded the group, living for maximum disruption and for pissing on the establishment.

Chris, however, was more serious than Sophia had ever seen him. He spent the time watchful, pointing out the best places to walk and steering them away from anyone who looked threatening. There was resistance – climate deniers, people who just wanted a fight, or members of the public who had been inconvenienced. They hurled insults and occasional fists. Horns were piercing, people were shouting. Cyclists were forced to dismount, joined the jeers.

'Get out of the fucking road, idiots!'

There was a heavy police presence too, and they tried to keep lines, keep order, but ended up shoving when the road bottlenecked.

'It's getting lairy,' Jude said jovially, pushing into Sophia because someone was pushing into him.

'Move on,' officers shouted when the group funnelled, became tight and slow.

'The police aren't helping,' Chris muttered. 'They should be directing traffic the other way.'

He turned his head to the several police officers walking alongside them, shoving the demonstrators forward.

'Hey!' he yelled. 'Take the cars over to Holborn!'

'You've made your point, mate,' one officer shouted back. 'Time to fuck off home and drink your chamomile.'

'Funny!'

They started to squeeze, tight sardines. Someone pushed against Sophia's back so forcefully that she tripped and dropped her picket sign. It landed on someone's head in front.

'Sorry!' she said.

'Hold back!' Chris shouted ahead.

'Go home!' someone else yelled from the pavement.

The pushing became a swell of movement. Sophia saw the police line break as they stepped forward to haul protesters out of the march – to help them or arrest them, she didn't know. Suddenly she was pushed to the ground, landing face first on the tarmac. Several others landed on top of her, crushing her cheeks into the grit of the road. She tried to speak but couldn't. The noise above became a roar.

'Up, up!' Chris said, dragging her up by her coat.

She put her hand to her nose, felt the rush of warm liquid and realized it was blood.

'Keep moving,' Johann said, and even he sounded worried. 'They're getting too much.'

'What the fuck was that!' Chris shouted at the police. 'Was that you, fucker?'

'Walk on,' the officer replied. 'You're a nuisance.'

'Don't you see what we're doing here?' Chris said.

'Keep walking, Chris,' Carlotta said.

But Chris was incensed. 'You're not doing your job, you piece of shit! People are going to get hurt!'

The police officer lunged forward with a baton, smashed it down on Chris's back.

'Oh my God,' Sophia said. 'Are you OK—'

But she'd not finished her sentence, because Chris had spun around and was shouting, a primal roar in her ears, and before she could properly register it he was reaching for the officer with his bare hands.

'Don't you fucking touch me!'

Sophia took Chris's arm, pulled him. 'Come on, let's go.'

'Listen to your bird,' the officer said. '*Move.*'

Johann stared at Chris, in shocked surprise, and Sophia steered Chris away, forward through the narrow line and then to the side of the march, where there was space. He was red in the face, fierce in the eyes.

'Hey,' she said. '*Hey.* Do you want to get yourself arrested?'

'I won't get arrested.'

'You will if you act like that.'

'This is turning into something too big, and the police are making it worse.'

'That scared me, just then. You scared me.'

He paused for a moment, looked at her. 'Shit, your nose.'

'It's fine,' she said, though she had no idea. She had probably smeared blood all over her face. 'War paint.'

She smiled up at him, wanted the look of fury on his face to disappear. He reached out, enveloped her.

'I'm sorry,' he said into her hair. 'Fucking savages.'

The smell of him was peppery and fresh, even through her busted nose. She gripped him tight, and then he released her as suddenly as he'd grabbed her.

'Let's call it a day and get a pint, yeah?'

She nodded, and they walked away from the march in silence, but close together, hands almost touching.

He ordered her a drink at the bar and came back with napkins. He held them gently to her face. 'You OK?'

'I'm OK,' she said.

His wild outburst with the police had shaken her, but there was something deeply attractive about how he'd squared up to the officer. And she couldn't deny that her body had lit up when he'd held her.

The thing is, exposing those undercover police — even their wrongdoings — means that public opinion is swayed against the entire establishment. Some of these people put themselves in real danger. Coppers in drug rings, gangs, whatever.
— @NickG, X

You're saying we need to protect these men??
— @Outtahere, X

I'm saying it's not black and white. Nothing is.
— @NickG, X

The media goes crazy for stories like this — makes it all worse.
— @whizzy, X

An integral part of being a journalist is to hold authority to account. Don't come at journalists @whizzy
— @MeganKimGuardian, X

Do you realize how much access they had to us? The private, most inner details of our lives? The police had *files* on us all, and it wasn't only our official records — driving licences, passports, addresses, etc. They had images of us going about our daily lives. Photos of my mum inside her house, pictures of me with friends at the pub – taken with one of those high-definition cameras. I thought that only happened in Hollywood films. Do you know how violating that feels?

    – Lola Coutelle, ex-girlfriend of former SDS police officer James Pearson, BBC True Crime Drama: *Into the Dark*, 2025

The 'establishment', as you call it, had a responsibility. Activists shouldn't have been infiltrated. Those police operations breached freedom of expression rights. End of story.

    – @MildrageMassiverage, X

The police in Surrey were very kind and helpful when I lost my handbag.

    – @EmiliaWentworth, X

Who invited you to the party, Grandma??

    – @MisterDis, X

My husband is in the police, and my cousin. They're both exceptional men and I'm proud of them.

    – @MeeraPTL, X

The police deal with the absolute scum of the earth every single day. I'd like to see you try it for one fucking second.

    – @heavysimponX, X

You're all missing the point. As a police officer he tricked Sophia into a relationship. IMMORAL AF.

    – @Outtahere, X

I thought I was a good guy. Wasn't I a good guy?
– [Name redacted], former SDS officer, BBC True
Crime Drama: *Into the Dark*, 2025·

10

He has dreams. Persistent and sweat-inducing and always the same — variations of his identity being revealed while he's undercover. He dreams of walking through woodland, lost in the blackness of trees, and there are voices, screaming. Sometimes he can hear Sophia. Sometimes he hears men. The dominant emotion is always fear.

He wakes suddenly, sticky and damp against the sheets, and his hand immediately reaches beneath his pillow, instinctual. There were some years when he was on deployment where he slept with a cricket bat under his bed and a knife under his pillow, terrified he would talk in his sleep and unveil himself. Not with the environmental activists from Green is Go. They weren't threatening, but that couldn't be said for the ones who came after. Those people could be hunting him, right now, and he is worried about them, terrified of them, but he cannot say anything to Jill.

He realizes then that Jill isn't in bed beside him. He looks at the alarm clock on her bedside table, sees that it's ten in the morning. He's never this late up. His head is banging from the alcohol, and from mixing it with the sleeping pills. He shouldn't drink; he's a bad drinker.

'Jill?' he calls.

There's a noise by the bed. Jackson has lifted his head, and now thumps his tail on the wooden flooring. Chris peers out of the window, sees the dinghy isn't by the bank.

'Mum's gone sailing,' he says. 'Did she feed you already?'

The dog whines.

'Maybe an extra biscuit or two then, just in case.'

Jackson's tail goes harder. *Whack*, *whack*, like a thick whip, like a drumbeat. Jill hates it when Chris calls her 'Mum' to the dog, so now he only does it in private.

For many years they hadn't tried to conceive very seriously – he was away a lot and Jill was busy working. But when they moved to Sardinia, they decided to try in earnest. They both wanted it; sometimes he wanted it so badly that he scared himself. Four years passed before they decided to try IVF. Three years of failed rounds followed, and then it was too painful and too expensive to keep trying.

The realization that they couldn't have children had been a grief like no other – holding hope each month and then holding each other when the blood came. When they eventually decided to stop trying altogether, he drove her to a house where there were five Great Dane puppies for sale, and Jill had burst into tears from both happiness and sorrowful acceptance.

'We will always have each other,' Chris had said quietly, and Jill had squeezed his hand.

Four weeks later, Jackson was home with them.

Chris wrinkles his nose. There's a smell in the air, sharp and chemical.

He stands, uses the bathroom, then puts on pyjama trousers and a hoodie. He's missed making Jill her morning cup of tea and hates himself for it because it's the little things that moor people when they are weathering a storm: a cup of tea, your pet butting its head against your leg, your favourite song on the radio. He goes downstairs, is almost knocked sideways by the sharp smell before realizing it's chemical and it's coming from the downstairs bathroom where they clean the mud from Jackson's walks. Jill must have cleaned it herself, when he was supposed to do it as a present to her. He opens the bathroom and sees it's spotless.

'Shit,' he says.

Jill will be fuming.

He gives Jackson some biscuits and then makes tea for himself, sits at the table, stares around in the quiet. He realizes that the lamp Jill uses to write by is on the side by the toaster. It's usually in the snug. It's a horse-head base, solid and wooden, with a cream-and-green shade. Beside it is her notebook.

He sighs. While she's not here, he takes the opportunity to call Oliver Hamilton.

'What's going on with Leila Roy?' he asks when Oliver answers.

'Leila is volatile. And the internet wants blood spilt.'

'They'll get it if all this carries on.'

'We're doing everything we can without also poking an angry bear.'

'There was writing on the wall of the house.'

'Writing?'

'Graffiti. "Fucking Killer Pig" in red on the wall.' Chris hears Oliver swear. 'It wasn't online and it's been painted over now, but . . .'

'Why didn't you tell me?'

I didn't have the energy, he wants to say.

'You're a sitting target there, Chris. We thought it would be good for you two to have some familiarity during all this, but the inquest has garnered too much bad press. I'm going to look into moving you to another house.'

'Where?'

66

'I don't know yet.'

Chris thinks of the figure in the woodland that may or may not have been his imagination. He feels like a target.

'Is there any news on Roper?' he asks. 'About where he is?'

There's a pause. 'Roper? Don't even think about Damian Roper. That's history.'

'It's not though,' Chris says. 'Is it?'

'Don't worry about him, OK?'

Oliver hangs up.

It passes midday. Chris makes himself and Jill a sandwich lunch, and then waits. At one o'clock he calls her phone, but it rings out. Given how they went to sleep last night, he wouldn't be surprised if she decided to stay out on the water for longer.

He spends some time re-reading the documentation he needs to read. As an interested party and part of the inquest, he has access to it, and he's most *definitely* interested in what it says. It's crucial he reads it all, but it's difficult to process – Sophia's heartache is acute in each sentence. When he can't take any more, he distracts himself by listening to the radio and continuing to whittle the wooden heart.

At two o'clock he watches the glinting light on the loch, calls Jill again, twice, and then a third time, but there's still no answer. He eats his sandwich, which has been waiting on the table. He wonders if she's with Harris or Susie, considers how he would check in with either of them. He would have to go into the village but is reluctant to.

'Where did she get to?' he asks Jackson.

He strokes Jackson's head, slips the silky ears between his fingers, and looks again at the loch, to try to catch sight of Jill out in the boat. But the body of water is so vast and the high clifftops either side obscure inlays and he can't see the boat. In fact, he can't see any boats. The sky is beginning to bruise over the water and a knot of worry pulls on his stomach; Harris had said there was a storm coming today.

At two thirty, his phone rings. But it's not Jill. It's Jawad. He doesn't want to speak to Jawad. He wants his wife to call, tell him to make some tea because she's a minute away and she wants to write, and then she wants to lie in bed with him.

'Chris, how are you doing?'

'Hi, Jawad. I'm doing OK.'

'Listen, I wanted to touch base.'

They're in touch constantly, as is Oliver, so they can get all their ducks in a fucking row, even though, at this point, Chris feels like they might as well just shoot them all. Little yellow feathers falling around his face.

'I wanted to update you on the permissions,' Jawad says.

Chris sighs, goes to the snug and sits on the sofa. Jackson follows, lays his head down on Chris's lap. The inquest is in a few days and they've applied for special permission for him not to be on camera. He's praying this is approved. He can't be seen on a global platform, not when he's spent so many years in hiding.

'I've heard from the coroner, and we're all good to attend the inquest via secure link,' Jawad continues. 'We've got the pandemic to thank for that. Before 2020, you would have had to attend in person.' He gives a surprise laugh. 'Did you see that lawyer in Texas who attended a case on video link as a cat?'

'What?'

68

'He had a filter on his computer and he couldn't remove it. He had to do the whole thing as a white kitten.'

The story is fluffy, like cotton wool taking up space in Chris's head. But perhaps Jawad is telling him this to put him at ease.

'I hope our systems are a little more mature.'

Jawad laughs. 'I won't let you put on a kitten filter, it's OK. How are you getting on with the diaries? I realize they must make for difficult reading.'

Chris bites at the inside of his cheek. 'Yeah.'

'Everything is filed in regard to your operation in Southampton. Your evidence, photographs and such.'

'Thanks, Jawad.'

'I'll see you in a few days.'

He hangs up, leaves Chris staring into the middle distance. Jawad can afford to be light-toned because he thinks he knows exactly how everything went, exactly what happened.

He doesn't.

The clock reads two forty-five. There's a storm on the horizon; he can see the sheet of grey in the distance and he is worried by it.

'Let's go and look for Mum.'

They should out the bastard. Why put that photo up on X to take it down again? Not tell us where he is? Which loch??
    – @Outtahere, X

It's an *inquest*, not a trial. What @LeilaRoyPR has as evidence against #chrisfletcher isn't factual. His initial statement said he wasn't there, that he was in deployment somewhere else.
    – @Mickeyblueeyes, X

@Mickeyblueeyes, considering who Chris Fletcher was, and what his role was, the finding of Sophia's documentation was enough to incur an inquest. I didn't believe it then, and I don't believe it now – Sophia wouldn't have taken her own life. She was in a bad way, but she hadn't spiralled that low. #sophiaroy #justiceforsophia #chrisfletcher
    – @LeilaRoyPR, X

But how do you know that? People hide parts of themselves from others all the time. How confident are you that your sister wasn't using?
    – @Marioboy126, X

Why would she go all the way to Derby to do that when she lived with our parents in Kent?
    – @LeilaRoyPR, X

I'd move far away and start taking drugs if I lived with my parents.
— @Rammifications, X

Look what I've found. [Image shows a house with red writing on the wall, FUCKING KILLER PIG]
— @AnonRC, X

Is this about him??? Where is this?!!?
— @Outtahere, X

In my village. This is where he's staying – buff.ly/305cwn2
— @AnonRC, X

@AnonRC, perhaps you could send me a DM? I would love to interview you.
— @MeganKimGuardian, X

11

The lights are off at The Black Horse, but the door is open and Chris can hear tinny music coming from the kitchen at the back of the pub. He didn't want to come out and risk being seen in the village, but he doesn't have Harris's mobile number and he's the only person Chris can think of who might know where Jill is.

'Hello?'

The ceiling seems lower in the darkness. Jackson butts up behind him.

The McGowan family has owned The Black Horse for three generations and Harris has run it for the last twenty years, previously with his wife, Kate. The atmosphere of the pub changed when Kate died – Harris painted the interior all black for one thing, and he stopped doing the Christmas Fair nights; stopped the children's Easter trails; stopped the Halloween Festival that drew in people from villages miles away. Jill said it was sad, but she understood. Everyone understood. What happened to Kate was a tragedy.

Chris follows the music, looks around the open kitchen door. Spotless stainless-steel countertops; a range and a microwave; two tall standing fridges; a double sink with an industrial dishwasher stacked next to it. The strip-lights, at odds with the ambient lighting in the pub itself, are harsh in his eyes. He walks further inside, feels a gust of wind on his face; there's obviously a door open somewhere. A pad of paper on the side lists vegetables down one column and meats down the other. Jackson's tail whips against the metal of one of the counters.

Chris can hear Harris's voice coming from outside, and then he sees him in the outbuilding a few steps from the main kitchen. He's dipped over a chest freezer, his phone balanced on his shoulder, a pen in one hand, shouting over the noise of the washing machine.

'Another leg should do it for the weekend. And ribs,' he says, and shuts the lid, turns, and jumps.

Chris grimaces, mouths an apology.

'No, lad. It's OK,' Harris says into the phone. 'Got someone here. That's all though. Tell your dad I'll collect it in an hour.'

He puts the phone in his pocket. 'Everything all right?'

'Sorry for the intrusion.'

'Lorna said the wall looks good now.'

'That's not why I'm here.'

Jackson steps closer to Harris and towards the huge freezer. Harris gestures to the kitchen door. 'Shouldn't have pets back here. Health and safety would have my licence.'

'Do health and safety come out here?'

Harris laughs. 'They come out everywhere.'

He shuts the outbuilding and they walk back through the kitchen and into the bar.

'Drink?'

'No – no, ta. I shouldn't really even be out, but I . . . Have you seen Jill?'

Harris pulls himself half a pint. 'When?'

'Today.'

'I've not seen the pair of you since yesterday at Meredith's place.'

'Jill's taken the boat out, but she's always back at midday. At first, I thought maybe she just went a long way out, but it's getting late. I've tried calling; it just rings out.'

Harris strokes the stubble on his chin.

'There's that storm due, isn't there? It's looking a bit grey out on the water.'

'Maybe she's gone to Susie's?' Harris suggests.

'She stocked up yesterday.'

'Maybe she forgot some things and docked the boat closer to the shop and forgot to call you? Maybe she had lunch out on the boat? Wanted time to herself?'

'Maybe. But she would have answered my calls.' Though, given their argument, perhaps she wouldn't.

Perhaps she wants to let him stew.

'I'll try her,' Harris says, and takes his phone out.

They look at each other in silence, the phone at Harris's ear.

'Nothing,' he says after a minute. 'I'll call Susie.'

He scrolls his phone to find her name, presses a button. 'Sus? It's Harris. You seen Jill today?' He pauses, looks out of the window. 'Aye, it is. Just started.'

Chris follows his eyeline, sees that it's raining.

'Perhaps another half-hour before it gets heavy? Aye.' Harris ends the call. 'Susie's not seen her.'

Chris feels a sharp edge of panic in his throat.

'I'll call Murray.'

'Who?'

'The coastguard,' Harris says. 'If she's out on the boat, she may have already got caught in some headwinds, or else she's taken shelter in a cove.'

'Thanks.'

'Can you tell me what she was wearing today so I can

74

pass it on to him?'

'Her sailing jacket is gone from the house, and her rucksack. I don't know what she had on otherwise, but the jacket is distinctive. The bright green one.'

Harris nods. 'Aye, I know it. You go back to Smoke House and I'll call it in, see what he thinks. I need to go to Gareth's to pick up the meat, so I'll ask around some of the shops too, shall I?'

Chris exhales, feels the constriction of the invisible shackles. 'That would be good. Thanks. I . . . I probably can't be seen out.'

'No. I understand.'

'Who else might have seen her? The newsagent? John Crossan? You were all friends, too, weren't you? Jill knew him.'

'She knows a lot of people up here. I'll put out a message.'

'OK. Thank you.'

Harris smiles reassuringly at him. 'Jill will be fine, Chris. She's a good sailor.'

'She probably is fine,' Chris agrees. 'She's probably punishing me.'

'Aye, she would too. You drive back and I'll swing round to you on my way back.'

'We walked over.'

There was a moment when he'd considered driving before worrying someone might slash his tyres. Perhaps this is paranoia.

'You might get wet on the way home.'

'I think you're probably right.'

He opens the door to the pub, and Jackson collides with someone coming in. It's Lorna.

'Sorry, Lorna. Jackson, look where you're going.'

'Mr Fletcher . . .' she says, and then stops. 'I'm sorry.'

'It's OK,' he says. 'The wall is fine now.'

She slips past him and into the pub, disappearing up the private stairs at the side of the bar.

12

By the time they've walked the twenty minutes back to the house, both Chris and Jackson are drenched. Long needles slant against the grey backdrop of the loch and render the line between the sky and the water invisible. The hills either side of it are shrouded by cloud and rain.

Inside, Chris grabs the towel they use to clean off Jackson's paws after a walk, but this time he throws it straight over the dog's head. The towel blooms with water. Jackson is patient, stays sedentary and then yawns, his breath like old meat in Chris's face.

Chris calls Jill again. No answer. He pours Jackson fresh water and puts some biscuits down for him, and then sits on one of the kitchen chairs. The thick arms of it provide comfort in their stability. Where the hell is Sophia?

Jill.

Where the hell is Jill?

His eyes come to rest on the kitchen counter, on Jill's notebook. He reaches for it, flicks to the pages she was last writing. Her familiar scrawl, the words made up of looping letters, and her beautiful doodles in the page corners – ink flowers and curling vines, eyes with heavy lashes and lids. He reads the last poem she's penned.

> *I once wished upon the universe,*
> *Show me the star that shines bright for me.*
> *And I reached and I clawed, but they all burnt out at the*
> *touch of my fingertips.*

Faded one by one into yawning holes.
Then I found something. Too bright, this truth! It scorched
my eyes.

Chris turns the page, but it's blank. He turns back to the beginning, starts to read every single poem with eyes he would have used as a police officer, but her poems are obscure, steeped in metaphor. He's never understood them.

He flips to the back of the book. Sometimes she makes notes in the back when she doesn't want to sully the beauty of the pages at the front, but there's nothing. No, wait. There's a page missing – ripped out.

He frowns.

It's an hour before Harris knocks on the door. He's brought another man with him who looks like he's stepped directly out of the sea – tall and broad, with gnarled hands and wiry grey hair. Chris places him at around seventy. There's a smell radiating off him, salt and brimstone. From the floor, Jackson lifts his head with interest.

'Chris, this is Murray Scott,' Harris says. 'Coastguard.'

Murray nods. They don't take their coats off. The rain puddles on the stone tiles.

'No one in the village has seen Jill.'

Chris's heart thrums. 'Then she's out there on the water, isn't she?'

'I've gone on the radio,' Murray says. His voice is gravelly. 'And asked for any nearby vessels that might have seen the boat. No one has seen your wife so far, but she could have seen the turn in the weather and holed up somewhere without a signal, or perhaps her phone battery has died.'

'I think something's happened,' Chris says.

Murray Scott watches Chris the way Chris used to watch others. Quiet and observing but with fierce intensity. The green of his eyes like emeralds.

'What do you think has happened?' Harris asks.

'I don't know.' Anguish slaps him round the face, makes him sway. 'Something bad.'

'We're going to go out and look for her,' Murray says.

Chris's eyes snap open. 'In this?'

'Aye, it'll only be getting worse later on. Best to try now while there are still a few hours of light. But we won't go into the mouth of the sea in this. She's angry.'

'Who's angry?' Chris asks.

'The sea,' Murray says.

'Let me come with you,' Chris says, reaches for his jacket.

Murray smiles, reveals the crack of a front tooth. 'You don't know this water, son. You leave it to us.'

'What if you don't find her?' Chris asks.

'Then there's a fine chance she'll already be back here with you.'

They leave, and Chris shuts the door behind them. The weight of the silence is heavy in his ears, like something physical.

13

The wind is howling down the chimney and the night is dark and wild with the storm. It's past nine at night and Jill is still not back.

He tells himself that she got caught out in the rain and has taken shelter somewhere. Or she'll be walking home. He's left the curtains open, hopeful that Jill might see the light if she's out on the water, or if she's making her way back on foot. She'll be cross that she's missed the day; she'll be itching to write about the swell of the water and of the air before the rain fell.

His breath hitches every time lightning forks across the sky. The storm is nasty, and he is filled with guilt that she is out there alone; while he is idling, better men are looking for his wife. Fuck, he's never felt so impotent. Or tired. He is dog-tired.

What would his father do in this situation? Chris thinks. He would be out there looking for Jill. He would be up all night, strategizing where she could have got to, or if she had fallen in, where the tide may have taken her. Edd Fletcher was a man who got things done, and Chris had strived all his life to be like him, but where Edd was a visible hero, Chris was now painted as a villain. Even if the truth absolute was shared, it would be impossible to be the good guy; there are too many layers to the story. He looks around for Jackson.

'Jacko?'

At the sound of Chris's voice, Jackson stands up from behind the sofa, where he's taken refuge from the sounds of the storm.

'You OK?' Chris asks, not sure if he's asking the dog or himself.

He kneels to Jackson, strokes his head. At eye-level the half-empty bottle of whisky stands on the wooden table by the window. It was stupid to drink last night; alcohol has always triggered paranoia and anxiety, blackouts too. There were times on deployment when he would drink an entire bottle with those he was infiltrating because drunk targets meant spilled secrets, but, akin to the fear of revealing himself when asleep, Chris worried about what details he'd spill when the alcohol started to flow. It took energy, so much energy, to keep focused when the drink wanted to slow him down, make him forget.

God, it was all so fucking heavy. Being undercover was more than putting on a different pair of jeans and growing his hair long. It was choosing which dead child to take the name of. It was crafting a backstory that was credible, weaving elements of his real past within it so there was emotional weight and depth to a created character. It was living in shitty bedsits, going on marches, drinking and scoring highs with people who were consistently suspicious of infiltrators. It was dealing with some terrible and terrifying people. It was all the fucking bad things he witnessed, all the things he *did*.

What he didn't realize until years later was that it was also so fucking *lonely*. When he was home with Jill and his real-life friends, he couldn't tell them about his work. He couldn't share stories about work colleagues, moan about his bosses. He couldn't begin to tell them about the things that threatened to undo him in the darkest hours of the night. No, the only people who kept him 'real' were the senior officers at Special Branch, the covert officers within other activist groups, and Oliver. But even within that group, there was pretence. No one ever wanted to say how shit-scared they were.

He gets up and looks to the window. Jill's absence in the house is like a missing limb. She should be here; they should be asleep together in bed. He can almost feel the warmth and comfort of her curled body in front of his. He imagines his arm around her waist. He wants her so desperately, even though, for weeks now, she's not allowed it.

A bolt of fear runs down his spine. There's a figure standing by the rocks leading to the loch, ten feet away. He can't tell who it is, if they're even facing the loch or the house, but it could be Jill. His heart is racing as he cannons through to the kitchen, pulls a torch from his rucksack next to the door and wrenches it open. A roll of thunder passes overhead, and the rain is hammering. He gets instantly soaked even though he's standing in the threshold.

'Jill!'

He shines the torch uselessly out to where the figure was, but the illuminated rain limits his vision. He steps out, walks towards the water.

'Hello?'

But the figure has gone and now he wonders if it was even there. Is he seeing things? He shuts the door, locks it, but within seconds there's a knock, and Chris jumps and backs away from it. The door handle starts to turn. Chris lunges to sweep a knife from the block, grips it like he's holding on for his life.

'Chris?'

It's Harris. Relief floods Chris's body.

'Can you open the door?'

Chris unlocks it, realizing only as Harris steps through that he still holds the knife in his hand. He hides it behind his back.

'I thought you'd seen me,' Harris says. 'You came outside?'

'I did – but I thought . . . did you find her?'

'We combed it,' Harris says. Rain drips from his hood, from his eyebrows, from his chin.

'Take your coat off, Harris. I'll put it by the stove.'

Harris obliges, turns out of the jacket, but instead of giving it to Chris, he hangs it up on a hook that juts out of the ceiling beam. Chris stares at it; he'd never even realized the hook was there and it makes him feel irrationally galled by Harris's familiarity with the house. But it makes sense that Harris knows it; Jill comes back every year to visit, and so Harris must come over here. What Chris doesn't like is that Harris knows it better than he does.

While Harris's back is turned, Chris puts the knife down behind the kettle and out of sight. He tells himself to get a fucking grip.

'If she's out there, we couldn't see her,' Harris says. 'We'll go out again tomorrow if we need to. She's most likely to be sheltering somewhere.'

'You think so?'

'I do.'

Chris sits heavily on the kitchen chair. 'I need to call the police.'

'Aye, I've already called Joseph Locke on my way over here. He's the local senior officer in these parts. He's fifteen

83

miles away, mind, and likely not able to get out tonight. The storm has been pulling trees across the roads.'

'But she's missing. She's actually *missing* now. What if she's injured?'

The other possibility hangs in the air between them.

Chris wants to go out and look for her. Jill is more important, the most important. Everything is off kilter without her. His mouth starts to water; he's not eaten for hours. He gets up, leans like he's on the ocean, and then puts some bread in the toaster. He puts some in for Harris too. His hands are shaking as he does so. Sweat beads on his brow line. Presently, a hand rests on his shoulder and he flinches – he's become so nervy after all the years undercover.

'It's going to be OK,' Harris says.

'Who else do we talk to? I need to be making lists. I need to be taking statements.'

'Joseph will come over tomorrow. Let him handle it.'

Chris pauses. 'Does he know about me? About what's been going on?'

'He does now.'

Harris moves to pick up his coat.

'I have to get back to Lorna,' he says.

Chris nods. Harris opens the door and walks back into the night.

14

He sleeps intermittently. Sometimes in the chair in the kitchen, sometimes on the sofa. He doesn't go to bed because going to bed feels like something has ended. Not just the day, but also his time with her, with Jill. Always he feels a presence – something ominous in the background, outside the house, and inside it too. He is swimming in half-sleep and worry.

At seven in the morning, the headache that has prolonged over the past twenty-four hours eventually wakes him for the day. Out of the window of the bedroom, the loch is now still. Debris from the storm has blown all over the grass surrounding the house and down to the rocks. There are entire branches snapped from trees, and slate tiles have come off the roof.

Next to him, Jackson woofs gently. 'You're hungry, I get it.'

They go into the kitchen and Chris fills Jackson's bowl.

Fuck it, the police won't come at seven in the morning after this storm. Jill is missing and the first twenty-four hours are crucial in finding her. He shouldn't have listened to Harris last night – he should have gone out and looked.

Chris pulls on his boots.

The storm has ravaged the fringes of the loch; there are trees leaning at unnatural angles, and others now dip sadly into the water, rocking and creaking with the lapping waves.

The wind blows, little and often, but in between the gusts, there is an eerie silence.

Chris can only hope that perhaps Jill made it to one side of the loch and then took shelter. Perhaps she made a Boy Scout hut from branches. She was always at home in nature – it didn't scare her – but if she had been out in that storm last night, how could she not have been frightened? Every crack of lightning was like a gunshot, the rolls of thunder deafening.

He stops suddenly.

What if someone has taken her, used the storm as a way to cover themselves? Damian Roper. No, no, he tells himself. He can't think that way. He's confusing the past and the present in his head.

Jackson noses the ground beside him.

'Is she here?' Chris asks. 'Can you find her?'

But the Great Dane isn't a bloodhound or a trained scent dog.

The sky is colourless but bright. The fallen and bent trees make the woodland more visible in parts, and Chris goes further and further in until the skin on his back begins to prickle. Someone is here in the woods with them, he could swear it. He stops, looks all around. The trees blend into darkness.

'Jill?'

There is an edge of agitation to Chris's breathing, but no one is here – apart from Chris's own demons.

Jackson trots up to him, bats his head against Chris's arm. The solidity of the Dane brings him back to himself. He will not be hurt if Jackson is here. He is once again thankful that they brought Jackson to Scotland.

They spend more than three hours of the morning

scouring for Jill and for any signs of the dinghy, but to no avail. At ten thirty he returns to the house to wait for the police.

It's as he comes out of the woodland and trudges back towards the house that someone steps out from behind the back wall. A boy – young, blond, keen-eyed.

'Are you Chris Fletcher?'

Chris stops dead. 'This is private property.'

'Are you Chris Fletcher? I'm Rory Campbell. I'm doing a journalism course.'

'Good for you,' Chris mutters, and starts walking again, head down now to shelter his face. He is only ten metres away from the house.

'Can I ask you some questions?'

'No.'

Suddenly the boy whips out a phone from his jeans pocket. Before the boy can flick the screen, Chris twists round so his back is turned. His image cannot be out there.

'Mr Fletcher!'

He doesn't follow, but his words are carried on the wind behind him –

'Did you kill Sophia Roy?'

Chris jogs the last steps to the house, like an animal retreating to a den, and shuts the door behind him and Jackson with a crash.

The stillness that follows is absolute. Chris can hear his own eyes blinking. Jackson stares up at him dolefully. Chris takes out his phone and calls the next best thing to a father figure; he calls Oliver Hamilton.

Oliver answers immediately. 'I've seen it.'

'Seen what?'

'The image on X.'

Chris freezes. Did that boy manage to take a picture of him?

'The house that you're staying in. You told me someone graffitied the house.'

'But that was yesterday – no, the day before. It was painted over.'

'Well, it's popped up a few times from various accounts. We're on it, but it's not going to go away. Nor is the picture of you from the pub.'

'That's back too?'

'That's back.'

'Listen, it doesn't even matter right now – I rang you because of Jill. She's gone.'

Oliver is silent for a moment. 'What do you mean, gone?'

'She took the boat out yesterday – there's a sailing dinghy that her friend lends her – and she's not come back.'

'How long?'

'I haven't seen her in twenty-four hours.'

'What? Why are you only calling me about this now?'

'Because we've been *looking*. Local police are coming.'

'Local *police*? What the hell—'

'There was a storm here overnight.'

'You think she went out in the storm?'

'No, before the storm. And maybe she got caught up in it. I don't know. Maybe she's sheltering somewhere. Or . . .'

He fades out.

'This isn't good,' Oliver says.

15

Chris refrains from shouting down the phone. Of course it's not good. How can anything be good if Jill isn't here? How can he think straight without her?

'I'll let you know when I hear anything,' he says to Oliver, and then hangs up.

He stares into the silence and his mind tracks back to the morning that Caroline Bonner's article broke. Oliver had called to tell Chris about it. He had been in the kitchen of their Sardinian home, and the afternoon sunlight was streaming in from the window, bathing everything in soft gold. He'd leaned heavily against the countertop, felt like his legs might give way.

He'd waited an hour before asking Jill to sit down. He had knelt on the floor in front of her, like a marriage proposal, but he had shattered her entire world. He'd told her that when undercover, deployments had been difficult to navigate, that infiltration needed levels of attachment. He'd told her that he had been intimate with an activist – Sophia – while 'on duty'. He could see that that information in itself was enough to floor her, but there was more to tell her – the added detail that the inquest into Sophia's death cited Chris's possible involvement. He'd told her that he wasn't in Derby the night Sophia died, that he was in Southampton on another operation, and Jill had listened, stunned, and then without a word she had got up and walked away. She'd locked herself in their beautiful bathroom, and stayed in there until the moon came up. He'd waited outside, sick with knowing how he had wounded her, sick with knowing that worse was to come.

Jill hadn't wanted to come back to the UK with Chris. Chris had wanted her well out of the spotlight, but Jawad had told them she might be needed at the inquest too. Unlikely, he'd said, but not impossible. The thought of this scared her witless, but their hands were forced. She'd asked if they could stay in Scotland, in Meredith's house, because she needed something familiar. She needed Harris, she'd said, and Chris remembers the look on her face and the tone of her voice when she said it. Harris, who was dependable; Harris, who would never have hurt her the way he had done. He'd fought with Jawad and Oliver to approve it – Jill returned to Scotland annually, Chris had said, and no one would need to know that he was with her, although they might suspect it. Jawad had eventually and reluctantly agreed, and Jill had been instructed to tell anyone who asked that she had wanted to be alone while the inquest happened. Chris had thought – foolishly – that she would be comforted by being in The Old Smoke House, but in the few weeks since they've been here, Jill hasn't appeared comforted by the house or the loch, or by Harris.

The reality of what they are now facing has slapped them both hard across the face. The media have gone mad for the story about the police officer who'd infiltrated the activist group, become frenzied over the discovery of Sophia's secret online diaries and, despite Chris's best efforts at telling Jill not to read the articles that spewed out like hot vomit, he suspects that she has been reading them. Of course she will have, because who wouldn't?

Who wouldn't want to know all the sordid little details, if only to arm themselves against a rising tide of accusation and horror? She's also been relentlessly bombarded by Meredith, who sends articles about unmasked undercover officers, who asks about Sophia and spits her own personal thoughts about Chris. Sometimes she texts Jill multiple times a day; sometimes Jill reads out what they say because, he thinks, she likes to punish him.

You need to leave him.

'Will you?' he asked once, timidly.

She had looked away, and that small action had almost broken him.

'You abused my trust,' she said.

How could he argue with that? She had been so trusting over the years; in October 2005 when Chris had told her that he was leaving policing, that they were going to take an extended holiday, she hadn't asked why. She hadn't questioned why, after all the years of gruelling training and the drive for undercover work, he suddenly wanted to leave it all behind. But he knew she was happy that he was finally *with* her, relaxing, walking around with nowhere to be and no phone calls to take. She had her husband back, albeit a slightly different version: more subdued, more reflective. But warm too, affectionate, needy even. He knew she liked this version better than the one who used to come home on days off from operations sullen and quick to anger. He had been so unfair to her then.

'Are we in witness protection?' she had joked after a fortnight of beach trips and lunches on beautiful terraces.

'No,' he'd said, and gave her a hug, but when he'd suggested they actually *buy* a place out in Sardinia, she'd frowned.

'What about your parents?' she'd asked. 'My dad and my aunt? Our friends?'

'They can visit,' he'd said.

She'd frowned. 'Dad can't. You know that.'

'We can go and see him. You can stay with Rani.'

His enthusiasm, his spontaneity and the considered answers to all the issues she brought up about moving there had convinced her. They bought a house on the coast. They went out for meals, they walked hand in hand through the markets, they made friends, they took evening classes to learn Italian. In the beginning, Chris's parents came out, even though Edd Fletcher said he didn't like the heat. But Marion loved it all, and on those visits, would pull Jill aside and whisper audibly so Chris could hear:

'Any news?'

'Not yet,' Jill would say, but she would be smiling because they hadn't given up hope then.

Jill went back to Scotland every year and stayed at The Old Smoke House, seeing Harris and other schoolfriends, and went regularly to London to see Robert and Meredith. But despite saying he'd come back with her, Chris made constant excuses for why he couldn't. He knew it hurt Jill; he'd been close with her father, after all. Occasionally Chris would ring Robert, but Robert got confused on calls, would press buttons and disconnect them by mistake. Jill and Chris argued about it, but still Chris would not budge, would not return for anyone.

On the whole, their lives became simple and happy. And if Jill noticed now and again that he was quiet, she mentioned it rarely. She chose to ignore his moods, live in the present, where they have their lives ahead of them. But Sardinia now seems like a lifetime ago, a pretence.

A sudden noise disrupts Chris from his thoughts.

The police, he thinks, and is about to answer the door when he pauses. He doesn't want to be seen by the boy again. Doesn't want his face captured on camera.

'Who is it?' he says.

'Christopher Fletcher?'

It's a woman's voice. A mature timbre, but not Scottish. He worries that it's a journalist, someone with a camera.

'Who is it?' he repeats.

'I'm Amanda Connolly,' says the woman. 'I want to talk to Jill.'

He invites her in immediately. Of course he does, though his mind is running on overdrive. Because Amanda Connolly is the ex-wife of Mike Emerson, another SDS officer, who had been unmasked a decade ago. Jill had told Chris that Amanda had emailed via Jill's literary agent when the news first broke with the simple words, *I've been through it all. I am here if you need to talk to someone.*

How has Amanda found them?

Amanda is a petite woman, brown hair streaked with silver. Her eyes sweep over the kitchen, the horse-head lamp.

'Is Jill here?' she asks.

'No,' he says.

'Is she out sailing?'

The way she says this, casual and knowing, makes him double-take.

He frowns. 'Have you seen her? Here?'

She nods. 'I've seen her.'

'When?'

'A few days ago.'

He shouldn't feel betrayed by this, and yet he does. His fingers curl into his palms and he can feel the nails imprinting into soft flesh. Jill has done the thing Chris had asked her not to – she has reached out to Amanda, and not only that, but she has told Amanda where they are.

'But not since yesterday? Since the storm?'

'No?'

'She told you where we were staying?'

'Jill called me around a week ago,' Amanda says. 'She needed to talk to someone who knew what she's going through. She said the feelings got so heavy that one morning, when she was out on the water and away from you, she dialled my number. And when I picked up that first time, she burst into tears.'

Why is this stranger telling him this?

'That *first* time?' Chris asks. He is unable to keep the ice from his voice.

'We've spoken a few times,' Amanda says. 'Always when she's out on the water.'

'Show me.'

'Sorry?'

'Show me evidence. Your phone record. I want to see her number on your phone.'

If she is surprised by this challenge, she doesn't let it show. She takes her phone from her bag and taps on the screen, turns it around to show him. There, sure enough, is Jill's number on her phone. Several calls. Daily for the last few days except for yesterday and the day before. He is stunned by this, can't believe Jill would have done something so stupidly reckless. But evidently, she has.

'I was worried because I haven't heard from her,' Amanda says.

'That's kind,' he says through gritted teeth.

'I shared my own story with Jill, and I encouraged her to voice hers. I want her to know I'm here. We're all here.'

'All?'

'There are three of us. All ex-wives of undercover officers. Maia and Connie.'

A party, no less.

'I told Jill how we'd become each other's support group. I told her that we meet once a month in London, have a drink, talk about how much better our lives are now.'

Chris is silent. Rageful. 'That's . . . lovely.'

He doesn't have time for this woman who is standing in the kitchen and making him feel like shit. He doesn't have time to hear that Jill needs someone that's not him. He wishes Amanda gone.

'I said I would hire a house for a few nights,' Amanda continues, 'and if she wanted to get out, then she could use it as her safe house, as it were. No one would have to know.'

Oh, Jill, he thinks bitterly. Safe houses are never *safe*.

'She said there was something that was worrying her, but she couldn't say what it was. She kept sobbing. She said she wasn't sleeping, was up all night. Three days ago, she called me in the middle of the night. I was awake, and I replied straight away. And I picked her up.'

He stares at her. 'You – you picked her up? In a car? From here?'

'Yes.'

'And she . . . went with you?'

'She said she needed a couple of hours to talk it all through face to face with people who understood, with people who wouldn't judge her. She needed *back-up*.'

Back-up, Chris thinks. Like he is the enemy and Jill needs a cavalry behind her. His heart is thudding.

'She got in the car. She said she should have left you a note, but she hadn't. I started to drive. And then . . .' She stops talking for a moment. 'Before we went even a hundred yards, Jill asked me to stop.'

'Why?'

'I thought she was going back to write you a note. But she told me she needed to do something with the boat.'

'The – the boat?'

'The boat that she sails. She said you wouldn't be awake for hours, but if you woke before she was back, she needed you to assume she'd be out on the water. She made me get out and together we went and we untied it. We pulled it through the water, dragged it so it was a hundred metres or so into the woodland. I helped her obscure it with foliage.'

He is very still. Astounded by Jill's cunning.

'She said that it was just a precaution.'

'Go on.'

'We came to get back into the car, and I was about to put it in gear but she . . . she changed her mind.'

'Changed her mind about going with you?'

'Yes. She said she couldn't do it. That she couldn't speak to me, to any of us. She got out and I watched her go back into the house, and I've not heard a thing since. I tried to call, text.'

Finally, Chris thinks. Some loyalty from Jill.

Amanda looks at him, almost defiant. Almost challenging. 'I'm here because I'm worried.'

Then it clicks. She thinks Jill is afraid of him, of Chris. Perhaps she thinks he's got her locked up somewhere.

96

'I'm worried about her too,' he says after a moment. 'Because I haven't seen Jill for twenty-four hours.'

Amanda's mouth falls open.

'She's missing. It's not on the news yet. But when I woke up yesterday morning, she was gone. I thought she was sailing. I've called the police. They should be here any minute.'

'Oh,' she says. 'Oh, I – I just wanted to know if she was OK.'

'I'll need to tell the police to contact you,' he says. 'You'll need to tell them about what she asked you to do. With the boat. Hiding it.'

Because perhaps she had done it again? Hidden the boat and gone out again, on foot? But where would she have gone?

He looks at Amanda with a new doubt. 'She's not with you now, is she?'

'No!' Amanda says, blustering. 'No, of course not.'

'Show me.'

'Show you? Show you what?'

'Where you took the boat.'

She says nothing for a moment and then nods. He takes a key and his jacket and cap. From his position on the floor, Jackson looks up expectantly and thumps his tail.

'Not you, Jacko.' Chris looks to Amanda. 'Come on.'

They walk out of the house together and he surreptitiously glances towards the ridge – no one is up there, but he is uneasy. They will come, he thinks. They will come for him.

'Where do you think she is?' Amanda asks.

'I don't know,' he says.

'I'm so sorry. I had no idea . . . I wouldn't have come over if . . .'

He says nothing and so she edges now into silence, leads

him along the bank towards the woodland he was in that morning, looking for Jill.

'It was dark,' she says. 'We only had the light of our phones. I'm not sure how far in we went, but it was under some of these trees – you see? Where their branches get thick, over the water? We left the boat somewhere around there.'

He starts to lift some of the branches.

'Help me look,' he says, because he's angry, and hurt by Jill's betrayal. Furious, too, that he's having to ask this woman for help, a woman who was party to Jill wanting to trick him.

She nods, and together they start grappling in the undergrowth. Time passes; perhaps they go some three hundred yards down, searching.

They don't find the boat.

'I don't think it could have been this far,' Amanda says eventually.

He stands upright, panting. His hands are red and hot, and his palms are scraped from lifting heavy branches. Amanda's hair is messy across her face.

'I have to go back and wait for the police,' he says, by way of acknowledging defeat.

Back in the house he gives her a pen, some paper out of Jill's notebook, and she writes down her number.

'The police will need to interview you.'

'I – yes.' She nods, looks spaced and wobbly. Tiny leaves and twigs are caught up in her hair. 'Good. I'll speak to them. I – I'm sorry.'

Then she bustles out of the door and he shuts it behind her. Exhausted by her, exhausted by everything.

He watches her drive away.

*

98

He sits on the kitchen chair, stares into nothingness. How had it happened, he thinks, that Jill had jumped in a car with a complete stranger, to a place she didn't know, leaving him asleep and unknowing in the pitch-dark?

His brain is addled with thoughts of their fight before Jill disappeared.

'I hate this,' she had said. 'I hate it all.'

'If I could take it back—'

'But you wouldn't. You wouldn't ever take it back because you loved that job. It meant everything to you. And you loved her, too. I don't believe that Sophia meant nothing. I don't believe that.'

She had rolled over. Why hadn't he said anything to her after she'd said that? Why had he gone to sleep and not comforted her? She would have been comforted by Amanda and by the other two.

She is still with them, Chris thinks suddenly. Jill is playing with him. Or perhaps the women have taken her elsewhere and are trying to throw him off the scent by sending Amanda here as the concerned friend? Perhaps after that night, after he had taken the sleeping pill and fallen asleep, Jill had texted Amanda.

Can I see you again? This time I'm coming with you.

Perhaps Amanda had replied immediately.

Yes. Be with you ASAP.

Jill would easily have slipped out of the bedroom. Maybe she had made a cup of tea and sat in the darkness of the kitchen. She probably would have raised the blinds enough to see the moon, thin and silvery in the sky, because she loved the moon. Possibly she went into the snug, took the horse lamp, brought it to the kitchen table and opened her notebook, to write. Possibly she ripped a page from it to leave Chris a note, but then paused. Because she hadn't left one that first time, so why would she leave one now? A note would mean an explanation and an admission that she had told someone else where they were staying, which they had agreed they wouldn't do. No note then, but she would need to move the boat again, just in case. She folded the blank page and put it into her jeans pocket, and, with a renewed sense of determination, she put on her green sailing jacket, slung the rucksack over her shoulder, and closed the door softly behind her.

Chris imagines the wind on her face – cool and pure – as she walked down to the water. The air smelt of salt, of the promise of rain. A small crab scuttled across the rocks. She would have hidden the boat, as she had done with Amanda – walked it a few hundred metres further along the riverbank from where they'd looked, into the wood and sufficiently covered by low branches, before walking back to the house, just as Amanda's car pulled up over the ridge.

She would have passed the sleeping house, deliberately not looking at it for fear of going straight back inside and back to him, and then opened the car door, feeling thrilled and terrified at her recklessness. Amanda would have driven them to a little flint cottage, where the two others, Maia and Connie, embraced her like a long-lost sister. Chris almost chokes at the thought of it – the simple warmth of a hug when she hasn't allowed Chris to touch her. How he longs to. How he would hold her for as long as he could if she would just let him.

He imagines that the women talked long into the morning, past the dark blues of night and into the colours of dawn. They talked about their god-awful husbands, and how the police unit could allow such behaviour. Cackled with glee at their husbands' comeuppances.

When the sun came up, perhaps they decided a walk would clear their heads, and out they went into nature's symphony. But Jill would know she should get back home, he thought. She'd know he would be worrying about her, but this was a group of women who had endured what she was going through and had come out the other side. Would Jill have got her phone out of her bag and seen that Chris had called her? Known that he was worried?

But she wouldn't have wanted to leave them, and how could he blame her? They were looking after her when she was tired of being the one who had to look after others. She was tired, most of all of looking after Chris. He can wait, she might have thought. And so Jill wouldn't have panicked that she wasn't back in Smoke House. She was in a different place – both physically and emotionally disconnected to Chris. Indifferent, almost.

He imagines that time passed and the storm gathered. The wind started to move the tops of trees and then later began to sway huge branches. Maybe they all listened to the rain drumming on the windowpanes until it got so hard and fast they couldn't hear themselves talking.

Perhaps they decided to make dinner. Four witches over a cauldron.

He thinks how, at eleven that night, as lightning flashed over the house and he was worrying about her, she might have been sitting with a blanket over her legs, belonging to a sisterhood that he himself had put her in. Was Amanda right when she said that the only people who could pull Jill out of the mess of her own head were the women who had lived it first-hand and understood what Jill was going through?

Had they encouraged her to leave him? Had they told her that she would deal with whatever came next because they were the proof of it?

Let him suffer.

'Stay with us,' Amanda might have said.

'There are phone records,' Jill might have said. 'Of our conversations.'

Maybe Amanda would have smiled. 'You think the police are the only ones that can play games? We'll cover you.'

16

It's two in the afternoon when the police finally arrive. The man – Joseph Locke, as his badge reads – is tall like Harris, and dips his head when entering the house. The woman is young, short and keen-eyed.

'Our apologies in getting to you,' Joseph says. 'There has been significant damage to the roads.'

His accent is heavy, but his voice is quiet and smooth. He is a police officer – Chris can tell – who's used to law and order and cooperation.

'I'm Joseph Locke, and this is my colleague, Karen Holland.'

Karen's eyes meet Chris's and burn with suspicion. She is a police officer – Chris can tell – who's looking for a story.

'Murray Scott and Harris McGowan are out on the loch, looking for Jill. Duncan Bruce and his sons are also out in their boats,' Joseph says. 'We've called for the police dive team too.'

The dive team. Chris feels sick. No good ever comes of having the dive team out.

'They're coming from Greenock; it's going to take them a good five or six hours to get here, I'm afraid. And that's if they don't run into trouble on the road.'

Chris swallows the nausea down. 'Would either of you like coffee?' he asks.

He doesn't need more caffeine – he is wired by adrenaline – but it's something to do.

'Yes, please,' Joseph replies.

'No, thanks,' Karen says at the same time.

Chris gestures to the kitchen table. 'Please, take a seat.'

The officers sit, and Chris puts the kettle on the stove, takes mugs from the cupboard.

'There's a woman I need you to speak to,' he says. 'Her name is Amanda Connolly and she's an ex-wife of an old friend of mine. Another officer. She's staying around here with some others and they arranged to see Jill a few nights ago.'

Chris picks up the piece of paper, hands it to Joseph, who stares at it.

'We weren't given this information last night when Harris called us?'

'I didn't have it then. Amanda came here this morning because she'd tried to ring Jill but couldn't get hold of her.'

Joseph nods. 'Might Amanda know where Jill has gone now?'

'She said not, but I don't – I don't necessarily trust her.'

'Why so?'

'Because she had tried to steal Jill away in the middle of the night.'

Karen raises an eyebrow. '*Steal* her?'

Chris realizes how accusatory he sounds, how garbled. 'I mean – not against her will. Apparently she wanted to go, but . . .' He takes a pause. 'I should have asked to go back with Amanda and check if Jill isn't there.'

'You think they're together now?'

Chris pauses. *Does* he?

'I don't know.'

'I would think it unlikely, if Amanda came here looking for Jill,' Joseph says. 'But we'll contact her immediately.'

He passes the paper to Karen, who nods and steps out of the room.

'OK,' Joseph says. 'Let's start at the beginning, shall we? Could you please explain your and Jillian's movements over the last few days? It will be useful for us to have a view of things both before and after her going missing.'

As the kettle boils, Chris tells Joseph about their trip to the pub, the photograph that was taken there, about the writing on the wall. He tells him that the next day he woke late and Jill and the boat were gone.

Chris doesn't tell him that they woke earlier in the night, that he disturbed her at three in the morning and Jill had told him that she knew he had fallen in love with Sophia. He chooses to omit those details because they make him look even worse than he already looks. A liar, a cheat. He doesn't want anyone thinking he has driven Jill away.

Karen returns from the snug.

'We spoke,' she said. 'I'll go over after we've finished up here and take an official statement, but she said exactly what she apparently told you this morning. She and Jill did speak while Jill was out on the boat. Amanda came over three nights ago and offered to take Jill back with her, but Jill didn't go. After that, Jill stopped answering her calls and messages.'

'Did she tell you that Jill almost *did* go? That they hid the boat together so I wouldn't find it?'

'Yes.'

'Don't you think that's odd?'

'Yes,' Karen says. 'To me it says that Jill was afraid of what you'd think of her talking to anyone.'

Chris stares at her. Joseph jerks his head, gestures for Karen to sit down next to him. She does so and then takes her black book and a pen from her pocket. Chris swallows down the urge to shove the pen down her throat.

'We'll talk to Amanda properly later,' Joseph says. 'Let's talk about personal items missing.'

'Her sailing jacket – it's green – and her rucksack and phone.'

'What clothes was she wearing? Do you know?'

'She's taken the thermals that she wears on the boat and a sweatshirt . . . nothing else is gone from her wardrobe or from around the house. Her passport is here. And the spare key. She never took it when she went sailing. I'm always here.'

Trapped, he thinks, bitterly. He gets the milk out, stirs it into the coffee.

'So the house wasn't locked when you woke up?'

'It locks automatically behind you when you leave.'

'Do you know what was in the rucksack she took?' Joseph asks.

'It's the one she always takes sailing. There's a small first-aid kit in it, some spare rope, tools for the boat, that sort of thing.'

'She had a life jacket, too? For the boat?'

'The boat has one in it.'

'And she wears it?'

'Yes.'

Joseph nods. 'Can you give us a description of Jill?'

'Five foot five. Blue eyes. Long, blonde hair. She's slight – weighs around eight and a half stone, I suppose? But she's strong. A good sailor.'

Karen keeps writing.

'And the dinghy, Harris McGowan told us, is a 1970s Miracle sailing dinghy, yes? That she knew the boat like the back of her hand.'

'They've sailed it together since they were kids.' He pauses. 'Do you take sugar?'

'No, thanks,' Joseph says. 'Any medical history we should be aware of?'

'No.'

'And she goes by Jillian Moore? Not Fletcher?'

'Moore, yes.'

Chris never minded that Jill kept her own surname when they married. She had wanted to go by Moore if she ever got published, which now, of course, she has been. He's relieved she kept it. Any association with the name Fletcher would do her no good now.

'And how was Jill when you last saw her? In herself?'

'We went to bed. She was anxious because of what had happened with the wall outside. You've probably seen . . .'

Joseph nods curtly. 'We're up to date with all the social media.'

Chris puts the mugs down on the table, too strongly, and the coffee spills. 'Shit.'

'It's fine,' Joseph says. 'Have you called any of her family?'

'Both her parents passed away. She's an only child.'

'Doesn't this house belong to her aunt?' Karen asks. 'That's what Harris told you, wasn't it, Joseph?'

Chris pauses. 'Yes, it does. Meredith.'

'And have you checked in with her?'

'I – no.'

'Why not?' Karen asks.

Why not? It's a good question.

'Surely, as an ex-police officer,' Karen continues coolly, 'you remember that contacting friends and family is a priority in these situations? Jillian may have contacted her. She might know where Jillian is.'

Chris clenches his jaw. 'Honestly? Because I thought Jill would be fine. I thought she was out on the water and she was stewing. I thought she would come back later, but when the storm . . .' He pauses. 'Besides, Meredith hasn't been supportive throughout any of this, unsurprisingly.'

'Have you got her number?' Joseph Locke asks.

'Yes.'

'Please call her now.'

'Right now?'

'Aye.'

Chris takes his phone from his pocket, finds Meredith's number and presses dial.

'On speaker, please,' Joseph Locke says.

Meredith answers after a couple of rings, her voice clipped and brusque. 'Jill? Why are you calling from *his* phone?'

'Because it's him,' Chris says dryly.

'Oh. What do you want, Christopher?'

'Has Jill been in contact with you?'

'What are you talking about? We've been in contact constantly ever since this news about Sophia Roy. It's broken her in two, Christopher. Were you there? What happened to that girl?'

'You're on speaker phone, Meredith. The police are with me.'

'Your undercover friends, or the actual police?'

'Meredith—'

'You never told her the truth. You never—'

Joseph Locke motions for the phone and Chris gives it up to his waiting palm.

'Meredith Moore?'

There's a pause. 'Who's this?'

'My name is Joseph Locke and I'm a sergeant with the Scottish police. I'm with your niece's husband, and we're in The Old Smoke House – your house, I believe. I'm wanting to know when your niece was last in contact with you.'

'You're in my . . . Why? What's going on?'

'I'm afraid that Jillian is missing.'

'Missing?'

'Can you tell us when you last had contact?' Joseph asks.

'I – I suppose a couple of days ago. We've been texting, emailing, that sort of thing. She texted me a few times after that photo of Chris in the pub went up online . . . And the picture of that wall . . . What do you mean, *missing*?'

Chris grits his teeth. 'The clue is in the word.'

Joseph switches the phone off speaker. 'I'll take it from here.'

He gets up, opens the front door, and disappears through it. Chris and Karen are left in the silence of the kitchen.

Karen gives a wry smile. 'Sounds like you're not Meredith's favourite person.'

'Our relationship has been like that for the last twenty-five years.'

'Wow. That grudge is as old as I am.'

Chris looks at her, sighs. At her youth, at the whole situation.

'I understand Jillian is a poet?' Karen says. 'She's won some awards.'

'Yes. She was also a nurse for ten years in London before she became a full-time writer.'

'Does she still have her licence?'

'Her nursing licence? She does, yes. She helped out with the vaccines in Sardinia.'

'You must be proud of her for doing that, and for her writing.'

'Extremely.'

'And is she proud of you? Doing what you did?'

He looks at her sharply. She blinks at him innocently, but he can read people well enough to know the comment was meant to bite.

'She was supportive of my work.'

'Hmmm.' She starts scratching away in her notebook.

You would fall asleep, and I would drag your heavy, naked body out to the loch and fill your mouth with stones until it was all you were made up of – dark, slick, smooth stones clicking together as I pulled you into the water.

'We are very happy together,' he says, but the lie is hard to get out with his mouth as dry as it is.

'I assume it's true about your relationship with Sophia?'

'It's true. I've not denied it. And yes, Jill was angry about it.'

'How did you explain it to her?'

He grits his teeth. 'Is this conversation about my past or about my missing wife?'

'I'd say the two are pretty tightly linked, wouldn't you?'

'When Caroline Bonner's article ran, I told her about the operation.'

'When you met Sophia Roy within Green is Go?'

'Yes.'

'And what did you tell Jill about what happened to Sophia Roy in 2005, when she died?'

'Nothing,' he says, feels his fists clench. 'Because I don't *know* what happened when Sophia died. I wasn't there. As my legal representative has already said to the press and the public, I was on another operation. In any case, when

110

I was working I was never allowed to disclose details of where I was. Not to Jill, not to anyone.'

Karen carries on scribbling. A lock of hair falls over her face and she suddenly looks like a schoolchild doing her homework. He's been in terrifying situations before, has been held at gunpoint, has had to maintain his cover to the point of breaking, and yet this young officer casting her aspersions is getting under his skin.

'We're going to need Jill's phone number and email address to look at her call log.'

'Fine.' He gives Karen the number.

'And we'd also like to access her emails. Do you know her passwords?'

'I used to. She said she was changing them.'

'When?'

'Probably the moment she found out about Sophia Roy and my affair with her. I don't know. But her email address is Jmoorepoet@gmail.com.'

She writes it down.

'Lastly, we're going to need some of Jill's clothing for a dog search.'

'OK.'

He goes upstairs, and she follows him. He hasn't made the bed; it probably smells stale and of Jackson's atrocious farts.

He hands her two T-shirts. 'Are these OK?'

'These are good. I'm going to check over the rest of the rooms.'

'Be my guest.'

He goes downstairs, and she remains up in the bedroom. He doesn't want her upstairs but knows the procedure, and he's relieved to be away from her intensity. He listens to cupboards being pulled open, and floorboards creaking as she wanders into the spare room and then the bathroom. After a few minutes she comes down, walks into the snug. He can hear the scratching of her pen on the notebook, and the sound makes him physically shudder. He turns his attention to Joseph, still outside on his phone. The phone he uses to call Oliver is zipped up in the pocket of his coat. Out of sight, thank God.

'Does Jill have a laptop here?' Karen asks, reappearing.

Chris shakes his head. 'No.'

'She doesn't use one for her writing?'

'She does, but she left it at home. She has her notebook.'

'You have that here?' Karen asks.

'Yes, it's . . .' He looks to the kitchen counter. 'It's there. By that horse lamp.'

She follows his eyeline. 'We'll need to look at that. It's evidence.'

'The lamp?'

'No. The notebook.'

'Evidence of what, exactly?'

'Her mental state.'

'Have you read any of my wife's poetry, Officer Holland?' He's getting riled, getting hot and angry. 'Jill's poetry is a mind-fuck, so I doubt you'll find much there other than pain and torment. It's not like she's concealed codes in it like Dan Brown.'

'*Da Vinci Code* it may not be, but, as well you know, people hide themselves in all sorts of ways.'

He narrows his eyes. She smiles gaily.

'How do you think the inquest is going to go? Are you worried about it?'

Chris stares at her. 'What?'

'What you all did back then was wrong,' she whispers. 'And you give all us officers a bad name.'

She's enjoying it, Chris thinks. Direct access to the villain.

'You don't know the half of it,' Chris mutters.

'I know enough.'

'But that's the problem. Everyone thinks they know *enough*.'

'All right in here?' Joseph says, appearing around the door.

'Fine,' Karen replies, snapping her black book shut.

Joseph hands Chris his phone. 'Meredith Moore is coming up.'

'What?'

'She said she'll get the train ASAP. In the meantime, have you got family to call? Friends? This must be a very stressful time for you.'

'Yes,' he murmurs.

Who, though? His parents are dead and his sister, who is much older than him, lives in America and they do not keep in touch. He has Guy, his cousin, but he doesn't need or want to trouble Guy, or Marco back in Sardinia, or any of the men from the previous life that he had to leave in a hurry. He realizes that there is, really, only one option – Oliver.

Joseph Locke nods. 'We'll be seeing you later when the dive unit comes out.'

Chris watches them through the window as they leave, and only when the car disappears over the ridge does he allow himself to release the pressure of anger that's built up inside him. He goes to the snug, punches his fists into the cushions of the sofa over and over, and then he sits, completely still, panting at first to catch his breath and then slowing into silence.

There's a whirring hum coming from somewhere. He looks at his feet and sees Jackson on the rug in front of the cold, unlit fire. Is the noise coming from him?

'Jacko? Have you swallowed something?'

The Dane lifts his head, looks at Chris with his kind brown eyes.

'Forget it,' Chris says, and he gets up, goes to the kitchen. Perhaps he's left something on in there, or maybe the fridge is deciding to pack up, on top of everything else. But it's not coming from the kitchen either.

It's coming from outside.

He leans to the window, cranes his neck and sees a drone hovering in the air, level with his and Jill's bedroom.

'What the hell—'

He watches it hang there for a while before it moves on, going over the roof. He moves with it, goes to the snug and opens the window to see it pause outside the spare-room window and then the bathroom. Whoever's controlling it isn't a professional – it's wavering and keeps dropping and rising. He watches as it comes down, obviously scoping out the first floor, but before it reaches the window, he turns and goes back to the kitchen.

But he can't risk being seen, being recorded.

He throws open the front door and runs around the house. The drone hovers at the snug window, facing away from him. Chris doesn't even need to jump to reach it. His fingers catch its humming, wasp-like body and he pulls it close to him, covering the screen with his clothing. Its rotor blades whine and stick. He bends one of them, at first by mistake and then on purpose. He hears a voice as he marches back around the house, the other way round.

'Hey!'

It's a male voice, but young. Chris turns and sees a lanky teenager – the blond boy from earlier – standing on the grassy ridge, holding a remote. His expression is one of dismay.

'Fuck you,' Chris yells back, and slams the door shut, drone clutched to his chest.

Snapchat

RoryCampbell: He took my drone!!!

MattChristie: What?

RoryCampbell: Fletcher! He swiped it out of the air! My dad's drone! He's going to kill me!

MattChristie: What do you mean? Where were you flying it?

RoryCampbell: Over Smoke House. He came outside and grabbed it!

MattChristie: Why are you surprised, you muppet? What did you think he was going to do?

RoryCampbell: I wanted to be the first to get him on film. Can you imagine what some of the papers would pay for a picture of him?

FionaWilson: My mum had a journalist ring up and book our free room.

MattChristie: I've seen some vans arriving, too. Everything's kicking off.

RoryCampbell: Can you go and get my drone back, Lorna? It's my dad's.

RoryCampbell: Lorna, can you get my drone??

RoryCampbell: Are you reading these messages??

17

2003

Johann had a New Year's party. He had one every year because he was the richest and most generous of them and didn't care about mess. Fifty people were invited, a free flow in and out, an open door. Drinks and drugs would be passed around, and music would be notched high in all rooms because Johann took his sound system as seriously as he did his commitment to Green is Go.

Sophia hadn't asked explicitly if Chris was going to be there. He had told her that he was away over Christmas – he had some jobs on and was visiting his uncle, who had dementia. But he hadn't said what his plans were for New Year. She'd turned down other invitations from friends at university, from schoolfriends back in Kent, in the hope he might show up at Johann's. She bought a dress she couldn't really afford, got her hair cut, bought a new lipstick. On the night, she took a long bath, soaked in perfumed oils and scrubbed every inch of herself. The anticipation of seeing him was heady and anxiety-inducing. She felt like a child on Christmas Eve.

When she arrived, she casually asked around for him. Jodie told her he was upstairs, Carlotta said he was outside, Peter said he was in the kitchen. But when she went to find him in all those places, it was as if he seemed to slip elsewhere and, after her third drink, she stopped looking.

He would find her, she thought, as he always did at the end of a night. So she drank a lot and pretended she was fine, even when her heart rate raced every time someone entered the room, and then fell again when it wasn't him. She smoked weed, and danced for hours to house music, drum and bass, people all around her, the room hot and close. Eventually it became unbearable and so she made her way through throngs of people to the kitchen, where she stuck her head under the tap and took great gulps of water, like a fish. It was when she stood straight, water running down her chin, that she realized he was there, in front of her, wearing a dark shirt and holding a can of Guinness.

'Hi,' he said, a smile playing about his lips like it amused him to have caught her under the tap.

Fuck's sake, she thought, wiped at her face. 'Hi.'

'Having a good night?'

'Very much so,' she said.

'I was watching you dance earlier.'

'You were? Why didn't you come and say hi?'

He smiled. 'Because I liked watching you. Besides, here I am now. Saying hi.'

Suddenly, the music all turned off, and from the living room came the sound of the television, with the volume turned up.

'Shhhh, everyone!' Johann's excited voice sounded throughout the house. 'It's nearly midnight!'

The other people in the kitchen streaked out, laughing, cheering, but both Sophia and Chris stayed, staring at each other. The countdown came. She found that she wasn't breathing properly.

'Three! Two! One!'

The bells chimed, and her heart alongside them. 'Happy New Year!' the house chorused.

She waited. He drank from the Guinness can. Fireworks sounded from outside, from all around. Ribbons of colour fell on to his face through the window.

'Why aren't you kissing me?' she asked, because she couldn't stand it, this connection between them that he wasn't acting on.

'Brazen.'

'It's New *Year*.'

'Happy New Year.'

'Fuck off,' she said. 'Why else did you find me a minute before midnight?'

He looked uncertain then, and so she decided to act. She reached up and pulled him in for a kiss. She felt a resistance at first, and thought with horror that she'd completely misread him all these months, but then he melted into her, kissed her back, and time unravelled. *She* unravelled; relished the heat between them, the scratch of his stubble. She closed her eyes, breathed in the smell of his aftershave, peppery with a tang of citrus. He pressed her against the sink, and she felt the muscle beneath his shirt, the leanness of him. Fuck, she'd never wanted anyone so much in her *life*.

And then, a minute later, she felt a breath of air as his body left hers. She opened her eyes, watched as he disappeared out of the room. She started after him but got snagged as people danced their way back into the kitchen for more drinks. Without a word to her or anyone else, he had left the party.

A week passed after New Year, and then two. He was all she could think about. Johann gave her Chris's number, but she stared at it and felt embarrassed, and didn't dare call or text him. Three weeks after New Year, there was a talk scheduled at the pub and, for the first time since joining Green is Go, she debated not attending, worried about seeing him, anxious that their kiss had meant more to her than it did to him. But she had to go to the talk, she thought crossly. This was *her* thing and she would not let a stupid kiss ruin it. So she got ready, did her hair nicely (in case, though she didn't care, obviously), and went out. She met him on the stairs – she was going up as he was coming down. The breath was knocked out of her at the sight of him in a white T-shirt, ripped jeans, an expression of faint amusement on his lips. Why was he always *laughing* at her? She didn't know whether to cry or hit him. She didn't have a chance to do either. Without a word, he took her by the hand and led her back down and out of the pub. In silence they walked along one of the small alleyways, and then he stopped, looked at her intently.

'What?' she said, expectantly. Heart in her throat with the worry of what he was going to say.

But he didn't speak. He kissed her, gently, and then harder, and she melted into him like mercury. His hands roved all over her, urgent and furious. She felt like she was floating out of her own body.

'I thought you didn't care,' she said after a couple of minutes. Breathless, lips numb, head spinning.

'Honestly,' he said. 'I didn't want to care.'

'What does that mean?'

'Come away with me,' he said, ignoring the question. 'To the Lakes, next month.'

She laughed. 'I'm not good in tents.'

'What about if you slept in the van?'

'And where would you sleep?'

'I'd sleep in the van, too,' he said. 'It is my van, after all.'

She smiled, and he kissed her again. They didn't return to the pub.

The SDS was something created from nothing, and that's important to know, because there was no blueprint for it, you know what I'm saying? They reported to Special Branch and thought they were above modernization, above the *law*. For decades, the unit had no rules and no regulation. The officers in the field were young twenty-somethings from Hendon who were let loose like dogs and thought they could do anything they liked. Some of them crossed the line when they were on deployment, sure. How do you think I did my job when I was in Narcotics? There were times I had to break the law and take drugs because they had to *believe* I was one of them. Did Chris Fletcher have to get into a relationship with Sophia Roy? I don't know. All I'm saying is that you don't get to judge it all without being in the situation. I'm speaking out about it; I'm writing a book. Ask me anything you want.

– Anthony Stewart, former SDS officer, BBC True Crime Drama: *Into the Dark*, 2025

I never crossed the line.

– Mike Emerson, former SDS officer, BBC True Crime Drama: *Into the Dark*, 2025

Mike Emerson was my boyfriend for three years. All the while he had a wife and two kids in Sheffield. If that wasn't crossing the line, I don't know what is.

– Michelle Farrow, former ALF (Animal Liberation Front) activist, and ex-girlfriend of former SDS officer Mike Emerson, BBC True Crime Drama: *Into the Dark*, 2025

Things had to be done that skirted the ethical boundaries. But who gets to decide what's moral anyway? You know what the unofficial motto of the SDS was? We were to obtain information 'by any means necessary'. I was doing my job. As was Chris Fletcher.

– Mike Emerson, former SDS officer, BBC True Crime Drama: *Into the Dark*, 2025

Does no one think for themselves any more?? Where are their morals?

– @Jumping JackRabbit, X

Hello?? How do you think the Nazis happened? How do you think soldiers do the things they do? Giving up personal responsibility allows people to do bad things. It's called 'The Agentic State' – which is when an otherwise obedient individual defers responsibility for their own actions. Instead, they attribute it to someone else, particularly a figure of authority.

– @theitheitheithei, X

Wow. Freud in the house!!

– @Outtahere, X

Actually it's from Milgram's psychological experiment from 1961, but whatever.

– @theitheitheithei, X

The question is, surely, who *was* responsible for signing off all this behaviour?

— @bemorelauren, X

I feel sorry for his wife. Isn't she that poet? #jillianmoore #sophiaroy #christopherfletcher

— @mootoo, X

There's something going on in the house they're staying at. I'm going to find out what.

— @AnonRC, X

Will you give the location??

— @shadowman, X

Jill was always on her own. That's what I remember from when we worked together at the hospital. Evenings alone, weekends alone. She liked shiftwork for that reason and, to be honest, for the most part, she seemed cool with it. She said she believed in what Chris was doing – not that I knew what that was, I just knew he was away a lot. Jill filled her time writing and gardening and whatever, and she was sociable, always out with friends and going on holiday with her aunt. Places like Iceland and Hawaii and Europe because her aunt is super-wealthy, owns an interior design company or something. One time though, Jill came into work after one of those holidays and she was really blue. I asked her if she was OK, if she had a good time, and she said that it was amazing but also that Chris would have loved it. She said she wanted to have a normal life and do normal things – with him. She said she was living with an invisible man. I'll never forget that phrase.

– Ella MacIntosh, nurse at St Thomas's Hospital, London, and friend of Jillian Moore, interview with Sadie Clarke, *Under the Cover*, 2025

18

Meredith Moore barrels through the door at ten to ten in the evening, a tornado of bags, expletives and dyed blonde hair. She is seventy-one and tiny, but lean like a whippet. Jill and Chris laugh about how Meredith is all hard edges, severe fringe and forked tongue, but Jill is joking and Chris is not.

'I'm gasping,' Meredith says without a hello.

Chris doesn't have the level of energy required for Meredith. After Joseph Locke and Karen Holland left, he'd gone into the woods again, looking for any evidence of the boat, but to no avail. He is completely exhausted, but Meredith will not take kindly to his exhaustion because she'll think it selfish. After all, she's worried, and so is he.

He fills the kettle. 'Good journey?'

She drops the bags to the floor, shrugs out of her coat – a bright pink and emerald puffa befitting of someone far younger – and swings it on to the back of a chair.

'Oh well, let me see. *No*. Because I've been worrying about Jill since I heard. I've given myself a splitting headache from the worry. And there were so many delays on the bloody trains because of the storm damage, and I had to stand there, absolutely *freezing*, with my head going at a million miles an hour. Hoping that Jill is OK. Hoping that Jill is *alive*. Then I couldn't get a connection from Birmingham, so I had to fly to Aberdeen. So. All in all, no. It's *not* been a good journey.'

He turns away from her to get two mugs out, exhales, and then sees the drone in the corner of the kitchen, lying crumpled by the door and half obscured by the mess of shoes and boots. He needs to move it or give it to the police.

'You look old, Christopher.'

'Thanks, Meredith,' he says through gritted teeth. 'You look as youthful as ever.'

'Botox and fillers,' she says unashamedly.

'I made up the spare room,' he says.

'How kind of you to make up the spare room in my house.'

I considered the dog basket because you're a bitch, Chris wants to say.

'Do you want the other room?' he asks instead. 'I can move.'

'I'll take the spare.'

He waits as the kettle boils, and she scuffles around in her handbag for her phone, taps loudly. He notices the necklace around her neck. She's worn the same one for years – gold and thin with an elegant pearl droplet at the end of it. There's something solid about this necklace, that it's stood the test of time.

She takes up the phone. 'I need to tell William I've made it here.'

'How are you both?'

'Still married,' she says faux-brightly. 'Though largely for convenience and money. He's decided to start shagging his forty-one-year-old skeleton PA which will no doubt end in a law suit. But for the meantime it keeps him busy and out of my way. Besides, he dropped me at the station, so, you know, chivalry isn't dead.'

'Oh. I'm . . . sorry.'

She laughs with sarcasm. 'Looks can be deceiving, can't they?'

He sighs. 'I haven't heard that one recently. Be more original.'

She pauses with the tapping. 'You *wanted* us to believe you had the perfect marriage. And that's what you wanted *her* to believe, isn't it?'

'I didn't say we had the perfect marriage.'

'Understatement of the century,' she mutters, and goes back to the furious tapping on the phone. 'Bloody hellfire, why can't I ever connect to the bloody Wi-fi?'

He makes tea. The recent news of Sophia had given Meredith yet another excuse to hate him, but Jill going missing is the final straw. He needs to give Meredith this time to process things, let her chew him up a bit and spit him out. They are in this together, like it or not.

She finishes on the phone and he holds out the tea for her, but she doesn't take it. Her arms are folded across her chest. He sets it down on the table in front of her and tells her what he has told Joseph and Karen already. He tells her that the dive team are on their way.

'No,' she says, holds up her hands and physically turns her face away from him. 'Don't tell me that. That means she's *dead*. Divers look for bodies.'

'Meredith—' he says.

Her whole body slumps forward. 'This is too much to take,' she whispers.

'I know.'

Seeing her suddenly look so fragile, so bird-like, is alarming. Like Edd Fletcher, Meredith has always been an adult in charge, but in this situation she is not. They fall into silence.

'What was the last thing she said to you?' she asks eventually.

'I don't know. "Goodnight", I suppose.'

He speaks the lie without a tell. Not a blink, not a shift. He has been trained so extraordinarily well. No one was there, no one will know. Plus, he doesn't like to relive it, how they last spoke to each other.

Meredith's phone beeps and she snatches it up, lifts the screen close to her face. Jill told him that Meredith needs glasses but never wears them, thinks they age her.

'Oh God,' she says.

'What?'

She gets up with urgency, looks out of the window, and he follows her.

'It's on social media,' she whispers.

'What is?'

But then he sees. The pale glow of a half-moon illuminates a huge black lorry parked at the water's edge. The dive team has arrived.

Christopher Fletcher's wife has disappeared without a trace. Police think she took a boat out on to the loch 2 DAYS AGO and she hasn't been seen since!! #jillianmoore #christopherfletcher #sophiaroy
  – @AnonRC, X

WHAT? Are you serious?
  – @Outtahere, X

We've got a dive unit out here. Lots of news vans coming over too. People are renting out their spare rooms and garages. Some people are getting mad about it.
  – @AnonRC, X

That's a whole lot of water out there.
  – @shadowman, X

@AnonRC, please see your inbox.
  – @FrankWalkerTheSun, X

You don't think this is a coincidence?? Christopher Fletcher was there when Sophia Roy died – that's what her sister is saying was in Sophia's diaries – and now he's offed his wife in Scotland.
  – @Overlordette, X

The initial statement from his legal representative said he was 'elsewhere'.
  – @Mickeyblueeyes, X

I don't believe him.
  – @Outtahere, X

How can you make a judgement about someone you've never met?
  – @Mickeyblueeyes, X

Isn't that the beauty of Twitter?! LOL #twittertrolling
  – @shadowman, X

It's not called Twitter.
  – @Mickeyblueeyes, X

Fuck off.
  – @shadowman, X

Two women missing. One defo dead. This is a true crime documentary, no?? Here for it. #sophiaroy #justicefor sophia #whereisjillianmoore #jillianmoore #documentary inthemaking
  – @SalleeeeA, X, GIF shows woman wearing sun-
  glasses, eating popcorn, and smiling

@Netflix, @bbcstoryville, are you reading this??
  – @Happyfeet, X

I've seen on here that Chris Fletcher's wife has been declared missing. I hope she's got as far away from him as possible.

— @LeilaRoyPR, X

19

Morning light filters through the kitchen window as Chris watches the boats out on the water. People will know, if they don't already, that it's Jillian out there, lost. And then what happens? Will he get blamed for that too? He doesn't dare check social media.

Last night the dive superior came to The Old Smoke House with Joseph Locke and asked Chris where Jill liked to sail, which direction she usually went, which coves she stopped at. But he couldn't tell them because he had never gone out with her – in those hours she could really have been doing anything. Admitting this was deeply uncomfortable, like he didn't know her. Like she had secrets. The divers are out again now, looking for her.

'I hate that we can see it.'

He turns to see Meredith behind him and knows without asking that she means the dive lorry, which sits on the horizon. An ominous mass.

'I know.'

She sighs, makes a cup of tea and comes to stand beside him. Having someone close feels comforting. He only wishes it was Jill. He closes his eyes and imagines for a moment that it's her.

'My God!'

His eyes snap open.

'There are people on the ridge up there at this time in the morning?'

He reaches to close the curtains. 'We should keep these closed.'

Meredith is furious. 'Is my niece's disappearance some kind of horrible *sport*? I probably *know* half of those people. Bloody *horrors*!'

There's a knocking at the door and he and Meredith stare at each other.

'The police?' she asks.

'Hello? Chris? It's Susie,' calls a voice. 'Susie from the shop. And John Crossan.'

Chris opens the door. Susie Hall stands with sympathy in her eyes and a bag of shopping in her hand. She's Meredith's age but looks maternal, grandmotherly and gently rounded. John Crossan stands beside her and looks solemn in corduroy trousers.

'May we come in?' Susie asks.

Chris ushers them inside. 'Please, yes.'

'I know we don't know each other and – well, it's a bit of a surprise to know you're here.'

'Like a fugitive, you mean?' Meredith says.

Susie leans to look round the corner to see Meredith. 'Oh, Merry!'

Chris almost laughs aloud. *Merry?* He watches Susie and Meredith embrace.

'How are you holding up?' Susie asks, stroking Meredith's arm.

'Terribly,' Meredith replies, and her voice cracks.

'It's a dreadful thing,' Susie says. 'Dreadful. We can't believe it. Harris called on us both before the storm hit and asked if we'd seen Jill, and then this morning we saw . . . the lorry.' She offers the shopping bag to Chris. 'I brought some groceries. I assumed you wouldn't want to go out for anything, what with Jill, and . . . and the other business hanging over your head.'

Meredith arches an eyebrow.

Chris nods, takes the bag. 'Thank you.'

Meredith looks to Susie. 'You saw Jill, Sus, when she came in to buy some food? How did she seem to you?'

'We didn't talk for long, but she was worried about Chris, obviously.' She turns to face him. 'I did think it strange that she would have come here and left you, Chris, in Sardinia. Turns out, she didn't . . . Anyway, it goes without saying that we don't believe for one second that you had anything to do with that girl's death.'

Chris sees Meredith raise her other eyebrow and they jointly disappear into her fringe.

'We've started to have a couple of journalists come in about it all,' John says. 'But we've closed our doors to them.'

'It all feels like it did when Kate died,' Susie says, lowering her voice, even though there's no one else here. 'All these strangers clamouring for details – the more sordid the better. No respect for her, for Harris and Lorna.'

Chris nods, thinks about Kate McGowan, Harris's wife. 'Jill was so upset about what happened to Kate.'

'We were all upset,' Susie says.

'Kate was a good woman,' Meredith agrees.

Chris notices John shift his weight from foot to foot.

'I saw Jill, you know,' he says.

'What?'

'Not since she went out on the boat,' John adds. 'But she came in to see me a couple of days ago. We talked about her poetry. And you.'

It takes all Chris's mental strength not to outwardly fume. Jill had promised that she would keep a low profile, that she would only see Susie and Harris. That was what they had agreed, but it was too much to expect, he realizes, to ask her to stay away from others.

'She said she'd been talking to people,' John says.

'People?'

'Women in the same position.'

Amanda Connolly.

'Yes. I know that,' Chris says, sharply.

Joseph Locke left last night with the dive superior before Chris could ask if he'd talked to Amanda. It irks him that they haven't told him what she's said, if it differs from what she told him.

Susie puts a hand to Meredith's arm. 'The police will find her.'

Meredith nods but says nothing.

'Thank you again for the food,' Chris says.

They turn to leave, and then John pauses. 'Have the police gone to End Stone?'

'End Stone!' Meredith exclaims, and claps her hands so loudly that Chris flinches. 'Yes, John. They should go there. Ring them, Christopher, right now.'

'What's End Stone?' he asks.

'An old haunt,' John says. 'I'm surprised Harris hasn't mentioned it.'

20

They drive five minutes through the thickly wooded valley towards the only house at the top of High Mount Lane – End Stone. The road leading up to it is little more than a narrow track, dappled by the midday sun and then eventually blotted out entirely by dense canopy. Within minutes they are plunged into fairytale darkness and Chris wonders if this might be the happy ending he wants – that Jill is waiting in the house at the top of the hill and he is coming to rescue her.

Chris joins Harris in his truck, with Joseph Locke and Karen Holland close behind. Before they left, Harris explained that End Stone was once a childhood hideout, and later a metaphorical teenage bike shed where the local kids took packs of broken biscuits and bags of weed. He didn't give any explanation as to why he hadn't mentioned it before, and Chris assumes it's because the house is an old, forgotten place, but there's something in the back of his mind that he can't put his finger on. A feeling of unease.

They pull up to the house, crumbled and quiet and lost to its surroundings. Joseph gets out of the car and walks up to the front door, inspects a rusty padlock and then the yawning windows beside and above it. They are boarded, their soft and rotted window frames sagging with neglect. The grass around the house is long and beaded with droplets of rain.

'It doesn't look like it's been disturbed,' Joseph says.

The others are behind him. Karen and Harris both hold torches.

'You say you came here as children, Harris?'

'Aye, but that was an age ago. It's not the safest place, as you can see. My dad warned me away from it when part of the roof came down in 1998.'

'You don't know if Jill ever came this way in the years since?'

'She never told me if she did.'

Chris shook his head. 'Nor me.'

'It's worth a look,' Joseph says.

He heads around the back, and they all follow.

'Is there any information about her call log yet?' Chris asks.

The tall grass and weeds reach to their knees, soak their trousers. Tangles of invisible brambles try to trip them.

'Nothing yet, but it's a priority.'

'What about Amanda? What did she say?'

'Jill isn't with her, if that's what you're asking,' Karen says. 'She and two other women went out for lunch on the day of the storm and came back around three in the afternoon. A local pub confirmed their booking.'

'But Jill could be there? At the house they're staying in?'

'She isn't there. There are security cameras on the rental: no one left until the morning after the storm when Amanda went out to see you. We've checked.'

Chris is silenced. A dead end. Part of him is relieved because it means Jill hasn't abandoned him, but the other part is terrified of what that now means: the weight of probability leaning towards her being lost in the water. He feels sick at the thought.

They stop by the back door of End Stone, which is also boarded and locked, the windows too.

'If Jill came here, I don't know how in God's name she would have got in,' Joseph muses. 'How did you used to get through, Harris?'

'The window by the front door,' Harris says. 'It wasn't boarded then.'

Joseph nods. 'It's a slim hope, but we'll do it anyway. We'll have to rip off some of the boards.'

They choose a window and use their weight to lever one of the thick, bolted plywood boards. It takes less than a minute before they stagger backwards. Karen falls to the ground and Chris offers his hand.

'You OK?'

She doesn't take it, instead scrambles up. 'I'm fine.'

'In we go then,' Joseph says.

The window they enter is into the living room, which boasts a huge bay window opposite, boarded now and gloomy. The fireplace is vast and empty but gives the room character and majesty. An old sofa, mouldy and fungal, sits opposite the fireplace. There are no footprints.

'Hello? Jillian?'

They are met with silence.

They go from room to room, and then into the corridor, where there is parquet partially visible through gathered dust and pools of stagnant water.

Joseph stops by the staircase. 'What's the upstairs like, Harris?'

'There's probably some loose flooring in places.'

'Karen, you check the rest of the downstairs. Take Chris. I'll go up with Harris, if you're comfortable with that, Harris?'

'Aye.'

Chris nods along to the instruction, but he wants to explore all of it himself. This is where Jill was a child, a teenager; where she hung out with friends. Maybe she smoked her first cigarette here, tasted alcohol for the first time, had her first kiss. He should have asked her more, should know every single detail about her. He suddenly longs for her, a physical stabbing pain in his chest. The fact that Harris is here, that he knows all about Jill when she was young, that he was *with* her when she was young, makes him envious. He watches Harris now, as he and Joseph disappear upstairs, gripping the banisters because the steps are slippery and warped from weathering.

'Where shall we go?' Chris asks.

'I don't even know why you're here. This is an investigation. Joseph shouldn't have allowed you to come.'

'Well, I'm here now,' Chris says, through clenched teeth. 'So I'll help find my wife, if that's OK by you.'

Karen turns without another word, and Chris follows her through to a large kitchen with stone flooring and a hearth where a range or an Aga might have once stood. From behind one of the window boards, a vine has snaked and unfurled, its fingers grasping at the walls and the free-standing dresser next to it. A large farmhouse table is in the middle of the room, with a random old teacup on its side, covered with a film of dust, unused for God knows how many years. Karen watches him, her eyes narrowed. Chris looks under the table, behind the doors, opens drawers and cupboards. There are remnants of a life lived here, but nothing is alive now.

They go to another room — a study perhaps, or a library where there are old books, spine-out on shelves. Most are curled with the damp. Above them, Chris can hear Joseph and Harris moving, their voices low and muffled, and Chris wonders what they might be saying, what information they might be sharing now he's out of earshot.

'There's nothing here,' Karen says, after a while.

'When was this place built?' Chris asks. 'Is there a privy outside?'

Karen nods. 'There might well be. Let's look around.'

They go back into the living room and out of the window. Karen vaults it like she's a deer, and together they walk the perimeter of the house.

'Was this the garden?' Chris says, coming to the back and staring into thick trees ahead. 'I can't see any walls or fencing.'

Karen shrugs. 'There are fewer trees this way.'

'But no privy.'

As they walk around, Chris thinks how strange it is, how uncertain and unbalancing it is to have lost a person. It is a very specific unrelenting, limitless agony, and unlike anything he's encountered before. Because everyone loses things in life; small things like keys, or sometimes things that weigh heavier; a brilliant mind to dementia like Robert. But the loss of a missing loved one is a constant physical pain. How would he cope, he wonders, with the loss of Jill after the loss of Sophia?

'Nothing,' Karen says, breaking him out of his thoughts.

'No,' he agrees.

'It was a slim hope,' Joseph says when he and Harris come outside ten minutes later. He looks up at the building. 'We'll need to board that back up. Don't want any youths getting in.'

'Do you want me to come back tomorrow and fix it all up?' Harris offers.

'We'll send some officers later,' Karen says. 'This place should be on the demolition list.'

'Keep thinking, both of you,' Joseph says. 'And ask Meredith if she can think of any other places Jill used to go. We have the dogs coming out tomorrow. They'll start from The Old Smoke House and go into the woods. Perhaps we'll suggest they come up here too in case we've missed something they could pick up on, but this is a bit of a hike from The Old Smoke House, even more if she was coming from the loch, so I'm doubtful.'

'You have the resources for a wider search?' Chris asks.

'We have some,' Joseph says. 'Our main search area is still the loch and the surrounding coves, big though that is.'

No one says anything for a moment.

Karen and Joseph walk to their car, get in. Chris walks towards Harris's truck, pauses as he sees Harris staring up at the house.

'Everything OK, Harris?'

'Aye,' he says, then turns on his heel and walks back to the truck.

Chris looks to where Harris was staring, up to the broken windows of the second floor, where there is an outline of a heart drawn in the window. Greasy and grubby in the dust, but unmistakable.

21

2003

After the day they kissed in the alleyway, Chris and Sophia spent every moment that they could together. A lot of the time was spent with the other members of Green is Go, or at least the core group of them, discussing plans, organizing marches to create maximum disruption. But they found time, just the two of them, for daytrips or the occasional weekend away in the van when he didn't have a gardening job scheduled.

In late February they went to the Lakes, where they spent the pale hours of the daytime walking, talking about upcoming protests, or about her university coursework, stopping in pubs to get merry. Chris often stopped them too, to point out ox-eye daisy, knapweed and meadow vetchling. She felt him change when they were alone in nature together; his eyes were bright, he got up early to make coffee on his camping stove, he gazed at the pale sunsets, stared up at the stars. He would smile easily and often, and in those moments she would look up at him with a full heart.

'This is what we do it for,' he said on the final night as they walked back from the pub to the van. 'This world is beautiful.' He laughed at himself.

'Don't laugh. You're right,' Sophia said. 'This world is ours to protect and nurture.'

'Sometimes I feel like a fraud,' he said quietly.

She frowned. 'I don't get why you'd think that. You care.'

He turned to her. 'Do you feel like any of what we do actually makes a difference?'

'Of course I do,' she said, and then paused. 'Big changes start with small ones.'

He sighed.

'Hey,' she said gently. 'Right?'

'Yeah, I know . . . but it feels . . . sometimes just a bit hopeless.'

'It's not hopeless when you have hope.' She smiled and then leaned into him. 'I want you to meet my family. My sister is clawing at me to invite you to Kent.'

He laughed. 'Serious?'

'Will you come?'

'Sure.'

She suddenly stopped walking. He stopped with her.

'You OK?'

'I think I love you,' she said.

He looked at her in silence for a long moment. 'Move in with me,' he whispered.

22

Chris spends the afternoon in the woodland around The Old Smoke House, striding with purpose with his jacket hood up against the rain. He wants to roar into the silence of the trees so that his lungs hurt and his eyes strain, bulging from his face, because he is done with being calm, done with rationale. Hurt and anger have been his continuous companions for years, dangerously lapping the brim of control, and he can't contain it for much longer. Something has to give.

In the silence of the woods, he can still hear the ravaged screams of the past, can feel the earth beneath his feet move when it is still. Things have been buried in the woods, and the truth will always try to dig itself out. He feels like it is digging itself from under his skin.

Don't think about them, the creatures of the night.

Jackson lollops alongside him, tongue out the side of his mouth, nose low to the ground.

Chris calls Oliver and his old handler picks up immediately.

'How are you holding up?'

'I don't know. Barely.'

'We found the little shit who posted the original photographs though. His name is Rory Campbell, and a caution is coming his way.'

The name clicks immediately. The kid with the drone, the one who accosted him when he walked up to the village. Everyone's a fucking journalist.

'Fuck's sake.'

'We're doing everything we can.'

'How about a public declaration that I was in Southampton the night Sophia died?'

He hears Oliver sigh.

'We've been through this, Chris. It's best not to engage with all this until the inquest, otherwise it turns into a slanging match and we'll come off worse, because we always do. No one seems to respect the police any more. I've been talking to the powers, and we've decided that we have to move you out of that house.'

'What? No, I can't move while Jill is still missing.'

'Journalists know where you are, and they know that Jill is missing. It's only a matter of time before one of them crawls down your chimney to get a picture of you.'

From out of nowhere, there's a sideways movement and an explosion of feathers plumes in front of his face. Jackson barks and Chris cries out, the alarmed shriek of a bird mirroring him, before he reels backwards. He sees it fly upwards, a grouse that he's disturbed from its perch in a tree nearby.

'Chris?'

'I'm here. Just a . . . just a fucking bird in the wood scared the shit out of me.'

'I've got some options—'

'I need to be near the investigation. Near to Jill.'

'I know. But listen, don't lose sight of why you're here.'

'What?'

'You're here for the inquest. Have you finished the reading?'

'I – mostly. But I haven't picked it up since Jill went missing.'

'You need to make sure you're absolutely watertight in what you're saying.'

'I know what I'm saying, Oli, but I have other things on my mind now!'

'That's what worries me.'

There's another noise. Not the bird; there's something that sounds human. A muffled moaning. Jackson lifts his head.

'Hello?' Chris calls out.

The noise stops abruptly.

'Chris?' Oli's voice is tinny from the speaker.

'I'll call you back,' Chris says, and hangs up, drops the phone into his pocket.

He walks on. His heart is hammering, but he pushes forward with purpose, following Jackson, who gallops in front of him until he reaches the curve of the wood where it meets the edge of the loch. Someone is sitting on the mossy bank of it, with their knees up and their arms wrapped around them. His heart leaps.

'Jill?'

But as soon as he says her name, he realizes that the person is too small to be Jill. It's Lorna McGowan, wearing a white-and-green sweatshirt, who has turned around to face him.

'Mr Fletcher. I didn't see you.'

'Sorry if I scared you. I didn't think anyone would be out here. I mean, I hoped Jill would . . .'

But what did he hope? That Jill would spring out of the ground because he was looking for her?

'Umm, yeah. I – I came here because there are reporters everywhere. They're all asking questions.'

Jackson trots over to her, lifts his nose to her hand. She pets him, smiles.

'It's a bit like when my mum . . . you know. How she died. Everyone asked their questions.'

'Jill told me what happened. It must have been so hard on the both of you.'

'It was horrible.'

They fall into silence.

'Shouldn't you be in school?' he asks.

'It's the Easter holidays,' she says.

'God, yeah. I forgot about Easter.'

They smile awkwardly at one another. Nothing about this conversation is normal.

'I'm sorry,' he says. 'For all this on your doorstep.'

'It's my fault. I – one of my friends took your photograph.'

'Rory Campbell?'

She nods. 'How did you know his name?'

'As it turns out, he's been posting a few things about me.'

Her eyes well with tears. 'I didn't know he'd done it, and I definitely didn't know that he'd put them up online. He's studying to be a journalist.'

'Is he?'

'You took his drone.'

'Yeah, I did.'

'He wants me to ask you for it.'

'I won't give it to you, Lorna.'

'You shouldn't give it to him even if he comes to you directly.' She strokes Jackson's head, slips his ears between her fingers. Everyone loves Jackson's ears.

He frowns, curious at this. 'And why is that?'

'Because he thinks you're . . . bad. He believes everything on social media . . . believes that you've done bad things.'

'And what about you?' he asks. 'What do you believe?'

'Umm. I – I don't know. I don't think we should judge each other without the facts.'

'I agree, though sometimes the facts are hidden from the public, with good reason.'

They are silent a while.

'What do you think has happened to Jill?' she asks.

He pauses, looks to the loch. 'I don't know.'

But his mind goes to the worst place, of course. She could be there, beneath the big and endless blue.

23

The thought of Jill beneath the water makes him shiver, but it's the most logical of explanations. Jill went out in the boat and got caught in the storm – couldn't wrestle the wind, couldn't navigate the rain, couldn't handle the waves. But she is a good sailor, so how could she have not seen the storm coming in?

Once again, he thinks about their heated argument that night. Any normal person would have sat up, turned the light on, and opened an honest dialogue. Instead, he had simply taken the sleeping pill and knocked himself out.

He wishes he'd told her that night that he loves her.

Was that what Jill had written on that ripped-out page of the notebook, he wonders. Might she have played around with some words that she would later give him – words of love and forgiveness? Might she have berated herself for the horrible poem she'd recited to him, about drowning him in the loch?

He needs to hold on to the belief that the inquest will go the way he needs it to. Neither he nor Jill wants their life altered by the inquest; they want Sardinia, their barefoot beach trips, their nights with Marco and Angela. Jill loves to teach her students. And Jill *loves* Chris. Doesn't she?

I love you, fool.

He has to hold on to this proclamation. He has to believe that she will appear any moment now, and when she sees him, she will throw herself into his arms and tell him that she never doubted him, that she will stand by him come what may.

But as he continues to stare at the loch, doubt slithers up his throat. He pictures her waking up that morning, the day of the storm, quietly dressing in her thermals and jeans, and going downstairs. He pictures her sailing along the shoreline in the Miracle, the very boat that she and Harris had sailed together as children. Jill has told Chris how they used to lie down in its wooden warmth, top to toe, and look at the colours of the sky, talk about their future and their fears.

He wonders, briefly, taking a sideways glance at Lorna, if Jill ever thought about marrying Harris. Theirs was a friendship that was bound by time and a love of water, and wouldn't it have been better, Chris thinks resentfully, if Jill had stayed in Scotland with Harris and lived happily ever after? But no, she had moved south, had wanted to spread her wings and go to London, which at nineteen years of age seemed to her to be the dazzling centre of the universe. Meredith was there building her interiors empire, the university scene was incredible, there were parties to go to. And then she met Chris and the rest was history. But what a life Chris has forced her to lead since that point – she has given him so much of herself and he has always kept her at a distance.

Perhaps out on the water Jill lay down in the boat as she had when she was a child, but removed the life jacket because it was uncomfortable. Maybe she fell asleep and didn't notice as the water began to swell with the promise of the incoming storm. And then what? Had she woken only when the rain started to fall – fat drops on her cheeks and her lips? Had she woken to a noise that sounded like a flapping bird, and then looked up to see the sail snapping back and forth with a powerful wind? She would have realized this was the beginning of the storm that Harris had warned them about. She would have tried to tell herself that she was a good sailor and that she would be fine, but she would probably have known that she had made a cataclysmic error of judgement.

Chris knows that Jill would have been too panicked to remember that she'd removed the life jacket if her sole focus was getting the boat under control. She would be thinking only of moving in the right direction, back to the safety of Smoke House. But with the waves growing taller and the rain lashing down, it would have been harder to wrestle, and in time she wouldn't have been able to see properly through the spray coming at her, wouldn't have been able to tell which way was home. The fog on the water would have descended, wrapped her up and whispered that it wouldn't let her go.

Chris closes his eyes, tries to stop himself from thinking of any more terrifying last moments, but the images come anyway – a huge wave catching the sail, sending it crashing down on top of her, knocking her unconscious or seriously injuring her. Another wave after it, tipping the boat and trapping her beneath it. Dragging her down in the water, unable to breathe.

His wife is lost to the sea.

He can't breathe for these awful thoughts. If she is down there he wants to dive to the bottom and lock himself into her lifeless arms. And when climate change means the rivers and lochs are all but evaporated, whoever is still alive in this weird, wonderful, frightening world might find their bones, next to each other. Lovers, they will say, in a final embrace.

*

'I understand,' says Lorna.

Chris looks at her, has forgotten she was even here next to him. He finds that he is breathing in short and shallow pants and she is barely visible because his eyes are swimming. He feels as if he's losing all sense of reality.

'I understand why you don't want to think about her being out there. It's too big to think like that.'

'She's a great sailor,' he says with more conviction than he feels. 'She hasn't . . . she isn't . . .'

Lorna nods, and then stands. 'I need to go.'

'Please thank your dad for me,' he says. I know he's going out on his boat whenever he can. I know all her friends are worried.'

Lorna looks at him then, a strange expression on her face. 'OK,' she says eventually.

She walks away, and her form is immediately swallowed by the trees.

Chris stays looking at the loch. Everything feels wrong and upside down and he's shaking now from cold and apprehension, the looping thoughts of Jill out on the water, scared. The imagination conjures such sinister things, and he knows he must shut it down before he is eaten up by it. After a while he too gets up, whistles for Jackson.

He returns to the house, but doesn't respond to Meredith, who calls for him from the snug. Instead, he trudges upstairs and shuts the bedroom door, wants to be alone with his thoughts.

He loves Jill.

Chris's fists clench. He loves Jill. Harris can't love Jill, isn't allowed to love her how Chris loves her. Jill is Chris's everything, his best friend, and he is hers.

He pops a sleeping pill and then wraps himself in the duvet, takes up his phone and opens a browser. He doesn't know why he's typing the words that he is, only knows that he needs to.

Links line up detailing the death of Kate McGowan. Chris clicks into the first.

> *Local woman Kate McGowan has been found deceased in what police have called a tragic and heartbreaking accident. Mrs McGowan was reported missing by her husband, Harris McGowan, on Tuesday, October 29 and was found three hours later by a search party at an abandoned house on High Mount Lane. It is believed that Mrs McGowan slipped and hit the back of her head on a rock and died from internal injuries.*

High Mount Lane. Chris has just been there to search End Stone. He keeps reading.

> *'We are breathless over her loss,' said husband, Harris McGowan. 'Kate was our everything.'*

The dive team has been out for eighteen hours and has so far recovered neither Jillian Moore nor the Miracle sailing dinghy that she sailed in every day. Family and friends, and the police, remain hopeful that she has pulled the boat up and is safe but currently unable to make contact. Local forces have been recruited to expand the search.

  – BBC Scotland, interview with Sergeant Joseph Locke, Scottish Police

I actually went to a reading of Jillian Moore's once. She was really good! I hope she's OK!

  – @catseyes, X

He's stashed her somewhere. SWEAR.

  – @Outtahere, X

Yeah, cos that's what he'd want to do in the middle of all the Sophia Roy stuff happening, right? Gimme a break.

  – @minniethemousercat, X

Doesn't look good for her either way, does it?

  – @shadowman, X

24

Chris wakes with a jerk, instinctively looks to Jill's side of the bed and sees that she's there, beneath the duvet. He's filled with a rush of emotion.

'You came back,' he breathes. 'Thank God you came back.'

He goes to hug the body beside him but realizes within half a second that it isn't Jill but Jackson. Out of the duvet comes a wet tongue that slops at his face and, although his heart sinks, Chris reaches to hold Jackson anyway, like he's a buoy in deep water.

The clock on the wall reads ten past five in the afternoon. He feels guilty for the indulgence of having taken himself to bed for a sleep, but he needed it. My God, he needs it still. Through the closed curtains there are little golden slithers on the wall. He remembers how he and Sophia used to lie in bed together in Notting Hill, stare up at the ceiling and watch car headlights cut through the room as they passed. A light show, she'd called it, made it sound romantic. He'd lace his fingers in hers; on some mornings, he would wake still connected to her that way.

He shouldn't be thinking of Sophia.

He gets up, risks inching back the bedroom curtain so he can glance out of the window. The dive lorry is still a big, black, hulking presence at the side of the loch. A little way away — but too close to be comfortable — are reporters' vans. There are a few tents pitched by the side of the water – trauma tourism – and Chris hopes that the police will move them on, but even if they do, there'll be more to replace them. He's properly under siege now. Maybe he should have let Oli move him after all. He releases the curtain and goes downstairs. Meredith is standing by the kitchen sink, staring outside.

'Meredith, pull the blinds down.' She doesn't answer.

'Meredith? Otherwise your face will be all over the media. Pull them down.'

She turns around, fury written all over her face.

'What do I care if my face gets in the papers? If *yours* does? You're already news. Again.'

She lunges towards him with her phone thrust out to him. He steps backwards, an automatic reflex.

'This,' she spits. 'What the hell is *this*?'

He takes her phone, scans the headlines.

Undercover police officer Chris Fletcher fathers child with unknowing activist girlfriend.

His stomach drops.

'Is it true?' she asks, and her voice breaks.

Sweat gathers under his armpits, slinks down his ribs. The words are fizzling on the screen. Not like this, he thinks.

Fuck. Fuck, *fuck*.

'Pull the blinds, Meredith,' he says again.

She yanks them and they fall with a crash.

Christopher Fletcher left Sophia Roy on 29 December 2003, almost eight months pregnant. His son was only twenty months old when his mother, Sophia, tragically 'overdosed' and was subsequently brought up by Leila Roy, Sophia's sister.

'My nephew has grown up knowing exactly the person his mother was,' Leila Roy says on social media platform X. 'She was beautiful

and kind and loving. Now he is the very heart of our family, and we are so proud of everything he's achieved despite his difficult and traumatic start in life. These recent weeks – finding Sophia's online documentation and discovering Christopher Fletcher's true identity as an undercover police officer – have been deeply shocking and unsettling. The inquest will provide us with answers and, hopefully, justice will follow.'

As yet, the police have not given any statement.

'Is it *true*?' Meredith screams next to him.

Chris's phone rings. He diverts from Meredith's glower, answers the call.

'Oli?'

'It was just a matter of time,' Oliver says, 'until this was released. I'm surprised it's not been sooner.'

'Christopher! You have a *son*?' Meredith is grabbing at his arm. 'How *could* you?'

Oliver starts speaking again, but Chris can't hear him. 'Meredith – please.'

He moves towards the snug to talk to Oliver, closes the door and leans up against it.

'I've found you a new place,' Oliver continues. 'I've booked it in my sister's name, three miles away from the loch. Rosewood Cottage. No neighbours for a mile, but you're close enough for Jill, OK? Mark will come for you at 1 a.m. – black van. I'll ping you his picture and the registration.'

'Hey! *Hey!*' Meredith shouts from behind the door.

'Is that the aunt?'

'Yes.'

'She'll move too. With you.'

'There are reporters all over the place, Oli. Staying in

the village, in their vans, in tents. They'll see us, follow us.'

'I'll deal with anyone who tries to follow you. Do you forget what bloody unit we were in, lad?'

Chris breathes, feels like his whole body is deflating. It's all falling apart. He's standing on the gallows with his head in the noose.

'Leave your car, let them think you're still there. One of our men will get you out.'

'We'll be ready to move whenever you say.'

'This is a shitstorm, Chris, I have to say. I'm going to come up tomorrow, OK? We're all in it together, aren't we? Come what may.'

Chris puts his hand to his throbbing temple, relieved that Oli and others above him are looking out for his well-being – after all, an undercover agent, or officer, gives their life, their very identity, to the state in return for protection. However, Chris's brain decides to remember, at this precise moment, that the French government hung their agents publicly out to dry after the bombing of the Greenpeace boat *Rainbow Warrior* and the subsequent manslaughter of one of the crew members in the 1980s. The irony of that situation and the one Chris finds himself in now isn't lost on him.

'I've been in touch with that sergeant – Joseph Locke, is it? I've told him where the new place is, and I'll keep Jawad in the loop, too. He's coming up on the train tomorrow. All right?'

Chris says nothing.

'All right?'

'Yes.'

'Don't lose your head. And keep me updated on Jill.'

Chris hangs up, exhales. Meredith is banging on the

door, and he's got to face her at some point. He opens it, sees her grief-stricken expression.

'Is it true? Is it true you have a son?'

'It's true.'

'Did Jill know about him?'

'I don't—'

'You kept him a secret from her?'

He says nothing.

She flies at him then, all nails and biting words. 'You wicked man! Wicked!'

He raises his arms to his face because she's going for him like she wants to rip his eyes out of their sockets. Jackson barks behind them.

'Meredith! Meredith! I know – I *know* it's bad—'

'Do you see him? Do you see your *love child*?'

'No.'

Her eyes blaze. 'I don't know if that makes it better or worse! You just left them?'

Yes. He just left them.

'What else?' she spits. 'What other abhorrent things have you done?'

Too many, he thinks.

'Jill picked out baby names. Do you know that? She never told you because she thought it would be too painful for *you*.'

This is nearly enough to break him. 'Please,' he says softly. 'Don't do this.'

'Claire for a girl.'

'Meredith—'

'And Tom for a boy.'

He shakes his head, tries to spin her words out of his head. He didn't know Jill had thought of names.

'I can't . . . I can't do this with you.'

'Why? Because I'm holding you to account?'

'You need to pack.'

'*Pack?*'

'There's a car coming to get us at one in the morning. We need to move out of here.'

She sets her jaw. 'Out of my *house*? I'm not coming with you, Christopher.'

'Staying anywhere in the village means you'll be mauled by journalists.'

'And you don't want me to say the wrong thing?'

'I don't want you getting stressed out by it all.'

She barks with laughter. 'Stressed! Like I could be any more stressed than I am already! You want us to leave in the cloak of darkness, like criminals!'

He feels like one. *Is* one.

'We need protection,' he says.

'There's that *we* business again, Christopher. You're wanting me to bunk up with a wanted man.'

He doesn't answer her, instead snatches up some paper, writes a note to Harris, explaining that they're going to leave.

'Who's coming to pick you up?'

'Friends from when I was undercover. My handler, Oli, is organizing it.'

'Your *handler*? My *God*.'

'We need to focus on Jill.'

'That's been the biggest problem, Christopher. You never *did* focus on her. And now you've decided, if we think hard enough, we can magic her up out of thin air? The dinghy has gone; there's the biggest chance that she's *dead*, and here you are, focusing on yourself. What have you got left to save?'

He says nothing for a moment and then comes up close to her, so close that she's immediately uncomfortable and takes a step back.

'Meredith, my job was something so strange. So . . . unreal. I don't expect you to understand. But there are still things I have to save. The unit I was in, all the other people involved.'

'What does that mean?'

He shakes his head; he's saying too much. 'I know I've fucked up – with Jill, and our life together. I know I treated her badly. I know I didn't tell her the truth . . .' He trails off, overcome by a swell of emotion. 'But I can't think of the "if"s. I can only think about what I have to do now and, at this moment, that's making you leave this house with me. I don't want to drag you into it any more than I already have.'

He thinks she's going to fly off into another fury, but she surprises him. Her expression suddenly changes.

'Fine,' she says quietly.

25

2003

Sophia moved in with Chris in April, and all but abandoned living with her university flatmates. It felt bigger, more grown up, to wake up to the bustle of Notting Hill. They would cook together – sometimes Chris cooked Mexican, his one culinary talent. Life was good. *Better* than good. It felt like she was putting everything she believed in into practice: she had a lifestyle and a partner who believed in things as passionately as she did. In May, Chris met her family, bowled over her mother and father with the effortless charm that had attracted her. Leila said she'd reserve judgement, because she always reserved judgement.

'We should get a cactus and name it after your sister,' he said, after Leila had met them one day in London for a beer.

Sophia laughed loudly. Leila was, and always had been, prickly with any of Sophia's boyfriends, and took her role of 'Big Sister' very seriously. She was older than Sophia by five years and so declared herself the authority on relationships. She was also the same age as Chris, and had said privately to Sophia that Chris should be dating someone his own age and not a student. That had pissed Sophia off no end.

'She's just overprotective,' Sophia said.

'Ain't that the truth,' he said.

She put flowers in a jar, placed it on the windowsill. They were building up a plant collection in his flat, which had been sparsely decorated when she'd moved in. He had been apologetic about how it looked, had explained that the rent was pretty high but that he'd loved the area. Over time she bought some prints to hang on the walls and a bright rug. They'd bought Carlotta the fern, Jude the spider plant and Johann the yucca. They even bought a parlour palm, called it Vera the Second.

When she wasn't studying and he wasn't off on jobs or visiting his uncle Robin, they spent their days together planning new protests and meet-ups with other groups. But there were whole days when they just spent their time dreaming. Late afternoons in bed, evenings in the pub talking about music and books, and about friends and family. She asked if she could meet his parents in Southend-on-Sea, but he told her that he didn't talk to his parents any more. His father had been emotionally abusive and his relationship with his mother had broken down.

'What about Robin?' she asked.

'I would love you to meet Robin,' he said. 'But it would confuse him.'

'Evan went with you to clear the garden there, the other month, didn't he?' she said, trying to keep the disappointment out of her voice.

'No. That wasn't Robin's place.'

'I'm sure he said—'

He pulled her close. 'Listen, you're the family I didn't have,' he said. 'You're the family I *want*.'

He released her, dug around in the bag he'd brought back in from his van.

'What's this?' she asked.

In his hand was a small piece of reddish-brown wood, whittled into a perfect, smooth heart.

'A heart,' he said. 'I made it for you.'

Everything felt like it was beginning. And it was. Because they weren't careful. They were too busy being in love, caught up in a whirlwind romance. And in late July, she realized what was different. She had skipped her period, twice, and she hadn't really noticed. She had never been regular. But after a third missed bleed, she did the maths. For a few days, she did nothing. She told herself that it wasn't what she thought it could be. But one early evening, in the glimmer of the summer sun, she stepped out of the shower and stood sideways to look at herself in the mirror. There was a small curve to her belly. No one would have known it to look at her. Even Chris wouldn't notice.

But she knew, and she was terrified, but the overarching emotion at seeing that curve was joy. Pure, unfiltered *joy*.

She waited a week to take a pregnancy test. She wanted to be alone, wanted to be sure, even though she was already sure. He had been away for five days on a landscaping job up north, but on the night he came home she was waiting for him. Nervous, excited, and holding the test as his key turned in the lock.

He'd not gone two paces before he clocked it.

'What's that?' he asked.

'I know it wasn't part of the plan – yet – and I know we wanted to travel, but—'

'You're pregnant?'

She beamed. 'A baby, Chris. This is what you wanted – a family! So what if we're starting early?'

He went very still and there was a second when her

gut lurched, like she'd made a huge mistake, because his face looked different, like a mask had slipped. But then he rushed forward, grinning with delight and throwing his arms around her.

'Fuck,' he said into her hair. 'A baby, Soph.'

He was holding her so tightly that her lungs were squeezed. She pulled away from him, took his hands.

'Are you happy?'

'I'm so happy,' he said, and then he started to cry.

HE HAD A SON!!! WHAAAAAAAAA
   – @Happyfeet, X

What did Leila Roy tell him when he was growing up about
Sophia? About Chris Fletcher?
   – @Frankiegoestobollywood, X

#findsophiasboy
   – @Happyfeet, X

I saw Chris and Jill early in 2004 – April, I think. I went for
lunch with them. He was about to move on to a different
job and he couldn't tell me what, obviously, but we toasted
it. He didn't seem happy though. Jill told me when we were
alone together that she thought he was working too hard,
that he was exhausted. She asked me something strange
too. She asked me if I'd ever heard Chris mention a young
woman who lived in Notting Hill. I said no.
   – Guy Fletcher, Christopher Fletcher's cousin, interview
   with Sadie Clarke, *Under the Cover*, 2025

26

At exactly one in the morning, headlights cut through the blackness of the house.

'Are you ready?' Chris asks.

Meredith nods. They haven't spoken since their argument earlier, but she seems to have listened to him and packed up all her things, and silently helped him with some of Jill's too.

'Pack enough for a few days,' Oliver had said on the phone. 'We can bring the rest later.'

Moving will mean that they're not as close to the action of investigation, which is both a good and a bad thing. Good, because he can't stand the sight of dive lorries and reporter vans, and bad because being in Smoke House feels like still being with Jill. The perfume of her body lingers on the pillows; he sees the ghost of her sitting at the table, writing.

Chris clips Jackson's lead to his collar, puts his rucksack on his back and picks up a small holdall of his and Jill's with his free hand before opening the front door. They walk quickly as a black van drives across the grass and pulls up right outside.

Chris slides open the door and a man, Mark, he ascertains, turns around in the driver's seat, flashes a police badge at Chris, who nods.

'Good to go?' Mark asks.

'Yeah, thanks.'

Meredith steps up, and Jackson follows, stands on the floor, unsteadily.

'Did anyone see you come down?' Chris asks.

'We created a little diversion down at the pub.'

'At Harris's?'

'That's right. All the journalists are down there for the juice.'

'What was the diversion?'

'A fight outside of it,' Mark says. 'Between two of our lot.'

'Bloody hell,' Meredith mutters.

'It's all right,' Mark says. 'They like a good scrap. Someone might even fall off the jetty for good measure, make it a real spectacle. Should keep the eyes off you for a good hour or so, I should think.'

Chris says nothing, but feels bad for Harris, who won't know the fight isn't real and will be dealing with it.

'And this van is electric – stealthy as they come. I've had the headlights off until now.'

'Not your first rodeo,' Chris remarks, which is something Jill might have said.

Mark laughs. 'Leave your car keys with me and someone will pick it up in an hour. If any reporters are out, they might follow, so we'll have a decoy. We'll deliver the car back to you ASAP, when everything has died down.'

'Oh! I didn't lock my window,' Meredith says.

'I'll do it,' Chris says.

She nods, gives him the front-door key.

Rucksack still on his back, he hurries to the front door, and then races up the stairs to close the spare room. It's as he's going back down that his eyes lock on to the horse-head lamp in the kitchen. Without thinking, he plucks the shade from it and picks up the base. He wants it, wants it because Jill loved it. He puts it into his rucksack and then double-locks the front door behind him.

'All phones off now,' Mark says when Chris gets into the van.

'What?' Meredith says, her own phone reflecting blue light on her face.

'Yours is a visible number, I'm afraid, Meredith,' Mark says. 'A business number. We're making sure no one can get hold of you that shouldn't. Chris, yours is locked down and secure, but we need you to turn it off anyway. At least for twenty-fours.'

Meredith looks at Chris. 'How am I going to communicate with William?'

'I've got a phone you can use,' Mark says. 'A burner.'

'A *burner* phone?' Meredith exclaims.

The car starts to move. Jackson sways.

'Memorize William's number,' Chris says. 'You can touch base with him when we get to the house.'

'Does it have the internet?'

'No.'

'What about dealing with my *business*?'

'Meredith,' Chris says quietly. He is exhausted by her. 'In a couple of days, if you want, you can go to a hotel and take the train back to London and get on with your life.'

'Without knowing what's happened to Jill? As if I would. Anyway, I would go back to Smoke House, thank you very much. I have nothing to hide!'

'OK. But right now, if you're staying, you have to comply with what we're telling you.'

The car moves slowly and silently across the grass, over the ridge. Chris looks out of the window at the house but, as he does so, spots a lone figure in the darkness, by the edge of the woods. His heart begins to thud. Perhaps it's a tree trunk and his mind is playing tricks on him. He leans so his nose is against the glass and cups the rest of his face so it's shaded. No, it *is* a person, but it's not Jill, the frame is wrong, too tall. Could it be a reporter? That idiot, Rory Campbell?

'There's someone out there, Mark,' he says.

'We've got two officers keeping an eye on the property.'

This is supposed to make him feel better, and it does, a little, but he's jumpy. Whoever it is though – police officer or not – can't follow them, because there's no car to be seen, apart from his, and the keys are with him. Chris sits back, allows himself to breathe, but he can't ignore the blade of panic that is slicing into his heart.

Christopher Fletcher will not be speaking directly to the press in regard to the disappearance of his wife, Jillian Moore. He is deeply concerned about her welfare and is cooperating with the local police in their investigation. He continues also to be cooperative with the inquest into Sophia Roy's death in 2005.

    – Jawad Khan, Department of Legal Services

Jillian is in hiding. #jillianmoore #christopherfletcher #sophiaroy

    – @Frankiegoestobollywood, X

YES @Frankiegoestobollywood!! You're so right! She's hiding!

    – @Happyfeet, X

Maybe the son has killed Chris Fletcher's wife??

    – @shadowman, X

OR, and maybe I'll get roasted for this, but I'm going to throw it out there! Maybe she's hiding from the police. Maybe Jillian Moore killed Sophia Roy all those years ago. #justiceforsophia #christopherfletcher #jillianmoore

    – @Outtahere, X

WHAT? #justiceforsophia #christopherfletcher #jillian
moore
– @Happyfeet, X

I thought Sophia Roy overdosed? How could Jillian Moore
have killed her?
– @DeaconMiller, X

It was Sophia and her son alone in that house in Derby.
Come on, are you telling me it's impossible?! Where was
Jillian Moore on the day Sophia died anyway? #justicefor
sophia #christopherfletcher #jillianmoore
– @Outtahere, X

27

Rosewood Cottage is tiny – a two-up, two-down flint cottage, pretty and neat. But even with the equally trim little courtyard garden, it feels like another prison. Chris longs to be back in Smoke House to feel a sense of familiarity, a sense of Jill.

He sits in the kitchen in the morning light, flicking his thumb across his phone screen. He probably should have kept the phone off for longer as Mark had requested, but Chris needs to keep track of what's been said online.

He can't stop doom-scrolling. He's found himself down a rabbit warren of conversation about where Jill could be; all the cruel hypotheses of what could have happened to her. He tells himself that assumptions lead to mistakes, and that he can't think too deeply about all these theories, even though some of them mirror his own – that she drowned, that she ran away from him, that she is lost or injured. His worst fear of all is that someone has taken her. He chooses instead to tell himself that Jill will come walking into The Old Smoke House at any moment and ask him to make tea so she can sit and write. Except he won't be there, of course. Harris will meet her. Harris is the man that his wife can depend on.

In his hand his phone rings and he drops it in shock, before bending down to retrieve it. He is momentarily stunned by the name on the screen – Rani, Jill's friend. He glances upstairs, can hear Meredith moving around in the bathroom, and so he hunts out the furthest corner of the tiny downstairs, where he will not be heard. He presses answer.

'Hello?'

'Chris?' Rani's voice is soft. 'I've seen the news.'

'Yes.'

Rani is crying now. No longer soft, but choking, heaving great sobs down the phone.

'What's happened?' she asks. 'Where is she?'

'I don't know,' he says, and then feels disproportionately angry at her. If he knew where Jill was, why would the divers be out? Why would any of this be happening?

He hears her blow her nose.

'I'm sorry I haven't phoned before now,' she says.

'Sorry I haven't been in contact,' he says, at the same time.

There is a silence between them. He pictures her, gripping the phone.

'There's something I need to tell you,' she says after a moment.

His heart rises. 'About Jill?'

'No,' she says. 'Well. Yes. But about you.'

He is confused. 'OK?'

She takes a breath; he can hear it.

'I saw you,' she says. 'I saw you once in London. With a girl.'

He goes very still. There is a rush of silence to his ears. Everything has gone white.

'Chris? Did you hear what I—'

'When?' he says.

'It was in the summer – 2003. You were in Notting Hill, coming out of a flat.'

Shit. Shit, shit. Cold sweat prickles his skin.

'I was on an operation around west London,' he says. He can hear that his tone is defensive, but suddenly everything feels strange.

'I wasn't sure it was you at first. You'd grown your hair.' Here Rani pauses. 'You had your arm around a girl, and now I wonder if it was Sophia Roy. I told Jill.'

Three words. *I told Jill.* He feels something crack inside of him. His lungs? His heart?

'You – you told her?'

'I thought that if it was me, I'd want to know about it.'

He opens his mouth to speak, but it's thick and tacky. He thinks that he might pass out. He reaches with a hand for something to hold, grapples air because he can't see properly. He finds the arm of the sofa, sits heavily. Jill *knew*? But what exactly did she know?

'What did you tell her?' he manages.

'I told her you looked more than friendly with a girl that wasn't Jill.'

'And what did she say?'

Rani was quiet for a moment. 'She laughed.'

'She – what?'

'Jill laughed. She said you were on a job and then she hung up pretty soon after. Said she was making lunch. And we never talked about it again. Actually, we never talked much after that at all. I think I really upset her.'

He is weak with relief and then feels immediately ashamed that Jill was so trusting.

'But I gave her the address of where I'd seen you. I wrote it down.'

'You gave her the *address*?'

'Yes.'

'I was on various operations in that year,' he says, though, of course, he had only been on one, and the girl would have been Sophia. 'Do you know what could have happened?'

He can barely keep the anger out of his voice, wants to scream at her. But he can't, of course. And now Rani is crying again down the phone.

'I don't think Jill wrote down the address. And now I feel so awful. Jill and I haven't spoken for so long. In 2004 she sort of lost touch with everyone. And then you moved, and I . . .' She pauses to blow her nose. 'I tried calling when all this . . . all this happened with you, but she wouldn't pick up my calls.'

Chris swallows.

'I should have made more effort. And now – now . . .'

'I need to go,' he says.

'I should tell the police, shouldn't I? About telling Jill.'

'To what end?' he asks. 'You saw someone you think could have been Sophia Roy in 2003. But it might not have been her. Correct?'

'I suppose . . .'

'So unless you can tell the police what happened to Sophia in 2004, or tell them how that small sighting relates to Jill going missing, I'm not sure you'll want to get tangled up in it.'

She is silent for a moment. 'I'll be the judge of that,' she says, coolly.

He hangs up, heart pounding. Rani has aimed a shotgun at his chest and pulled the trigger. He had been certain, *certain*, that Jill hadn't known about Sophia, that she had heard about her for the first time only a few short weeks ago, when Caroline Bonner's article broke and Leila discovered Sophia's online diary. Even with Rani telling her that she'd seen Chris with a girl, she wouldn't have known it was Sophia.

But what if she *had* found out? What if Jillian had known about Sophia for years?

Jill had never said anything to him about this phone call with Rani. Surely she would have confronted Chris immediately, wouldn't she? There is no way that on the days – or hours on occasion – that he returned from a job, Jill would have played dumb, because Jill was no one's fool. She was outspoken, upstanding. She hated liars.

He winces at this.

Jill had known that Chris was a police officer, obviously – she had supported his years of training, the gruelling periods of shiftwork, and later the secrecy of his assignments. She had accepted the precious few days they had together when he was on leave, accepted that they wouldn't be doing all the daytrips she longed to do because he was so tired. Accepted, too, that his appearance switched, depending on his operations – he came home long-haired, skinny and smelling different. Throughout all of this, she trusted him completely and utterly.

Or so he had thought.

But what if Jill's suspicions about what Chris really got up to when he was away working got the better of her after Rani told her what she'd seen? What if Jill had written that address down and had gone to London, to the street? What if she had sat on one of the benches down from the flat and watched him? His chest feels tight at the thought of her seeing him with Sophia. Would she have assumed that Sophia was in police protection and needed safeguarding? That Chris was employed as a big brother of sorts? What if Jill had seen him *kiss* her? What kind of a big brother or police escort would allow *that* kind of behaviour? Because he *had* kissed Sophia in public, many times. He had totally disregarded the potential for his two lives colliding because Sophia was in London, the bustling metropolis, and Jill was miles away, safe in rural north Essex. Worlds apart. His skin crawls with the arrogance he'd had in his own invisibility. He had been so confident, so cocky. Stupid, stupid man.

If this had happened, if Jill had indeed seen them together, what if, instead of confronting Chris, Jill had decided to collect evidence against him? What if Jill had returned every few days to London and tortured herself by sitting rigid and predatory-eyed, documenting each touch between the two of them, every lingering kiss? Had Jill heard Sophia's name spoken on his lips? On the days Chris came back to Jill, had she started to analyse every single thing he said? Waited for him to call her Sophia, waited for him to trip up? *Had* he ever tripped up? Perhaps she would smell his clothes and his hair for Sophia's perfume. Would she have found it? His stomach rolls at the thought.

What if she'd gone further? Ransacked Chris's study, examining all the documentation that she could find. This was forbidden, of course, because the job required secrecy. People could be compromised, he had told her seriously, back when he qualified. She'd agreed never to go inside.

Had he kept it locked securely?

Even if she had got in, what would she have found? He was confident that he had never written anything on Sophia. There were no files, no photographs of her. Jill wouldn't have been able to access his computer. What else? What else had he kept in the study? It was so long ago now. Documentation in drawers, perhaps. A list of safe houses? Details of operations? Surely not. Surely not.

But what *if*?

He had left Sophia in late December, and Jill and Chris had spent New Year together. She had been fine with him, hadn't she? He tries to think what they had done – had they been out with friends? In the house, just the two of them? Try as he might, he can't remember, because he had been so in his own head, in anguish over Sophia. For days, weeks, he was moody and sullen, snappy, and restless at night. He hadn't wanted to go out anywhere or see any friends. Much to Jill's displeasure, he hadn't even found the energy to see Robert. Was Jill still touching him, laughing with him at that time? Were they still communicating, sleeping together? Were they happy? Was she?

He does recall that during that time she was up at all hours scratching out poems. He remembers because every night for months he lay awake, seething and sorrowful, and Jill wouldn't be in bed beside him but downstairs writing pages and pages of poems, prolific and frenzied, filling up notebooks. He recalls too, that at some point in that year, or possibly the following, packets of pills started to litter the cupboards – Sertraline, Citalopram. He remembers commenting that she seemed to forget to sleep, ignored mealtimes. She told him she was writing.

But it was more than that. When Jill brushed her hair it seemed to come away all by itself. Clumps in the shower, clogging the drain, and it annoyed him because pulling out wet ropes of hair made him retch. But was all that because of what he had done to her? That both of them were suffering with his guilty secret? Because if she had believed Rani, and had indeed gone to see for herself Chris with Sophia, she clearly hadn't told anyone of his betrayal. Perhaps she couldn't bear the pity, couldn't stomach the pain or the inevitable *I told you so* from Meredith, who made it no secret that she thought Chris was a lousy husband for being away so much and wasting Jill's life.

Had Jill started to follow *Sophia* alone? Tried to glean anything she could about her? He can't imagine her doing so, but anger is a powerful drive. Perhaps she had followed for only a few hundred yards before getting frightened and turning around again, but then the hours stretched and she started to follow Sophia to the shops she visited, to restaurants. Maybe even to the impressive buildings of Kingston University. And then, the worst thing he could imagine – that Jill had realized Sophia was pregnant. If she'd tracked Sophia, she would have noticed over the months that her belly began to swell.

A lump forms in his throat and then his breath zips in. He realizes – with a bright and dazzling certainty – that there *was* something he'd put in the drawers of his study. There was a note Sophia had left him when he left her. Her parents' address in Kent, a phone number, and words of love that burned in his eyes as he read them.

Please call. I love you.

No. Impossible. Because he had asked Jill never to go into his study. He had always locked it. Hadn't he? A shooting pain stabs so deep and so hard inside his chest that he can't breathe. The note is long gone now, of course, but when had he got rid of it? What if she *had* gone in and found it? He imagines Jill reading it, gripping it so hard that her thumb nearly went through it, and the words shouted at her in the ringing quiet of their house. He imagines that the clock ticked over, the light changed in the study, and it was somehow evening before she finally moved and calmly put everything away.

But what if she'd kept the note? Gone to see Sophia. What if she'd seen his baby?

Stop, he thinks. Your head is running away. Jill would never have done that. Rani might have told Jill about seeing him with Sophia, but she hadn't seen them physical together. Jill had laughed it off. She had known he was on a job, and had respected his work.

Whereas he had not respected Jill at all and had not cherished her as he should have.

He opens X again, eyes skimming the latest comments, latest wild theories. Why won't they stop? Why won't he stop himself incessantly looking?

It was Sophia and her son alone in that house in Derby. Come on, are you telling me it's impossible?! Where was Jillian Moore on the day Sophia died anyway?

He reads on, aghast at the speculative, gleeful and gruesome words from these strangers. How Jill must have engineered Sophia going to that house in Derby, waited for her to arrive and administered a fatal dose of heroin. Jillian was a nurse, knew how to find a vein. These disgusting speculations made him want to be sick. Because yes, Jill knew her own mind and spoke it, but her heart was kindness and compassion itself. She would never, ever do anyone any harm.

She's on the moors, hiding! Doing a runner!

She's putting the blame on #christopherfletcher and he deserves it.

The scales have already tipped towards sending him down; a climactic ending to his jaunts as an invisible man.

He turns the screen to black. Jill had no connection to Derby. It's all absurd.

Though one thing is true — Jill is the invisible one now, not him.

Snapchat

MattChristie: Lorna, what happened at the Horse? Tommy next door said something kicked off???

RoryCampbell: Lorna, does your dad know where Chris Fletcher has gone?

RoryCampbell: Did your dad find my drone?

FionaWilson: Shall we come to the Horse tonight to see you, babe?

RoryCampbell: I got offered 200 from the Daily Mail for that picture of The Old Smoke House!

LornaMcGowan: Leave it the fuck alone, Rory.

RoryCampbell: Oh, *HI LORNA*!

LornaMcGowan: You shouldn't be speaking to anyone about any of it. Can't you see you're making everything worse? We had a fight last night at the pub by some blokes that must be here for the circus it's all become. Two lamps got smashed, and my dad had to call Joseph Locke.

RoryCampbell: This is all putting us on the map!

LornaMcGowan: It's exactly what happened before with Mum. All the speculation. I hate it. I wish they were all gone.

28

2003

Chris surprised Sophia, and not in a good way.

Initially, he had been happy about the baby. For the first few weeks after she told him, they spent hours talking about what gender it would be, what it would look like, and how they would welcome it into the world. But as summer turned to autumn, Chris's mood seemed to shift. There were days where he was untalkative, solemn even, and then prolonged periods of time where he would no longer entertain decisions about the future. She put it down to nervousness, that he didn't want to jinx anything, but increasingly he would lurch – so suddenly – into what could only be described as bouts of depression that it began to worry her.

By the end of October, it was as if Chris was going through some sort of breakdown. He became lethargic, started to drop out of attending Green is Go meetings. He would leave the flat and not return until the following day, and when she questioned him about where he'd been he told her that he'd been out on a job or at the pub, stayed over with a friend and forgotten to text. He never told her who it was he'd stayed with.

On weekends he would go and visit his uncle in the care home and, when he returned, he would be almost inconsolable. Robin was slowly getting worse, he told her, and she was understanding and supportive, held him as he cried on her shoulder. She offered to go with him to see Robin, to shoulder some of the emotional burden because Chris didn't have family he was close to, but he always said no, told her that it was something he had to do alone. He would hold her and whisper *thank you* in her ear. *I don't deserve you.*

But still the random overnight trips persisted, once a week, sometimes twice. There were times when she was so worried she would call Johann, Carlotta, Jude, tell them with fake laughter that she had 'misplaced' him and ask if they'd seen him, but they never had. She didn't have any details of his family back in Essex, didn't even know where the care home was that Robin was in because he'd never told her, and Evan, who had gone with him once, couldn't remember. And then Chris would come back again.

She began to fear that he had met someone else, or that he was taking harder drugs than weed. Perhaps, she thought, he was struggling with the thought of becoming a father because he had a bad blueprint with his own. She asked him to consider antidepressants or therapy, but he outright refused her suggestions. Increasingly, he took up jobs in further-away towns, often leaving for a week at a time and not telling her where he was. He wouldn't return her calls, and she would go mad with anxiety, then with anger. It made her dizzy, and the baby would roil inside her, like it knew her sadness and echoed her distress.

'Can't you understand?' she shouted when he'd been away for three nights with no contact. 'Can't you see what you're doing? You're shutting down! Shutting me out! Why are you doing this, Chris, when we love each other? When we have everything going for us? Look at me!'

She grabbed his face, and he turned his eyes on her, but it was like he wasn't there behind them. He wouldn't acknowledge that he was actively sabotaging their relationship and she called him cruel. She lay in bed with her back to him and wondered if they had made the most colossal mistake. She wondered if she had completely misjudged the man he was.

On that last night in their bed – and it was 'theirs', not just 'his', because the flat had become their home over the months she'd been there – she took his hand and placed it on her swollen stomach.

'Chris,' she'd breathed. 'I don't want to do this without you.'

The very next day he left her for ever. It was 29 December 2003.

29

Chris had seen Oliver on 5 January 2004 for his final debrief. They met in the café they always met in, where Chris passed on information and Oliver sat quietly and made notes. It was small, with metal tables and chairs and the smell of greasy breakfasts hanging in the air. Tradesmen passed through; old people sat in window seats with the daily tabloids.

He could see Oliver take in his unwashed hair, his crumpled clothes and bloodshot eyes.

'You've done it then?' Oliver asked.

Chris nodded.

Oliver leaned across the table, his hand out. Their fingertips were inches apart, but they didn't touch. Not the done thing, of course, but the gesture was there. The sympathy.

'It's for the best, son.'

Chris stared out of the window. Outside, an empty crisp packet swirled along the street with the wind. Blue: salt and vinegar.

'You're an officer, first and foremost. You got in too deep with that girl, when she was a target.'

'Don't call her that, Oli.'

Oliver sighed. 'No. But she *was*. Except she's not any more, is she? She's got your baby in her belly.'

There was no denying the obvious, but Chris was angry, defensive.

'But it was always part of the role.'

Oliver forced a laugh. 'You made out that group was

much more threatening to public order than it was. You pushed to stay there month after month because of *her*, and not the job. You jeopardized your well-being, and that of your family. What about Jill?'

'Please,' Chris whispered. The mention of Jill, of his betrayal, was like a needle to his eye.

Oliver looked around, spoke low and quiet. 'Some officers, some handlers – hell, even some *seniors* – might allow this sort of thing, but I'm here to look out for *you*. What you did was reckless, but look, it's done now. Right? You're going to tell yourself that Christopher Flynn is gone, for ever. OK? That's how you get through this. Chris Flynn never even existed.' He picked up his tea. 'I'll arrange a desk job for you.'

Chris looked at him in alarm. '*No*, Oli. Fuck no. I want to go undercover again.'

'I don't think that's wise right now, do you?'

'But it's what I trained for. It's what I wanted to *do*. I don't want to be pushing papers. I want to be out there doing what I'm good at.'

'You need to be doing something easy—'

'I need to be *busy*. I need to be out in the field, OK? Distracted. I can't think about . . . I don't want to think about Sophia, about what we could have had.'

'Chris—'

'Put me out there. I want to be somewhere . . . I want to do a job where I can be ruthless. Where I can't care about anyone.'

Oliver paused. 'How ruthless?'

'I want to bury myself in something big and nasty.'

'There is something,' Oliver said after a while, glancing around the café, and then leaning forward. 'Have you heard of the group Dawn?'

30

Chris can hear Meredith pacing her room upstairs, moving around like a fly trying to get out of a window – erratic and irritating. Just past nine, she comes down, looking flustered and out of place.

'Shall we have tea?' she says.

Their argument from the previous day still smoulders behind her eyes, but the offer feels like an olive branch.

'I'll put the kettle on,' he says, and gets up to fill it.

'All this endless waiting,' she sighs.

'Is this what it's like in an old people's home?' he muses.

She snaps her head round, a cross owl. 'Why are you asking *me*?'

Olive branch broken.

'I didn't mean you. I know you have the elixir to endless youth.'

The kettle boils in the silence. She gets up and starts taking over, aggressively pushing the teabags against the mugs with a spoon. He gets the milk.

'I suppose it could be worse,' she says after a moment. 'There could be paisley-covered chairs in the lounge and biscuit crumbs in the beds.'

'And *Pointless* on TV.'

'Ironic.'

They smile at each other then, a rare moment of solidarity. He goes to pour the milk and, as he does, there's a knock on the door.

'Will you get the door?'

Meredith pauses. 'What if it's someone bad?'

'Tell them we don't want to see anyone bad today.'

She rolls her eyes. 'Christopher, I'm not answering the door.'

'Hello?' says a voice. 'Chris?'

'It's Joseph,' Chris says to Meredith.

Meredith sniffs. 'I'm not *deaf*.'

Chris opens the door and Joseph comes in, followed by Karen.

'Is there any news?' Chris asks.

'No news in regard to finding Jill, I'm afraid,' Karen says. 'We wanted to know if you brought a laptop here. I know you said Jill hadn't, but perhaps you did?'

'Only my phone.'

'We'd like that then, please.'

Chris nods. 'That's fine.'

And it is fine because he has another, secret phone, so he can still contact Oliver. Not that he'll be telling that to Joseph Locke.

'Do you need mine?' Meredith asks.

'Just Chris's at present.'

'Has there been any luck accessing Jill's emails?' Chris asks.

Meredith raises her eyebrows. 'Her emails? Why do you need to check her emails?'

'Routine procedure. This is an investigation.'

'Not a criminal one though,' Meredith says. 'If you have any information, you can share it with us, can't you? Because we could help? Why do you think it's necessary to be looking through her private things?'

'Everything is relevant,' Joseph says. 'We're stepping the

investigation up a gear; we need to look at Jillian's disappearance from other angles.'

'And what does that mean?'

'We're not ruling out foul play,' Karen says.

Foul play. The words make Chris feel physically sick.

Meredith blanches. 'Foul . . . foul play?'

Joseph shoots a look at Karen, visibly annoyed by her bluntness. 'As I said,' he says, 'we're considering other angles as to what might have happened. Meredith, would you give us permission to send a forensics team into The Old Smoke House?'

Meredith blinks. 'I – of course, but is that necessary?'

'We know someone came to the property and wrote on the wall while you were out on your walk. People know that you were there. We need to make sure no one got into the house.'

Chris is taken aback. 'And what? Abducted her? I would have noticed.'

But Karen shakes her head. 'Would you? We know that you stayed asleep when Jill left to go with Amanda that night.'

He is speechless because she is right.

'And someone takes sleeping pills. I saw them in the bathroom cabinet in Smoke House.'

'I take them,' Chris says. 'But only sometimes.'

'How many at a time?'

'I—'

'Why didn't you tell us the first time we were round?'

'I didn't think it was relevant.'

But perhaps it *was* relevant. How many had he taken that night? One? Two?

'What about alcohol?' Joseph asks.

'What about it?'

'Were you drinking the night before Jill disappeared?'

He starts to shake his head and then remembers the whisky, remembers Jill's words.

You've drunk nearly half of it.

He berates himself internally. Drink makes his mind fall away to strange places, though, if he's being honest with himself, his mind wanders on its own sometimes anyway. It tangles itself into knots, occasionally whispering to his body to move without him knowing. Sometimes he's felt like he's in a different skin – not just another identity on the outside but on the inside too. A version of himself that isn't him. Sometimes he's woken in places he's not gone to sleep. The strangest sensation, and a horrifying one.

'I can't remember,' he lies.

'This is procedure, Chris,' Joseph says. 'As you know. No one is casting aspersions. We just need the full picture of that night.'

'You really think someone might have come in?' Meredith asks.

'In all honesty,' Joseph says, gently, 'we still believe the likelihood is that Jillian became lost at sea, but this is turning into a high-profile case. The media are jumping on her disappearance. I'm getting questions asked.'

'What kind of questions?'

'Is there anyone you know who would want to attack Jill?' Karen asks. 'Someone that might have known you were here?'

To hear someone say it aloud, his worst fear of what might have actually happened, chills his blood. He thinks about the figure at the hedgerow, the person who stood outside the window in the pouring rain, who he's more and more convinced wasn't Harris about to knock on the door. What about the person who watched them drive away? Was it definitely one of the police officers that Mark said was stationed to watch Smoke House?

Chris's heart hammers. 'I – I don't—'

'If you're asking if Jill had enemies, then of course not,' Meredith cuts in. 'She's a poet, for goodness' sake. And she's no Salman Rushdie.'

'From your other undercover operations? Or from your life in Sardinia?'

'No, and no,' Chris answers, but that's not true. Damian Roper. Oh fuck, oh fuck.

There's a silence. 'OK.' Joseph nods. 'If you think of anything, let us know.'

They leave, and Meredith turns to Chris.

'Oh God, oh *God*! You take sleeping pills?'

'I – yes.'

'Heavy enough to knock you out?'

'Sometimes. Sometimes I'm half awake and half asleep, but . . .'

'*And* you had been drinking?'

'I just had a bit, Meredith. Calm down.'

'Don't tell me to calm down! There's no one who might want to do her harm, is there? What Officer Holland said? There's no one who could have come in and taken her from under your nose?'

'No,' he says.

But what if, after all these years, Damian Roper has found him? The man he's been constantly afraid would track him down. The man who haunts his dreams. The man responsible for the creation of Dawn. What if Roper has taken Jill?

Christopher Fletcher has left The Old Smoke House!! Am trying to get the intel on where he's gone!
— @AnonRC, X

What do you mean? He's done a runner?
— @Tankerman, X

There was a fight at the local pub. All eyes were turned. I think he left then.
— @AnonRC, X

WTF? This is INSANE! #sophiaroy #christopherfletcher
— @Happyfeet, X

You know what they say. If you want a proper investigation, don't go to the police. Get a reporter on to it.
— @Mickeyblueeyes, X

I'm studying to be a journalist :)
— @AnonRC, X

I found their son!!!! His name is ALEX #sophiaroy #christopherfletcher #policespies #justiceforsophia
— @shadowman, X

31

2004–2005

In the days and weeks after Chris disappeared, Sophia tried in desperation to find him. But his number wouldn't connect, and her texts and emails repeatedly bounced back to her, undelivered. Chris had taken his bags and all his clothes. Even in previous depressive episodes, he'd never cleared out his things, and that is what scared her — that he could actually have gone for good this time. She went everywhere she could think of and spoke to everyone they had in common, but no one had seen him or heard from him. She rang hospitals and police stations, terrified that Chris might have hurt himself. She contacted all the care homes in south London, looking for his uncle Robin, but couldn't find anyone who matched the limited details she knew of him. Evan from Green is Go couldn't remember where the care home was when he'd been to clear the gardens once with Chris. She even tried to trace his van registration, but now it belonged to a private owner who had bought it from a company that couldn't tell her who had owned it formerly. There was no paper trail of him. Nothing. She prayed every night to a god she didn't believe in to bring him safely back to her, but it was as if he had fallen off the face of the earth, and she was devastated, utterly stunned, by this betrayal. She couldn't remember what the last thing was that she said to him. Was it *I love you*? Was it *I hate what you're doing*? It could have been either, or even both in the same breath.

With heavy reluctance, she left the flat in Notting Hill in January and moved back to Kent. She was six weeks away from giving birth and needed the support of her family, even though she was paranoid that he would return and find her gone. She left a note on the pillow with her parents' address and number on it, and the words, *Please call. I love you.*

She had no idea if he would come back and see it, but it was her only hope. She took all their plants with her, and Vera the Second sat on the windowsill of her childhood bedroom. She felt a mixture of grief and anger every time she looked at it. In the evenings she sat on the sofa and watched television, her mother stroking her arm, her father oddly quiet and sad-looking, which made her feel worse. She had been going to change the world for him, follow in his footsteps of exploring green energy, and now she had left university, her course, everything, and was having a baby with a vanished partner. The weight of responsibility became as physically heavy as the baby who turned inside her. What had she been thinking, to meet a man, move in with him and fall pregnant? She cried, nightly, exhausted by having a baby, exhausted by grief, for that was what it felt like. It felt like he had died. A shock abandonment. Rejection.

She wondered how she had got it so wrong.

The sun rose and dipped, the moon waxed and waned, and she became bigger and bigger, more and more uncomfortable until, on 14 February – a kick in the teeth that it was Valentine's Day, she thought at first – she gave birth to their son, Alexander James, with Leila holding her hand.

It turned into the most romantic day of her life. Within moments of him being placed on her chest, she fell in love, this most perfect thing she'd ever seen, dark-haired, soft.

'Oh, Soph,' Leila breathed, tears in her eyes. 'I love him. I fucking love him.'

Her whole family delighted in him. They took him for walks, held him while she bathed, rocked him when she was too tired to rock him herself. They were the best support network she could ever have imagined having, but, as ungrateful and ugly as she knew it was, she didn't want *them*. She wanted Chris, and only him. She wanted the promises he'd made, her independence, her own family unit. She wanted his smile, the focus of those liquid eyes on her, and on *Alex*. But that was not her reality any more. What else could she do but survive the loss of him?

She found distraction in the monotony. She got up every day, sang to Alex and cuddled him, loved him. She went out with the pram, would meet people on the streets who'd peer into the pram and coo at him. She would attend local baby groups, go to the park to feed the ducks. It was a dull existence, but he was loved, and she was safe.

And then, out of the blue, she was thrown a curve ball. A lifeline. In May, a letter came for her, via Jude, and she recognized at once that the writing was Chris's. Her heart constricted as she tore it open to read it.

He wrote that he had gone to Slovenia. He said that he wanted to do good out there, that he couldn't cope with being in the UK when Robin was so unwell. He said that he wasn't planning on coming back. He said that he was sorry, that he loved her and their child.

Sorry.

This was worse than having no letter at all. What did 'sorry' mean when he had gone and ripped her heart out? His words of love were meaningless. She crushed the letter in her hands, and then went to rip it up, but stopped herself and hastily smoothed the page out. Those words were all she had of him. She kept it under her pillow. Pitiful, she thought, pathetic.

But after the anger had subsided, the letter ended up galvanizing her. She rang all the airlines that flew out to Slovenia to ask them about their passenger lists for the months of January and February, but they wouldn't give them to her. She contacted the Passport Office to see if she could get any information on whether Chris was still abroad, gave them Chris's details – his birthday and his parents' names – but they told her a code had come up against it.

'What code?' she asked.

'Can you hold?' the woman said.

Sophia held, but when the woman came back on she sounded more puzzled than before.

'The file isn't available,' she said. 'It just shut down.'

'What was the code?'

'It was "CE", but I don't know what that means. I've not seen it before. My supervisor tried too, and we can't access it. I'm sorry.'

The following day she went to the Family Records Centre to see if she could get hold of any other information for Chris, or Robin, or any other members of Chris's family. After an hour, she found his details and filled in an application for his birth certificate and got it three days later through the post – a copy of Chris's birth certificate with his parents' names, Colin and Lynda, and their address in Essex. He had talked about growing up in Southend-on-Sea, and how much he'd loved the coast. Excitedly, she rang the number, even though there was a chance they had moved. She gripped the phone as it connected, white-knuckled.

She was told they had moved. No forwarding address.

Everywhere she turned, she hit walls.

'Piece of shit,' Leila spat when Sophia cried on her shoulder. 'That letter did nothing but give you false hope, Soph. He's not coming back, and you need to forget about him, OK?'

She nodded.

'I mean it. Who the fuck leaves a pregnant woman and goes to Slovenia to "do good"? I never liked him, Soph. I always thought he was a creep.'

'No, Leila—'

'*Yes.* One of those charming men who think they can do what they like and to hell with the consequences.'

'You don't know him,' said Sophia, and then she stopped talking, realizing that she had clearly not known him either.

'He gave you Alex,' Leila said, putting her arm around Sophia. 'Alex is all you need.'

32

It's the afternoon, hours after Joseph and Karen drove away with Chris's phone. Meredith went for a walk shortly after and took Jackson with her, but it's been a long time and Chris is getting worried. He can't call her phone because then she'll know he has another that he didn't hand over, and yet she was so agitated over the visit that he's concerned she'll start talking to friends or family on the illicit burner phone they were given by Mark. He's worried that she'll give their location away.

In one respect, however, Chris is glad that Meredith isn't here because, finally, Oliver has arrived. Chris watches him, in the kitchen of Rosewood Cottage, flipping a cheese sandwich over in the pan. The inquest is only a day away now.

'What if he's found her?' Chris says, sitting at the table, watching the smoke from the pan. 'What if he's taken Jill away?'

'Who? What are you talking about?'

'*Roper*. What if he's got Jill? I think Damian is here, in Scotland, and I think he's taken her.'

'Roper isn't *here*, Chris. Don't be ridiculous.'

'But how do you *know*? Don't you think it could be a possibility?'

'No.'

'Why not?'

Oliver slides a burnt offering on to Chris's plate. 'Do you want ketchup?'

'On a toastie?'

Oliver shrugs.

'No, I don't,' Chris says. 'I'm just saying that he could have come back and tracked us and—'

'Stop. You're paranoid.'

'With good reason.'

'I *know* with good reason,' Oliver says. 'But even if he had come back, why would he take Jill out of your house when he could take you?'

'To punish me?'

'The police will find Jill. It might take time if she's . . . but they're searching all over, and have extended their search, you said so yourself. It's all over the news. God help us.'

All the muscles behind Chris's eyes hurt. 'Do we know where Alex is?'

'As far as we can tell, he's gone to ground,' Oliver says. 'We're trying to find him. As is Leila Roy, apparently, because he's not told her where he is either, and she's beside herself. People on X have found out his name, and she thinks they're going to try and locate him.'

'To what end? Alex doesn't have anything to do with any of this.'

'Nothing and everything,' Oliver says. 'But before you ask, no, I don't think Roper has found him either.'

Chris bites into the grilled sandwich. It's at once crisp and sharp, but the dough is thick and sticks to the roof of his mouth.

'Do you know anything about what's happening at Smoke House?' he asks. 'With the forensics team?'

'They're in there now. I'm all over Jill's investigation too, all right? I've got your back.'

Oliver puts the second toastie into the pan for himself. Smoke rises from it, curls into the air.

'We need to go over the inquest one more time.'

'I know.'

'You need to be absolutely rigid in what you're saying.'

'I *know.*'

'We have evidence. We have pictures of you in Southampton, on that operation.'

Chris nods. 'We have alibis.'

Chris swallows. Hot cheese and grease flood his mouth, make him want to throw up. Evidence, alibis. It's all there.

'You left the country in 2005, and it was a smart move. We just have to hope it was smart enough. My worry is that someone is going to out you from somewhere completely left field. A friend in Sardinia, a friend from school who has old pictures. Someone. We've got alerts set up, manpower directed to monitor all this, but – as we saw with the photograph taken at the pub – it's difficult to keep track of every conversation thread popping up.'

'Yes.'

'Your car has arrived too,' Oliver says. 'Mark's parking it up, OK? Not that you can go anywhere for the foreseeable.'

'I think he's taken her.'

Oliver looks angry. 'What?'

'I think Roper has Jill. I do. It all adds up—'

'It does *not*,' Oliver says sternly, and flips his toastie over. 'The boat was missing, her bag, her jacket. I'm sorry, Chris, but it all points to . . . Well. Get Damian Roper and Dawn out of your head. No one from Dawn knows you as Chris Fletcher, and they didn't know Sophia.'

'Damian knows.'

'Stop it. I'm serious. You're letting your head run away.

I'm sorry this is happening to you, but don't go thinking Roper has anything to do with Jill.'

Chris pushes his plate away. 'I can't eat this,' he says. 'I'm sorry.'

He drops the sandwich to the floor and Jackson moves to hoover it.

'Oh, Chris.' Oliver sighs, puts his toasted sandwich on his plate. 'I would have eaten that.'

'Did we do the right thing, Oli?'

'What?'

'Did we do the right thing by the activists? Spying on them?'

'Are you serious? That was the objective.'

'I treated Sophia badly.'

Oliver hesitates. 'You did.'

'And I left her. I didn't take personal responsibility.'

Oliver bites into the cheese. 'You need to get your shit together.'

33

2005

An entire year passed in a blur, but at the little party that Sophia threw for her boy's first birthday, time stood still. The day was supposed to feel so special, and it was, in some ways; Alex was adorable with his presents, so sweet in blowing out his candle. But Sophia hit a level of sadness she'd not reached before.

Chris was missing every single thing.

She took photographs of the day with her camera – she had, in fact, taken pictures every day, was storing them for Chris – but as Alex smiled at her while picking up a glob of icing, she lowered the lens. Chris didn't deserve the kindness. She had told Leila that she wouldn't bother trying to find Chris, but Alex deserved to know his father. And *she* deserved answers.

A week after Alex's birthday, Sophia left him with Leila for the day and told her that she was seeing a friend.

Instead, she took the train to Southend, to Chris's old family address. When she'd called months previously, she'd been told that they'd moved, but what if they hadn't? What if Chris had *been* there at the house and told his mother to lie to her? Or, what if they had moved, but neighbours knew where they had gone? She had been stupid to give up on the trail back then, but she was a new parent and emotionally and physically exhausted. Now she was ready.

She sat on the train but couldn't read the magazine she'd bought at the station platform kiosk. She couldn't seem to do anything but stare out of the window at the passing landscape, worrying about what she might say when she got to the house. When she reached Southend-on-Sea, she was practically shaking. She hadn't eaten anything all day, hadn't even thought to bring a bottle of water.

It took her a dizzying amount of time to find the street. Not because it was far away but because she kept misreading the map and walking in the wrong direction. The sky was blue, and there was salt in the air from the sea. Seagulls wheeled overhead. The houses were mostly white, some pebble-dashed; there were trees lining the roads. In any other situation she would think that perhaps it was a nice part of the world, though she remembered that Chris's childhood had been far from it. The alcoholic father, the broken family.

At last she reached the street, and stopped outside number forty-six. A pale grey door, a brass knocker in the shape of a bumblebee. She knocked it and then stood back on the pavement, until a petite woman opened the door a moment later. Mid-fifties, perhaps, hair a strawberry blonde and her eyes pale blue.

'Hello,' Sophia said. 'I'm looking for Lynda Flynn.'

The woman appraised her. 'They moved, lovey. I don't have a forwarding address, I'm afraid.' She paused. 'Was it you who rang before?'

'I – yes.'

'Is she a relative?'

'No, I'm a family friend.'

The woman looked at her curiously. 'Some of the neighbours might know where they went. I think Maureen might have known them.' She nodded to the house opposite. 'Number forty-three.'

'Thank you,' Sophia said, and the woman closed the door. She turned, looked at the house over the road, and then marched with purpose towards it before she lost the courage.

An elderly woman answered a minute after her knock, wearing an old-fashioned housecoat and a frown.

'Hello. Are you Maureen?'

'Yes?'

'Sorry to disturb you, but I've been looking for the Flynn family and was told you might know where they'd gone.'

The woman's frown deepened. 'That was all a long time ago. Nice family. Their son was a sweet boy.' She shook her head. 'It was awful what happened to him.'

Sophia's heart rate quickened. 'What do you mean?' she asked. 'Is he OK? Have you heard anything from his parents?'

Maureen looked at her oddly. 'The accident,' she said. 'I meant the accident.'

'What accident?'

Maureen hesitated. 'Are you from the papers?'

'No—'

'My phone is ringing,' Maureen said, though Sophia couldn't hear anything. Maureen went to close the door.

'Can I – can I come again and talk to you?' Sophia called as it was shutting on her.

'I don't like to talk badly about people,' the old woman said, and then the door was shut.

*

All night Sophia lay awake, the thoughts in her head turning over and over. An accident. What could that have meant? The woman – Maureen – hadn't even said Chris's name, so could there have been a brother? Chris had never mentioned one. She went online and tried to find anything she could about accidents relating to their name, or incidents on the street. There was nothing but dead ends.

A few days later, she got up early and had an instinct to return to Islington, to the Family Records Centre, but this time she was going to look at the death records. She didn't have a name for any brother, but she searched Chris, just in case he had, God forbid, died recently, and Maureen had been in touch with his family. Just in case, just in case. She wanted to rule out the possibility. She entered his details – his name and his date of birth – and then she waited, her teeth chattering with nerves, as time seemed to stand still and the computer timer turned.

The screen changed, and there he was. The same address, the same parents, but Christopher Flynn was dead. She cried out in anguish, the noise permeating the silence of the room, and then she was rendered completely soundless. Christopher Flynn was six years old when he died, after falling into the pond at the back of their house. So who was the man she knew?

She didn't tell anyone what she'd discovered about Chris but wrote it all down on a password-protected Word document. She made lists, notes, desperate to find out who he was. She had spent the best part of a year of her life with a nameless stranger, and she would not rest until she knew Alex didn't have a criminal for a father, or a spy.

Interspersed with her documented findings were

outpourings of grief, of anger, of worry, but also declarations of love. Because, despite it all, despite these bombing truths that were exploding, she still loved him. She still loved him! She wished she didn't – wouldn't it have been easier just to have let him go? But there were days when Sophia looked at Alex and started to cry because it wasn't fair on him, on either of them. And what made matters worse was that Chris was out there somewhere. Perhaps he hadn't even gone to Slovenia.

After months of dogged perseverance and endless calls and emails, she eventually got a break. In August, Evan from Green is Go rang her to say that he'd found the care home he'd been to with Chris. He told her that when they'd arrived, Chris had spoken to one of the nurses, who appeared to know him, and then a few minutes later an old man was wheeled out in his chair and watched them work from the patio. Chris had waved over at him, told Evan that he knew the man, and that he was called Robin. Sophia's heart and stomach both lurched. She asked Evan for the address, and then called the care home and made an appointment for that very afternoon. She borrowed her mother's car and drove a hundred miles.

The care home was quiet, a place of comfort. There were delicate pastel colours on the walls, and on window-sills were vases with fresh-cut flowers, though when Sophia looked closely, there were a few fake stems bulking out the real ones. Tea trolleys with cakes in glass-topped stands in the common room, people sitting in armchairs and playing cards, watching television.

'You said on the phone you were looking for a place for your grandma?' the nurse said when Sophia had checked in for her tour.

'Yes,' Sophia said as she signed her name. 'Grandma had a friend here. Or has a friend. I'm not sure if he's still alive.' The nurse gestured for Sophia to follow her, and they started to walk down a long corridor, bright with natural light. There was art on the walls, photographs of flowers on canvas.

'His name is Robin,' Sophia said.

The nurse gestured to one of the bedrooms that was open. 'We don't have anyone here called Robin.'

'Oh,' Sophia said, glancing in for a second, out of pretence. 'Perhaps he died? He was becoming very unwell.'

They walked on. They passed an old lady, who smiled and told them she was off for her monthly haircut. The nurse beamed at her, told her she'd look a million dollars, before turning back to Sophia.

'I've been here for five years and I've never had a Robin. Did he perhaps go by another name? We had a lovely old gent in here called Gary, but his real name was Albert. They all used to call him Gary in the war because his second name was Garrett.'

'I don't – I don't think so? He was in a wheelchair. Maybe he went by Rob?'

The nurse shook her head. 'I don't think so.'

Sophia wanted to scream. Was Robin another lie that Chris had told her and Evan both? But Evan had seen a man in a wheelchair that day. Perhaps he had merely been at the right place at the right time? But why would Chris come here if not for Robin? Suddenly Sophia couldn't smell flowers, and nothing looked nice. Instead, everything smelt of chemicals, of weak tea, of damp knitted scarves.

She was dragging her legs, so tired of it all. All the lies.

But she followed on, limply, out to a pretty little courtyard and garden.

'I had a friend,' Sophia said softly. 'Who sometimes came here. Helped with the garden. He knew Robin, too.'

And then, suddenly, as the sun shone through clouds, the nurse turned and smiled at her.

'Oh! You mean Robert! Robert Moore? He's still here. He has dementia, poor soul, and is in his wheelchair. Your grandma knows him?'

'I – I'm not sure if it's Robert . . .'

'Yes, yes. His daughter and son-in-law visit him,' the nurse carried on. 'And his son-in-law clears the gardens sometimes, though I haven't seen him in a while. That's your friend?'

Sophia stopped walking, shock having seized her limbs. 'Son-in-law?'

'Yes. Chris, I think.'

Sophia's body became numb, as if it had been plunged into cold water.

'Chris?' she asked. 'Are you sure?'

'Yes. Chris and Jill.'

Any hope that Sophia might have had of Chris returning to her disintegrated. He was married, and that's why he had left her. She had never been hit by a cliché before, but it hurt like hell.

'Moore?' she asked. 'His name is Christopher Moore?'

The nurse frowned. 'No. He has another name . . .'

'Flynn?' she asked.

'I don't know. He's a nice young man,' the nurse said. 'He and Robert spend their time carving hearts together out of wood. There's a name for it . . .'

'Whittling,' Sophia said quietly. Whittled hearts. She wanted to be sick.

'Whittling. That's it. It's good at keeping Robert's hands dexterous. He seems to love it.'

The nurse gestured for them to continue walking towards the small river at the back of the gardens. The sun was glistening on the ripples of the water. Sophia stepped forward, small steps. All she could manage.

'She's a poet,' the nurse continued. 'Jillian is. Jillian Moore, Robert's daughter. Lovely girl. Have you read any of her books?' She beamed at Sophia. 'Isn't the garden beautiful? The residents love it out here in the summer.'

'Are they still married?' Sophia asked.

The nurse frowned. 'Who?'

'Jillian and Chris?'

'Oh yes, I think so. I saw Jill here only the other week.'

'I've seen enough now,' Sophia said, nausea inching up her throat. 'Thank you.'

She got home and shut herself in her room. She could hear Alex screaming downstairs; she had walked through the front door and upstairs without even saying hello to him or her parents. Her mother called up to her.

'Sophia? Everything OK?'

'Hang on,' she shouted down. 'I need the bathroom.'

Sophia logged on to her computer, typed 'Jillian Moore' into the search engine and then watched as links popped up immediately. Jillian had her own website – there was a photograph of her and details of her books, and her date of birth, because she had recently blogged about the birthday books she had bought on the day. In the privacy of her bedroom, with her heart thumping, Sophia wrote it all down.

'Sophia!'

'Coming!'

Finally she had a lead – a birth date and a name. And a possible link to Chris.

She was able to return again to the Family Records Centre and gather new information. Even if it went nowhere, it was something. The certificates arrived five days later. She had applied for all of them: Jillian's birth certificate, her parents' certificates, her marriage certificate, all of it. The stomach punch came a few moments after she'd started reading.

Jillian Moore was married to a man called Christopher Fletcher, and under his occupation was 'Police officer'.

34

Jawad arrives at Rosewood Cottage at exactly eleven o'clock the next morning. He accepts a glass of water from Oliver and then gets his laptop out of his bag, placing it on the coffee table, just so. Meredith is out again with Jackson, took a sandwich lunch with her and a flask, and Chris had watched her go with envy. He's been awake most of the night and is now sweating beneath his shirt.

'You bearing up OK?' Jawad asks as he starts clicking around the keyboard. 'I'm so sorry to hear about Jillian.'

'Thank you.'

'What's the latest with the investigation?'

'The forensics team have completed their sweep,' Oliver answers clinically. 'The divers are still out and the dog handlers are in the woods, have gone up to the valley too, but there's no further information.'

'It must be awful,' Jawad says. 'I'm sorry.'

Chris clenches and unclenches his fists. 'I want to get this over with.'

'Sure, everyone understands that. I'm surprised they didn't postpone it, if I'm honest, what with everything going on, though, unfortunately, interest in Sophia Roy's death has begun to snowball, given the news about Jillian.'

'They're not related,' Chris mutters.

'Obviously, but people are loving the drama. Trying to keep them separate in the papers or on social media isn't possible.' Jawad directs Chris to the chair. 'You sit there – that's it. We'll start soon.'

Chris sits, feeling like a small child, while Jawad leans over his shoulder, clicking into things. Oliver sits in the armchair, opposite Chris.

'The good news is,' Oliver says, 'despite all the drama, your face is still out of the papers.'

'But this is also *adding* to the drama,' Jawad adds, unhelpfully. 'People want to see you, Chris. It's a good thing we got you out of that house on the loch.'

'I've got Oli to thank for that.'

'Lots of speculation on socials,' Jawad says. 'Which is always going to be the case now, I'm afraid.'

Oliver leans forward. 'The files from the investigation have been raked over, original statements scrutinized, and the family has also called for all officers that were at the scene to give their statements again. Your statement and alibi for that night remain watertight. You only need to answer the questions.'

Jawad nods. 'Exactly. As I've said before, you won't be cross-examined. This is an inquest, not a trial, and you have to remember that.'

He types on the keyboard and the screen changes. Oliver looks at his watch.

'We'll start in a few minutes,' Jawad says. 'A reminder that we'll turn the camera on – not so it can see you but so that both Oliver and I can verify you, and then we'll turn the camera off so you can speak clearly into the microphone. Your face won't be online at any point.'

Chris nods silently, though he is suddenly bone-weary.

'Here, Chris. Take a swig of this.'

Oliver hands Chris a glass of whisky. Jawad looks disapproving.

'Calm down,' Oliver tells him. 'It's for nerves. Take it, Chris, go on.'

Chris takes it, knocks it back. 'Thanks.'

'Fire in your belly.'

It makes him feel sick.

The minutes tick by and they communicate in small sentences until Jawad nods, adjusts his tie then clicks on the link. Chris knows he's not in the direct range of the camera eye but looks away nonetheless. His heart feels like it's beating out of his body.

'Good morning, all,' the coroner says, onscreen.

'Good morning, ma'am.'

'Can you state your names clearly, please?'

'Jawad Khan,' Jawad says. 'From the Department of Legal Services.'

'And Oliver Hamilton. SDS officer.'

'Thank you, gentlemen. And you can confirm that Christopher Fletcher is with you in person?'

'Correct,' Jawad says. 'He's next to me and will be answering your questions once the camera has been turned off.'

'Please speak, Mr Fletcher.'

'I'm here, ma'am.'

The coroner nods. 'Thank you. Please turn off your camera and we will proceed.'

Jawad leans to switch it off, then Oliver sticks Blu-tack over the top. Jawad looks surprised but says nothing.

'For the record, and for the benefit of the others present at this inquest, special permission has been given for Christopher Fletcher to conduct his interview with the camera turned off. Undercover officers are recruited with the clear expectation that the law enforcement agency they are working for will protect their identity during deployment and afterwards, including into their retirement and even after their death. Let's begin. Christopher, can you confirm your full name and also your name when you knew Sophia Roy.'

'My full name is Christopher Samuel Fletcher. My ID when I was part of the Green is Go activist group was Christopher Flynn.'

'Thank you. And you met Sophia Roy in the August of 2002, correct?'

'Correct.'

'And you became close, eventually forming an intimate relationship.'

'Correct.'

'This was not unusual, I gather, for obtaining evidence while undercover.'

'Regrettably, no, it was not unusual.'

'Let me be clear that I will not be going into the complexities of the infiltration of the SDS into activism. I am purely interested in the circumstances of Sophia's death. We do, of course, need the background to your relationship.'

'Yes.'

'Sophia Roy moved into your flat in Notting Hill – which as we now know was a police-funded flat – in April 2003, and you were living together until the day you left, 29 December that same year?'

'Yes.'

'As an interested party, you have been given access to what Leila Roy found of Sophia Roy's online diaries. Have you read them?'

'Yes.'

'All of them?'

'Yes.'

'And what do you make of the documents that you've read?'

'I'm shocked that she tried to find me. I didn't know she had tried.'

'And did she? Find you?'

'I never saw her in person after I severed the relationship on 29 December 2003.'

'When she was pregnant with your son?'

'Yes.'

'But you were in touch between 29 December 2003 and her death.'

'I sent her a letter saying I had gone to Slovenia. It was part of a withdrawal strategy. That was it.'

'When was that letter sent?'

'May 2004.'

'And there was no contact beyond this? You didn't write again? You left no address for her to get in touch with you?'

'No. That was the first and only time.'

'We do not have the letter here to clarify what was said, but both parties – yourself and Leila Roy – have confirmed that, to the best of your memory, there was no message embedded within it to indicate your whereabouts or your true identity.'

'Correct.'

The coroner continues. 'On 12 October 2005, at approximately nine fifteen in the morning, Sophia Roy told her parents that she was going out for the day with Alex. Looking at her bank records, it shows that she withdrew two hundred pounds from an ATM in her parents' town of Wye, and then we know that, at some point in the day, she got to Derby. Her family insist she had no connections with anyone in Derby – no family or friends. They checked with university friends and also her friends from the activist group Green is Go. Do you know of any personal connections she had there?'

'If she had any, she never said.'

'Her whereabouts before getting the train to Derby are somewhat unclear. None of her friends have come forward about seeing her that day and, unfortunately, given the amount of time that has passed since her death, we do not have any CCTV records.'

Chris swallows. His mouth is dry, but he can't reach for the water.

'It was, according to Sophia's family, unusual behaviour for her to take out a sum of cash like that. To your knowledge and in your experience, was this unusual behaviour?'

'Yes,' he says. 'It was unusual. I never saw her taking out large amounts of cash, nor did I ever see her with large amounts of cash.'

The coroner nods. 'We cannot ascertain why she went into that house. By examining the online diaries, we cannot link Derby to the series of documents and trails that Sophia had put together to try and find you. She got as far as tracking your wife, Jillian Moore, being the daughter of Robert Moore, deceased. She had found him through the care home he lived in. She had done impressive detective work.'

'Correct.'

'But that is where the trail stops.'

'Correct,' Chris repeats, and it's almost a whisper.

'Did your wife ever say anything to you about Sophia Roy in the years between 2002 and now?'

'No. She hadn't heard of Sophia until Caroline Bonner and Leila Roy broke the story last month.'

'How sure of this can you be?'

'Certain,' he says. 'I'm absolutely certain. It broke . . . I broke her heart with all of this.'

'Your wife is – I'm sorry to hear – missing.'

'She is.'

'She was on our list of people to interview at this inquest.'

'I know, and she would have helped in any way she could. I know that.'

'Indeed. Do you know where your wife was on the day Sophia Roy died?'

The question surprises him. 'At home, I believe.'

'To clarify, you mean your home address in Essex?'

Chris looks to Oliver, who is frowning. 'Yes?'

'Thank you.' The coroner turns a page in her file. 'From the original police report filed – and we will be hearing later from three police officers who were on the scene – there was an anonymous phone call made to 999 asking for police to check the house because a child had been heard crying for two hours and the property was known in the town as being unoccupied, though sometimes used by squatters. When police arrived at eleven thirty-three in the evening, Sophia Roy was found dead and Alex was beside her – hysterical.'

Chris closes his eyes.

'The house was unlocked. An appeal back in 2005, asking for that caller to come forward, resulted in a deluge of people all saying they made the call. However, none were deemed credible, and it remains a mystery as to who might have actually made it. There were also question marks as to why that person didn't try the door.'

Chris looks to Oliver, who sits statue still, staring at the screen.

'Inside, there was only one sofa and Alex's pushchair in the room, with a change bag underneath. No bag for herself, no overnight things for her son. There was no one else in the house. There was, however, evidence of people having been there.'

There's a pause before the coroner continues.

'The house was council-owned. We investigated historical tenancy, but records were patchy at best. For long stretches of time the property was empty, and it appears to have been this way at the time Sophia was found there. As previously stated, squatters and occasionally drug users took over the property. There were some personal belongings found: items of clothing, sleeping bags, needles. DNA was taken from these items, but nothing matched police databases. There was no one found at the property. There was no CCTV of anyone entering or leaving the building when it was taken by police in 2005.'

The coroner turns another page.

'We will now move on to the particulars of Sophia Roy's death. As stated, Sophia Roy was found with a needle in her left arm. In 2005 the coroner ruled that she died of a pulmonary oedema, later found to be a result of heroin.'

He can't breathe. He is cold and clammy and Sophia is in front of his eyes – so real that he could reach out and touch her. A ghost.

'Did Sophia do drugs when with you?'

'The odd joint, occasionally.'

'Were you aware of any past occurrences where she may have done harder substances, perhaps when you weren't together?'

'She was at university for most of the time we were together so I can't say no for definite, but I think it's highly unlikely.'

'We have heard from friends and family already who have testified that – to the best of their knowledge – Sophia did not take drugs of any kind. They do not know where she could have got the heroin or the needle. They have, however, said that her behaviour in the lead-up to her death was extremely erratic. Her sister, Leila Roy, suggests now that this was due to her desire to locate you but keep it hidden from family and friends. However, it begs the question, was Sophia ever irrational and secretive with you?'

'No.'

'I will now ask you about your whereabouts on that day, Mr Fletcher. Please could you tell us where you were working at that time, including on 12 October itself?'

'I was on an operation in Southampton.'

'This has been confirmed by senior staff at your unit, and we have been given photographic evidence of your time there,' the coroner says. 'However, as an undercover officer, you work alone, with little communication between you and your unit or handler for days at a time. We will therefore need to hear your account of your movements on the day Sophia Roy died.'

'That day in question I was with a group of homeless men in The Sailors' Home.'

'Can you verify it?'

'My legal representative gave a name—' He pauses, doesn't mean to. Oliver stares at him. 'Mike Emerson, who was working there at the same time as I was.'

'I have his testimony here. He was also undercover, I believe? His name at the time was Mike Tallow.'

'Yes. We were working as a pair.'

'It says here that on Wednesdays, the two of you went to the local curry nights at the Saints, a pub in Southampton.'

'Yes.'

'We asked the landlord of the pub if he remembered you. He said yes.'

Chris's breath hitches. 'Yes.'

'What we don't know – he couldn't be completely sure – was if you were there on 12 October 2005.'

'Nineteen years is a long time ago and I cannot confirm that with evidence either.'

'Indeed.' The coroner shuffles papers. 'Thank you, Mr Fletcher. Please stay online while the rest of the inquest is conducted.'

Jawad closes his file, and while his head is bent, Chris looks over at Oliver, who meets his eyes and gives the smallest of nods.

I listened to the whole inquest and found it completely fascinating.
— @NickG, X

@NickG but do you believe it?? Do you believe him? #justiceforsophia #sophiaroy #policespies #corruption
— @bemorelauren, X

@bemorelauren Honestly, I don't know.
— @NickG, X

He was lying. I could tell by his voice.
— @shadowman, X

After three hours of inquest and deliberation, Dr Strout has ruled that Sophia Roy died by a fatal dose of heroin, causing a pulmonary oedema, most likely administered by Sophia herself. However, given that the property was used by squatters and drug users, 'suicide' is not to be included as cause of death. Any certainty as to whether anyone else was in the property at the time of death will regrettably never be achieved. Regardless of direct cause of death, the circumstances of how Sophia came to take her own life have now raised questions about the morality of SDS infiltration. Sophia Roy was a victim of police tactics. Her death was a tragedy.
— *Observer*, article by Caroline Bonner

I guarantee you that Chris Fletcher didn't tell the truth at that inquest.

– James Pearson, former SDS officer, BBC True Crime Drama: *Into the Dark*, 2025

This isn't over. Trust me. #justiceforsophia #sophiaroy #christopherfletcher

– @LeilaRoyPR, X

35

2005

Christopher Fletcher.

The name rolled around Sophia's mouth and mind when she was both awake and asleep. For the first three days after finding out that Jillian Moore's husband was a police officer, Sophia limped through the daytime hours with Alex, went through the motions of meals and play and naps, but as soon as he was in bed and asleep for the night, she poured herself a glass of expensive Riesling from her father's chiller, and took it and the rest of the bottle to her childhood bedroom.

She was swallowed up in a whale's belly of confusion. She didn't have concrete proof that this Christopher Fletcher was her Chris, but didn't the confirmation of the son-in-law gardening in Robin's – or Robert's – nursing home, prove it? Didn't the certificates? Didn't the *occupation*?

She tried to search for Chris's 'real' name online, but nothing came up, no information on him and no pictures, and it exacerbated her most private terror – that he had been undercover and his objective had been to spy on her. She had heard of police infiltration within activist groups, but never in a million years would she have believed the police to be interested in Green is Go. Nor that the police would go to such lengths to deceive someone into an intimate, loving relationship. Because theirs *had* been loving, hadn't it? It had been *real*. They had shared a life together, had conceived a child. Their relationship had meant the world to her, but perhaps to him it had been nothing more than a means to an end. The police had wanted information, a source, and he had targeted her. The possibility made her stomach turn, made her rage at night, when the rest of the house was asleep.

Jillian's address on the marriage certificate had been blacked out, but Sophia had come all this way, and now her only hope of finding the whole truth was to track down Jillian Moore. It was a stroke of luck that Jillian was a writer and had a public profile. Somehow Sophia would figure out where Jillian lived, and then, in turn, she would know for absolute definite if Christopher Fletcher was her Chris Flynn. She was exhausted by the relentless 'what if's but was fuelled by a steel will to find him. She would find out if she had fallen in love with a liar.

Sophia began to visit Jillian's website even more obsessively than before, clicking every day to read both new and old blog posts and poems. She clicked on pictures, zoomed in on Jillian's shock of blonde hair, her beautiful eyes. She gleaned personal information: Jillian was half Scottish, had spent the first nineteen years of her life living in the Highlands, before moving to London. She had been a nurse, was a keen sailor. She didn't mention a husband, and it was a hope, albeit a thin one, that even if Christopher Fletcher was her Chris Flynn, perhaps they had divorced, or that he may once have been a police officer when married to Jillian but had left the force before meeting Sophia.

Two months passed before Jillian posted on her blog that she would be publishing a new collection of poems and touring for bookshop readings. She listed shops in

Hampshire, Essex, Shropshire, Derbyshire, Cumbria and Scotland. This was the opportunity Sophia had been both waiting for and dreading.

On the day of the reading, she left the house early and, at the ATM at the train station, she withdrew money. She was worried, given all she'd found out so far, that the police might be tracking her, so she had started to pay cash for anything related to her findings. She bought a ticket and told no one she was going, nor documented it online. Alex sat on her knee, staring out of the window, and she laid her chin on the softness of his hair.

It took all her courage to walk into the bookshop. It was busy, with people taking seats for the reading, but she hung back from joining them. She had the pushchair, and Alex might make a noise. She was also afraid Chris might be there, and what might happen if he saw her. What would happen if she saw him. She scanned the space, over and over, but didn't see him, and part of her was relieved. Part of her was desolate.

Jillian Moore was introduced by the bookseller, and she smiled warmly out at her audience. She was every bit as beautiful as the pictures on her website, perhaps more so in person, because a photograph can't capture movement, and all of Jillian's were graceful and elegant. She thanked her audience for coming and started to read in her beautiful Scottish lilt. An hour passed with Sophia captivated as Jillian stood with the light from the window cutting shadows across her slender frame and down her long-sleeved paisley dress. This woman, she thought, was like a goddess. Her voice even soothed Alex to sleep in the pushchair.

Afterwards, Sophia watched as Jillian signed books and

talked to the people who had come. She watched as she gathered her things then called goodbye to the bookshop staff, and it was only as Jillian was heading to leave that Sophia felt her legs move, spurred, at last, for what she had come to do. As Jillian reached the threshold of the shop, Sophia drew up to her with the pushchair.

'Excuse me,' she said.

Jillian turned and smiled at her.

What do you want me to say? Yes, we should have realized that it was Sophia looking for Chris when all the triggers went off on our systems. But we didn't.

— Oliver Hamilton, SDS officer, BBC True Crime Drama: *Into the Dark*, 2025

The thing you need to know — the fundamental part of this whole thing — is that they [Special Branch covert units] underestimated the hurt and anger and betrayal that people felt. They didn't appreciate that people would be wanting answers, wanting closure. They [undercover officers] thought they had tight withdrawal strategies to disappear — mental breakdowns, skipping jail — but it wasn't enough. They didn't realize that the best motivation for finding someone is driven by all-consuming, raging love. Isn't that the reason for all the things we do? People kill for love, people die for love. We rage because we don't have love, or we're miserable because it's taken away from us and we want it back. That's the key to it all. They all underestimated the women they deceived.

— Lola Coutelle, ex-girlfriend of former SDS police officer James Pearson, BBC True Crime Drama: *Into the Dark*, 2025

36

It is evening. Jawad left as soon as the verdict came in, but Oliver stayed to have a celebratory beer. They have done it, crisis averted, but Chris feels hollow. He didn't touch his bottle, but if Oliver noticed, he didn't pass comment. Now Chris sits in the lounge with Jackson's head on his lap, his eyes staring at the fire that someone has built – possibly it was Oliver before he went, possibly it was Meredith. The flames lick upward and shadows dance along the walls.

Despite the verdict, he feels no relief, only shame, because he lied of course, just as he was supposed to do.

He wishes Jill was here, writing with the horse lamp on. He wants to hear the scratching of her pen, wants the scent of her perfume – bright, fresh, clean on the air. Instead, Meredith sits down beside him with her sharp smell that claws at the back of his throat.

She hands him a whisky. 'I thought you could use this.'

It's the same bottle that he drank from before Jill went missing. Half full.

'Where did you get this?'

'It was in Smoke House,' she says. 'I brought it with us.'

She chinks his glass with her own. He doesn't want to drink it but does, neatly, all in one.

'That can't have been easy,' she says.

'It wasn't.'

There's a part of Chris – a huge part – that wants to tell Meredith everything. The way she's leaning towards him, giving him permission to speak freely, makes him want to spill it all and purge himself. But undercover work is exactly that, and talking about operations is strictly forbidden. Sometimes though, it has come out. In the dark nights, in his sleep. He knows that he has nightmares about his time undercover because there have been times when Jill woke him from them and told him he'd been speaking. Just a dream, he'd tell her, and try to smile reassuringly, but she would look at him with undisguised fear in her eyes. He never knew what he might have said, how much of those operations he might have given away. But she had never said anything about them.

'Christopher,' Meredith says solemnly. 'There's something I need to say.'

He lifts his eyes to her face. 'What?'

Her fingers go to the pearl-drop chain. 'I don't know if it's relevant—'

But she's interrupted by a knocking at the door and Chris stands to open it.

'Can we come in?' Joseph asks.

'Have you found her?' asks Meredith, who is suddenly behind Chris, so close that he can feel the heat of her against his back.

They stand awkwardly in the tiny kitchen.

'The dinghy has been found.'

Chris's throat constricts. 'And Jill?'

Joseph shakes his head solemnly. 'There was some driftwood spotted ten miles down the coastline. It was caught, and Harris McGowan has confirmed it's from the Miracle.'

'Oh my God.' Meredith is panting, little shallow breaths. 'Oh my God. She's drowned, hasn't she?'

Chris puts a hand to Meredith's arm, wants to freeze the

moment between hoping that Jill is alive and being told that she's dead.

'Please,' he whispers, but he doesn't know what he's saying please for, or to whom.

Meredith makes a whimpering sound. 'She's lost! Our poor girl!'

Chris looks at Joseph. 'What now?'

'The diving unit are out where the boat was found, but, obviously, there is a huge search area to cover. It won't necessarily be possible to recover her.'

'So we just . . . wait?' Meredith says, tears running down her cheeks. 'Until she's spat out by the sea?'

'We do hope to find her.'

'Alive?'

Joseph shakes his head. 'I mean that we hope to find her body,' he says gently. 'I'm sorry, but at this point it doesn't look good for Jill being found alive.'

Meredith sinks to the floor, howls with anguish. Chris puts his hand to her shoulder, not sure if he's comforting her or leaning on her to support himself.

He's in the betwixt. Not awake but also not asleep. Everything around him is unfamiliar, but he's up, stumbling around a room. Pale moonlight filters in from the windows. There are trees outside, a towering line of them. Keeping people out, keeping him inside.

In this half-state of sleep, he's looking for something that he put away the night they arrived in Rosewood, when Meredith was very much asleep. He kneels at the built-in fridge-freezer and tugs at the bottom of it, where the air vent is, because in that gap under the fridge Chris put his rucksack.

His days undercover made him good at hiding things.

He reaches into the cobwebbed corner and drags it out. He needs to open it, his brain tells him, because he believes the thing inside will hold answers to Jill's disappearance. The zip comes away when he pulls it – a clean, satisfying sound – and he picks up the base of the horse-head lamp that he took from The Old Smoke House. He turns it over in his hands. This. This is what he needs. It takes up nearly the whole bag with its size. He should take it to the bedroom and put it on so that Jill can be called to it, like a moth to a flame.

'Find me,' he whispers. 'You need to come and find me.'

He presses the cold wood to his cheek, hears the rush of the pulse in his ears against it. Like a shell and the ocean, he thinks, and then it comes out – a guttural moan from his throat. Jillian is lost in the sea, and it's all his fault.

'I did a bad thing,' he says. 'I did something bad.'

He puts the vent back in place and crouches with the lamp, clutching it to his chest, rocking on his heels. If he could take it back, he thinks. All of it.

Had Jill found out what happened in 2005? Had she found out about Damian Roper and what they all did? Chris cries silent tears, gulps air.

Then a shape moves within the room, black and foreboding. He twists his head and then, suddenly, there's a blaze of light in his eyes. He jerks with fright, thinks he must have turned the lamp on, but how could that be so? It's not plugged in. He drops it quickly into the bag and, still crouched on the floor, starts to shout in fear.

'You! You took her!'

But Damian Roper moves like lightning, behind him again now, and Chris wobbles as he tries to turn. The light is blinding, disorientating. He is between worlds, between Sophia and Jill. He swipes his arm out, and his nails catch on the skin of Damian's calves.

'What have you done with her?!' he shouts. 'Where's Jill?!'

'What are you doing?'

Chris scrambles up, sways with fright. A dog barks – Jackson is here.

'Get him, Jacko! Get him!'

There's a whooshing sound in his ears. 'Where's Jill?!'

He lurches forward, swipes again, but there's water now in his face, in his eyes and up his nostrils. He blinks, chokes, and something switches in his head. The light changes again, flick, flick, and suddenly he sees clearly that in front of him isn't Damian Roper but Meredith, dressed in flannel pyjamas and holding a water jug to her chest. She's thrown the contents of it in his face. Droplets rain down on the floor.

'What in the bloody hellfire are you *doing*, Christopher? Are you awake?'

'Meredith?'

She bends to her leg. 'You hurt me, you arse!'

He looks blankly at where her hand clamps at her calf. A long red scratch mark.

'Oh God, Meredith. Was that me? I – I'm sorry. I wasn't—'

'Why did you hurt me?'

'I'm sorry. I thought you were someone else.'

'*Who?*' she cries.

But he can't say. He cannot say.

'What on *earth* are you doing down here?' she says when he doesn't answer her. 'What's in that bag?'

He glances down at the rucksack. 'I – nothing.'

'Let me see.'

'No—'

'I think you should give me whatever is in the bag.'

She makes to take it, but he pulls it away from her. 'There's nothing in there.'

'There's definitely *something* in it,' she says. 'What is it?'

'There's nothing. Our passports, our documents. That's it.'

Meredith purses her lips, says nothing. Jackson whines, butts his head into Chris's hands.

'I'm sorry I hurt you. I wasn't . . . I wasn't myself.'

Meredith doesn't wait for him to say more. She marches up the stairs and slams the door shut, leaving him staring at the bag, stroking Jackson's ears, over and over. The lamp inside is radiating, pulsing, like something alive. He takes it upstairs, shoves it as far into the wardrobe as he can.

37

When he wakes, he doesn't know where he is. The bed is different, the angles of the room are all wrong. He first thinks he's in The Old Smoke House, then his house in Sardinia, then in the flat with Sophia. Moments pass before he realizes he's in the new place, Rosewood Cottage.

'Jacko?'

He hears a skitter of feet as the dog heaves himself up, feels a knock against the bed, and then Jackson's head rears. The clock reads midday.

'I need to feed you,' he says. 'Has Meredith already fed you?'

Chris takes his dressing gown, wraps it around himself as he and Jackson go downstairs. The steps are steep, and difficult for Jackson, but his bony pelvis just about manages.

'And you need to go out, I know. Tonight. OK? We'll take a walk.'

Meredith is in the kitchen, sitting at the table with toast and a cup of coffee. Upon seeing her, he remembers – like a bolt of electricity in his mind's eye – the events of last night. Her holding a jug of water. He'd scared her. He'd thought Damian was here.

'Meredith. Last night. I . . .'

'You scared the bejesus out of me, that's what. And you scratched my leg with your nails like some sort of deranged animal.'

'I wasn't . . .'

'Yourself? No, you were Gollum.'

Chris gets some dog food out, fills a cereal bowl up for Jackson.

'You bruised me.'

'I'm sorry. Please, don't . . .'

'What? Tell the police?'

'Please don't,' he says. 'I'm sorry. Sometimes I don't feel like myself. I take pills to sleep. I . . .'

She is silent a moment.

'Clearly, you're traumatized,' she says. 'That job, Christopher. It's made you completely paranoid. You have all the symptoms.'

'The symptoms?'

'The clinical definition of paranoia is that the individual believes that harm is occurring, or is going to occur, to him or her. I was reading up on it all. It's not normal to live as someone else, is it? Your sense of self is the core of your very being – the very heartbeat of you – and that job flips it all upside down.'

'Thank you for the psychoanalysis, Meredith.'

'Being a faceless, nameless person all those years. You didn't talk to friends in the force? That man, Oliver?'

'No.'

'The police aren't allowed feelings, is that it?'

He laughs a little. 'It was tough love back then.'

'What a load of old codswallop. Acknowledging trauma isn't weakness.'

'No undercover officer ever talked openly about feelings, Meredith. No one wanted to open the floodgates.'

She says nothing for a long while and then she pulls up the chair opposite him.

'I actually feel sorry for you,' she says. 'I didn't, but now I do. I think you're a broken man.'

'Wow. OK. Thanks.'

'It's all broken.' She inhales deeply. 'Christopher. About what I was going to say before they came . . . Joseph and Karen. When they told us about the boat . . . I – I sent her an email. Jill, I mean. But it was nothing. I don't know.'

He frowns. 'What email?'

Her fingers worry at the thin gold necklace at her throat.

'It was a photograph,' she says. 'When all this happened . . . you know, with the article, about Sophia, and the date she died . . . the date was 12 October 2005. I started looking . . . where I was on that day. What I was doing. What Jill was doing.'

'In 2005? How would you even know?'

'I went to a reading,' she says. 'Of Jill's. She was touring with her publication of *New*. We had lunch after. But it was . . . it was the day that Sophia Roy died. When that article came out, I sent Jill an email about it, with a photograph attached. It was of Jill at the reading. A local journalist took it.'

'OK?'

She licks her lips.

'What aren't you telling me, Meredith?'

She looks anxious. 'Joseph Locke will see that email, now they have access to Jill's emails.'

'And why is it a problem if he sees it?'

'I – well, it's not a problem . . .' she says, but fades away.

'I strongly suggest that if you are worried about something, or you have something you think might be important to the investigation, you tell me. I might have used this information when the coroner asked me about Jill's whereabouts at the inquest.'

She looks surprised. 'They asked you where she was?'

'She was going to be called up to give evidence, did you know that?'

Meredith shakes her head. 'I didn't . . . she didn't tell me. But – look – it doesn't matter, does it? She never told me otherwise.'

'I thought Jill was at home. She never mentioned a reading. You're sure it was the same day?'

'Positive.'

'Where?'

'It was – it was in Essex.' She gets up. 'Anyway. It was only a picture . . . it's just . . . Well.' She inhales. 'Would you like tea?'

'I should take the dog out.'

'Fine. Yes.' She pauses. 'Christopher?'

'Yes?'

'You weren't in Derby, were you? The night that girl died.'

'I was in Southampton,' he says. 'How many times do I need to say it?'

He picks up the lead and walks out of the door, Jackson skittering behind him. Grateful to leave. Because he hadn't been in Southampton that day. From April 2004 until October 2005 Chris had been deep undercover, infiltrating Dawn, the far-right activist group headed by Damian and Malcolm Roper in Derby.

Snapchat

RoryCampbell: This place is swarming with journos. I couldn't even ride my bike through the village this morning! There were so many!

LornaMcGowan: You're not speaking to them though?

LornaMcGowan: Rory?

RoryCampbell: My uncle said his pal has got a right weirdo staying over in their town. Says he's a journo for The Mail but you wouldn't want to get on the wrong side of him.

LornaMcGowan: Rory, don't talk to them. They're talking about Chris Fletcher and Jillian. And my mum. They've started asking questions about Mum.

FionaWilson: What's your mum got to do with any of this??

LornaMcGowan: Exactly. It's horrible.

RoryCampbell: Journalists are people trying to do their jobs. Your dad has been friends with Jillian years and the journalists are trying to get new angles on things they should leave well alone.

LornaMcGowan: Dad has banned them all from the pub. They're not welcome here, and nor will you be Rory if you talk to any of them.

FionaWilson: Is your dad OK, babe? I saw him the other day at John Crossan's and he looked like death.

LornaMcGowan: He's worried.

RoryCampbell: I thought your dad hated John Crossan, Lorna? With good reason obv.

FionaWilson: Ignore the journalists, babe.

LornaMcGowan has left the group

MattChristie: Fuck sake, Campbell.

RoryCampbell: What?? Why did she leave?

FionaWilson: Babe, we love you but you can be a bit *much* Everyone knows Lorna's mum and John Crossan had a thing – why would you bring it up with Lorna?

MattChristie: You don't know when to quit, man.

RoryCampbell: There was always a question mark, though, right? My uncle and aunt saw Harris and Kate arguing literally hours before Kate died.

FionaWilson: Kate McGowan's accident has nothing to do with what's going on now. Show some respect, dickhead.

RoryCampbell: Except they were all friends. Harris, Kate and Jill. What if Jill disappearing isn't even about Chris Fletcher?

FionaWilson: What are you talking about??

MattChristie: You don't believe all that shit about Mr McGowan, do you?

FionaWilson has left the group

38

Jackson leads them through a belt of trees, along a narrow track that looks like it was made by animals and not people. There's relief in that, because Chris doesn't want even a trace of people here, wants only to be by himself. It's only one in the afternoon, but the canopy plunges everything into darkness. He pauses after a while to switch on the torch of his phone, and the beam illuminates the towering trunks and branches. He thinks he should have brought his coat because there's a chill in the air now and it smells like it's going to rain – there's that particular scent that no one can quite describe but everyone can recognize instantly. Jackson nudges up to Chris and he snaps out of his thoughts, leans down to put his face to Jackson's neck. The smell of this lumbering creature, so real and grounding.

'I've got to warn you,' Chris whispers gently. 'That Mum might not be coming back.'

Jackson doesn't acknowledge him, moves away and cocks his leg to urinate against a tree.

'And I might not be with you for ever. I might have to . . . I'll have to leave you. Who would you go to? Marco?'

Jackson bounds away.

Everything is so tangled and muddy. Chris has lied to the coroner, to the public, and to Sophia's family. He was told to lie by Oliver, by the senior members of the unit, but hasn't that been the entire problem? That he was always

242

obeying orders and not thinking for himself? But when should obedience and duty give way to an individual's moral compass? An undercover officer, an agent, a soldier, they are all in a difficult position where duty overrides all else.

Until this point, Chris has never needed to lie under oath before. He knows plenty of undercover officers who have, but being called to court was rare, given that most charges against them would be mysteriously dropped. If ever they had to appear in court, they were there under their fake identities, which was a literal get-out-of-jail-free card.

He thinks about Dawn.

When Chris left Sophia on that December day in 2003, he shed the identity Christopher Flynn – as Sophia had known him – and a few months later became, instead, Chris Callaghan. A very different operation called for a very different approach, but nothing could have really prepared him for the constant feeling of terror he'd have while working in the world that SDS then put him in.

Cleverly, Dawn had begun by promoting a romanticized idyllic Britain, one without poverty and with an emphasis on community. They were organized, disciplined, gave impassioned speeches and delivered flyers to target universities – Loughborough, Nottingham, Sheffield. They wanted loners to join them, young men who could be easily manipulated. Their messaging garnered sympathies and provoked subtle outrage. In the town people would turn a blind eye to the things they did: throwing bricks through windows, spraying doors with graffiti. But over time they became more sinister. Members of Dawn started to follow people home at night. There were reports of beatings and stabbings. And that was when Chris got involved.

In April 2004, Chris's unit had him living in a one-bed flat in central Derby and doing a fake job, working shifts on a laminator at a local cardboard factory. He bought track-suits and shaved his head, listened to death metal, read a lot of documentation, a lot of dark manifestos. Watched a lot of films, went deep-tunnelling online. Physically he did nothing for a few months, simply got the lie of the land, and occasionally went to the pub that Dawn went to, but never at the same time. He wanted to be recogniz-able to the landlord as a bloke who came in and read the *Sun* and had a few pints and chips. He shopped in the local supermarkets. He became someone who 'just lived there'.

In June and July, he attended the marches that Dawn organized in Loughborough and in Derby, observed their messaging.

Local jobs for local people
Reclaim our community

On both occasions Chris stood on the sidelines, observ-ing the group and, more actively, the two brothers who had started it – Damian and Malcolm.

After a few months he started to make eye contact with some of the men who walked past him in the street, nodded his head. *Solidarity*, the nod said, *understanding*. In September he listened to a speech given by Damian in the pub they frequented. More than twenty people were there, but Chris had hung back deliberately, wanted to seem shy and vulnerable – the kind of man they targeted. He sat in the corner, nursed a pint and listened. Damian was the more vocal of the two brothers, wiry and jaunty with his gesticulation. He had a pale face and pale grey eyes, and a wide mouth with small teeth, pointed incisors. Through the speech he paused often and gave inflection and drama in all the right places, was an impressive speaker. He was dressed in a black tracksuit – most of them were; it was like a uniform – and had a skinhead cut and a rose tattoo on the back of his neck. Later, when he was embedded within the group, Chris saw that the word 'Dawn' was written within the folds of the petals.

He started attending speeches and meetings regularly. He volunteered to deliver flyers to the universities and set up local marches. He volunteered to take photographs, keeping behind the camera instead of in front of it. By December he was getting drunk with them, smoking weed and talking about smashing in the faces of anyone who wasn't white. Over the next few months, he joined Damian in destroying the glass windows of the local corner shop, witnessed Malcolm and others light fires in the gardens of ethnic families. He drank with them outside the supermarket, leering at the checkout woman, who was from Ghana. He planned marches with them, drove them all around in his van.

How strange it was to live in a skin this way; to wake up every day and remind yourself you were good but spending the day doing bad. To laugh – at times, genuinely – with people that you also found abhorrent. Chris clung on to seeing Oliver every week and visiting Jill whenever he could. The only two people who could truly tether him back to his real self.

One April night, six of them got stoned and, at three in the morning, they ended up walking the streets and stopping outside a house that Chris immediately recognized as a home for refugees.

'Let's go in,' Damian said.

Chris grinned. 'And do what?'

'Do fucking *harm*.'

And before he'd even had the chance to steer them away from the idea someone threw a stone through the window, shattering it. Immediately there was screaming from inside. Chris went to turn away, but to his horror, members of the group started to smash the glass with their elbows and climb through.

He had a split second to decide what he was going to do. Reveal himself as a police officer and risk the operation before he'd obtained all the information the unit wanted, or join in with what was unfolding? As he hesitated, there was an enormous bang, and then people started running out of the door – a woman wearing a nightdress, two men and a little girl in bed clothes, gone, gulped up by the dark. There was an acrid burning smell – had someone let off some sort of firework? Some sort of home-made bomb? More people rushed past him in a blur as he stared after them in disbelief. Where were they going, he thought, when that safe house was the *safe* house?

He ran inside the house, was immediately met by thick and lung-choking smoke.

'Hey!' he yelled. 'We've gotta get out!'

There were thudding footsteps and shouting above him. Damian appeared at the top of the stairs.

'Someone's called the police,' Chris said.

'Fuck, already?'

'Someone yelled it across the street.'

They ran down the road like a pack of stray dogs, whooping and yelling, to the children's playground, where they sat on the swings. Malcolm lit up a joint, passed it around. They heard a siren ten minutes later. Someone had, obviously, called the police.

'What was that?' Chris said. 'The smoke?'

'Just a little scare tactic.'

Chris managed to grin, though it felt like someone had sliced through his mouth and was pulling at the corners. 'Worked a treat.'

Damian looked approvingly at him, the blue of his eyes like shards of ice. 'There's a camp out in Germany in a few months,' he said. 'Combat 18 are going, and I want us lot to join them.'

And that's how Chris found himself, a year into his infiltration, in the Black Forest with over two hundred far-right activists from all over Europe. A weekend with access to international far-right groups was invaluable, but also exceptionally dangerous. He would doubtless be the only undercover officer there but, regardless, no one would dare tip someone the wink in a forest full of violent men. He would have no back-up if he needed it. The nearest unit officer was in a hotel in Stuttgart for the weekend.

Different groups arrived throughout the day and Chris made mental notes of them as they came: names, appearances. He, Malcolm and one of the other Dawn members went on a hike with one of the Combat 18 men who was half German and had grown up trekking the forest with his grandma. He helped them cross the steep inclines, was funny, polite and considerate, and Chris thought how insanely disorientating it was that these men believed and promoted such hate, and yet, here they were, sharing beers on a hillside and laughing over a story of Petey's dear old German grandma. It was fucked up.

In the afternoon they set up their tents. Chris was sharing with two other members of Dawn, both intelligent, bulky youngsters tattooed with swastikas and 88s.

Damian and Malcolm were next to them. Chris had packed a small hunting knife, put it under his pillow and prayed he wouldn't have to use it.

The afternoon hours bled into the night, when impassioned speeches were delivered and alcohol and meat passed around. The trees flickered in firelight, shadows roved across faces, and Chris sat, his fingers raking the moss beneath him as he listened to the hate and vitriol spewing from the mouths of the men around him. He kept accepting beer because it was expected, and he was desperate to drink it all to obliterate himself, but he couldn't. He had to carefully monitor his intake and mentally record every terrible word, every terrible desire.

He went to sleep at three.

At four in the morning, he was woken by hands on his shoulders. Damian was in the tent, standing over him.

'Get up,' he said.

Chris looked around, bleary-eyed. The other two Dawn members who had been in the tent when he'd gone to bed were now nowhere to be seen.

Dread crawled up Chris's throat. 'What? What's going on?'

'I want to take you somewhere.'

'Where?'

'Come.'

The hunting knife was below Chris's pillow. How could he take it while Damian stood there?

'Here. Get your clothes on.'

Fuck, had they found him out? But how? Clumsy, half drunk, completely terrified, Chris pulled on his jeans, a jumper and a jacket.

'Where are we going?'

'I got wind of something happening down in the woods.'

'What? What's happening?'

Damian's face split into a sinister smile. 'They've got something.'

Chris laced his boots, mind racing to figure out how to bring the knife. 'Who? Who's they?'

'Here, take this.'

Something small was placed in his hand and he knew what it was before he looked down. A pill in his palm.

'No, mate.'

Damian looked surprised. 'No?'

'We're driving back tomorrow.'

'So we'll stay another night. Isn't this what you want? Bit of adventure, bit of fun?'

It was a challenge, a threat to his place within the group, and they both knew it. Chris couldn't throw the pill away, couldn't hide it, so he put it to his lips and Damian watched as he swallowed it down. The bitter aftertaste was sharp. What the fuck was happening?

'What was that?' Chris asked.

'Fuck knows. Mal got them.'

'I'm going to have such a fucking hangover,' Chris said, and Damian laughed, pulled him forward.

Everything became slow and buttery in his ears. Chris could feel his hair on his neck, the ends of it rope-like with the sweat that was pouring from his scalp and body. He could hear the rustle of his clothes, the leaves in the trees. Everything was sharply focused in one moment and then blurred the next. He looked down at his hands and turned them over, thought he could see his fingernails growing. His skin was patterned like a kaleidoscope, and he laughed at this thought and then wondered if he'd laughed aloud.

He must have done because, beside him, Damian was laughing too, but his mouth seemed too large for his face and was twisted into something monstrous and evil. He was both those things, and here Chris was, trapped in a forest with all that was wrong with humanity.

'Come on.'

Damian ran deeper into the woods, and Chris followed. There were men carrying fire torches, which melted in and out of the trees like fireflies. Chris's feet were flying like they didn't belong to his body. He looked down and saw they were bare but couldn't remember removing his shoes. The conscious part of his mind was slipping, eel-like, away from him. Keep yourself together, a voice whispered in his head.

'Where are they going?' he asked Damian.

'There's going to be a sacrifice.'

Chris laughed, his heart lurching. 'What?'

'Keep going.'

Something pulled. He looked down to see a leather strip of material in his hand, wondered if he'd always been holding it or if it had been given to him. He followed the length of it with his unfocused eyes, tracking it like it was a lazy river, and at the end of the leather strip was a young man in handcuffs.

'What's this?' Chris said. 'Who is this? He's saying something. What's he saying?'

'He's praying to his gods,' Damian said, suddenly behind him, and he took the length of leather from Chris and passed it over to another man.

'Who is he?'

The man who now held the leather strip spoke. 'He's the lamb. We cut them up and feed all the creatures that come out at night.'

39

Fuck that night, Chris thinks. Fuck the memory of the man's screams, of the light that bounced from the fire torches on to the machetes they used. Later, when he'd told Oliver what happened, Oliver had retched.

The looping fear of his time with Dawn, in those woods, is exactly why Chris goes walking now, because he refuses to let that night defile an environment so wonderful. But even after all these years, he is haunted by what's beyond the black shadows of any tall, silent woodland.

The eighteen months he spent with Dawn were the most traumatic time of his life. Every day he lived as someone who promoted hate and violence and they all called him 'friend'. And, to his horror, at times, they almost were friends. He drank with these men, smoked with them, shared jokes, played football with them. It was the most confusing and disorientating thing to live as one of them. He had to remind himself that he *wasn't* Chris Callaghan. Oliver, too, would remind him. But how easy it was to forget who you *really* were.

He realizes that he's been walking for two hours – it's nearing three in the afternoon. Jackson has tired of running around and is now walking beside him.

There's a noise in the trees and Chris whirls around, balling his fists. By his side, Jackson stands, ears pricked.

'Did you hear . . .' Chris swallows. 'Who's there?'

His eyes search out the gloom of the trees – the phone's torch can only reach so far – but he can make out nothing.

He thinks that if this is going to be how it happens, his reunion with Damian Roper, he is ready. He is older now, and not as fit, but surely Damian will be the same. How will the years have weathered him?

'Hello?'

A minute passes and then another, but there is no other sound. Jackson puts his head down again, carries on walking, whatever noise forgotten, and this brings Chris's heart rate down. Perhaps it was a bird in the scrub or a deer passing. Or perhaps they're both going mad. Chris has already gone mad in front of Meredith. He hid the rucksack at the back of the wardrobe in his bedroom, where she'll never reach. He doesn't even know why he took it, because it was a crazy thing to do, to take Jill's lamp.

There's another noise – the snap of a twig behind him – and he turns. There's a man through the trees.

Panic seizes Chris by the throat. He starts to run, wildly and blindly, his skin ripping on brambles and his feet bumbling over twisted roots. He doesn't know if he's heading out of the woodland or further into it, but all he can think of is getting away from the man behind him. Or is he now in front of him? There is screaming, and it sounds like the man from the Black Forest, but Chris realizes that it's all coming from inside his own head.

There's now another noise, a soft thudding that whispers alongside him, and he looks to the left, sees a darker shadow in the deep blue of the woods. A man. A man on all fours like a werewolf. Chris trips over, lands heavily and winds himself. There's dirt up his nose, in his mouth, and the smell of decay. The throb in his shin tells him that he's hurt himself, but there's no time to see if it's bleeding or whether he's got something embedded in it.

Jackson comes to stand by him and barks at a figure approaching them.

'I can see you,' Chris says in a voice stronger than he feels.

The figure comes closer. He wonders how they'll find his body. Maybe no one will find it. Maybe Damian Roper will cut him into tiny pieces. Maybe he'll set Chris alight so there's nothing but his teeth left.

And then, a face.

The shock of it – like looking into the silver of a mirror and seeing himself from years ago.

'Hello, Dad.'

'How . . .'

'She told me to come. Jillian did.'

40

Chris has dreamt of this moment, over and over, but never thought it would happen like this – in the darkness of a Scottish woodland. He wants to step forward, wants to embrace his son, but how can he? Alex looks like Chris genetically – dark hair, a square jaw, bow lips – but, to his shame, there's nothing of Chris that's gone into the making of who he is. Pulling him to his chest would not be the right thing to do. Besides, Alex's words have also back-footed Chris. Alex has heard from *Jill*. The combination of shock and joy sends him off kilter.

Chris had admitted his affair with Sophia after Caroline Bonner had published her article, and at the same time he had also admitted to having fathered a child, because it was only a matter of time until it came out. The look of utter devastation on Jill's face when he had told her these things was absolute, but she didn't scream, nor did she cry. She simply turned, walked to the bathroom and locked herself away.

They didn't speak for days afterwards. They moved around each other quietly and he went to the spare room to sleep. Less than a fortnight later they were at the loch, trying to make sense of the parasitical lies he'd invited into their lives and their marriage.

Yet despite this, she had found Alex. Why had she done it? For answers for herself? Or had she done it for Chris?

'Jill told you to come here?' Chris asks. 'Have you seen her here? In Scotland?'

Alex shakes his head. 'No. I've never met her. I got an email a week or so back and she asked me to come.'

'Jill has disappeared. Did you know?'

'I saw on the news.'

Alex looks like he is about to say something else, but refrains. Droplets of rain have started to fall in little clinks against the leaves above them.

'I don't know what to say,' Chris says. 'I've thought about you for so many . . . How did you know where to find me? Here, at this house. We moved in secret. Was that . . . did you come up to The Old Smoke House when we left?'

Alex smiles. 'Yes. But that's not how I found you here.'

'How then?'

'Your dog.'

Chris frowns.

'The older woman walked him the other day in the woods when you were at the other place.'

'Meredith?'

'I don't know. She's older, got a fringe like it's a mono-brow. Looks like a ball-breaker.'

'That's Meredith.'

'She lost the dog for a while and I – I put a tracker on his collar.'

'A tracker?'

'Apple AirTag.'

Chris wants to laugh, so he does. All the intelligence of the unit on his side and they can't even move Chris securely.

'Fuck.'

'I know that's weird, but I thought you might move,' Alex says with a boyish half-smile, though he's not really a boy any more.

Oh God, Chris thinks, he's an adult. Chris has missed his boyhood, has missed it all.

'Jillian said you might move around, depending on what happened with the inquest. She said you'd want to talk to me. She said you spoke my name – for years – in your sleep, but she didn't know who it was you were talking about.'

'She never told me I did that.'

'She said you used to say some really strange things. About the woods, about a man called Damian.'

Chris swallows. So he has said Damian's name in his sleep. Jill never once mentioned that in nineteen years. Why has she never asked him? Sweat slinks down his back. Had he ever mentioned being in Derby? He changes the subject.

'Who else knows you're here? Leila?'

'No one.'

'Where are you staying?'

'I rented a cottage not far from here.'

'In – in your name?'

'No,' Alex says, then pauses a moment. 'I thought I'd come under a pseudonym. Like you.'

Chris feels an intense stabbing shame. All his son knows about him is his ability to deceive.

'I wish our first meeting hadn't been like this,' Chris says.

'It's atmospheric.'

'I suppose it is.'

'Did she know? Did my mum know who you really were? Did you see her before she died?'

Chris swallows. The rain is steady now; a droplet falls between his neck and collar.

'Come back to the cottage with me,' he says suddenly. 'We're not . . . I don't think we're safe here.'

'I won't hurt you.'

Chris pauses. 'I didn't think you would. But there are people out there . . . maybe out here, who wish me harm.'

Alex says nothing.

'Please,' Chris says.

'What about the woman? Is she here too? Meredith?'

'Meredith is Jill's aunt. She'll be surprised to see you.'

'As much as you are?'

'I'm happy to see you.'

'Really? You've had over twenty years to be happy to see me.'

He deserves the sting. 'I always knew how you were doing.'

'How?'

'I have a network of contacts.'

'Spies?'

He sighs. 'If you like.'

Alex regards him coolly for a moment, then, 'I'll come.'

Chris opens the door, gestures for Alex to go in first, but Jackson barges in ahead of them. Wet paws, claws clicking on the wooden floor, going straight for his water bowl and slopping it about.

'Hang your coat up on the chair here,' Chris says. 'Do you want anything to eat? Drink?'

'I'm OK.'

'Are you warm enough? I haven't got the heating on . . .'

He's suddenly nervous, like his son is an animal about to be scared off, which is the last thing Chris wants, because, selfishly, he wants this moment not to be about Sophia or Jillian but about him and Alex together. He wants to know Alex's favourite band, his favourite meal, his brightest childhood memories, if he's in a relationship. He wants to know if Alex is happy or if his life was set on a trajectory of misery the night Sophia died. He wants to know if Alex hates him.

'I'm fine.'

Chris nods. 'Right, right. Sure.'

Jackson whines, and Chris feeds him biscuits.

'Are you sure you don't want anything?'

'I don't eat dog biscuits, if that's what you're offering.'

Chris laughs. Too long and too hard, because he's giddy now. He grabs a bar of chocolate from the side. He hasn't seen it before, it might be Meredith's, but he needs to eat. He's becoming light-headed. He reaches for it – a Snickers – and unwraps it.

Alex pulls up a chair, sits down.

'What's going on?' a voice calls from the staircase.

Chris chews madly, swallows the mouthful.

'Meredith,' he says as her footsteps descend. 'You have to promise not to do your nut.'

'Do my what? Who's here?' She appears around the door, gasps. 'Good *God*.'

'This is Alex,' Chris says. 'My son. Jill made contact with him.'

'I – your . . .' She stares at Alex and then marches towards him. 'You spoke to Jillian?'

Alex is silent, looks up at Meredith, then back to Chris.

'Meredith, come on – give the kid some room.'

'When did you speak?' she demands.

Alex looks back at her. 'I got an email a couple of weeks ago. She told me to meet her up here. To come to Scotland to talk to Chris. But I've never met her in person.'

Meredith thrusts out her hand. 'Show me.'

Alex takes his phone out of his pocket and starts to click. He turns the screen around. 'Here.'

Meredith studies it. 'That's not her email address.'

Chris leans to see it, frowns. Meredith is right; the email address isn't Jill's.

'Can I read the message?' he asks.

'Sure.'

He skims it. It's only a short introduction and the address, but there are no giveaways that it was written by Jill. Perhaps she created the email address and hid it from him. How else would Alex know to come here? Chris rubs at his temple, thinks of the boy, Rory Campbell. What if they're all in it together? The media, the ghoulish social media trolls, all out to get him? The thought makes him sick. He should have been the one to check the validity of Alex's claim, not Meredith, but he's been bowled over by this boy – *his* boy – because this is Alex. There is no doubt.

'Do you know where Jill is?' Meredith asks.

'He's already answered that. He hasn't seen Jill since he came here.'

She narrows her eyes but says nothing.

'I'm sorry she's missing,' Alex offers.

'You're sorry,' Meredith snaps. 'I'm sorry, and Chris is sorry. Everyone is sorry. That doesn't help us.'

'Meredith.'

She ignores Chris. 'Tell us what she said to you.'

Alex shrugs. 'You read what she said to me.'

'And now she's gone.'

'*Meredith.*'

She whirls round to Chris. 'Oh! I'm sorry. This boy here might have been the last person to speak to my niece, so

I'm going to want to know about it. We have to talk to Joseph Locke.'

Alex looks at Chris. 'Who's that?'

'He's the local police officer looking into Jillian's disappearance.'

Chris sees Alex's eyes widen. 'I've never even met Jillian—'

'But you might have information that will help move the case forward,' Meredith says. 'These emails, for a start—'

'I brought Alex here to talk about Sophia,' Chris interjects.

Her mouth twists with disgust. 'Oh! Oh, OK. Don't mind me. I'm just here panicking that my niece has died. Your *wife*. Remember her?'

'Please—'

'No, no. You go ahead and have your happy little father–son moment. For Christ's *sake*.'

Something that looks like hurt crosses Alex's face. 'You think I hurt her?'

'No. Meredith isn't saying that—'

'I bloody *am*, actually.'

Chris takes her by the arm, pulls her into the little living room.

'Chris! What the hell are you doing? Ouch!'

He shuts the door. 'How dare you say all that to him!'

'How *dare* you speak to me like that!' She wrenches her arm away. 'This is a young man who's had a completely messed-up childhood because of *you*. And now maybe he's out getting his revenge.'

'Revenge? For fuck's sake, listen to yourself.'

'I thought you used to be a police officer, Chris. Engage your *brain* cells.'

260

'He has a right to know me.'

'What if he's done something to Jill? We need to go to the police at once.'

'She told him to come. That's what he said.'

'And we believe that, do we?'

'I—'

But he trails off. Because he doesn't know for sure. He doesn't know anything.

'He's my son.'

She glowers at him. 'And what reassurance does *that* give me?'

'Come on, Meredith—'

'No, *you* come on. You don't know your son, Chris. He's a grown man who has been brought up hating you because that's what his aunt has fed him. You want to have your bloody cake and eat it – and that's you all over, isn't it? I'm giving you one hour, then I'm calling the police myself. Also, that was *my* Snickers bar, you bloody thief. Don't think I didn't see the wrapper on the sideboard.'

She goes upstairs, slams her bedroom door, leaving Chris with the sound reverberating in his ears. He opens the door into the kitchen, where Alex is now standing, his arms by his sides but his fists clenched. Chris wonders, briefly, if this might have been how he looked when he was a little boy on the verge of upset.

'I'm sorry. I guess you heard all that.'

'Should I go?'

'No! Please. Please stay. Meredith is – understandably – worried about Jill.' Chris moves to the cupboard. 'I'm going to have a drink. Would you like a whisky?'

'No.'

'Coffee, then?'

'I don't like coffee.'

'What do you like?'

'Red Bull?'

'I haven't got any Red Bull. Water?'

'OK.'

Chris nods, pours Alex some water and himself a tumbler of whisky. 'Come out to the courtyard.'

They step out, sit opposite each other. It's all Chris can do not to stare at the young man in front of him. Handsome, assertive, keen in the eyes. The sun is low now, and makes everything about him glitter, but maybe even in the darkness he would glitter for Chris. Alex's face has the shape of Sophia's, the same cheekbones.

'It's weird being here,' Alex says. 'With you.'

'Yeah,' Chris says. 'It is pretty weird.'

'Will you tell me about her? About my mum?'

The word 'mum' spoken from his son's mouth makes Chris's heart constrict.

'She was an amazing woman. She wanted to change the world.'

'I'm in solar energy. My aunt says Mum would have loved that.'

'She would.'

Alex pauses. 'I know a lot about her from Leila, but I don't know anything about her life with you.'

'Well, you wouldn't. By the time you were born, your aunt would have put black marks against my name for life.' He remembers, then, how he and Sophia had bought a cactus and called it Leila. The memory simultaneously brings a smile to his lips and an ache to his heart. 'And rightly so, I guess,' he admits.

'What do you remember about her?'

Chris sighs. 'Your mum sang in the shower. She named her pot plants. She was a great hiker, she loved sunsets. She and I talked about travelling together – she wanted to rent a van and live life on the road for six months, to go to Europe. She was interested in history, in nature, in abandoned buildings.'

Alex frowns. 'I know all this. Leila told me. I want . . . I don't know. Something else.'

Chris pauses. 'OK,' he says gently. 'Then I'll tell you some things about the three of us.'

At this, Alex is silent. Waiting.

'When she was pregnant with you, she fell in love with oranges. She'd eat five or more a day. I was always picking them up from Sainsbury's – daily, at points. Sometimes, when we were bored of an evening, we'd play catch across the living room with them. We'd suggest baby names for you, every time we threw to each other. At night, I used to circle her bellybutton with my finger and you used to push your feet back at us.'

A lump forms in Chris's throat. Alex is so still that he could be stone.

'She went on a march when she was about five months pregnant,' Chris says, 'and I was scared shitless because it got rough. When we came home she told me not to be a wuss, and we had a massive fight. She threw an orange at my face, and it almost broke my fucking nose – and then we laughed. We laughed and laughed and laughed.'

Chris laughs himself at the memory, then almost chokes at the sadness of it. The waste of her life. He meets Alex's eyes.

'We talked about what you might look like, what you might do with your life. We wanted to shelter you from Leila recruiting you into PR.'

Alex gives a ghost of a smile.

'Soph wanted you to be happy, above all else. Have you been happy?'

He's asking for himself, because his guilt is overwhelming.

'I'm OK,' Alex says, and then pauses. 'Do you regret it? Leaving Mum? Did you regret leaving me when you found out she'd died?'

Tears spring to Chris's eyes now. 'Oh God. Every single moment.'

Time had healed some wounds, but never that one. Every day since he left, he has thought of them. There were days in Sardinia when he and Jill would go and lie on the beach, and Jillian would laugh at Chris, unmoving on the sand. She thought he was relaxing, but in truth, he suggested those beach trips because on those days he was physically paralysed by heartache and couldn't bear to speak or move. He could do nothing but listen to the sea and concentrate on breathing.

There were countless times too, when he and Jill had held each other when their attempts at having a baby had failed, that Chris felt not just grief but heavy shame. Because he had a child, but he wasn't a father.

He had wanted to live both lives – his life with Jill, who was his everything, and his life with Sophia and his baby. He had been both people at once and had loved two women completely, yet differently, at the same time. But the cold, simple truth was that he couldn't have both. He chose Jill because that's what the unit wanted – what they expected – but perhaps he would have chosen her anyway. Or maybe he would have run away and done that thing the unit found repugnant: gone native.

Plenty of officers had gone native in situations where

their undercover lives had become more real to them than their actual ones and they had left their legitimate families to be with their activist ones. There was a price to pay, of course. Not only did they leave their families devastated, in time they were written off by the unit. And afterwards, both parties lived in constant fear of exposure.

'Why didn't you ever try to find me?' Alex asks, in a voice that quavers.

'I was watching you from a distance,' Chris says. 'I knew you were safe.'

'But you didn't know if I was happy, because you just asked me. So maybe you weren't watching closely enough.'

'If I had come closer, I might have put us both in danger.'

'I don't get it.'

Chris shakes his head. 'I can't explain.'

'You know something about the night my mum died that you didn't say in the inquest.' Alex's eyes were accusatory.

'Why don't we talk about you?' Chris says. 'I want to know about you.'

'Why won't you answer?'

Chris looks at his watch. It's six thirty in the evening and the sun has bled pink into the skyline.

'Do you want some food?' he asks.

'You won't tell me?'

'I could make you a sandwich?'

'Chris.'

Chris, not 'Dad'. He is a stranger, of course. He doesn't have to be, he thinks. He could just say it all – the whole truth of what happened – to this boy in front of him who wants answers. Chris owes it to Alex above all others, so why does he feel he needs to protect Oliver and the rest of SDS? He remembers then what Edd Fletcher said –

It's a job of servitude. And it sucks you in. Being part of the police is like having a love affair. It's a commitment, for ever.

'I'm sorry about the inquest,' Chris says.

'What does that mean?'

'Let me make you some food, OK? Pasta and some sauce? We don't have to talk about . . . you know.'

'What about Jill?' Alex asks. 'Where do you think she is?'

'We don't know where she is, and it's . . . it's all . . .'

He is starting to choke up, but cannot. Not when Alex is standing in front of him, upset about Sophia.

'We don't know if she's still alive.'

Alex nods. 'I'm sorry.'

Chris pinches the bridge of his nose, wants to stop himself from showing emotion. 'No, it's fine. I mean, it's *not*, obviously. I need to get out and find her somehow, but it's still very difficult to be out there, to know what to do.'

Alex tilts his head, as if in thought. 'I am hungry.'

'So am I. So am I. And Meredith will be too. I'll make something and take hers up to her. A peace offering.'

'What about the police? Are you going to call them? About me?'

Chris glances upwards, at the room where Meredith is hanging above them, an invisible wraith. She's right to want to call Joseph and Karen about Alex because if there is anything to help find Jill, then the emails are worth tracking, but Chris needs to be soft.

'No,' he says. 'No, I'm not.'

Alex nods slowly.

'You could stay here?' Chris asks.

'I shouldn't—'

'I know I shouldn't be asking this of you,' Chris interrupts quickly. 'But we could talk some more about your mum later on. The good times, because we had so many, Alex. I want you to know that. I want you to know how much I loved her, because I did.'

'Then why didn't you choose us?'

There – that little boy again, asking that same question. Perhaps he'll ask it all his life.

'We could still get to know one another,' Chris says. 'I am so sorry. For everything.'

Alex nods. 'OK. I'll stay.'

Chris's heart dances.

'On one condition.'

'What's that?'

'I have your dog with me. He's cool.'

Chris looks to Jackson, smiles. 'He is.'

Chris has told Meredith that he's phoned Joseph, told her that he and Karen will be over tomorrow to ask Alex some questions, but he hasn't. He knows that he should – any potential lead to Jill could mean finding her – but he's worried that if he does, then Alex will bolt and Chris will lose him.

He's in a state of euphoria, lying on the sofa, listening to his son walking around upstairs. It's a curious thing, when everything else in his life is in utter turmoil, to feel so excited, so full of joy, but there it is. Chris hears a soft murmuring, like a hum or a lullaby, and then experiences a tremor of worry that Alex is on the phone to someone, but then there's the thump, thump of Jackson's tail on the floor and the creak of Alex's weight as he moves on to the bed. Chris wonders if his sheets will take on the smell of his son, whether he might lie in bed tomorrow and inhale whatever sweet aftershave and shower gel he uses. He wonders if Alex is sleeping in the clothes he had on or if he might have taken up Chris's offer and put on one of the clean T-shirts he'd laid out on the bed. He's desperate to go back up and see him, talk to him – hell, to just *look* at him. He knows this is strange, but maybe it's not – maybe this is what it's like when people say that you fall in love with your child. He considers going into the room in a few hours and taking a photograph of him to study in detail later. He won't, of course, but he so craves to. He can't believe that Alex is here, after all these years. It is all thanks to his wife, who has now disappeared from the face of the earth.

He doesn't have Jill, but for tonight at least, he has his son.

41

But with the slow, creeping hours of darkness, euphoria turns to unease. Meredith's words about Alex have earwormed into Chris's head.

What if he's done something to Jill?

Chris doesn't want to believe this could be possible, but as the minutes tick by and the excitement of the evening fades, he realizes that it's not *im*possible. Because Meredith is right that Chris doesn't know who Alex is. He only knows the man he wants him to be.

What if Jill *had* made contact with Alex since he'd been staying in the cottage? Alex said the rental wasn't far from The Old Smoke House – presumably because Jill had engineered it that way – so would it be too far a stretch to think that she might have secretly visited him?

His mind begins to crank. She couldn't have driven to Alex the morning she disappeared because their car remained at Smoke House. The only logical explanation is that she took the boat and moored it in one of the small beach inlays near where Alex was staying before hiking up the steep clifftops and towards the house. It would have taken a while to get there and she would have been caught out in the rain. Maybe it was really starting to pour by the time she eventually reached the house.

Chris turns over on the sofa and the thin blanket that he found in a cupboard slips from his body and pools to the floor. He reaches for it and pulls it back over his shoulder.

He hadn't felt like he'd needed it when he first lay down because he was warm and fuzzy, but now he shivers. He wants something heavier, wants the weight of a thick duvet to bring him comfort. He doesn't want Meredith's words buzzing around his head.

Maybe he's out getting his revenge.

He gets up, goes to the kitchen, pours himself a glass of water and then stands in the darkness, thinking.

Would Jill have reached out to hug Alex? Would he have let her? Chris wonders if Jill might also have been shocked by how similar he was to Chris. And then what? Would they have talked? Would she have stood up for Chris? Would Alex have been receptive to her, or would he have been defensive? No doubt any conversation between them would have been stilted and jerky, because it was a bizarre situation that neither of them knew how to steer – the betrayed wife and the child Chris didn't want.

But I did want you, Chris thinks. I just couldn't get to you.

These thoughts are too much. Why is he trying to imagine the two of them talking about him? He feels like a narcissist, a psychopath. Besides, Alex is *here*, isn't he? Jill had convinced Alex to come. Yes! Of course she would have done, because Jill would want that for Chris – perhaps she would want that also for herself. The chance for a child because they could never have one. There would be years of hurt and anger to navigate – Chris knows that – but they could salvage something, couldn't they? His mind races to the thought of the three of them in Sardinia. They could take Alex to Marco's, to the beach.

Chris drains the glass of water, returns to the sofa and then falls into a fitful sleep.

*

He dreams that Alex and Jill are in a little house on the clifftop. The loch is some way below; the boat rocks on the water as the wind starts to whip up from the North Sea. It causes the windows to rattle in their frames, and a high howling noise spins down from the chimney and into the empty fireplace.

Alex and Jill are sitting in a dimly lit kitchen – the horse-head lamp from The Old Smoke House at their side. Chris is there too, but also not there. He is like a ghost, like smoke, above, watching. He cannot speak and they cannot see him.

Alex and Jill look rigid, uncertain. There is a heavy unease in the air. Alex is drinking Red Bull from a tin; Jill sits opposite him with her hands on her lap, shivering because she is soaked from the rain. Huge puddles of water are at her feet and the water is not clear but dark. Her hair looks strange, and Chris can't work out why.

'I know that your aunt has probably told you things,' Jill says. 'But Chris is a good person and he'd love to meet with you.'

Oh Jill, Chris thinks, above them. You are compassionate and warm and kind. You will bring us all together.

'Did he say that?' Alex asks. 'That he wants to meet me?'

She hesitates, and he laughs, but it sounds hollow and unhappy.

'Chris doesn't know I'm here, does he? You wanted to vet me first?'

'Please,' Jill says. 'Chris wasn't with your mum when she . . .'

'Overdosed?'

'Yes.'

'How do you know that? He's a professional *liar*.'

She glances upwards then and her eyes seem to find Chris's, even though it is impossible.

You believe me, Jill, he whispers. *Don't you?*

She looks back to Alex. 'Would you come back with me? Give Chris a chance? He's not how the papers are making him out.'

Alex says nothing for a while. 'OK.'

Jill smiles, and Chris smiles with her.

'Yes!' she beams. 'That would be great. I've got the boat, moored by some rocks near one of the coves. No one would even know you'd come to The Old Smoke House. It could all be done privately. In secret.'

Alex is silent, stony.

'Secret' was the wrong choice of word, Chris thinks.

'I'll come with you,' Alex says. 'On the boat. But I need to get a few things from the next room. I want to give something to Chris. Can you help me?'

He walks to a dark living room and both Chris and Jill follow, eyes adjusting to the gloom. It smells of mould. There are no windows. Chris is immediately worried. Alex is hunched by a chair, rummaging in a bag.

Careful, Chris whispers, but Jill can't hear.

'What can I help with?' She feels along the wall. 'Have you – is there a light?'

But before she has time to register what is happening Alex steps forward, arms outstretched, and shoves her so hard that she stumbles backwards, landing heavily against a low wooden table. She cries out with pain, but he is already retreating from the room, shutting the door.

'Alex!' she screams, getting up. 'Hey! What are you doing?'

What are you doing? Chris shouts too, but his desperation is unheard.

The only sound in reply is the door being locked, and Chris can only watch helplessly as Jill throws her weight against it. But it is solid and doesn't move.

'Let me out!' she cries.

There is another noise then – the front door shutting and locking. Chris feels Jill's raw panic as if it's his own.

'Alex!'

Silence. She is alone. Alex has left her, and both Jill and Chris realize with fear that she has told him where to find Chris back at The Old Smoke House – she's told him about her boat and where she's left it. What might he do now? She puts her hand to her pocket for her phone, but her pocket is empty because her phone is zipped up in the raincoat that Alex hung in the kitchen. She breathes into the darkness, and then starts to run her hand along the walls to find a light switch.

Don't do that, Chris says, because he is suddenly sure that something or someone is in that room. *Please, Jill.*

The walls are beamed, and in between them they are textured with flimsy paper. She keeps banging into things – a sofa, a bookcase. Finally, after a few minutes, she finds it, a small protruding plastic wedge on the wall, and snaps it on, illuminating the room.

She blinks furiously to adjust to the light, and then looks around. An ordinary room except for the coffee table she tripped over, which is covered with documentation – newspapers, photos of Chris as a younger man, printed pages of what must be Sophia's online diary.

Don't look! Chris shouts, despairing now, but she can't hear him. He flies to her side but cannot move her hand away, cannot shield her eyes. He is still a ghost, still like mist.

To his horror, Jill sits down to read and discovers the missing piece of what really happened to Sophia that night.

Chris wakes up, drenched in sweat.

Alex has locked Jill inside the house. She is still in that room.

No, it cannot be the case. Chris swings his legs so that he's sitting, holds his face in his hands and tells himself to breathe, to calm down but, fuck, his heart is racing. The blanket has fallen to the floor. His body is pouring beads of water. He takes his hands from his face, holds them out in front of him. They are bone-white, thin and skeletal. They don't look real and yet he's moving them. He laughs, and then clamps his lips shut. Everything feels like a dream. Is this one? Is this whole thing a dream? One sick joke?

Quietly he takes the stairs two steps at a time, and then he's nudging his bedroom door open. There, in the doorframe, he stands very still and stares at Alex, who is wrapped up, fast asleep, with the duvet pulled to his chin. Next to him on the floor is the huge snoring bulk of Jackson.

Chris lets out a shuddering breath.

He's your boy.

He goes back down, sits on the sofa and tries to quiet his thudding heart. He tells himself that his mind is running away, that Alex is not here to hurt him, nor has he hurt Jill. It was only a dream, and Jill is not locked up in any room. She has not read or seen anything she should not read or see.

All the secrets are safe.

42

When Chris wakes, the house is quiet and the living room is flooded with light. He glances at the clock, sees with disbelief that it's nearly nine in the morning. His sleep is so irregular. Jackson should have woken him long before now for his breakfast and to be let outside. Perhaps Meredith has already fed him. Or Alex. His heart leaps.

He gets up quickly, wraps his dressing gown around himself and walks into the kitchen. It's as they left it last night – pots and pans in the sink and plates on the side.

'Hello?'

He goes upstairs, knocks softly on the bedroom door. 'Alex?'

There's no sound. Chris pushes it open to find the room empty. Confused, he glances across the tiny corridor to the bathroom, but the door is wide open. Chris walks the few steps to the other bedroom – Meredith's – and realizes her door is open too.

'Meredith?'

A feeling of dread steals over him. Maybe Meredith called Joseph Locke and they marched in while Chris was asleep and took Alex to the police station. But they would have woken him, surely, for questions. Where is Jackson? Have Meredith and Alex gone out together with him? Chris goes back downstairs and looks out of the kitchen window, but there is little to see aside from foliage and the stone courtyard. He needs coffee; his bafflement is making him cloudy.

He switches on the kettle, takes a mug from the cupboard and, as he puts it down, he sees a piece of paper that reads *FOR YOU* and gives a URL. He cocks his head, frowns. Is this Meredith's writing? Alex's? In his nightmare, Alex wanted to give Chris something, deliver it by hand. A shiver runs down his back.

He picks up his phone from its hiding place under the living-room sofa and is about to input the URL when a knock at the door disturbs him. He closes the note within his palm and pockets the phone in his dressing gown.

'Hello?' he says through the wood. 'Meredith?'

'It's Joseph Locke.'

'And Karen Holland.'

His heart starts to race. Meredith has rung them. 'I – hang on. I need to get some clothes.'

He rushes back up the stairs, grabs underwear, jeans and a T-shirt. He transfers the piece of paper to his jeans and smooths down his hair.

'Sorry,' he says, opening the door. 'I was . . . Is there news?'

'Can we come in?' Joseph says, by way of reply.

'Of course.'

Joseph sets down a bag, and in it Chris can see a loaf of bread, a pint of milk, some bananas.

'Is Jill's aunt here?' Joseph asks.

'No. She's . . .' He hesitates, looks around for Jackson. 'She's out with the dog.'

He doesn't know for sure, but that can be the only answer. Where is Alex though? He could walk through the door any moment and be taken away for questioning.

'Did she call you?'

Joseph frowns. 'No. But we have some questions for

Meredith about an email she sent to Jillian a couple of weeks ago.'

'An . . . an email?'

Was this the email Meredith had been alluding to the other day? A photograph taken on the day Sophia died?

'Can you tell me what the email said?' he asks.

'No,' Karen replies curtly.

'It's something we need clarification about,' Joseph says. 'But that was only part of the reason we've come to you, and this can't wait for her to return, I'm afraid. We wanted to tell you in person that the dive team have been called to another job.'

A new weight descends on Chris's shoulders. 'They're giving up?'

'They have an immediate call. But . . .' Here he pauses. 'They can't look indefinitely, Chris. The body of water is enormous.'

Chris clenches his fists.

'We haven't given up,' Joseph says. 'We'll keep looking for Jill, and Murray Scott is out every day on the loch. One of the other fishermen – Cal Mellors – is taking his boat out too, and Harris McGowan has been out every day that he's not been in the pub.'

'Fuck.'

Joseph gives him a sympathetic nod. 'I'm sorry, Chris. I know that's not the news you want to hear, but we're doing all we can. On a different note, the team have done a full inspection of The Old Smoke House.'

'Oliver Hamilton told me. Nothing came back.'

'No. But we'd like to talk to Meredith about that too.'

'Can I ask why?'

Joseph pauses, seems to weigh up speaking. 'We asked

Harris McGowan to come to Smoke House this morning to answer a few questions.'

'Questions like what?'

'He was the person Jillian saw most of here, both historically and recently. We were asking him routine questions about their interactions.'

Chris bites at the inside of his cheek. Because what kind of interactions did Harris have with Jill?

'While in the house, he commented that there was a lamp missing.'

Chris frowns. 'Oh?' But as he forms the shape of the word, his brain catches up.

'More specifically, the base of it,' Joseph continues. 'The shade is at the property. It's a lamp that looks like a horse's head. Wooden. Do you know the one I'm referring to?'

He swallows the lump that's formed at the back of his throat. 'Yes.'

'Was it in the property when you were there?'

'No. Yes. I mean, I have no idea. I remember it though. Jill liked it.'

Karen narrows her eyes.

'Was everything else present and correct?' Chris asks.

'It appears so,' she replies.

Chris turns away, needs to distract himself, needs to busy his hands. Why is he sweating all of a sudden? Why is there a heat of worry at his chest and burning up his throat?

'We'll update you if we hear anything else,' Joseph says. 'I'm sorry about the dive team.'

They turn to leave, but Joseph pauses.

'When Meredith gets back, can you ask her to call us as a matter of urgency?'

*

Chris stands still in the kitchen for a full ten minutes before darting upstairs and making for the wardrobe, pulling out the rucksack and unzipping it. There is the wooden horse-head lamp, the one he took because it reminded him of Sophia.

Jill. *Jill.*

He smacks himself in the face, over and over. Why can't he get his brain working right? Jill. His beloved Jill. He gives a shout of frustration and loses his grip on the lamp. It drops to the floor with a thud and rolls to the side.

That's when he notices there are specks of blood on the base.

43

For the longest time, Chris stares at the spots on the lamp until they begin to multiply in his eyes. Whose blood is it?

Did he *hurt* Jill?

A threat of vomit rises up his throat. Immediately his mind goes to their whispered argument in bed. He'd drunk whisky and taken sleeping pills that night; he wasn't of sound mind and hadn't been for weeks, ever since the inquest had landed at his door. Could he have blacked out and done something awful?

'You believe me, don't you?' he'd asked. 'That I had nothing to do with what happened to Sophia?'

'You were in Southampton and your unit has evidence of it.'

'Yes.'

She'd looked at him, like she was examining him for cracks. 'But we left for Sardinia not even a week after she died.'

'That was a coincidence. Nothing more.'

'I hate this. I hate it all.'

'If I could take it back—' he'd said.

'But you wouldn't,' she'd interrupted. 'You wouldn't ever take it back because you loved that job. It meant everything to you. And you loved her, too. I don't believe that Sophia meant nothing. I don't believe that.'

Her anger and weary acceptance of how things were

weighed like lead on his heart. She'd turned and he had rolled over and taken another sleeping pill.

Yes, that's what had happened.

Except everything was slippery in his head. He doesn't have a grip on anything. What if he *hadn't* rolled over but instead stayed staring at her, at her silhouette under the duvet, and her hair splayed on the pillow in ribbons of gold. He suddenly remembers the half-second when he'd wanted to pick up that pillow, put it over her face, because he was angry, scared. In his anxiety-induced state, and with the mix of alcohol and sleeping pills in his blood, Jill had become the embodiment of all the pain and the terror and the judgement, and he wanted the mess of what he'd done while undercover and Jill's disappointment in him to be wiped away.

The thought of this makes him retch, and he moans aloud.

Never. *Never.*

But he is capable of doing bad things. He has been so many people; has lived different names, crafted different mindsets. Perhaps that night when they argued, something had tipped in his head and he had become a man with a shaved head and a tattoo of a rose at the back of his neck. A man who wanted to do harm.

His mind takes him there now, to his hands on the pillow and to the most frightening of all possibilities – complete dissociation from himself.

Jill jolted immediately, and cried out, but the noise was muffled and strained, because he was crushing her windpipe. She managed to twist herself fully so she was on her back, and her eyes locked on to his, at first in fury and then in horror as she seemed to understand what he wanted to do to her. She started to flail against him, kicking up her legs, trying to prise his hands away, but he was strong.

'It's for the best,' he said.

Jill continued to thrash against him, but he pushed down harder, wanted to drown out her fish-like gulping noises from beneath the pillow. He almost laughed at how strange it was – the disconnection between his hands that pressed so firmly down on the softness of it and the love he felt for her, even in the moment of trying to obliterate her.

There was a sudden noise, a bark, and it momentarily snapped him back to himself. He glanced around, and in his confusion Jill managed to lift his little finger from the edge of the pillow – and where the little finger goes, the rest must all follow – and in that split second, she rolled and kicked him hard, the heel of her foot catching him in the face.

He let go entirely.

She scrabbled off the bed and ran for the door. There was barking again – Jackson, now standing at their bedside, his eyes wide with fright.

'Shut up, shut up, shut up!' Chris shouted.

In the seconds of distraction, Jill threw open the bedroom door and disappeared through it. Chris managed to barge past Jackson and hurtle out after her, shutting the door behind him and barring Jackson inside. Then, one step, two steps, he flew down the stairs.

Jill was in the kitchen, about to open the front door, but he lunged for her and brought her down, heavily. She smacked her face on the stone tiles, whirled around, blood all over her nose and running in rivulets across her cheeks, down her chin.

'Chris! Please!'

She kicked out again, scrambled up and ran for the knife block, grabbed a knife. They stood on opposite sides of the circular table, Jill holding the blade, Chris looking at her like she was an apparition.

'It's me,' she cried. 'OK? It's *me*. Are you *asleep*?'

He ran to one side, forcing her to run in the opposite direction and into the snug. By doing so, she trapped herself in the room. She whipped the knife through the air, uselessly.

'Stop! Chris! Wake up!'

But he picked up the horse-head lamp that she loved so much and easily deflected the knife as she thrust it out in front of him. With a silver ting, it made contact with the metal, and she dropped it. They both watched it fall.

Then he swung the lamp and smashed her skull.

It was later, but he didn't know when. Everything around him was grey and shimmering and there was a sound – a muffled barking noise. His head throbbed.

He found that he was dressed in a hoodie and trousers and he was crouched beside Jill, but she wasn't in bed. She was on the floor of the snug and there was a dark, pooling liquid around her head. Not much, but enough. Some of it had been soaked up by her hair, had stained the white of it so that it was dark and unusual. He reached to touch it, then jerked backwards because it was sticky and he knew what that meant but couldn't quite grasp hold of it.

'Jill?'

She didn't look up at him, didn't open her eyes.

He spoke into her ear. 'Are you going to wake up?'

But still she said nothing. His heart thumping, his breath

in ragged pants, he lifted Jill from her armpits and dragged her to the downstairs bathroom. Then he returned to the kitchen, dimly noted that the horse-head lamp was in there, on the side, out of place.

He chose the biggest knife from the knife block.

'This is what we do.' His voice was gravelly, deep, belonged to someone else. 'We cut them up and feed all the creatures that come out at night.'

He walked back into the bathroom and calmly hacked Jillian's body to pieces.

He took her somewhere – a garden, a wood – he couldn't remember, but there was dirt under his fingernails.

He needed to clean up the house.

He was in different clothes, though he couldn't remember changing. His hands were like foreign entities in front of his face, but they knew how to clean, knew how to work hard to polish the lie that was beginning to build in the swirl of his mind. His hands kept time with a ticking clock somewhere in the house as first a rag and then a sponge moved back and forth, over and over. The strong chemicals inhabited his nostrils and his eyes, making them drip with water, the tiles pulsating in front of him. But soon, the bathroom and the stone flooring in the snug and kitchen were spotless.

'Happy birthday,' he said, standing up.

There was silence, heavy and strange. Something had happened here – an incident of some kind – and he couldn't remember what, but there came a dawning realization in the deepest corner of his mind that something dark had happened here, something unspeakable, like what had happened to the man in the woods. Like what had happened to Sophia. The anger he knew he'd felt earlier gave way to something else, a knife-sharp, inexplicable sorrow.

Knife. He had seen one somewhere.

He saw that on the side of the sink was a clean butcher's knife. I should move that, he thought. Jackson might swing it with his tail and it could hurt someone. What was it doing here? He returned it to the kitchen then opened the front door, pushed a stop in front of it so the chemicals could clear, and walked out.

'Jill?'

Confused, he wondered if Jill was out on the boat. Was she with Harris? Why would they be out at gone four thirty in the morning? Something was odd between the two of them. Fury twisted inside Chris's stomach.

There was a low mist hanging like a shroud over the loch. As he walked out, he felt the bite of cold air – there was going to be a storm later, that's what Harris had said. Chris walked down to the water and through the swirl of fog, saw the little dinghy bobbing. Jill wasn't out in it, so where was she? Was she at the pub? Was she walking to Harris? No, he thought in his addled mind, he had seen her somewhere and she had been sleeping. Though perhaps she had been pretending and any moment she would get up and leave him. Fury turned to pure, cold panic.

He unhooked the rope that secured the boat, pushed it into the water and walked along the rocks towards the woodland, pulling it behind him. He wanted to hide the boat from Jill, didn't want her to escape him – his biggest fear was being alone. He picked his way along the bank, and the boat followed behind on the water, like a subdued animal. It made him think of a leather strip, another time, with a man's wrists tied at the end of it, but where had that been? What had happened, exactly? He couldn't remember, but there were trees and men and talk of a lamb. He laughed aloud then. Because that didn't make sense, did it? Why would there have been a lamb in the woods? His skin prickled, a deep and aching fear. His body knew, even if his mind did not.

The hems of his trousers became soiled and heavy with mud as he dragged the boat, but he didn't register the weight or the smell of the boggy water creeping up the fabric. He walked for an hour until the woodland density forced him to stop. Panting for breath, he looked behind at the dinghy and thought that this would be the spot to be rid of it. A pity, he thought then, because the varnished wood would make such a beautiful heart for Jill. He let go of the rope for a moment and looked around for a rock. Something big, something strong that would break the boat apart, so that he could take a chunk out and whittle it. It would be better than the piece of wood he'd found on the walk before, and Jill deserved the best.

He eventually found a rock with a sharpened flat side. He eased into the water until he was shin-deep in the swampy mud, then brought down the stone. The wood didn't even crack. He brought it down again, harder and faster until the boat began to dent and splinter. He continued, smiling to himself, because there was a pleasure to rhythmically destroying it. Maybe because it was Harris's boat and there was something he didn't like about Harris. Hearts in windows. Broken hearts. Jill, all broken up by Chris's lies. Did Chris even *like* Harris McGowan? Did he trust him? Jill always returned to Sardinia after being in Scotland with a lightness about her that made Chris wonder if there was something there, between the two of them. He thought then that he would bury the lamp in the pub garden of The Black Horse, let Harris McGowan take the blame.

On and on Chris smashed until the ruined boat began to take on water and slip away beneath the black. The white of the folded sail appeared like a long thin bone down its length. He would have to come back another time, he thought, and push it further into the water so it could be taken by the storm due later on. Would he even remember, tomorrow, where it was that he'd walked? The blackness of the woodland was haunting, and all the ghosts were watching.

He stood still. Was Roper here, somewhere?

He walked quickly back to The Old Smoke House and arrived just as the sun was beginning to rise over the loch, and then he stood inside the warm kitchen. He couldn't remember where he had been or why his clothes were wet. He didn't know, either, why he was moving, shedding his clothes, and putting them into the washing machine. There were other clothes in there too – dark and stained. He frowned, turned the machine on.

'Jill?' he called. 'Where are you?'

He walked naked up the stairs, got into the shower and washed himself. In the heat, everything began to dissolve, the mud and the memory, until eventually the hot water ran out and he stepped outside and into the bedroom, refreshed. Reset.

He was immediately pinned to the wall by Jackson, who licked madly at him. Happy tears rushed to Chris's eyes as he wrapped his arms around the dog.

'Oh!' he said. 'Where have you been? Have you seen Mum anywhere?'

Perhaps within this twisted possibility of what might

have happened that night, Chris got some fresh pyjama bottoms out of the drawer and crawled into bed. The memory of what he had done only hours before now belonged to a version of himself he wasn't aware of, locked up in the part of his mind that housed all the dark things.

44

He blinks and refocuses his eyes on the lamp that he's holding. The droplets of blood are dark on the wood. He needs to get rid of them but feels a distinctive and familiar tremble in his jaw. He knows what's coming. He catapults up the stairs, sticks his head into the toilet bowl and throws up.

Terror, panic, it all comes out in a hot stream of sick.

He cannot have done it; he could never have hurt Jill. He wipes his mouth with his arm, and stands too soon, sways a moment and leans against the wall. But there is no time to lose. He feels a necessary, white-hot urge to scrub out this heinous possibility, right now. Because what if he has hurt her? What *if*?

He goes downstairs with the lamp, sets it down on the table, and then opens the cupboard at the bottom of the sink and gets out some cleaning spray. But as he's about to erase the spots of blood, there's a voice outside the door.

'Come on, Jackson, you muddy dope.'

Meredith and Jackson have returned. He shoves the equipment back into the cupboard and the lamp into the rucksack, dropping it behind an armchair just as they walk in.

Meredith looks at him. 'Where's the boy?'

'What?'

'Alex. Where is he?'

Alex. He'd forgotten about his son. Has he also done something to his boy? His heart beats wildly.

'He's . . . he's gone.'

'Gone where? Did you call the police about him?'

'I – they came over.'

Meredith doesn't need to know that he didn't tell them about Alex, and he won't tell her.

'Good. It was the right thing to do, Christopher. I'm sorry, but it was.'

She bustles, oblivious to his rigidity and the grey pallor of his face. His vision is swimming, but every sound is crystal clear. He hears the rustle of her coat as she removes it, the clip of Jackson's lead. He hears the slop of Jackson drinking his water, the filling and turning on of the kettle.

'Did they update you?'

He closes his eyes, hopes to refocus, reset. What has happened to Jill?

'Sorry?'

'Was there news on Jill?'

'News?'

She is in front of him then, so close that he jerks back in surprise.

'Your *wife*? Are you all right, Christopher?'

'I'm fine.'

He is not. *I might have killed her*, he wants to say, but how can he? How the hell could he have done something so monstrous?

'What did they say then? Joseph and Karen?'

'They said . . . that the dive team needed to move on.'

She baulks. 'Move *on*? Move on where?'

'They have other jobs.'

'Other *jobs*?' she explodes.

He can barely keep upright, and her screaming is making him dizzy. He sits, heavily.

'The attention on this case is huge! What are they thinking?'

'They said Joseph needs to speak to you.'

She pauses. 'To me?'

'About an email.'

She is suddenly still. 'It's completely irrelevant, but I'll phone them. Obviously.'

He wants to tell her that it's all OK – he knows now what happened to Jill, and it's nothing to do with an email. He licks his lips, tastes salt. He realizes he's crying.

'Meredith, I think maybe . . . I think you should go elsewhere.'

'Pardon?'

'I think maybe you should go back to Smoke House on your own. Or somewhere else. I'm . . . not coping.'

The lamp is in the corner behind the armchair – nowhere near him – and yet it's banging against his skull. Would Meredith also notice that it was missing, if she returned to The Old Smoke House? Would Harris tell her, or the police?

'Move? Where on earth to? For goodness' sake, Christopher, you need me with you. The email wasn't anything, I promise—'

'Please, Meredith. Whatever happens, I'm finished. They're not looking for Jill in the water. Where else will they look? You have your family, your business.'

He puts his head in his hands. Did he sleep that night they argued? Or did he put his hands around her throat like he had so wanted to, silencing her anger? Or was it Roper who had come for Jill, and Chris had been too comatose to hear the struggle? But the house the next day had been clean. It had been *cleaned*. He thought Jill had done it, mad at him because she'd asked him. But he must have done it. He has killed her.

'Why are you giving up, Christopher?'

'What?'

'What's got into you? Are you all right?' he hears her say. 'I think we should call someone. A doctor? Oliver?'

'You should get your things. You're not safe here. Neither of us is safe.'

'Safe from what?' she asks.

'All of it. The men. Me.'

'What are you talking about?' she whispers.

Sweat slips down his back. He's shaking.

'I'll arrange for someone to pick you up,' he says.

'But you don't have a phone—'

'I have a phone, Meredith. A secret phone. Secrets. So many dark fucking secrets.'

She looks like she is about to speak but decides not to.

'Please, Meredith.'

She nods. An hour later she is packed and closes the front door behind her.

She leaves at four in the afternoon, taken by a police escort back to The Old Smoke House. He wonders if Joseph Locke will go to her. He wonders what he needs to ask her about the email. But what does it matter when the answer to Jill's disappearance is staring at him in the mirror. Himself, but not.

Where did he put her? And where is Alex?

The day is fading now. He retrieves the rucksack from behind the armchair and takes out the lamp, stares at it as he turns it over and over. Is it misshapen in any way? No, it's the same as it's always been, a smooth wooden horse head. There is no dent, nothing that looks out of the ordinary.

He goes to the sink, puts on the tap and, now alone, scrubs at the lamp with a sponge. He can hear his breath in his ears, a shallow panting. He wants to faint. If it was Jill's blood, there might also be evidence of who killed her, and he's destroyed it.

What will he do about the lamp? He can't return it to Smoke House. Maybe he'll tell Joseph and Karen and Meredith that he never saw it and he'll bury it somewhere. Maybe he'll burn it in the fireplace. Yes, that's a better idea. But that would look worse, wouldn't it, if traces of it were found. Who would find it though? Who would know to go looking through the ash? He can't call Oliver; he can't call anyone. When it boils down to it, he's got no one left. He cracks then – emits a noise that doesn't seem quite human. He grabs the bottle of whisky and sits on the sofa, drinks and stares dumbly at the soft yellow stone walls. Presently there's a breath on the back of his neck. Jackson, his faithful companion. He buries his face in the dog's fur.

'What did I do, Jacko? What happened?'

The light has changed; it's now dark. How many hours has he been sitting there? He needs to find the place where he buried her. His legs are cramped and shaky from being in one position for so long, but he gets himself up somehow. He swigs a mouthful of whisky from the neck, then another for the road. He shouldn't have more because his head feels like it's on fire, but he does so anyway, feels the familiar and comforting burn at his throat. He's so drunk he can barely see, but it doesn't matter.

He grabs his car keys from the kitchen counter. Jackson barks.

'Come,' Chris says, and they leave Rosewood Cottage.

Snapchat

RoryCampbell: Guess what I've seen.

RoryCampbell: GUESS WHAT!!!

MattChristie: Why are you texting at 2 in the morning?

RoryCampbell: I've seen a truck going up the High Mount Lane.

MattChristie: Are you kidding me? You woke me up for this??

RoryCampbell: The only place up there is End Stone. Why would anyone be going up there? The police searched it with dogs.

RoryCampbell: Lorna's mum used to go up there. Oi oi.

RoryCampbell: What if it was John Crossan who killed Kate McGowan? What if he killed Jillian Moore too?

RoryCampbell: What if it was LORNA'S DAD and he's stashed her away up there? I'm gonna go up there.

MattChristie has left the group

45

She is there in front of him. His love, his lifeline, his Jill. He is so close to reaching for her, but something is making a noise and frightening her, and she is shrinking away into a place beyond, where he can't follow.

His eyes flicker open. His neck is twisted at a funny angle, his face is sideways on the hard kitchen table and he unsticks his cheek from it, turns his head. He was dreaming of her, and the thing making the noise in his dream was Jackson, who is pawing at his legs and whining. In his hand is the wooden heart he was making Jill. It feels like a lifetime ago since he first picked it up. Its rough edges have left imprints in his palm.

He glances at the clock on the wall. Time has become slippery and, somehow, it's six o'clock in the morning. He's still in yesterday's clothes and they're dirty with earth. A sliver of fear runs down his back: where did he go last night? He recalls an urgency to go out in the car but, God, he was drunk. Adding more offences to the list against himself. The terror of not being able to trust himself or his memories feels like something physical clawing at his eyeballs. Was he in the woods again? He has a vague and drifting image of a black horse. Then he remembers—

The lamp. The blood. Jill.

His phone is next to him on the table, and he looks, bleary-eyed, at the notifications. Messages from Oliver telling him to call. Where is Alex, he wonders. Could he have gone to the police? Perhaps he found out, somehow, what Chris did to Jill. He shivers at the thought, and stands, wobbles. He needs air, so he opens the kitchen window, then walks up the stairs to shower and change into fresh clothes. He needs to start thinking rationally.

It's when he's peeling off his mud-sodden jeans that he sees it fall to the floor – the note with the URL he pocketed before Joseph and Karen came over, before he realized that the lamp . . . He swallows. The lamp.

Standing in his T-shirt and boxer shorts, with the smell of the outside on him and all around him, he picks up his phone again and puts the URL into the search engine.

To his confusion, he sees that it's a video file labelled '12 October 2005'.

The day Sophia died.

With rising dread, Chris clicks into it and it starts to play. It's blurred and badly focused, but he can make out that whoever is taking the video is walking towards a building. It's a familiar house. It's the council house in Derby. And there is a man walking into view, going to the door, unlocking it, and he knows this man.

He recognizes himself.

He drops the phone in shock. This can only have come from Alex, which means that he knew from the very beginning Chris was lying about being there that night. Alex knew Chris lied at the inquest, and this video is the evidence.

He needs to call Oliver. Dizzily, he picks up the phone from the floor. It's already ringing.

'Oli—'

'Don't go *anywhere*.'

Chris can hear that Oliver is on speaker phone, realizes that he must be in the car.

'There's a video – Alex has . . . I think it's a threat.'

'A threat? Are you joking? It's no longer a *threat*, it's a bomb that's already exploded.'

'What do you mean?'

'The fucking *world* has seen it. It's on the news, and now everyone knows. That you were there, and that we've lied.'

We, Alex and I, thought long and hard about our strategy, and what it would take to blow this all up. We decided not to reveal the video earlier because we wanted to see what the inquest kicked up. What lies they would spin. The date on the footage that Sophia recorded on her phone was 12 October 2005, the day she died. The image is blurred – the technology then wasn't what it is now – but it's undoubtedly Chris Fletcher outside the council house. Sophia sent this image at just before nine in the evening, to the email address she'd set up to record all the documents. The phone she sent it from wasn't on the list of her personal belongings when she was found, and when we asked what had happened to it we were told it wasn't there. We assumed it had been lost, or that Sophia had thrown it away because she was not in sound mind. We presumed that after she took this video and sent it to herself she went into the house to confront Chris. I hope this is evidence enough to prove to the coroner not only that Chris Fletcher needs to go on trial before a criminal court but also that the police need to look at their own moral compass when it comes to protecting rogue officers. Did they know he was there? What happened between him and my sister? It's my strong suspicion that they had an altercation, but then what? She ended her life? Perhaps it was more sinister than that.

    – Leila Roy, interview with Megan Kim, *Guardian*, 2025

Here is the link to my blog and to ALL of Sophia's documents that show the tireless effort she went to to find out who Chris Fletcher was – buff.ly/3GTbd #sophiaroy #justiceforsophia #chrisfletcher #lies
— @LeilaRoyPR, X

Have you seen the footage?? All the DOCUMENTATION Sophia Roy had collected??
— @theitheitheithei, X

WTAF!
— @Frankiegoestobollywood, X

@LeilaRoyPR, you knew they'd lie! You knew they would cover their arses! YOU DID IT! #sophiaroy #justicefor sophia #chrisfletcher #christopherfletcher #nowhere tohide
— @MMOP, X

What if the police needed to cover themselves in that inquest?
— @Mickeyblueeyes, X

Oh, it's a dirty world.
— @shadowman, X

46

Chris answers the door to Oliver and, on seeing his handler's ashen face, he starts to laugh. Manically, hysterically, because he's slipped somewhere beyond reality, where nothing really matters. He hasn't got Jill, hasn't got Sophia. He has lost any chance of a relationship with Alex. He has removed himself from the crushing anxiety of the repercussions ahead.

Oliver slaps him round the face. 'You think this is fucking *funny*, Chris? Everyone has lied for you.'

He barges into the house. 'Where's the aunt?'

'Gone.'

Oliver slams shut the door, turns to face Chris. His face is the colour of plum.

'I didn't know they had the footage, Oli.'

'No shit. It must have been Leila Roy's plan the whole time to wait for the verdict and then counter it. She's in PR, for God's sake.'

His eyes scan the room, come to rest on the bottle of whisky.

'Is there any of that left?'

'No.'

'Fuck's sake.'

Jackson trots over, goes to sniff at Oliver, but Oliver bats the dog away and sits heavily.

'Christ on a bike. My emails are *alight*.'

'I deserve it, don't I? I deserve everything coming to me.'

'Has there been any news about Jill?'

'Nothing.'

'Your life, Chris. Jesus. I don't envy you.'

Chris whistles to Jackson and gently pats his lap. The Dane walks over, puts his head on Chris's knee.

'You know what's going to have to happen, don't you? Listen to me. This is important.'

'I know what you're going to say, Oli. You're going to say that you'll have to hang me out to dry.'

'Leila Roy has hung us *all* out to dry, Chris! Even if people realize that you were part of a bigger operation, the fact remains that we all lied about what really happened to Sophia. Every single person on that operation was sworn to the version of the truth you gave in that inquest. It was about saving your skin, and others involved in the wider operation.'

'Maybe I shouldn't have been saved. My selfishness is what got Sophia killed.'

Oliver tuts. 'You're guilty of falling in love when you shouldn't have and jeopardizing not only your deployment but the entire unit's. But *we're* guilty of not covering your back properly. Hell, I suppose I agree with Leila Roy there. The whole thing was imperfect, obviously. But that's what we do in this department, Chris. We *lie*.' He sighs. 'You weren't to know that Sophia would come looking for you. None of us ever imagined she would. It blew the whole thing apart.'

Chris stares out of the window, at the verdant greenery outside. What good is the real truth anyway? What good is the truth when no one wants to understand all the complex layers of it? He is a puppet on a string, and always has been.

'What do you need me to do?'

'We need you to put out a statement. That you were there in Derby – I'll work out the details of why and how the fuck she found you – that she confronted you and you told her you weren't interested in pursuing the relationship. Then you left her and returned to Southampton for your deployment – we can't drag Mike into the courts for agreeing to lie for us. From there, it'll be the obvious jump that Sophia was so upset she topped herself.'

'That's not what happened though,' Chris says quietly.

'No. But it's going to be the new version of the truth. OK? The establishment can't be the bad guys here, you understand? The media don't need another reason to blame the police for everything wrong in the world. We all go into the police to be the good guys, but it's not fucking Hollywood, is it? We're all human. We make mistakes.'

Oliver stands.

'We'll work on the statement together, OK? ASAP. In the meantime, stay put while I deal with all the other shit. You talk to no one until I come back, understood?'

47

12 October 2005

It rained all day, a steady downpour of fat, cold droplets, and there was a gusting wind that rattled the roof tiles of the house. Some of the outside bins had overturned in the street, and litter was washing in a dirty stream down towards the guttering, swirling with dead leaves.

Chris sat in the damp kitchen, his hoodie soaked from the rain and his trainers squelching on the grubby linoleum flooring as he moved his knees up and down with nerves. It was just past nine in the evening and he was waiting for the other members of Dawn to arrive. This was the night they were meeting to plan a jump on their target – a local MP who was sympathetic to refugees and wanted to expand job opportunities for people from minority backgrounds.

Over the last six months, Chris has encouraged meetings in a building away from their own houses and any prying eyes. The building was on the quieter and rougher side of the town, a known squatters' house, and totally secluded. But, unbeknown to the others, it had been commandeered by the police two years before and now it was serving as part of the operation. It was not wired because the risks were too great, and nor was Chris, but on that night there was a surveillance team in a van a hundred yards down the road to take pictures of who came in, and on the road parallel there were two unmarked police cars.

Chris had planned this meeting meticulously, had thought of every detail.

Except her.

When there was a knock on the door Chris assumed it would be a member of Dawn, even though he knew most of them would be coming past ten because the football was on. But when he opened it, it wasn't one of them but Sophia, standing there like a mirage, with a tiny child on her hip – dark-haired, with large hazel eyes. A boy. His son. He should have slammed the door shut in her face, should have shouted at her and scared her away, but he was so shocked at seeing them that she took his moment of hesitation and pushed the buggy past him, over his feet, and into the house.

He went to grab her, missed, grabbed air. Without a word, she walked the small, narrow corridor and turned the pushchair into the disgusting kitchen. He ran to follow.

'What the fuck is this?' she breathed, standing in the doorframe and staring around.

'Sophia—'

She thrust Alex at him. 'Do you know this is your son?'

He took hold of her arm, gripped it hard. 'Get *out*,' he said in a low growl.

Her eyes blazed. 'No way. You'll meet your son properly. His name is *Alex*. Had you forgotten that was the name we chose?'

She was speaking with such a loud voice, and it was clanging around the empty, grotty house. He started to drag her then, out of the kitchen and back into the corridor. Leave the buggy, he thought, heart banging, just throw them out of the house.

'Get off me! What are you *doing*?'

She twisted and flailed. Alex started to cry.

'You *lied* to me!' she cried. 'All this time! A false name and a false address? What—'

'Shut up!' he hissed. 'Shut the *fuck* up!'

'You're hurting me, Chris! Oh my God, you're *hurting* me!'

He looked to the back room, quiet, with the door partially closed, and then looked back at her with frightened eyes.

'Fucking *stop*.'

He gripped her arm so tightly she looked at him with real, animal fear, and then she opened her mouth to scream. Before she did, he clamped it with his dirty hand. But she bit down then, hard, on the soft flesh beneath his thumb. It took all the fibres of his being not to cry out. He started to push her out of the kitchen, Alex wobbling in her arms.

'Stop it!' she screamed. 'What are you doing!'

'Sophia,' he whispered, but she was not hearing him. 'There are people here—'

And then, a sound. Someone had emerged from the back room behind them and spoke the words no undercover officer ever wanted to hear.

'You're a copper.'

He turned, and there stood Damian Roper.

'What the fuck, mate?' Chris laughed. 'You can piss off with calling me that scum—'

'You're a fucking copper.'

Chris positioned himself between Sophia and Alex, them in the kitchen and Damian in the corridor.

'This skank is high,' he said. 'She doesn't know what she's saying—'

'I think she knows *exactly* what she's saying.'

Behind Damian, Malcolm Roper, the two of them now in the corridor and blocking any escape through the front door. Why weren't the surveillance team here, hammering down the door? They couldn't possibly know who Sophia was, he realized, so would be running checks. How long until they came? *Would* they come, or not want to jeopardize the entire set-up?

'Chris,' Sophia whispered from behind him. 'Oh God.'

He knew then that she'd realized what she'd done, what danger they were all in. His two worlds had collided. Fear wound itself, oil-like, around his throat.

'This place is being watched, is it?' Damian said. 'Fucking son of a *bitch*.'

'We need to get out of here,' Malcolm said, his hand on Damian's arm. He was high, Chris noticed, on something stronger than weed. His pupils were enormous, like pools of black water.

'Not fucking yet.'

The malice, the determination to stay, triggered Chris to shout.

'Get out, Soph!'

She made to bolt towards the kitchen window, holding Alex to her chest, but Damian stepped around to grab at her. At the same time, Malcolm jumped Chris and took him down to the floor at such an angle and with such force that Chris felt a rib pop and a deflating in his chest. An intense pain followed, and he gulped at air like a fish taken from water. Beneath Malcolm's weight, he jerked his head round to see if Sophia had made it to the back room, but with horror saw that Damian had his fist in her hair and was snapping her backwards. She dropped Alex as she fell and they both landed with a smack on the floor. Alex started to howl, blood pouring from his nose. Chris twisted himself, caught Malcolm awkwardly on the ear. Malcolm hit back, spitting on him and ramming Chris's face into the floor. The metal tang of blood gushed from Chris's lips.

'Alex!' Sophia screamed, now held up by one arm like a string puppet.

'Bitch, whore,' Damian hissed, and started to drag her into the back room.

Alex's howls were like knives in Chris's ears. He started to inch his way across the floor, clawing with his fingers to reach them, his *family*. Every breath was a fight. His vision began to swim.

'What are you doing, Daim?' Malcolm yelled on top of him. 'Come on!'

Chris lifted his eyes and saw that Damian was holding a needle. And then his vision went out.

There was a dull thundering sound in Chris's ears. He opened his eyes and found himself still on the floor. Everything was coloured in purplish hues. He realized he'd been out cold, but for how long? Minutes? Seconds? He could make out voices. Malcolm Roper was on the other side of the room, face down on the grotty floor, people on his back who Chris then realized were officers. Thank God. Thank God they had come. He turned his head to see three next to Sophia, who was on the floor, Alex crying by her side. He could hear the urgency in the rise and fall of voices even though he couldn't hear the words – the throbbing of his own pulse and Alex's ragged wailing drowned them out.

'Sophia?' he whispered. It hurt to speak, to breathe.

'Someone attend to Chris,' a voice said. 'He's come round.'

'I told you to get him in a car, for Christ's sake.' It was a familiar voice.

Oliver knelt beside him.

'You've gone blue, we think you might have a punctured lung.'

'Sophia came – I didn't . . . I didn't know she was . . . What's going on?'

Malcolm shouted out then, and someone talked back sharply.

Oliver moved around to help Chris up to sitting, positioning himself like a shield in front of his eyes. 'We'll get you out of here, lad, that's it. We've got to move fast.'

Chris craned his neck to look round. 'Oli, what's . . . Is Alex OK? Is he OK?'

'Can you stand? We should go.'

And then Chris saw what Oliver was trying to protect him from – a needle sticking out of Sophia's arm.

'What's that?'

'We're dealing with it.'

'She's all white, Oli . . .' Chris panted. 'Why does she look like that? Why isn't she moving?'

'Don't look,' Oliver said. 'OK? Don't look.'

'What's he done to her? What's he done?'

'Up you get, come on.'

'Alex—' Chris reached uselessly for his son, but the boy was hysterical next to Sophia, blood smeared across his face.

'Come to me,' Chris whispered.

Alex couldn't have heard, but at that moment he looked over. Their eyes locked, the first time they had looked at each other in Alex's short life. Electricity ran through Chris's body.

'To me,' he breathed.

'Here,' Oliver said. 'Chris, we need to go.' He looked over his shoulder. 'Take the boy away.'

A woman picked Alex up, and Chris could only watch as the boy's face crumpled into more sobs, little fists curled.

'Please,' Chris wept quietly. 'Give him to me. He's mine, my boy.'

But no one was listening. Conversations were had, decisions made, all above his head. The woman walked out of the room, walked his boy out.

Oliver took Chris's forearm, pulled him up, and held him tightly. 'Can you walk?'

'Yeah – I – wait, fuck, that hurts, Oli.'

'We'll get you straightened out.'

'Are we going with them?'

'We're going to a car, OK? We'll go together.'

'But Sophia—'

'Please. You need to come with me.' Oliver was now steering him down the corridor. 'Emily will get Alex back home.'

Chris tried to pull away. 'Who's Emily? I have to be with Alex. With Sophia.'

Oliver dragged him back by his shirt. 'Listen to me, Chris. Your son doesn't know you. And he can't know you. Ever. Do you understand what's happened here? Sophia exposed you. Damian went out the back window.'

'What?'

'Malcolm is going straight to the station with our lot. He'll be denied access to anyone but a lawyer because we can't have him spreading news about you. But we didn't get Damian, and until we catch him, you're in danger. He's going to tell all the other members of Dawn about you, and that places a mark on your head, do you understand? You need to disappear.'

'Is Sophia going to be OK?'

Oliver paused, put his hand to the back of Chris's head and drew him into an embrace. Tender, private. 'I don't think so, son,' he whispered. 'I don't think so. I'm so sorry.'

Chris slumped against him.

'It's done now,' Oliver said. 'OK? You don't need to see this. We need to go. It's for the best.'

What's that buzzword everyone's falling over themselves for now? *Well-being*. Therapy wasn't a thing when I was undercover.

– James Pearson, former SDS officer, BBC True Crime
Drama: *Into the Dark*, 2025

Before he left the unit in 2005, Christopher Fletcher declined a psychological debrief.

– Oliver Hamilton, SDS officer, BBC True Crime
Drama: *Into the Dark*, 2025

Declined it? He didn't have time for it. He had to fucking go. Leave the country. Him and Jill, they had to disappear.

– [Name redacted], former SDS officer, BBC True
Crime Drama: *Into the Dark*, 2025

When you've been in that sort of role – the undercover roles where you're scared for your life most days – you get fucked up. You barely sleep, and when you do, you have bad fucking dreams. But at the same time, you love it because it keeps you totally in the present, everything happens in slow motion. Every day, you're thankful to be alive. But when you come out of that deployment, it's like you don't know what's real any more. You're always looking over your shoulder. Once a copper, always a copper. Always looking for odd behaviour. Always waiting

for things to kick off. A permanent state of fight or flight.
  – Anthony Stewart, former SDS officer, BBC True
  Crime Drama: *Into the Dark*, 2025

At one point on the job, I had the thought that my life
could be properly over. Three blokes in a gang I was infiltrating found me out. They broke two ribs, my arm and my
nose, and they were going to tip me into a fucking dump-
ster. I was hanging, half over the lip of it, when my unit
got to me. I was offered counselling but said no because I
thought I'd be marked out as a wuss and wouldn't be sent
on any more operations. That's the culture, or it certainly
was when I was in the unit.
  – [Name redacted], former SDS officer, BBC True
  Crime Drama: *Into the Dark*, 2025

People think that sort of thing only happens in films, but it's
not true. There are people out there, risking their lives for you.
  – [Name redacted], former MI5 agent, BBC True Crime
  Drama: *Into the Dark*, 2025

Chris didn't come back to the UK for his parents' funerals.
For his dad's, I sent him pictures, you know, of the family
and everyone who came. He FaceTimed me afterwards,
and he cried. I'd never seen him cry. He said he'd wanted
to fly back but he couldn't, and he didn't say why, but I
guessed it was because of work.
  – Guy Fletcher, Christopher Fletcher's cousin, interview
  with Sadie Clarke, *Under the Cover*, 2025

You don't want snowflakes in the police anyway.
  – @RaquelNorth, X

48

Chris is downstairs in the tiny cottage, sitting on the sofa in the darkness, Jackson lying heavily against him. Now and then, the air is punctuated by Jackson's dreaming woofs, or his smells, but Chris doesn't say a word, and doesn't move. Oliver didn't return as he said he would, but sent a curt message:

Trying to sort it. Don't you dare go anywhere.

Chris drifts in and out of sleep, the nightmare of the situation he now finds himself in pulsing with every tick of the clock on the wall, and with every heartbeat. Jill is dead. Sophia is dead. They are all gone.

He tries to marry himself now with the person he'd been before that night in October 2005. Who was that man in the SDS who was cocksure and arrogant and surefooted under extreme pressure? He's definitely not that man any more. Did he even have the chance to know who he really was before he moulded himself into different people?

It doesn't matter who he was then, though, because he is soon to be a nobody.

Oliver came back, they worked on a statement, and then Oliver disappeared again on the promise of coming back the following morning. Chris will take the fall and the police will issue a statement, and in return Chris will escape elsewhere with a new name, a new identity, because his real name and reputation are now tarred beyond measure. If he wasn't so exhausted, so sad, he'd be furious that he wasn't allowed to fight back. The footage is damning evidence, but it's not the truth.

He reaches for his phone and dials a number.

It takes a while for his call to be answered and, when it is, the voice at the other end is deep with disturbed sleep. Chris realizes the time – it's one in the morning.

'Hello?'

'Harris, it's me. Chris.'

There's a beat of silence. 'Chris, I don't know what to say.'

'No one does. But it's true. I was there.'

'Right.'

'I didn't kill Sophia.'

'OK.'

'I did *not* kill her.'

'So why did you lie?'

'Because there was a bigger picture . . . There's always a bigger picture.'

Harris is mute.

'I took the lamp, Harris.'

There's a pause. 'The what?'

'Meredith's lamp. The horse-head lamp from Smoke House. The police said you'd told them it was missing. I don't know why, but I packed it in my rucksack.'

'Why are you telling me about a lamp?'

'I took it because she loved it. Jill did. And I was . . . I don't know. I didn't want to leave Smoke House, Harris. I didn't want to leave the memory of her there, so I took it with me. She used to write with it on. Always. And I . . . I wanted it with me. I thought that if I put it somewhere, I'd come down one morning and she'd be there with it on beside her. Writing again.'

And that's what he *had* thought, before he'd seen the blood. Now he knows otherwise.

'Perhaps you need to be talking about this to Meredith—'

'I know you're worried too, Harris. About Jill.'

'Aye. I am.'

'I don't know if I can . . .' He doesn't finish his sentence, moves to another instead. 'Did she say anything to you? At any point?'

'No.'

Chris thinks, then, of the shape of a heart, drawn with a finger in a grubby window, and frowns, trying to remember where he saw that image.

'What do you think, Harris? What do you think happened to her?'

He hears Harris sigh deeply. 'I think she drowned, Chris.'

Maybe she did drown, or maybe this call to Harris, telling him he took the lamp, is Chris's admission of guilt that he killed her. Suddenly a thread of a memory of where he'd been the previous night and why his clothes were dirty weaves itself into his head. He went somewhere in the woods, and he'd taken the lamp and he'd buried it. Jill had loved it, and this was his offering to her because he had cut her into pieces and put her body somewhere. He doesn't know where, only that he's done it.

Chris hangs up without a goodbye.

He goes to the kitchen, stands there in the silence. On the table is the wooden heart he never got to give to her.

49

It's raining, and the noise of it on the windscreen is like a thousand drumbeats. It's three in the morning and Chris has driven to the turning to High Mount Lane. On foot he will walk up the track to End Stone, but he wants to leave the car somewhere that someone will find it when dawn comes. He needs someone to find Jackson, who, right now, he is holding on to for dear life – it's the end of the road for the two of them, but only one of them knows it.

'You'll be OK, my friend,' he says quietly, and he lets go of the dog's huge head and moves to slash open a food bag.

Jackson looks delighted.

'They won't let me take you wherever it is they want to send me. It's for the best.'

Chris gets out of the car and puts a hand to the glass of the door. Jackson is already hoovering up the food, his tail rhythmically thumping away, and doesn't notice him. Perhaps this is also for the best – no long goodbyes. Chris has left a window partially open, and a bowl of water, and a blanket, but Jackson won't be alone for long.

He doesn't know why exactly he has come here, but something about the building jars him. He starts up the track, slow and zig-zagging, only realizing halfway up that he's not wearing a coat, just a T-shirt and jeans. No trainers either – how did he drive without his shoes? The track is muddy and soft, but there is a wind, and his body suddenly registers the swirl of cold, and of potential danger.

His mind, however, is lazy because an hour before he left, Chris took a handful of pills, enough to be sleepy but not comatose. Enough to get here. His phone is slowly running out of battery, its light is trying its best.

Like me, he thinks. Running out of time. I tried my best, too, but I fucked it all up.

He's lied all his life – to the court, to his loved ones and to himself, and now he's in an impossible situation. He doesn't know or understand himself any more, doesn't know how to navigate the world around him. He has done something evil, he is sure of it, added to an already long list of awful things. If Jill is dead, by his own hand, he doesn't want to carry on. Doesn't deserve to live.

But why has he come here to End Stone, when he could just walk into the water? Isn't that what Jill had wanted for his end?

You would fall asleep, and I would drag your heavy, naked body out to the loch and fill your mouth with stones until it was all you were made up of – dark, slick, smooth stones clicking together as I pulled you into the water. And then I'd watch as you sank down into the depths. Into the blackness. Into nothing.

He could almost laugh, but he's too tired and full of sorrow. Regret, too. Yes, there is so much regret.

He reaches the front door of the house, breathless and dizzy, and takes a moment to steady himself against it. There is police tape across new boards that have been put over the windows – *Do Not Enter* – but he has brought a large sharp knife in the pocket of his jeans and can easily slash through the chipboard. Perhaps it is the same knife he used to murder Jill. He gulps down bile that has immediately flooded his mouth.

He starts to hack the board apart, but it takes him longer

than it should because his mind and body are slowed by sleeping pills and coldness. Eventually he manages to prise the board open enough so that he can climb inside and then he half jumps, half falls in. His phone clatters to the ground, lands face down, and he is engulfed by a thicker darkness. Shadows move. He starts to panic.

He grabs the phone and stands up, wobbles on his feet, shines the light around. No one is here, but he stays still for a moment in the living room, just to be sure. He listens to himself breathing.

He walks through to the hallway and goes upstairs. He didn't go up when they were here last because Joseph and Harris had taken the top floor, but he wants to see it. A noise sounds as he treads the boards and quickens his heart, but it is only the soft exhale of the rotting staircase underfoot – there is nothing alive here except for him and the nature that has encroached from the outside. Nature always makes its way.

To his left is a small bedroom, and to his right a dirty rusted bath and toilet. He walks on and then picks his way over the flooring of the main bedroom, which looks to have once been a plush carpet but is now blooming with mushrooms. There is a broken bedframe by a wall and a stained double mattress which has been pulled to the window. A gust of wind hits Chris's face and he realizes that all the windows are broken.

He frowns. But there were hearts in those windows, he thinks. This is the bedroom that overlooks the front of the house. Broken hearts. Broken promises. He recalls Harris looking up at this window when they left.

Where are the hearts? Who had they belonged to? Are they why he has come?

He turns out of the room and ascends a second set of stairs. They are more precarious than the first, sodden and moving beneath his dirty feet. Rusted nails poke up like spears and he is careful to avoid them. It is an attic room, but the roof is partially caved and has taken out half the brick work on one side. The elements have destroyed anything that might have been kept up here. Cardboard boxes have all but melted away, old clothes like puddles.

Cautiously, he walks towards the side of the house that almost does not exist. Below is pitch-black, an empty void. Above are the stars. He leans and turns his head to stare up into the sky and thinks that the world is so beautiful and also so awful. Is he still a good person even though he has done bad things? How many bad actions tip you into being a bad person?

His phone dies. The light goes out.

He swivels again, stands upright and stares ahead. From up here he can see down to the harbour and its two rows of small boats. A couple of larger fishing vessels. The Black Horse sleeps behind it. Beyond are the houses of the village. He can see too, some way across the valley, a lone building near the shore. There is a light on in The Old Smoke House. Perhaps Meredith doesn't like sleeping in the pitch-dark. Perhaps she is looking for her horse lamp. He doesn't know where he buried it. He doesn't know where he buried Jill, but he can't have buried her here because he didn't know about it then, and besides, the police have come out since then. Dogs have come.

The image of a black horse suddenly returns to his mind. The sign on Harris's pub. Had Chris driven, blind drunk the previous night, to The Black Horse to talk to Harris? He can't remember speaking to him, but perhaps he hadn't even knocked? Had Chris buried the lamp there, somewhere in the pub garden, in order to blame Harris for Jill's murder? Had he buried Jill there, too? His mind whirs.

Harris, the best friend. The better man. Broken hearts. Jill's broken heart. Why hadn't Harris told him about End Stone when Jill first disappeared? Kate McGowan died here. Is Jill here, somehow? Too many racing thoughts.

He leans forward, catches himself on the remaining brickwork, but it's soft and he steps back again. And then, in the corner of his eye, he sees a dense black shadow of a person creeping up behind him.

A pale face in the gloom. Pointed incisors like wolf's teeth. He is here, finally. Roper has come for him at last.

'I knew you would find me,' Chris says. 'But it's too late now. They've all gone.'

He steps forward and out into nothing.

THERE IS ACTION HERE!
  – @AnonRC, X

I read this morning that #christopherfletcher tried to throw himself from the roof of a building. He's guilty of murder. FOR SURE. #justiceforjillian #sophiaroy
  – @Frankiegoestobollywood, X

But get this. His SON pulled him back.
  – @AnonRC, X

OMGGGGGG Why though?? Alex doesn't believe Chris killed his mother?! #jillianmoore #sophiaroy #alexroy #hero #policespies
  – @SalleeeeA, X

I don't know. It's all kicking off up here. The previous night I saw a truck going up at 2am to the same place and it was the local pub landlord up there! I'm sure there's something going on.
  – @AnonRC, X

Hang on, the pub landlord went there one night and then #christopherfletcher went there the next night??
  – @Outtahere, X

The night I went, the landlord threw a brick through one of the top windows. I freaked and left.
— @AnonRC, X

WHAA? What's going on?? What's in this place??
— @SalleeeeA, X

It's an old house called End Stone. The police have already searched it and found nothing.
— @AnonRC, X

But there are two sets of police in all of this. Good cop, bad cop. She's there, isn't she? #jillianmoore is dead in that house.
— @Happyfeet, X

Who's the landlord??
— @Outtahere, X

What hospital is Chris Fletcher at? @AnonRC see if you can get some more info!
— @shadowman, X

50

Chris wakes in a hospital bed. He's connected to wires, to machines, and they are bleeping – a little chorus of chirrups, singing that his body is OK and that he didn't manage to hurt himself.

He blinks, tries to push through the muddle of his brain. Images play out in front of his eyes – the darkness of an old building, his hands raking through shredded leaves to bury the lamp, of Damian Roper catching Sophia's hair, of the man who walked with handcuffs. Jill, on their wedding day.

The room is painted a bright white, which is supposed to give the reassurance of cleanliness, but the starkness burns his eyes. At least he's alone and not on a ward – Oliver must have sorted that for him – because there must be people outside, wild beasts hungry to bear witness to his undoing.

Damian.

'Chris?'

He turns his head, surprised at the voice, and a sharp pain shoots down his neck. Meredith is sitting in the corner of the room, looking fragile. Her hands are neatly folded in her lap.

'Why did you do that?' she asks.

He is silent, stares at the ceiling. She gets up, walks over to him.

'You complete *idiot.*' Her words are brusque, but her delivery is watery, upset. 'You wanted to end things? Really?'

'He was there,' Chris says.

'Yes, he saved you.'

'What?'

'Alex.'

He is stunned. His boy, his *son*?

'But . . . what happened to Damian?'

She frowns. 'Who's Damian?'

Chris shakes his head. 'I saw——'

He had seen Damian in the shadows. But if it had been Alex that had pulled him back from the rooftop, had Damian never been there at all? He is muddled, and so full of grief.

'How did Alex know I was out there?'

'A tag on the dog's collar! He said that you had gone to The Black Horse the previous night, with the dog in the car. Apparently, you stayed there for an hour.'

He remembers now. He went to The Black Horse to bury the lamp. Didn't he?

'And then you went back to Rosewood Cottage. But Alex thought you might do it again – he's been tracking your movements since you met him. Last night you went up to End Stone – the dog was asleep in the car at the bottom of the lane, and then Alex found you just . . . teetering at the top of that rotting place like a bloody madman about to jump! Bloody hellfire, Christopher! What were you *thinking*?'

'I don't know . . .'

'Well, you weren't thinking at all, were you? Because you were dosed up on all that nonsense from a bottle. You stupid man.' A tear falls from her eye. 'What would have happened if you'd fallen? What would have happened . . .' She stops talking, takes a moment to breathe. 'But you didn't, thank *God*. Because he got there and pulled you down.'

'I can't remember,' he says.

'Because you hit your head on a piece of wood that was jutting out,' she says. 'Knocked yourself clean out and scared the poor boy even more. He ran to the pub and got Lorna and Harris McGowan and they all drove you here to hospital.'

'Where's Alex?' he asks. 'Is he here?'

She hesitates. 'No. He came to the hospital, but now he – he's gone. I'm sorry. I don't know where.' She leans, picks up his hand. 'Christopher, this isn't the end for you, you hear me? There's something you have to know—'

But the warmth of her gesture, of her hand, is almost too much. He needs to talk to Joseph Locke, needs to explain what he's done – that he's killed Jill and cut her up into little pieces. That he's buried the lamp at The Black Horse.

'I can't live with knowing what I did,' he says.

'What do you mean?'

'I did—'

There's a soft knock at the door, and then it opens. In steps Harris.

'You're awake,' he says.

He draws up to Chris's bedside, his towering height and his dark eyes glaring down at Chris.

'There are a lot of journalists outside,' Harris says. 'And police.'

Chris shifts, his body prickling with an unexplainable cold fear as Harris leans in, so close that Chris can feel the heat from his breath.

'I know what happened to Jill.'

51

This is what happened to Jillian Moore.

Both Jill and Chris had slept, uneasily, until three in the morning, when he woke up and started talking to her. She was exhausted and didn't want to talk to him, but he was adamant – he wanted to make things right, he said, wanted to explain things to her. It was always about him.

'You believe me, don't you?' he asked. 'That I had nothing to do with what happened to Sophia?'

She could smell the whisky on his breath, despite him having brushed his teeth. Her whisky from Harris, which she would have shared with Chris, of course. But he hadn't asked, just taken, and that had angered her.

'You were in Southampton and your unit has evidence of it.'

'Yes.'

'But we left for Sardinia not even a week after she died.'

'That was a coincidence. Nothing more.'

'I hate this,' she said. 'I hate it all.'

'If I could take it back—'

'But you wouldn't,' she said. 'You wouldn't ever take it back because you loved that job. It meant everything to you. And you loved her, too. I don't believe that Sophia meant nothing. I don't believe that.'

She rolled back away from him, her heart hammering and her head full of fury. His *job*. Amanda had told her that Mike Emerson used the same line over and over. That the 'job' excused all behaviours. Maybe the men genuinely believed it. Maybe they thought it was all for the greater good because that way they could sign it all away and live the best life they could. Beads of sweat prickled her back, stuck her T-shirt to her skin. She read once that a person gets ill when they can't communicate a problem – they can't speak out so they get mouth ulcers, hold resentments until their stomach acid builds. She was sick in the heart, so would it stop beating one day, in a click of a finger?

She felt a cold breath of air between them as he rolled to the other side. Physical distance had always had a presence in their lives, but she had felt, with the bright, shiny, optimistic eyes of a young woman, that she and Chris would always be emotionally tethered together, even if by a single thread. It had severed now. The tapestry of their lives was frayed and unravelling with each passing day.

Chris fell back to sleep, but she didn't. Instead, she quietly took her phone out of the bedside drawer, took her dressing gown from the bathroom and went downstairs. She was angry at Chris, and angry at Sophia, who was dead, and she'd been so upset about the paint on the wall of the house and the photograph taken in The Black Horse that she needed to get all her feelings down in words before they strangled her. There was no way she was going to go back to sleep.

She took the horse-head lamp into the otherwise dark kitchen and sat in its spotlight writing line after line but messing them up because she was muddled. Trying to make sense of the predicament she now found herself in was impossible. Because she was angry, yes, but at the same time, she loved him. She berated herself for the awful poem she'd made up about drowning him, because what she had really wanted was for him to reach for her, to *talk* to her. She wanted their connection back, knew their biggest problem was that they'd stopped communicating at the very point they needed to voice their feelings the most. But how do you voice something so huge? How do you work out the right words to use? She should know, she told herself, she was a poet, and yet she was surprisingly ineloquent when it came to speaking her feelings aloud. Perhaps she should write to him instead. She ripped a page from her notebook, played around with some words that she could give him, and then she folded the paper in two and put it in her pocket. She stared out of the window, at the blackness beyond, and then at her own reflection in the glass from the bounce-back of light. Dark shadows under her eyes, her mouth turned down, her hair unbrushed.

It would only be another hour or so and the sun would be up and a new, horrible day would dawn. She thought briefly about messaging Amanda Connolly, who had been kind to reach out when the mess erupted from Caroline's article, but what good would it do to talk to Amanda now? She couldn't believe that she had almost gone to Amanda's rental that night. How stupid to let herself believe she could share her vulnerabilities when she couldn't tell anyone the whole truth – her own secrets needed to remain secret. Since that night, she had kept Amanda at arm's length, hadn't answered her calls.

But she picked up her phone now. She would text Harris, she thought. Who else, but him, could save her sanity?

Could we sail today before the storm comes in? Is it due tomorrow or later today?

She was surprised when the ticks turned blue as soon as she'd pressed send and the words 'Harris is typing' appeared.

What are you doing up?

I can't sleep.

I'm getting up in an hour to go out. The storm isn't due until late afternoon.

Can I come with you? I'm in desperate need of getting away from Chris.

He didn't write for a moment and then started typing again.

Come to the east side of the jetty. It's cold out. Wear something warm.

Her heart sparked. That's what she needed – a get-out, an escape for a while, and on a bigger boat, where she could be properly out on the sea. The dinghy wasn't strong enough for the tides, the north wind.

I'll make a flask, she wrote.

I've got biscuits, he replied.

She went to go upstairs but then stopped. The downstairs bathroom door was open and she noticed that it was still splattered with mud from Jackson's walks. Seething, she snatched up a cleaning rag and some spray from the cupboard beneath the kitchen sink and started cleaning.

'Prick,' she muttered aloud.

Afterwards, she went upstairs, quietly used the bathroom and splashed water on her face, brushed her teeth and hung her dressing gown on the back of the door. She crept past Chris and Jackson, both breathing deeply, then took her clothes from the wardrobe. She reached up and pulled out Chris's favourite hoodie, debated wearing it because she wanted to inhabit him, smell him – that peppery scent – wanted to taste him. But she didn't put his jumper on.

She changed in the snug, turning the horse-head lamp

on to dress. She thought briefly that if someone was outside, they'd see the light, because the snug faced the ridge, so she unplugged it and took it to the kitchen. While the kettle boiled, she dressed in thermals, with her waterproof trousers over the top and two sweatshirts.

The kettle started to hiss and she momentarily worried it would wake Chris or Jackson, or both. She didn't want to talk to him, didn't want to tell him where she was going. She stared out of the window, bit at her fingernails then told herself firmly to stop, because now they were bleeding and she would have to bind them again. She moved the horse lamp to open the drawers, looking for plasters.

Blood dripped down the base of the lamp. She didn't notice.

After securing plasters around her bleeding fingers, she returned to making tea. She wanted it the colour of a digestive biscuit and made it so, then put the flask in her rucksack, some tissues and the emergency first-aid bag she always carried: a packet of paracetamol, a gauze for dressing, sun cream, a spare pair of gloves, a pocket knife. She debated taking her notebook, but didn't.

She checked the time, then turned off the lamp, pulled on her boots and sailing jacket and opened the door to the early morning. The sky was dark and star-wild and the wind kissed her cheeks as she walked away from the house and over the ridge towards the village's tiny harbour. The sense of freedom was wonderful; no one out there watching her. No one at all.

She heard the harbour boats before she saw them – the chink of the metal sails in a slow wind, the creak of wood as the water gently rocked them. No one there. She walked to the end of the jetty and presently she heard a noise – a steady *put-put* along the water – then shortly after saw a light come towards her out of the dark.

She raised her hand in greeting but didn't know if Harris would see her.

'Can you jump on without me stopping?' he called as he neared her.

She nodded and leapt up as the boat approached. He caught her arm.

'Like a pro,' he said.

'Not my first rodeo.'

He smiled.

The boat smelt of the sea, of fish and netting, and metal and salt. To some, it would have been overpowering, but she loved it. The rawness of it.

'Let me set the course and we can have that tea.'

She followed him through the door to the cabin. Every bit of space inside was utilized; the cockpit at the front was messy, with two old computer monitors, a map and a radio, and bled into the galley: a length of yellow wooden countertop, a stainless-steel sink on one side and a bolted narrow table and benches on the other. On the table was a bottle of water, Harris's phone and an opened bag of broken biscuits.

'We always loved broken biscuits,' she said.

'We did, and still do.'

The floor was scuffed, dirty, dust balls gathered along the sides. On the walls were framed photographs with varying degrees of sun damage – some of Kate, and of Lorna. There were pictures too of fish, of crabs, of places the boat had sailed. Above them mugs hung on hooks, like tankards in a pub. The cabin was rough around the edges, but utterly charming in its honesty, and to her surprise, Jill found tears springing to her eyes.

This. This was what she wanted in her life. Here in this tiny space, she could see all of Harris – a simple man with a simple way of life. An *honest* life. For years, she realized now, she had been living with a stranger. Her husband had secrets from her – and she'd known his job had demanded he keep them – but he had gone beyond secret-keeping. He'd betrayed their vows. He'd had a girlfriend, and a *son*. Jill had wasted years with Chris – that's how she felt. She could have become a mother, or a wife to someone better. She should have taken the chance when she had it. He'd abused her love, had abused her trust. She blinked back the tears, really didn't want to start this trip as an emotional wreck.

'Tea then?' she asked.

'Aye.'

He reached up for two mugs and she poured the tea.

'Chuck me a biscuit,' he said, and she threw one high.

He caught it in his mouth.

'Like a pro,' she echoed.

'Not my first rodeo,' he grinned.

He went back to the cockpit, checked the screen. She watched him and wondered what it would have been like to have married Harris. She watched his fingers glide over the wood of the wheel, the lightest of touches. She wondered what he'd be like in bed and then laughed at herself. Why these thoughts? Why now? Had she always, on some level, been attracted to Harris, or was this her brain on overdrive, trying to claw back some sense of self, some identity unattached to the mess Chris was in? The mess that Chris *was*.

'What are we fishing for today?' she asked.

'We could get some real beauties up here. Thornback rays, coalfish, mackerel, pollack. We'll launch some weights with whole mackerel using some big old hooks and see what bites. You can help me with the hooks?'

'I want to be useful.'

'Do you feel useful back on shore?'

'No,' she said. 'I feel distinctly unuseful.'

'Is that a word?'

She laughed. 'No.'

'Thought you were a big-shot poet.'

'I'm a no one.'

'That's not true,' he said softly. 'How's it all going then? Chris said you could do with an ear.'

'Honestly? I feel like I'm watching my life fall apart in front of my eyes and I can't do anything about it. It's as if it's all happening on TV.'

'Aye. That's bad.'

She nodded. 'Yeah. It's bad.'

'I'm sorry it's happening to you, Jill. You don't deserve any of it.'

She opened her mouth to speak and then closed it again. He watched her, and then, when she didn't say anything, he spoke.

'In a bit, we'll go outside and watch the sunrise, and you can forget – for a while.'

'It's my favourite thing about being here. Nautical dawn. It's like magic.'

'It's thirty minutes to the mouth, so we'll be there when it comes up.'

They puttered across the loch, and she was energized by being on a boat that was not sailed by her, drinking tea and eating broken biscuits and staring into the promise of a new day. She unfolded the paper she'd ripped from the notebook, stared at it for a moment and carefully folded it up again.

'I love this boat,' she said after a while.

'You love it?' He sounded amused. 'It's dirty.'

'But it's real. Nothing fake. I'm surrounded by things that aren't real, Harris. I live in a version of the truth that isn't real. All my life there were all these mirrors that deflected the truth away.'

He was silent a moment, and then she laughed. 'Sorry. You don't want to be dealing with this.'

'Don't be sorry, Jillian—'

'I am. I've made you uncomfortable.'

'You never could. I'm struggling to find the right words for you, and it's because I'm not used to having someone tell me things like what you've told me. Lorna doesn't tell me what's going on in her life, or her feelings – she's got her friends for that. Since Kate died, my life has been about keeping everything afloat. Ordering meat, sorting rotas, sticking things in washing machines. I'm sorry you've had a hard time, Jillian, I am. Chris is navigating a path no one can follow him down. Not even you, and that's isolating for both of you.'

She nodded. 'That's it,' she said quietly. 'Exactly it. I feel like it's him and me against the world, except it's like we're on different planets, trying to shout to each other.'

'Sometimes silence is restorative.'

'But I've had too much silence. I wanted my life to be filled with noise – with kids.'

'Aye. I know you did,' he said gently.

'I was on my own when Chris was on deployment. Every day and every night in the silence. And now I'm in silence still.'

'Aye. And me, Jillian.'

She felt ashamed. 'Of course, Harris. I'm sorry. I know you miss Kate all the time.'

He shrugged. 'It's like a black hole that you have to step around.'

'I miss her so much too.'

His face changed then, crumpled slightly, as if in pain. 'There are folk here that still think I hurt her,' he said.

She went to him, put her hand on his arm. 'Stupid people, Harris. You know who your friends are.'

'Kate and I argued because of John Crossan,' he said.

She nodded slowly.

'Did you know about Kate and John?'

'Yes,' she whispered. 'I knew.'

'How long did you know?'

'About six months.'

She saw his jaw tighten. 'Why didn't you tell me?'

'I told her to tell you. And she did. Eventually.'

He scowled. 'Aye, eventually. You know how long it went on for? Three years.' He was quiet. 'They used to go to End Stone, Jill. Where we all used to go as kids. Can you imagine it? Like teenagers – they even drew hearts to each other on the windows.'

'Oh, Harris.'

'She told me, when we argued. She told me all the details. She wanted me angry, and she got it. I was raging. Livid.'

'I wish I'd been there for you.'

'When I came back from our fight, I wanted to go and find John Crossan, but I got caught up having to work the lunch shift, and then . . . you know the rest.'

'Kate slipped on that rock.'

'She went and slipped on that rock near End Stone.

Maybe she was even going to meet him and tell him that I knew. Whatever she was doing, I didn't even get to say that I loved her, that we could have worked things out, if that's what she wanted. Or got a divorce but been friends, you know? Or . . . I don't know. But she died, Jill. She went and died, and the last thing I said to her was that I hated both of them.'

'Harris, it wasn't your fault.'

'People think I pushed her, left her to die.'

'Those people are idiots. We all know what the coroner's report said. The time of death was at least an hour after you were back working in the pub.'

'But people don't believe it.'

'You can't change how people think, Harris.'

They were quiet.

'I don't think I've ever talked about it so much,' he said.

'You haven't.'

'But you understand.'

'Oh, I do.'

'The hearts are still there. At End Stone. On the bedroom windows.'

'Maybe you should throw a brick through them,' she said, and he laughed.

'Maybe I should one day.'

'Harris, you should. I'm not joking. Break the spell it's held over you all this time. Their affair wasn't your fault, and nor was Kate slipping.'

'Aye,' he said softly. 'But the pain of it, Jill . . . All the things left unsaid.'

'Don't I know it,' she said.

They sailed on. She refilled their mugs with the last of the tea. They talked about Lorna, about the ocean, about sailing.

'Here now,' he said quietly, after a while. 'Come outside.' She followed him to the prow of the boat, and there, she saw it. The dawn of a new day, unfurling in ribbons of gold and pink across the dark sky.

Her soul lifted. 'I feel like all my mistakes melt away in the face of beauty like this.'

'Aye.'

She turned to him then. 'Harris,' she breathed. 'I want to leave.'

He frowned. 'Leave?'

'I want to leave Chris. Now, today.'

'Why?'

'Why? Because I don't see how I can go back. I don't see how it can be the same – and it wasn't even the same when I thought it was. We've just been living a lie this whole time, and I can't do it. I want to leave him, but I . . . I don't know how.'

'Jill—'

'I thought I could make things better, you know? I even contacted his son. Yes! He has a son, Harris! Can you believe it?'

'Oh, Jill. I'm sorry.'

'His name is Alex. I wanted them to talk to each other, build a connection. I set up a secret email address, just in case Chris looked at my phone or something, and I told Alex to come up here and meet us. I sent him links to cottages, if you can believe my naivety. But I didn't hear anything back from him . . .' She looked at Harris. He was unmoving, watching her. 'I've got my rucksack and my jacket, and I . . . I don't want to go back. Do you understand? It's all unravelling, it's all . . . surrounding me like some sort of black fog, and I don't know

337

which way to go, but I can't stay there with him. Not any more. I've tried, I've tried to be there for him, but . . .' Her voice faded.

'Do you want to come back to the pub with me?'

'No. I mean . . . I would love nothing more than to be in that pub with you. Drink wine, forget it all. But I want to disappear. I want not to be found.'

'You can't do that to Chris, Jill. He's broken.'

'I'm broken!' she shouted suddenly, her voice cutting through the quiet. 'I'm broken! Did he ever think of me? Did he ever come close to admitting what he'd done all those years? That he'd led a double life? I have these horrible thoughts day in and day out, and I have to – I need to . . . I need to escape all this.'

'But you love him, Jill.'

'I do. But sometimes love can destroy us. Can't it? Sometimes love isn't enough.'

She collapsed into sobs, and he watched her, saying nothing, and put a hand to her shoulder.

She looked up at him. 'I did something terrible, Harris.'

52

Chris stares at Harris.

'You mean . . . she's alive? Jill is alive?'

'She was when I last saw her, aye.'

'I didn't hurt her?'

'What are you talking about, Christopher?' Meredith says. She looks at Harris. 'He's talking nonsense. It's the drugs they've given him.'

'I didn't physically hurt her?'

'I dropped her at Crag's Head. I gave her some food and some money I had on the boat. She didn't have a plan; she didn't have anything but the clothes on her back and her rucksack. I don't know where she is now.'

'But you went out with Murray Scott in that storm?'

'I bought her time.'

Chris is silenced, dumbstruck. She did it, then. She abandoned him. He had been unable to keep her, when she should have been the one piece of treasure he valued above all others. She slipped through his fingers like quicksand.

'I'm sorry, Chris.'

'Did you know, Meredith?'

'Not until an hour ago, when Harris told me.'

'Does anyone else know about this?'

'Only Lorna,' Harris says. 'Lorna was up early that morning – the morning Jill went. I told her I was picking up Jillian in the boat because – at that point – I had no reason to lie to her. I didn't know what Jillian would say. When I came back, I told her what happened, that Jill had decided to leave, and I swore her to secrecy. Because she was now complicit too. We were never going to say a word to anyone, and I'm only telling you now because . . . because . . .' He pauses. 'When that boy came knocking at whatever time it was in the morning today, when he woke me and Lorna up by shouting at our window and we followed him up to End Stone and saw you on the ground . . . that boy was sobbing, you understand? He was inconsolable, saying you were going to jump, and I knew you'd gone up there because of Jill . . . and I had to tell you that she'd left. That she wasn't dead. I couldn't have your death over my head. I needed to tell you what had really happened.'

'I don't know what to say, Harris.'

'I'm sorry for putting you through it. She was upset about everything. But there was one thing she said that I couldn't understand. She said that she'd done something terrible.'

Meredith's fingers go to the thin chain at her throat.

'And that's where I need to tell you what *I* know, Christopher,' she said in a whisper. 'What I should have told you before. Jillian had no idea Sophia Roy had died all those years ago. No idea, and it's important you know that. Sophia's death hadn't been reported in any of the papers because it had been ruled a suicide, and a week after she'd died, the two of you left for Sardinia. But when the article came out, Caroline's article, Jill called me right away. We googled relentlessly. We weren't sure if it was . . . Oh, but she was so upset, Chris. She kept saying it was her fault.'

Chris sits up, Meredith's words tangling in his head. 'Meredith, you're talking in riddles. Slow down.'

'The email that I sent to Jill. The picture I was trying to

tell you about. It's from the day of the reading, but . . . I saw them together, Chris, outside the bookshop, and I'm worried . . . I'm worried the police might find out . . .'

'Who did you see together?'

'Jillian and . . . and Sophia Roy.'

53

One last time, Jill thought. Remember the terrible thing one more time and then never again—

On 12 October 2005, on the threshold of the bookstore in Essex and on her way to meet Meredith for lunch, a young woman approached Jill, with a little boy in a pushchair. She must have been early twenties, pretty and dark-haired.

'Excuse me?' she said.

'Hello,' Jill said warmly, and smiled at her. 'Did you want a book signed?'

'I – no. But it was a lovely reading.'

'Thank you.' Jill looked down at Alex in the pushchair. 'Oh, what a cutie. Hi, darling.' She looked back at her. 'Are you a writer?'

'No – I'm – I'm studying. I was studying . . .' She faded out, switched direction. 'Can I talk to you for a minute?'

Jill glanced over the road, to the restaurant where Meredith had booked a table to celebrate the beginning of Jill's book tour.

'I'm meeting my aunt for lunch; I can't be long.'

'Please. I'd appreciate a few minutes of your time. Can we go somewhere private?'

Jill frowned. 'Private?'

'I know this will sound strange. And it might . . .' The young woman stopped again, looked over her shoulder into the bookshop, behind them. 'Perhaps we should step out of here a minute?'

Jill found herself walking, out of the shop, out into the street, the younger woman close by her side. There was something unsettling about her, a nervous energy. They turned the corner, stopped near the pedestrian crossing, where there was room for people to walk around them. Jill looked over at the restaurant, where she could see Meredith through the huge glass windows, tapping on her phone.

'What's this about?' Jill asked,

'Have you got a husband called Chris?'

This was not the question Jill had expected. Perhaps it had been the last thing she expected.

'I – yes?'

'Have you got a photograph of him?'

'What?' Jill laughed, but nothing felt funny. The conversation had turned, had taken on the colour grey, and felt glassy underfoot. 'Why would you want—'

'He's an undercover police officer. Isn't he?'

Jill stopped laughing. 'Who are you?'

'My name is Sophia and I was part of an environmentalist group called Green is Go. I believe that your husband, Chris, joined us and spied on us. He pretended to be one of us for eighteen months, and he and I . . . we . . . I thought . . . I didn't know he was married.'

Jill blinked Sophia in, her heart rate increasing. 'What?'

'We were together.'

At that moment, Sophia's eyes went to the pushchair, to the child inside it, and Jill looked down with her.

'Together?' Jill echoed, and then, suddenly, she understood. 'Oh God,' she whispered. 'Oh, fuck, no. Is your baby . . . No way. No, he wouldn't do that—'

'Have you got a photograph of him?' Sophia asked. 'I need to know if it's the same man. I've been looking for him for so long.'

'It's not going to be my Chris,' Jill said. 'He would never—'

'He told me he had an uncle in a care home,' Sophia said. 'He called him Robin, but now I know that it was your father, Robert. Chris went to clear the gardens. He said his uncle taught him how to whittle wooden hearts.'

A sob escaped Jill's mouth. 'Is this . . . is this a joke?'

'No. I'm sorry. Chris left me pregnant with our son. He disappeared without telling me why. I had no idea he was a police officer until recently.'

Jill fumbled with her bag to get out her phone, her hand shaking as she went to scroll through her pictures. Show her the picture and let her fuck off, she thought. Show her the picture and let it all be a mistake. She turned her screen around and Sophia gave a short cry of despair.

'Yes. Yes . . . it's him. That's Chris . . .'

Jillian's legs became fluid.

'I'm sorry,' the woman, Sophia, said. 'That's him. That's Chris Flynn.'

'That's not his name—'

'No. I know that now. It's Chris Fletcher.'

'I need . . . I should go . . . I . . . When did this happen?' Jill said. 'Your boy? When was he born?'

'Alex was born in February 2004. Chris left me late December 2003. He just – he disappeared.'

Jill almost laughed. All the pieces of the puzzle slotted together – why, in early 2004, Chris was at home when neither of them expected him to be, why he had been moody and anxious. Why he got another posting elsewhere a few months after.

344

'I'm sorry. I know this is . . . a shock.'

Sophia reached out, tried to make contact with Jill, but Jill snatched away her arm.

'I've been trying to find him,' Sophia said. 'I just want answers. I'm so sorry.'

A flash of the church where Jill had walked up the aisle towards Chris, and of him putting the ring on her finger, reading his vows. What had 'for ever' meant to him when he'd said those words? That *she'd* stick around for ever while *he* lived his life how he wanted?

Jill wanted to be sick, right there, on the pavement. She held her hand to her mouth, tried to regulate her breathing. Rani had rung her, had *told* her that she had seen Chris with a young woman in Notting Hill a couple of years ago, and Jill had simply laughed it off. In fact, she had been riled by Rani's suggestion that Chris could be anything but loyal, and Jill had cut her out. She had trusted Chris and believed in their marriage so completely, but here was evidence that it hadn't been true both ways.

'Can you tell me where he is?' Sophia asked.

Jill blinked. Was this girl still *here*? Hadn't she done enough?

'I have to go. I'm having lunch . . . my aunt.'

'Please, he's never seen his son.'

'I have to go.'

She started to walk, but Sophia rushed to walk with her. The wheels of the pushchair bit at Jill's heels.

'Please stop following me.'

'I need to see him.'

Jill stopped at the crossing, jabbed at the traffic light button. She could see Meredith, studying a menu. It felt like she was another dimension away, shimmering and unreal.

'Have you got a number for him?' Sophia asked.

'He's working. I can't contact him when he's working.'

The lights bleeped and Jill made to cross, but Sophia pulled at her arm. 'Please, listen. Chris had a son under a *police* guise. Don't I deserve to know the truth of how that happened? Why I was targeted and discarded like that?'

'I don't want to talk to you.'

'Our son was the product of a lie facilitated by the police.'

Jillian glanced down at the little boy. At that innocent and beautiful face.

'Fuck,' she whispered. She moved away from the crossing and started to tap on her phone. 'Chris is in Derby. I don't know what he's doing, but this address . . .' She paused. 'This address is a police safe house. I'm not supposed to know about it, but I saw a document when he came home a while back. He can be so careless with his . . . I saw the dates he was supposed to be in different places . . . and . . .'

Why was she telling this woman? What did she owe her? Angry tears rushed to her eyes. Sophia was nodding, her eyes on the screen.

'Thank you,' she whispered.

'If you go, you cannot go to the door, do you understand? You have to wait for him to come out, I don't know how long. I don't know if I should even be . . . but there. It's done. That's it. I . . . Oh my God, I have to go.'

'Thank you.'

Jill reached again for the button of the crossing and pressed it so hard that the tip of her finger turned white. 'I'm sorry you had to find out like this,' Sophia said. 'I'm sorry that—'

The lights were changing. Jill started to cross, but over her shoulder, she spoke.

'Tell him that our marriage is over.'

Moments later she sat down opposite Meredith, dazed. What had happened? Already it felt like a dream. She stared out of the window, thinking she might see the ghost of the girl and her pushchair, but there was just life. Ordinary people stepping around each other. Rain had started to spot the pavement – pathetic fallacy doing its thing for her.

'It was a lovely reading,' Meredith enthused, not noticing that Jill was suddenly, irreversibly, changed. 'Lots of people. And the local journalist was there – did you see? George what's-his-name. Took lots of pictures for the paper!'

Jill nodded, although she hadn't noticed any journalists. She thought maybe the whole thing hadn't even happened. That it had been someone else giving a reading. The Jill then and the Jill now were like two completely different people; severed, now existing in different worlds.

'So exciting, darling! It's all happening for you. After all your hard work.'

Jill looked down at the menu, but the words were blurring as her eyes teared. Her life was disintegrating, and there she was, at Prezzo with Meredith, who had ordered them a bottle of crisp white wine and some olives. Some fucking *olives*. The sting of Chris's betrayal was too fresh, too humiliating, for the niceties of olives and white wine. She told herself to get through the meal and then she could go home and collapse. And then what? She didn't know.

'I'm going to get a salad,' Meredith said, closing her menu. 'And chips.'

'OK.'

'What are you getting?'

To eat something – anything – was beyond her. 'The same,' she said.

'Who was that you were talking to outside?'

Jill looked up. 'What?'

'The young woman with the pushchair?'

'She needed . . . she needed directions.'

Meredith nodded. 'Ah.' She smiled and held out her glass. 'A toast,' she said. 'To your fantastic publication.'

'Jill?'

Harris was looking at her with concern, she knew it, but she continued to stare out at the glitter of dawn on the water. There was no hiding from the sun, or from lights being shone in the darkest corners where you hide your secrets. She'd been hiding hers for too long.

'Jill? What do you mean, you did something terrible?'

'Please help me,' she whispered.

'Is that really what you want? To leave?'

'I just need to be gone.'

'OK,' Harris said. 'I'll help you.'

Time was of the essence. They did not throw the nets out for the fish. Instead, they threw her phone into the water, each having deleted the conversation thread between them from that morning. If the police tracked the phone to its last location, it would be lost to the depths and people would assume she had drowned. Harris said that he would find a way to sink the Miracle when he returned.

'No, Harris,' she said. 'That boat is our childhood.'

'It needs to look like you've gone, Jill. The boat isn't as important to me as you are.'

She couldn't speak. He would destroy the boat, his father's boat, for her.

'Lorna saw me this morning,' he said. 'I said you were coming out with me. She might even have seen me pick you up, so I can't say you changed your mind. I'll need to tell her. OK?'

She bit her lip. 'That's a big lie for her to keep.'

'She can do it.'

'What about anyone else?'

'Cal Mellors went out twenty minutes before me this morning at the harbour,' he said. 'But he was going out east. No one else was sailing today. I know all their routines.'

He changed course from the mouth of the loch, and they sailed towards Crag's Head, an inlay a mile away from the village and obscured from view by the hills. There was no one to see them except the seabirds and Poseidon. Her heart was soaring and dipping with emotion. Harris was tight-lipped as they went.

'You'll have to go up the cliff and through the wood,' he said as they neared the rocks. 'Then across the moorland. Get to the shepherd's hut there, remember it? And wait out the storm.'

She nodded. They had gone to the hut only a few times as kids, but she remembered it – straight up on the ridge, a mile beyond the woods.

'The cliff is a tough climb,' he said.

'I'm a tough woman.'

'Is that really so?'

She smiled, but it wavered.

He knew her.

'Are you sure you want to do this?' he asked.

'Yes.'

'I can't get closer,' he said. 'Will you be able to jump down and make your way over?'

'Yeah.'

'You'll get wet.'

'It's OK. I'll get wet anyway in the storm.'

'Hang on,' he said. 'You should take another jumper—'

'No,' she said. 'I don't want to take anything of yours. I don't want to implicate you in any way.'

'Food then,' he said. 'And money. I always keep a bit here.'

Harris gave her the food he had on the boat – not much, some tins of beans, some bread rolls, some cheese. Then he took the lid from a battered tin from inside a cupboard, gave her a roll of money.

'There's just short of a few hundred here.'

'Harris—'

'Take it,' he said. 'Go on.'

She packed the food and the money into her bag.

'Where will you head to?' he asked.

'North. Try and barter passage towards Scandinavia.'

'Without a passport?'

'I don't know. I'll try and find a way.'

He was quiet a moment. 'If you want to get across the sea, you'll need to barter-board from Uig. I know a man – Archie Robertson – who's got a boat. I'll send him word in a few days to look out for you – it'll take you a day or so to cross the Highlands. I'll tell him you're Beth, yes?'

She smiled. Her middle name. 'OK. Yes.'

'Maybe he'll know who you really are by then, but chances are he won't. He's not got time for "mainland nonsense", as he calls it.'

'Thank you,' she whispered. 'I don't know what to say.'

'Say I'll see you again.'

She looked at him, saw the boy she'd grown up with.

'You know I adore you, Harris McGowan.'

'And you're my closest friend, Jillian Moore. You always have been.'

They stepped forward at the same time and embraced for a few short seconds. He held her so tightly that she almost changed her mind. He smelt of the memories of better days.

He sighed when he released her. 'Chris will suffer, Jill. I know you might want him to now, but . . .'

She swung the rucksack on to her back. 'I'll contact him. And Meredith. A few years down the line. I don't know.' She dug into the pocket of her jeans. 'Can you give Chris this?'

Harris looked down to her hand. A single page, folded over.

'Give it to him when it's safe,' she requested. 'When the time is right.'

'When is the right time?'

'You'll know.'

He nodded, took it, then offered his hand and helped her to stand on the lip of the boat. She jumped down on to the grey rocks and the waves crested them white. They would flood violently when the storm hit.

'OK then,' he said after a while, as she stood there.

'OK then,' she said.

He steered the boat back around. No goodbyes. The waves lapped over her boots, and she watched him go. He raised one hand and kept the other on the wheel, and she saw that his face was contorted by an emotion that was indescribable, and only knowable in the feeling – something like desolation, like purity of love. Soon he was nothing but a lone figure on a toy ship.

Her heart stumbled. A jumble of emotions: anxiety, regret, hope.

She remembered then with shock that she hadn't deleted the picture Meredith had sent her from her emails. She laughed at herself all the way up the moor.

54

Chris sits up. 'Show me the picture.'

'I deleted it,' Meredith says. 'Remember? I was worried . . .'

'Tell me about it then. Every detail.'

'It was of Jill at One More Story in Saffron Walden, in Essex,' Meredith whispers. 'The local journalist took it, and it's of her speaking with the audience in front of her. I keep everything of hers, you know? All the articles and press releases of her publications and things. I started doing it when Robert got unwell and went into the care home so I could show him. In the photo, in the audience . . . well, no . . . at the back . . .'

'It was Sophia?'

'No. But the buggy is pictured.'

'Alex is in it?'

'It's only the buggy. It's off at the side, towards the back, but it's there – you can see a bit of it in the picture. She was *there*.'

He's confused, like she's throwing arrows of information and he can't catch them. 'How can you be sure it was Sophia from that?'

'Because I *saw* her and Jill together, Christopher! They talked on the street after the event. I saw them from the restaurant window while I was waiting for Jill to meet me for lunch. I had wanted to secure a table while she finished up signing and talking to people.'

'Tell me exactly what you saw.'

'I was writing notes on my Blackberry so I wasn't watching them the whole time, but they talked for a good few minutes.'

'You're absolutely sure it was Sophia? Jill told you her name?'

'No. But I asked her who the girl was when Jill sat down. I thought she might be a fan. Only . . . Jill looked agitated. A bit . . . I don't know. Strange. She said the girl asked her for directions.'

Directions.

'And then that same girl got on the train to Derby. I know now because of all the pictures of her that have come out. It was Sophia Roy. I didn't know Alex was your *son* though. Oh, that was a surprise.'

He shakes his head. 'You think Jill told her where I was? How? Jill never knew where I was when I was away. I kept everything in my study . . .'

Meredith glances at Harris before she speaks. 'She *did*. She used to tell me she'd see documents in your study – lists of safe houses and what have you. You would leave all of it just sitting there, she said.'

'You think that Jill knew all this time who Sophia was? She's known for nineteen years?'

'Yes. But she didn't know, until recently, that she'd *died*. And especially not how. Not until this all blew up from Leila and Caroline Bonner's article.'

The breath is taken from him. Jill knew about Sophia. About his child.

'Joseph Locke found my email to Jill. I sent it with a subject line . . . I wrote . . . I wrote, "On the day she died".'

354

'Did Jill know you'd worked it out? That it was Sophia that day?'

'No. I mean, perhaps she suspected after I'd sent the email, but she never replied to it. I thought she might tell me herself, but she didn't, and then I thought maybe I'd got it wrong . . . and then she disappeared and I just . . . I just . . .' Meredith closes her eyes, exhales. 'I thought maybe I sent her over the edge. Maybe she felt there was no safe place to be.'

'Have the police said anything to you about it?'

'Yes.'

'And what did you tell them?'

Meredith looks crestfallen. 'I – I panicked, Christopher. I told them I'd been looking through everything since the Sophia fiasco surfaced, and I'd sent it to Jill saying, gosh, that's when the poor girl died. I didn't tell them that I'd seen Jill and Sophia talking. I didn't tell them. But I worried about the buggy – that there was enough of it in the picture to make out the brand of it, and then I thought someone might recognize it as the one Sophia had, I don't know . . . Oh, God. I *lied* to the police.'

He laughed then. An explosion, a firework. 'Meredith, I have spent my entire *life* lying.'

'It's not OK.'

He looks out of the window, serious again. 'No, it's not. But all that the police have is a picture from the paper, taken at the bookshop where Jill did a reading. There is nothing connecting Jill to Sophia there apart from a brand of buggy. The online diary entries have nothing about her going to meet or having met Jill. We need to keep it that way. Wherever Jill is, we keep her from all this. She played a part, but she didn't kill Sophia.'

'Neither did you,' Harris says. 'They're going to make you take the fall for this.'

'I'm the collateral damage,' Chris says. 'But I wasn't blameless. I had an affair, for Christ's sake. I left documents unsecured that Jill found. But we don't need to make her a victim of a witch hunt. No one can know about you helping Jill leave, Harris.' Chris looks at Meredith. 'And no one can know that she and Sophia met that day. We have to hope that no one will ever make the connection.'

Both Harris and Meredith nod.

'The police can have their secrets,' Chris says. 'And we can have ours.'

Meredith emits a little noise. She is, Chris realizes, crying. 'Where will you go?' she asks.

'I don't know yet.'

'Will you stay in touch with me?'

'If that's what you want.'

'I do, actually,' she says.

'Will you take Jackson?' he asks.

She takes a tissue from the sleeve of her top. 'Oh, stop, Christopher.'

'I won't be able to take him with me wherever it is that I go.'

'I've got him at the moment,' Harris says quietly. 'He's a good lad.'

'He was everything to Jill.'

'I could keep him if you like? Then he could mean everything to me.'

'Thank you, Harris.'

'And listen . . .' Harris holds out his hand. 'Jill gave me this – to give you when the time was right. I don't know if the time is right, but here it is.'

Chris opens it, sees that it's the missing page from her notebook – the ripped-out last page.

Beneath the midnight blue, somewhere undisclosed. If the ember is still alive, love will find a way.

55

In less than twelve hours, Chris Fletcher will vanish into thin air, but for the short time that he is still Chris Fletcher, he is back at the kitchen table in Rosewood Cottage. Across the table sits Oliver Hamilton, and between them is a pile of paperwork – statements and legal documents, all things Chris needs to concentrate on. But all he can think about is what Meredith told him.

Where does he attribute the blame now for Sophia's death? Squarely with Damian Roper? Does he blame Jill for any of it, for telling Sophia where he was? Is it all his fault? Oliver's? Perhaps it's a combination of them all. Or perhaps it was fate with its cruel hand moving pawns across the board, skittering them this way and that because it didn't matter what order the moves were played in – the endgame was predestined.

'Jesus, I'm sorry, Chris, I really am. Jill is still missing, and now . . . now you have to disappear.'

Chris drags his eyes to Oliver. 'It's OK, Oli.'

'I've got . . . you know, some counselling lined up for you.'

Chris almost laughs. 'It's too late for that, don't you think?'

'But you need to talk, don't you? Get it all off your chest?'

'I can tell the truth to a counsellor? The whole truth?'

Oliver looks sheepish. 'Well, no. But you can talk about your feelings?'

Chris laughs. 'My feelings. OK. Sure.'

Oliver pushes a paper towards Chris. 'Sign here.'

Chris leans forward, signs his life away, then he puts the pen down and starts to shake uncontrollably.

'Ah, shit,' Oliver says, reaches to pat his shoulder. 'This is all . . . Well. It's bad, I know. Everything spiralled.'

'I lost them both, Oli. Both Jill and Sophia. And he's still out there. With all this media attention, he's going to find me, isn't he?'

'Who?'

'*Roper.*'

Oliver takes a breath. 'Damian Roper is dead, Chris.'

'What?'

'He's been dead sixteen years.'

Time stands still.

'He went to ground after what happened the night Sophia died. But we know he told all the members who you were – albeit not your real name, because he didn't know it. We tracked him down after three months. He'd gone to America to join a right-wing group there. We shared intelligence with the Americans on him. The next thing we knew, he'd ended up in a fight somewhere in Tennessee and got bottled. He died in the hospital a day later.'

Chris can't seem to find any words. They are jumbled, huge, in his mouth.

'We didn't tell you because – well, because we believed you were a liability. Because we thought if you knew he was gone you would come back and try to make contact with Alex, blow your cover and out the truth that we'd tried to protect for so long. The truth is that, through all our negligence, a young woman *died*. We could have said she was murdered, because that's what happened. But then all the documentation, all the shit we were wrapped up in . . . We had to go with the suicide. We had to give him up when we knew he'd killed her, and that was wrong, *so* wrong. But what else could we do, without compromising everything else?'

'When?'

'What?'

'When did you find out that he'd died?'

'The Americans called us the day after.'

Chris is silent for a long time. 'You're telling me that you've known for sixteen years? Do you know how many sleepless nights I've had?'

'I know this is hard to swallow—'

'I didn't go to my parents' funerals, you know that? Because I was too worried that Roper might have found out about me or Jill. I thought – I thought we were friends, Oli?'

'We were. We are. Didn't I pull you back from the fucking abyss when Sophia died? Didn't I keep you updated on how your boy was getting on all these years? I did it because I always had your best interests at heart.'

'Keeping me away from Alex all this time wasn't in my best interests. What the *fuck*?'

Oliver is quiet for a moment and then nods. 'I'm sorry. For all of it. It came to find us anyway, didn't it? The truth. Jesus Christ almighty. In this job there are shadows and lies and all manner of fucked-up things. We only ever try to do the right thing, and sometimes it's not right, but we don't know it at the time, do we? Or maybe we're trying to protect the bigger picture – the police and all that they stand for. That's why people get so upset with the police. Because it's an establishment set up to *protect*, to be brave, and yet sometimes we get it so fucking wrong, and people are failed.'

Oliver's phone rings, and he stands. Chris looks up. 'Where are you going?'

'There is unbelievable bravery within the police, I truly believe it, Chris, and loyalty too. You were loyal, and we are repaying you by giving you a new name and a God-awful legacy. But your service was invaluable, never forget it.' He sighs. 'I arranged something for you, and it's at the door.'

It's Alex. His son, his hands shoved in his jeans pockets and wearing a polo shirt that's creased. Chris feels overwhelmed with joy at seeing him. He stands up so abruptly that the chair behind him falls to the floor.

'Call me when you're done,' Oliver says.

He leaves, and the front door closes. Alex hovers, unsure, by the table.

Chris rights the chair, then clears his throat. 'Will you sit?'

Alex nods, draws up a chair. Chris wishes with his entire being that they were anywhere but here. He wishes they could be skimming stones together on a beach in Italy. He wishes he could go back in time to when Alex was little. But would Chris be with Sophia, or Jill? Would he still be trying to straddle both lives? He tells himself not to think of the 'what if's, because they are too dangerous, and now, pointless. Alex, though, is in front of him, real.

'You saved my life,' he says.

'Yes.'

'After you and Leila posted the footage. After you knew that I was there in Derby. You still came.'

'Yeah.' Alex looks at the table. 'The footage was Leila's idea. And I was angry. I'm still angry. I don't know if you had anything to do with Mum dying.'

'I didn't. I never would have hurt her.'

Alex's jaw clenches. 'I thought I wanted you to go down, but when it came out and everyone jumped on you, I was . . . I don't know. I'd met you, and you told me all those things. About Mum. About the oranges.' He sits on his hands. 'Oliver Hamilton told me I wouldn't be able to see you again.'

'No, I need to leave.'

'Where will you go?'

'I don't know. Would you have wanted to see me again?'

'Yes. No. Maybe. I don't know.'

'I want you to know that I think you're an amazing kid. *Man*. I think you're an amazing man. I'm so proud of how you turned out.'

'But you don't *know* me.' Alex looks at him, sorrowfully.

'And I'm sorry I never got the chance to. It was, and will be, the biggest regret of my life. But I'm glad we talked about your mum. I'm glad you found me, that Jillian emailed you.'

Alex doesn't reply for a moment. 'I have to go. Leila has come up here. She doesn't know I'm with you, but she'll ask questions if I'm not back soon.'

'Not yet,' Chris says. 'Alex? Not yet.'

Please don't go, he wants to say. *Everyone has left me, and I know you're going to leave me, but let's prolong it. Let me pretend, let me have a moment longer to be with you. Let me have a moment to make it up, somehow.*

His eyes rest on the wooden heart, sitting on the table. He picks it up, turns it over.

Alex frowns. 'What is that?'

'It's something I made.'

'Mum had one,' Alex says. 'Leila gave it to me when I

362

was five. She said it was one of Mum's favourite things. Did you . . . did you make it?'

'Yes.' He puts it down again. 'I was making this one for Jill.'

'I'm sorry about Jill,' Alex says.

'So am I.'

Chris thinks then about what Oliver said to him about arranging a counsellor.

You need to talk, don't you? Get it all off your chest.

He pauses for a moment and then takes in a breath. 'I'm going to tell you something, Alex. OK? About your mum, and about what really happened that night.'

Alex turns his eyes towards Chris. 'What do you mean?'

'You need to hear the whole story. And you can decide what, if anything, you think should come out in the press.'

Alex pauses. 'What would happen to you if I did tell the press?'

What would happen? Perhaps a level of understanding. Perhaps a level of sympathy for him, and for what the unit had tried to do, which was to bring peace to the streets. But they'd messed up, because they were fallible. If the truth came out – minus Jill's involvement in it – perhaps there would be a level of understanding for the police about the handling of violent groups like Dawn. Or perhaps Chris would be hunted not only by his senior officers but by others too – more dangerous, shady people. He thinks of Sardinia, of the house waiting for him, but it wouldn't feel like a home without Jill in it. He will move, but he doesn't know where. Perhaps this is his penance – wandering the world, for ever looking over his shoulder, for ever a loner. But here, right now, he has a choice.

'The version of events we told at the inquest was a lie.

You know that; you knew it from the start. You had the evidence I was at that house that evening.' Chris pauses. 'The statement we put out tonight – that I saw Sophia, we argued, I left and she injected herself – is also a lie.'

Alex stares at him.

'Your mum didn't commit suicide.'

Alex inhales sharply.

'Do you want the truth?'

Alex nods. 'I'm listening.'

I remain dedicated to the memory of my sister, and to the women destroyed by unforgivable police 'tactics'.

— @LeilaRoyPR, X

Has Chris Fletcher fallen off the face of the planet?! Where did he go? #findchrisfletcher

— @Outtahere, X

He's gone. Chris Fletcher has disappeared, and I can't find him. No one can.

— Caroline Bonner to the *Observer* senior editor, Fenella Wu, 23 April 2024

I am now in possession of the notebook of my cherished niece, Jillian. Her publishers and I will be publishing her poetry collection. It will be entitled *Visible* and will be out in September 2025. Wherever Christopher Fletcher may be, I hope that he reads it. I hope wherever Jillian is – in heaven, elsewhere – she might know how we all love her.

— Meredith Moore, Jillian Moore's aunt, interview with Sadie Clarke, *Under the Cover*, 2025

You think we do it for fame? No one knows we exist. All the things we do in our lives undercover are concealed in files, and only accessible years after our deaths, if at all. By which time no one will care. We do it for King and country, but also for those closest to us – our family and friends. We do it to protect those we love. It's about service, bravery, courage. You have no idea.

   – [Name redacted], MI5 agent, BBC True Crime Drama: *Into the Dark*, 2025

I have something to say.

   – Alex Roy, speaking to Cass Halliday from *The Times*, 5 May 2024

Epilogue

On the day of the storm, after Harris had left her on the rocks, Jillian managed to scramble up the cliff edge, walk through the vast woodland and eventually reach the moors. It was three in the afternoon before she found the shepherd's hut on the ridge, and then it started to rain.

The hut was small and weatherbeaten, and inside were bits of broken stone and leaves that had blown in over the years and turned mulchy. In the driest corner, Jill ate some of the bread and decided to cut her hair with the penknife in her bag, putting the dead hair in her rucksack, because she didn't want anyone to find it. She sliced it to her chin, added a choppy fringe, and it was a crude cut, but perhaps it would be different enough.

Soon, everything would be different.

She thought about her life and her bad choices; she thought about Sophia, who was dead, and Sophia's boy, poor Alex, who Jill had strangely and desperately wanted to meet. In time she listened to the violence of the wind that came howling through the open gaps in the stone. She thought it sounded like someone was screaming at her, but she deserved that. She deserved to feel guilt and shame. At seven the sky was a steel grey and the storm was whipping itself into a frenzy over the sea. In only a few hours, it would be in full force. She huddled down on the rotten leaves to shelter as best she could, but each time the lightning flashed and the thunder roared her heart lurched because nature was raw and she was afraid. But wasn't that the beauty of it? Wasn't this what she wanted? Complete and utter freedom?

She started up again when the storm had passed, one foot in front of the other, the hope of the future pulling her forward through the hurt and heartache she was causing herself and doubtless Chris too. Over the next thirty-six hours she managed to hitch a lift with two truck drivers and get a bus to Skye, where she found Archie Robertson. He had been expecting her, but looked at her with no level of interest whatsoever. He made her a cup of strong tea and then left her to herself in the cabin. They sailed from Uig to the Isle of Harris. She had now been gone a full day and night. She allowed herself to imagine a new beginning. She'd find a way to sail to Norway, somehow travel to Iceland, somewhere she'd told Chris repeatedly that she wanted to take him because she had visited years ago with Meredith and it had been singularly the most beautiful and tranquil place she'd ever been. Chris and Jill hadn't been abroad together since they moved to Sardinia. He'd told her initially that it was because he loved Sardinia, that he didn't want to return to the UK, but now she wondered if it was because he *couldn't* return. He hadn't even gone back for his parents' funerals, and that, she knew, had torn him apart.

Enough about him. She wouldn't worry about him. She'd start her new life in Iceland, introduce herself as Bethany Moore – taking her middle name as her first. She would find work in a hotel, a bar. She would visit the lava fields, the Blue Lagoon. She would be a poet, single and with no pets, even though it was breaking her heart that she had left Jackson, the only precious baby she ended up having.

No, she thought. Don't cry. Jackson would be OK. She had to believe it because she had to look *forward*.

But the tears she didn't want to come sprang to her eyes anyway, because she already missed him – she missed Chris and she missed Jackson and she missed her life, even though it had been a lie. How silly it was, she thought, to run away from the thing you loved. But running away would be the thing that saved her.

Perhaps in a year she will make contact with Harris again, and Meredith, and they will meet in secret. Perhaps in a decade she will make contact with Amanda, and Amanda will ask Jill to come for tapas and meet her two friends Maia and Connie – still close friends, all these years later. This time she will go.

Perhaps, once Jill has learnt to forgive herself for the part she played in what happened to Sophia and accept the life she now has – quiet and finally contented – she will find Chris, and she will admit what she did. Neither of them had been honest with each other in the long years of their marriage, but perhaps they will reunite under a midnight sky, somewhere undisclosed, and they will talk about all the things they got wrong, but also the things they got right.

Perhaps none of this will come to pass. But perhaps it will.

Author's Note

This is a novel about love. It is about putting your trust in those who then betray you. It is about trauma, and the loss of identity. It is about trying to do the right thing when the right thing itself is murky and unclear.

Police infiltration into activist groups is an emotive subject and has affected many lives. The independent inquiry into its morals – or indeed, the lack thereof – is ongoing and full of complexities.

The SDS was born out of an unstable time in history, out of the Second World War, the Cold War, and was founded to try to maintain public order when activism was increasing at an alarming rate. Some groups were hell-bent on creating chaos and spreading violence. Others, however, were just trying to make a positive difference.

The unofficial motto of the SDS was 'to obtain information by any means necessary'. As such, regulations were not put in place, and in some cases officers went to extreme lengths to deceive their targets. Sometimes extreme lies are absolutely necessary; after all, undercover police officers risk their lives for others. But at other times they are not. Sometimes these lies do more harm than good.

It is not only the activists that have been impacted by these lies but also the families of the undercover officers and, indeed, the undercover officers themselves. As such, it is not a simple hero-and-villain story.

To Love a Liar is a novel about out-of-control people in

out-of-control situations. Although it is about real events from the world in which we live, it is completely fictitious.

I sincerely hope that you enjoyed reading it.

Acknowledgements

When I was seven, I wrote and illustrated a book about a girl who found out she was a witch. On my behalf, my mum sent it to Penguin, and for several weeks I waited with bated breath until, unsurprisingly (!), it came back to me, but with a letter. That letter told me to keep going, and the kindness and encouragement to a little mind determined on becoming a writer was everything. I wish I still had it, wish I knew who had sent it. I wish I could frame it alongside the cover of this book – because this book is a Penguin book!

Some readers may know that I worked in publishing many moons ago, first at Bloomsbury and then at Penguin, which later became Penguin Random House. To publish this book with Penguin Viking feels very special indeed. Thank you to my wonderful editor, Rosa Schierenberg, for bringing me to the imprint; I can't put a price on your vision and eye for detail and our friendship, and also your patience (!!). I hope we will have many more books together. To you and everyone at Penguin, my gosh there are so many to mention, but here goes – thank you to Lucy, for everything. Thank you to Kayla Fuller in Marketing and to Juliet Dudley in Publicity. Thank you to Charlotte Daniels for the incredible cover design, to Sarah Day for the copyedit, to Leah Boulton, and to Sarah Barlow, Anne Cook and Emma Adams for the proofreads. Thank you to the wonderful sales teams who sell across UK, international, digital and audio markets. Thank you to Production and Inventory and Operations. None of this could happen without you, and I'm so grateful!

This book is dedicated to my agent, Camilla Bolton at Darley Anderson, who I have been with for eight years. Cam, your capacity for providing feedback and support is seemingly a never-ending well. I know I speak on behalf of all your authors when I say that you are worth your weight in gold. You must be part machine and part wizard. To Jade, for your tireless spirit in all things, and to everyone at Darley, thank you so much. Within this, a big thank you, too, to Katy Loftus, for reading an early draft. Your feedback – 'You have something really special here' – spurred me to make it even more so.

This book is inspired by a non-fiction book I read called *Undercover* by journalists Paul Lewis and Rob Evans. I've always wanted to write about undercover officers and, in 2013, Jonathan Parker (an old Penguin buddy) gave me a proof of this book. It captivated me. I was so inspired to write about undercover officers – somehow – but it took me more than a decade to work out how to write it well. I also read *Deep Deception*, written by the female activists who lived those police tactics and their consequences. Some of these women tracked down the men who betrayed them and thus inspired Sophia's story, though of course Sophia's story had a very different ending. Research on this topic was so important to me – not only to get the facts straight but also to give each party an authentic voice. On that note, thank you to my lovely friend Helena Wood for getting me in touch with Mick Creedon. Thank you, Mick, for your insight and experience within the ongoing inquiry into police infiltration – your expertise was invaluable. Thank you also to Imran Mahmood for talking me through how inquests work. Any inconsistencies or glaring errors are mine!

To my writing friends who keep me company. You're the most inspiring and witty group of colleagues I could ever have asked for. Emma Christie, Nikki Smith, Karen Hamilton, Sophie Flynn, Emily Freud, Charlotte Duckworth, Lizzy Barber, Gytha Lodge, Claire Douglas, Jack Jordan, Sarah Turner, Mira Shah, Sam Holland, and to Frankie Pellatt, who is a champion of all writers.

To my husband and my boys, and to my parents and brother, and my wider wonderful family, and my beloved friends, what else is there to say other than 'I love you'? It's immeasurable. You are everything to me and more. Special shout-out to my dad, who has single-handedly shifted hundreds of copies of my books over the years. Salesman to the last!

To all the many bookshops and booksellers here in the UK, and beyond the seas, thank you so much for supporting my writing. To have my books on a shelf is everything I ever dreamt of. Special thanks to the indies: P&G Wells in Winchester, Hart's in Saffron Walden, and Harris & Harris in Clare.

Thank you to the bloggers and reviewers who champion books online. And lastly, thank you to every single person who buys books, borrows them from libraries and shares their enthusiasm for the books they adore. Books are escapism, an adventure, a joy. We can learn so much compassion from them. They educate us, fill our souls.

Long live the written word.